THE
PEOPLE
BEFORE

Charlotte Northedge is joint Head of Books for the *Guardian*. Charlotte has previously written for a range of newspapers and magazines, including the *Guardian*, *Psychologies* and *Cosmopolitan*. She has an MA in Modern and Contemporary Literature from Birkbeck and is an alumna of the Curtis Brown Creative writing course. Her first novel, *The House Guest*, was published in 2021.

 @charnorth

Also by Charlotte Northedge

The House Guest

THE
PEOPLE
BEFORE

CHARLOTTE NORTHEDGE

HarperCollins*Publishers*

HarperCollins*Publishers*
1 London Bridge Street,
London SE1 9GF

www.harpercollins.co.uk

HarperCollins*Publishers*
Macken House, 39/40 Mayor Street Upper,
Dublin 1, D01 C9W8, Ireland

This paperback edition HarperCollins*Publishers* Ltd 2023
1
First published by HarperCollins*Publishers* Ltd 2022

A catalogue copy of this book is available from the British Library.

ISBN: 9780008402600 (PB)

This novel is entirely a work of fiction.
The names, characters and incidents portrayed in it are
the work of the author's imagination. Any resemblance to
actual persons, living or dead, events or localities is
entirely coincidental.

Typeset in Sabon LT by Palimpsest Book Production Limited,
Falkirk, Stirlingshire

Printed and Bound in the UK using 100% Renewable
Electricity at CPI Group (UK) Ltd

MIX
Paper | Supporting
responsible forestry
FSC™ C007454

This book is produced from independently certified FSC™
paper to ensure responsible forest management.
For more information visit: www.harpercollins.co.uk/green

To my family

Prologue

It's that flash, the lightning movement at the edge of your vision, no more than a flicker, so that you don't know whether you've imagined it. Is it your mind playing tricks, or maybe there really is someone there, darting swiftly enough to go undetected by all but you? Someone who doesn't want to be seen, doesn't want to make themselves known. Or perhaps they do, and this quicksilver movement is their way of alerting you, only you, to their presence. Marking out their territory. Making sure that you, only you, never feel completely at ease, relaxed, at home.

It's the noise you hear, late at night. The knock that sits you straight up in bed. That makes your heart beat and your pulse race, your hands cold and clenched, as if ready to fight. There are always noises, of course, but this is the kind you recognise. A noise you can't ignore. The warning shot fired before an attack.

It's the smell that lingers when you rush outside, marking the presence of another human. That intimate odour that isn't a scent but an essence of otherness. The night air laced with it. Unfamiliar, unmistakable. Undetected by anyone but you.

It's the knowledge that you left that object in a particular place or position: the watering can with its spout just so. You can picture it clearly, and yet you turn around and it isn't there. It's facing the other way. Or it has disappeared entirely; but everyone else just shrugs their shoulders. It's no big deal. Who cares where you left it, anyway? Anyone could have moved it.

But you *know*. It's a knowledge that's moving inside you, rippling out from your core to your fingertips, traced along the fine layer of dust on the windowsill that has been disturbed and resettled, imperceptible to anyone else. Only you are sure of it.

Or are you? That's the question that plagues you late into the night. Are you sure, or is it your imagination? Is it real or hysteria? A mania that gripped you and has you in its clutches.

Maybe everyone is right, and you are going mad. Or maybe you are the only one who sees the truth.

PART ONE

PART ONE

Chapter One

SOLD

The sign, red with white lettering, looms above the ragged hedge like a warning. It's the only reason we don't miss the gap entirely, the high, overgrown bushes barely parting either side of the uneven driveway. We round the corner, the car rolling slowly to a stop. That's when it really hits me what we've done.

We've beaten the removal van. We're alone on the grounds of our new property, the bare branches lining the drive so much darker now, leaves collecting beneath them in sodden heaps. Already, the weather seems wilder in Suffolk than when we left London this morning, the light drizzle giving way to relentless sheets of rain. Pete switches off the engine, and I listen to the steady drumming on the car roof. But otherwise, not a sound. No buses, no cars, no voices. The building in front of us, the only dwelling visible on the flat horizon, is blurred through the rain-streaked windscreen. The Maple House. Our new home.

'Well, it's big enough, isn't it?' Pete turns to me, his eyebrows raised. Excitement, or anxiety perhaps. He's lost weight these last few months. I can see it in the hollow of his cheeks, his stubble darker, his eyes sunken from the stress of it all. There's more grey at his temples. There would be at mine, too, if it wasn't for the bleach.

'You could fit our house into it four times, at least.' I force a smile. It's only after I've spoken that I realise my mistake. Our *old* house. This is our house now.

Pete catches my eye. 'Let's find those keys then.' But I'm already half out of the car. The rain has slowed. I want to get a better look.

My stomach feels tight with nerves. All these months we've been poring over pictures online, scrolling through the 3D tour, sketching out what we could do to the place, and now we're finally here. I lift a box from the back seat and approach the house. Crumbling redbrick, two storeys, though the tall sloping roofs make it look much higher, small windows dotted here and there, tiny square panes in that Arts and Crafts style that won me over in the summer, when the air was still and warm, the sun-dappled lawn a respite from the scorched city. Now the wind shakes the splintered shutters and rattles the panes. I see that the circular window above the front door, the one that lodged in my mind all those months ago, finally selling to me the dream of rural living, the lure of a unique period home, has a crack running right through the middle. Was it there when we viewed the house? Perhaps it just didn't catch my eye when the house was still hypothetical. A possibility. Full of potential.

I shelter on a bench in the arched porch as Pete drops off two boxes and returns to the car, patting his pockets and swearing under his breath. 'Where are those bloody keys?' He climbs back into the Skoda, searching under seats and in the glove compartment. How has he lost them already? The estate agent sent them recorded delivery to us yesterday.

The office in Ipswich was closed today, apparently. And the house was empty. We could get straight in.

Only now he can't find them, and as I watch him clamber around the car, I sense a movement from the corner of my eye, over by the barn. I jolt my head to the side, expecting to see a cat slink away, or a bird nearby, but there's nothing. My heart rate quickens. It was probably just a reflection in a pane of glass I'm not used to yet, but for some reason I clutch the box closer to me, shuffle in nearer to the front door.

What's wrong with me? Here we are about to go into our dream home in the countryside for the first time – bigger, grander than I ever could have imagined. And all of a sudden I don't feel ready. I look across the expanse of field to the front of the house, giving way to the woods that wrap around the back of our land, the broad sweep of horizon, the sky turning from charcoal to a washed-out, watery grey, trying to ignore the feeling, just at the edge of my awareness, that something about this place isn't right.

There's a crack in the distance. A flock of birds rises into the sky, wings thrashing in a flurry of movement and then silence descends again. Suddenly I feel it, as surely as if someone had whispered the words in my ear. We are not alone.

'Pete, what's taking so long?' I want to get inside now, to close the door behind us and create an illusion of familiarity, unpacking the few boxes we've squeezed into our Skoda, filled with all our most precious belongings – the photographs and certificates, the laptops and iPads. I know it will feel different once the removal van arrives with our old yellow sofa, the sideboard we inherited from Pete's mum, the teal chairs I upholstered on that evening course. When Mum gets here with Rose and Archie and we can start to get settled while they run around with all their six- and eight-year-old energy, bagsying rooms and filling the air with their excitement.

I put the box to one side and look around. Maybe there's a spare key hidden somewhere. That's what people do in the countryside, isn't it? Beneath a plant pot or under the doormat. I move closer in, and that's when I notice the latch. It's been lifted. The door is open, just an inch or so.

'Pete?' I say, my voice sounding high, unfamiliar to me. 'Come and have a look at this.'

He approaches, dangling the keys triumphantly from one hand, but his smile dies as he sees the look on my face.

'The door's open. It wasn't locked.' I watch as the anxiety transfers from my voice to his face. His eyes widen, just as they did when I woke him that night in London to tell him I'd heard a noise, that someone was downstairs. Only this time we're the ones outside, trying to get in. God knows who might be waiting for us in there.

'It must have blown open.' Pete inspects the latch, carefully, as though it might hold evidence.

'I guess so.' I'm trying to keep my tone light, but I can't bring myself to go in, all the fears that usually lurk in the early hours rolling into my waking mind like fog off the sea.

'Come on, Jess.' Pete sits down heavily and puts an arm around my shoulder. 'It's probably nothing. The house has been empty for a while. Someone's just forgotten to lock it. Let's have a look around.'

He gets up, lifting my box, and I follow him through the heavy front door, moving slowly, eyes flicking left to right, searching for signs of movement. The high-ceilinged entrance hall is dark, damp, the panelling more splintered than I remember, the smell of rotting wood overwhelming. Our footsteps echo on the uneven tiles as we cross to the bottom of the large stairway that winds up one wall. Pete holds up a hand and we stand perfectly still, listening for movement upstairs – the creaking of floorboards, a door clicking shut. But there's nothing. Only the steady drip of rain outside.

'See, there's no one here,' Pete says, but his voice is low and I'm not convinced. It's as though the air has been unsettled. Something or someone has moved through it. The silence holds an echo.

'Let's look in the kitchen,' I say, keen to escape the musty smell. But it follows us through to the long, cold room lined with cheap pine units we'll be ripping out straight away. At the far end is the mildewed conservatory we plan to knock down and replace with a sleek glass box extension, and I focus on that, trying to imagine an uninterrupted view into the garden, the sunlight streaming through bifold doors, an immaculate stretch of hardwood floor replacing the torn, mouldy lino.

'I suppose it was summer when we last saw it,' Pete says, rubbing his hands together as he looks around him. 'But we'll get it cleaned up in no time.' He puts his arms around me, and I bury my head in his shoulder, trying to hold back the tears that have threatened to overwhelm me all morning.

I'd barely been able to look at him as we locked up our home in Walthamstow for the last time. The two-storey terrace we'd returned to with each of our new babies; the one that held birthday parties and barbecues and Christmas drinks. All the way up the M11, he'd kept me busy discussing plans for the kitchen-diner, the boot room, the conservatory. I'd been caught up in his enthusiasm again – the visions of our new rural life, leaving behind all the problems that had stacked up around us in London. But now that we're inside, the enormity of the project has taken on solid dimensions.

We move through the hallway into the large living room on the other side, with more splintered wood panelling, the carpets stained and threadbare. Upstairs, the banister is broken, the wall under the circular window at the back damp and uneven. The five bedrooms are in various states of disrepair, all peeled wallpaper and loose floorboards, and the mouldy bathroom has a cracked cistern. Everywhere, the air is heavy with damp and decay. By the time we've done the full tour and returned to the kitchen, any worries about the half-open front door have given way to a state of shock about the size of the renovation job we've taken on.

'There's a lot to do, but we'll manage it,' Pete says, joining me as I look through our boxes for the kettle, the tea bags.

'Yeah, I know.' I'll feel better once I've made a drink, sat down, gathered my thoughts. But I can't find where I packed them, and Pete watches as my search becomes increasingly frantic. Eventually, he lays a hand on my arm and I look up, seeing the concern, the guilt, in his eyes.

It had been Pete's idea, this move. He'd convinced me that a house in the country would be the new beginning we all needed. We'd made so much on our place in Walthamstow, after all, and one by one our friends had started to slip away in search of more space, greenery, fresher air, better schools. It was the break-in that finally clinched it, but I'd already been seduced by the idea of a new beginning. Leaving behind what was becoming an increasingly difficult situation. The prospect of rambling walks, weekend visitors, the children running wild in the garden. I hadn't allowed my mind to dwell on the months and months of renovations, miles from anywhere, entirely alone.

'It's just a lot to take in, isn't it?' I say, finally giving up on my search and sitting heavily on a box. 'And that's before we've even got started on the barn, the garden, the orchard, the weeds . . .'

Pete had seen the Maple House first, on his own, shown around by the owner. An odd guy, he said, something off about him. But he must have done quite a number on Pete, because the house was all he could talk about for days afterwards. He'd even got caught up in some family psychodrama – they'd owned it for generations apparently, there was some controversy over whether to sell it or not. The guy had already taken it off the market once and then put it back on. Pete was desperate to snap it up before he changed his mind. By the weekend, he'd set up a second viewing, this time with the estate agent – I'd assumed he didn't want the weird owner putting me off. And he arranged for the kids to stay with Mum so we could really get a sense of the place, together.

It was a Saturday in late August when he first brought me here. A heatwave had made the city steamy and unbearable, all brown, scratchy parks and heaving paddling pools, and as I stood in the long grass in the shade cast by this imposing building, I felt I'd exhaled properly for the first time in weeks. From the outside, it was easy to see how impressive the house must have once been, with its gable windows and vast gardens stretching towards the woods. But it was the little details that really sold it to me – the small window frames, the shutters, the wood panelling. Walking inside, I felt a tingling in the pit of my stomach – as though this house I'd never seen before, never set foot in, was somehow familiar to me. An image surfaced of the poster that hung above the table in Mum's tiny London kitchen. The one we'd picked up at the William Morris exhibition at the V&A when I was seven that had first sparked my interest in art, in design. It's still there, yellow with age now. I couldn't say how many mornings I'd sat eating my corn-flakes, transfixed by the old redbrick house in the picture, Morris's house – so big, yet welcoming, with its quaint little chimneys and wooden doors, its lush gardens a world away from the double-deckers that rumbled past our first-floor flat.

11

It was the circular windows in the Maple House that clinched it, the same kind I'd seen in Morris's red house when we'd visited in south-east London a few months after the exhibition, cementing my obsession with Arts and Crafts design. I never would have believed I'd one day be viewing a house with not one, but two of them – the round frame above the front door mirrored by an identical one at the back, on a large landing overlooking the long lawn. As we stood, peering out, I'd pictured myself sitting there on a summer's evening, book in hand, gazing out at the rustling trees.

'There is a slight sticking point,' the estate agent, Brian, had said as he led us back around the outside of the house, tall and thin in his shiny blue suit, and I'd rolled my eyes at Pete. Everywhere we'd seen had a catch – a box room instead of a bedroom, rising damp, some obscure land rights issue relating to a local church. I knew there had to be something here. It was so big, so sprawling. How could we possibly afford it otherwise?

'Just over there is a small patch of Japanese knotweed. We've got to let you know about it,' he'd said in that whining, nasal voice of his as he guided us quickly past the problem area to the side of the house, 'but it's not half as bad as people make out. And if you're willing to take it on, you can cash in.' He gave us a wink. 'It knocks thousands off the asking price.'

On the journey home, I'd allowed Pete to keep the dream alive. Maybe we could tame the garden and restore the old house to its former glory. Just imagine the two of us, owning a rambling place like that – all those rooms, all that land. Then we'd got back to our realistically sized terrace, our small, barely tended garden, and read up on the reality of knotweed. Extremely invasive, very hard to ever really get rid of without specialist help and many courses of treatment. The dream was over, for me at least. 'Think about it, though,' Pete had insisted. 'The knotweed's the only reason we can afford that place – and the state of it. But it's so much better than anything else we've seen. We could do it up, a proper modern renovation, sort out the garden – we'd double the value in a couple of years.'

But it seemed like too big a project, too much of a gamble. As keen as I was by then to make a clean break, I was holding out for a place without any major problems, or weird owners who took it off the market at a moment's notice. I wanted to wait for the right house, at the right moment. Then a few weeks later, we were woken by an intruder in the night, and suddenly it felt like just the right moment.

I can picture us now, standing with Brian outside the Maple House on our second, and final, viewing, the bricks bathed orange in September sunlight, golden maple and oak leaves fluttering in the breeze. I was wearing my usual bright colours, a yellow slogan T-shirt and red New Balance, I think. Pete probably looking distinctively north London in his roll-up jeans and neon trainers, no socks. Brian must have struggled to keep a straight face as we told him we planned to offer on the house. Two clueless, naive Londoners snapping up this enormous, remote, ramshackle building, with its weed infestation. We got it for a bargain in the end, far lower than the asking price, but even so, there had been no competition.

'It just all looks so different to the last time we were here,' I say, looking at Pete, who's pacing the room.

'But remember how excited we were? You saw it then, too, the potential, didn't you? You're just feeling overwhelmed. Remember how much you loved those windows? You'll see – it'll be amazing. It won't take long.' I can't help but smile at his skills of persuasion, the optimism – as if he can will

13

this place into shape. 'Come on, the rain's let up a bit, let's check out the barn. We can size up that rental property.' He turns to me with a grin, but I've known him too long to mistake the anxiety in his eyes, too. He grew up in suburban Manchester. He might know more than I do about living in a large house. I felt like we were rattling around in Walthamstow compared to the upstairs flat I'd spent most of my life in. But he knows nothing about living in the countryside, in deepest, darkest rural Suffolk. Neither of us do.

Pete's already through the back door, and I follow him down the path towards the outbuildings: a run-down garage and a large, abandoned barn, with missing roof tiles and a boarded-up window on one side. But as we reach the entrance, I stop. It's the same feeling I'd had by the front door. As though someone is watching me. That instinct, the prickle on the back of my neck, the involuntary shiver. I look behind me, quickly, as if I might catch someone in movement. But there's no one. Just rain dripping through the leaves, puddling on the uneven ground. I think again of the open latch. What if the person who let themselves into the house is lingering just out of sight? They must have thought the house was empty. What will they do now we've disturbed them?

I listen to the rattle as Pete opens the barn door. Is that something moving in the garage, through the small window? I hear a cry and my eyes dart again. But it's just a bird – large, dark, unidentifiable to my city eye – rising from the gloom of the trees. I turn back to the barn. All is still. Pete has managed to force the door open, but I stand on the threshold, unable to take another step.

'Can't you feel it?' I ask Pete, my voice hushed.

'What's that?' He turns to me from inside, where his neck is craned, surveying the crumbling building.

14

'Don't you feel like we're being watched? Like there's someone else here?'

'Jess, come in, won't you?' His voice echoes. 'Honestly, there's no one here. Why would there be? The house is empty. The front door had blown open. This isn't like in London – we're miles from anywhere.'

But that thought only makes me feel worse. I think about the nights when Pete will be working late, when it will just be me and the children in the darkness, among all these trees. A ten-minute drive to the nearest village. Even further to the town, to the doctor's surgery. Who knows how long it might take to get to a hospital. Why hadn't I thought any of this through?

I run back to the kitchen, alone, trying not to look towards the darkened garage windows, pulling my oversized sweatshirt around me against the wind. I can hardly believe it, after everything I've said to Mum all these years about her woo-woo nonsense, but I feel it. There's no other way to describe it. A negative energy.

'Come on, love.' Pete closes the back door behind him. 'It's cold feet. Buyer's remorse. You'll feel differently once we're all set up, all our stuff around us.'

'I know, I'm sorry.' I take a deep breath and turn away so he can't see my eyes. I'd give anything to be back in our warm kitchen at home, Becky round for a cup of tea, the kids watching Netflix, a train rumbling past. 'Let's get the rest of the boxes in, shall we?'

We haul everything in from the car, but the removal van still hasn't arrived, and we can't get any reception.

'How have we managed to move into a mobile blackspot without even realising?' Pete mutters, dumping the last of the bags in the kitchen and holding his phone up to the window.

'Maybe it's the weather? Why don't we go to the pub in the village? I can't find the tea bags, anyway. We can get a

15

drink. Find out where our stuff's got to. Check how the kids are doing with Mum.'

I can't wait to get away, even for half an hour. But as we roll down the driveway, I begin to see that Pete was right, I'm being paranoid. The oppressive weight that pressed down on my shoulders as we arrived begins to lift. The redbrick looks cleaner, less imposing, in the rear-view mirror. Perhaps it was just a shadow at the garage window, nothing more. The front door could have blown open. That latch does look loose. The whole place will feel different when it isn't pouring with rain, when Mum arrives with the children. I try to see it through her eyes – this huge house with so much land, so many features. Surely she'll be impressed. This is the new beginning we all need; I've got to give it a fighting chance.

As we stop at the end of the drive, Pete indicating to turn right, I feel an easing in my chest. Some of the excitement returns as I try to remember what the village looked like, the pub, the tiny shop. I look back at the house one last time as Pete turns onto the road, and then I feel my stomach lurch. I hear a gasp and realise it has come from me. Pete swerves and rights himself, turning to me in alarm.

'What the hell, Jess? What was that about?'

'The garage door,' I say, desperately trying to remember. 'It was closed, right? We left it closed.' I can picture it. I was standing outside the barn looking at it. We didn't go in. 'When I looked back just then, the door was open. We've got to go and check it. Make sure there isn't someone in there.'

But Pete keeps on driving, shaking his head. 'Those doors are old, Jess. It's windy. They need securing. I know you're spooked after what happened in London, but you've got to put that behind you now.'

He puts a hand on my leg, and I see that I'm shaking. I know it's true. I'm not being rational. But as we pull into the village, past the shop, the small green, the hand-painted sign for The Stag swinging in the wind, my heart doesn't stop pounding. The unsettled feeling lodges deep in my chest, under my ribs, churning my stomach and catching my breath. What if this move, this house, isn't the answer? What if our problems have followed us here? What if this is just the beginning?

Chapter Two

Mum can't wait to get away. 'It's so big,' is all she says as she steps carefully around the boxes and dust and loose floorboards in her low-heeled boots. But I see her skinny hands tremble as I join her out back, where she's retreated for a cigarette, taking a deep drag as she tucks her short silvery blonde hair behind her ears. 'If you're sure you'll be happy here?' She looks at me, the question lingering in her pale blue eyes.

She knows, I can tell, that I'm *not* sure, not now. She probably knew before I did what a gamble we were taking. Definitely, since I'd only fully realised this morning when we arrived with the first of our boxes. But I think she knows why I don't feel comfortable here, too. She feels it – her eyes drawn towards the garage and the barn, just as mine had been. In through the cracked windowpanes and to the darkness beyond.

'What are you going to do with those buildings?' She waves her cigarette at them. I haven't even told her about the garage door, still swinging in the breeze when we got back from the village, after we'd located the removal men in a hold-up on the M11. I haven't told her about the front door, either. It didn't seem worth giving her any more to worry about. She's already appalled by the state of the place, by its size, by its remoteness.

'The plan is to renovate them, turn them into rental properties.' I'd actually been thinking Mum might want to move into one of them, eventually. A granny flat for when she can't live on her own any more. But I can see that's never going to happen.

'And how are you going to afford that?' Mum shakes her head, a look of bemusement on her face at this turn of events, her city-raised daughter washing up in some abandoned country estate. I haven't told her how cheap we got the place. I didn't want to alert her to the knotweed, for one thing. As if saying it out loud would only confirm what a mistake we've made. But she knows that our area of Walthamstow gentrified beyond recognition while we were living there, so we've got enough left over from the sale. 'Especially with you not working. What are you going to do with yourself all day?'

'I'm going to retrain, Mum. And oversee the build. We made sure we kept back enough money to cover it all. Honestly, you don't need to worry. This place will keep me busy enough.' I look around, feeling a heavy weight settle inside me. It's true, I'd been complaining for years that they didn't appreciate me at the gallery where I'd worked as a fundraiser for nearly a decade, that I earned next to nothing since I'd gone part-time. And with two children, there was no way Pete and I could both commute to London. Something had to give – and his job in advertising sales earned four times what I made, so it was always going to be my career. The money we'd save on after-school care would pretty much cover the loss of my salary. And hadn't

19

I been saying for years I wanted to spend more time with the children?

'It'll be so much better for Archie and Rose,' I say, looking through the kitchen window to where the two of them are slumped on beanbags, prodding at iPads. I turn back quickly enough to catch Mum's grimace. She hadn't been convinced, like our friends were, like Pete's parents were, by our 'escape to the country' schtick. So good for the children, all that fresh air, the small class sizes, the absence of gangs, of intruders. She brought me up in London, after all, and I'd turned out all right.

'Yes . . . I suppose you want to give them the childhood you never had?' Mum tips her head back and exhales a cloud of smoke into the cold air.

'That's not what I meant. But, you know, after the break-in and all that. We needed to get away, especially Rose.' I swallow hard, remembering the bang that woke me that night. The unmistakable scrabbling. Pete flying downstairs, shouting. Me reaching the landing just in time to see the back of a head as the man escaped through the front doorway, that thick hand, dark wiry hairs, pulling the door shut behind him. Pete had interrupted him before he managed to take anything, but Rose had been at the window upstairs. She'd seen him look up at the house before he ran down the road. My sensitive six-year-old, haunted by night terrors, visions of large, looming men, black eyes, heavy stubble. The police interviews, the e-fits, and all for nothing. They hadn't caught him. But the trauma of it all had been the push we needed.

'Burglars do exist outside the city, you know,' Mum says, her voice gravelly from the smoke. She moves closer, putting her hand on my cheek. 'Just listen to how you're feeling, okay? Put yourself first occasionally. You're not just a mum. A wife. You're a person in your own right.'

I nod and cup her hand in mine. I've heard this speech so many times. Mum rejected those restrictions put on her by society back in the Sixties – refusing to marry, to settle down, to become a traditional wife and mother – and she can't believe I've so willingly accepted them. Welcomed them, even. Only this time, something in what she's saying resonates. I *had* been prepared to rush back from work, make home-cooked meals, be the one who remembered birthday cards and organised parties, who coped with the endless juggle – when it was on my own terms. When I could do an interesting job, see my friends nearby, live how I wanted to live. I didn't mind when Pete worked late, had client drinks, slept off his hangovers on Saturday mornings, because I had my own social life, my own hangovers. Now, cut off from my work, my colleagues, my friends, even my mum, I feel an isolation, a desperation, I hadn't anticipated.

'I'd better be off now.' Mum grinds her butt underfoot, a habit I know infuriates Pete, so I pick it up and cup it in my hand.

'Aren't you going to say goodbye to the kids?'

'Bye, kids!' Mum shouts. 'They're not interested in me any more. They've got their *mansion* to explore.' She says it with a glint in her eye, but I know the implication. This house is an outright rejection of her life, her choices. She sacrificed space to give me a childhood in the heart of the action, surrounded by people and events and culture.

'Of course they want to say goodbye. Kids, Pete, Granny's leaving!' I call as Mum lowers herself into her blue Micra. They appear at the door, just in time to see her reverse across the drive.

'Bye, Granny! Did you know there's a *river* in the garden?' Archie shouts, running up to the open window. I see Mum smile indulgently and give him a kiss, and I feel Rose's cold hand squeeze mine.

'I don't want Granny to go,' she says quietly, and I find

21

I can't speak past the lump in my throat. I don't want her to either. We've always lived in the same city. I hadn't realised until this moment what comfort that has given me. But there's something else, too. Mum feels what I feel about this house. The sensation Pete won't even acknowledge – that had hit me again as soon as we'd returned from the pub and found the removal team waiting for us outside. That we shouldn't be here. That something is wrong with the place.

It lingers long after Mum leaves, as I listen to Archie and Pete racing around the house upstairs, while Rose joins me in the kitchen. 'There's the barn *and* that whole garage,' Archie shouts. 'Can I have that for a den, Dad? I can get that drum kit!'

'Hang on a minute, Archie. We need to work out where everything's going to go. I've got to find space for my turntables, all my vinyl . . .'

'And your shoes, Dad. You could have a whole trainer *room*!' I hear Pete laugh. His extensive trainer collection has always been a running joke, one that used to seem a lot funnier before the kids came along – back when we had the disposable income for designer footwear and record collections. When the coke-fuelled late-night DJ sessions seemed exciting, rather than exhausting. Still, there won't be anyone coming back to ours after the pub all the way out here.

Rose trails behind me, watching me heat up baked beans on the dirty stove and helping me butter toast, sniffing the air uncertainly.

'There's a funny smell in here, Mum.'

'I know, love. It's because it's been closed up for a while. We'll open the windows for a bit and get the heating on. We'll soon get it cosy.' I give her a squeeze and try to make my voice as cheerful as I can. It weighs heavily, this need to keep my youngest child afloat as well as myself. The inescapable fact of motherhood – that none of your decisions, your moods, your anxieties, are ever just about you. Not any more. There's a whole fleet of small ships that need to keep sailing. If you go down, you might take them all with you.

'You could fit the whole downstairs of our house in this room.' Rose looks around, clearly doubtful about its cosiness.

'You could, couldn't you, Rosie?' Pete appears at the door, grinning. 'We've had a look round upstairs, worked out all the rooms.'

'Yes, I hear you're getting a DJ booth *and* a trainer room, so I guess we'll have to squeeze in around all your things.' I smile.

'Well, yes, of course, there's the VIP lounge, the dressing room, but there's also quite a few bedrooms, so I think we'll be all right.' Pete winks at the kids.

'I'm getting the one with the sink in it,' Archie announces.

'But that's not fair,' Rose whines. 'I want a sink.'

'Nobody really needs a sink in their room,' I snap. 'I grew up in a two-bed flat. You're lucky to each have your own room, I don't want to hear fighting about whose is biggest.'

'Come on, kids. Let's have more of an explore upstairs, give Mum a chance to get things sorted out down here.' Pete flashes me a look as he ushers them both through the door, somewhere between *Are you okay?* and *Don't spoil this*. I listen to them troop upstairs, and sink against the work surface, allowing my cheeks to fall.

I know it's too late now, but did we really need to take on a project this size? Why do we need such a big house anyway? I'd asked Pete the first time we'd walked around

23

it, and he'd looked at me like I was mad. 'Why wouldn't you want all the space you can afford?' I didn't have an answer for him then, but I do now. Because big houses are cold; there are dark corners and whole rooms you don't need to go into. You can't find things. There's no way of knowing who else is there. You can't hear your own family when they're only upstairs; and they can't hear you.

I call them for dinner, again and again. And then, swearing under my breath, I walk into the utility room, looking for the cutlery that has been tucked away somewhere. The moment I switch the light on it blows, but I can make out a pile of boxes dumped in the corner.

It's black now outside the curtainless window and I try not to imagine a pair of eyes looking in as I edge through the darkness, avoiding obstacles in this unfamiliar room. I never felt like this in our old house, where it was statistically more likely that someone could be watching. Even after the intruder, I somehow kept my fears in check, during the daytime hours at least. But we had curtains there, and small cosy rooms, and lights that switched on, and comforting noises from the neighbours who lived in every direction.

Reaching the boxes, I bend to open the top one, my hands feeling the worn cotton of our sheets; the familiar smell of our washing powder taking me straight home as I lift them to my face, revealing the knives and forks beneath. But as I straighten up, I feel it again. A presence. A shifting at the window. My eyes have adjusted to the darkness now, and I step quickly towards it, sure that I will spot the culprit, solve the mystery. A cat perhaps, or a fox.

When I look out, all I can see is the garden in darkness, the moon bright, the lawn floodlit. There's no movement, aside

24

from the rustle of trees, and I shake my head sharply. I have to get over this. It's silly. I'm not used to being in the middle of nowhere, surrounded by nothing. I've lived my whole life in a city, being looked at, spoken to, brushed up against, observed by dozens of people every day. Now, here I am, alone but for my family. It's just my mind playing tricks. Getting accustomed to the withdrawal from bustling life. I need to keep it together for the kids. They'll never settle if I don't.

As I turn to leave the room, a fork clatters to the ground, making me jump. I feel around on the floor in the corner, trying to locate it, and my hand brushes on something soft. It must have fallen from one of our boxes and I pick it up, carrying it with me. It's only as I move towards the light of the kitchen that I realise it's nothing that belongs to any of us. In my hand is a small knitted bootie, for a baby, light blue and frayed at the edges. It looks old, worn, the colour faded. I lift it to my face and inhale the scent of mildew, dust.

It definitely isn't ours. Any baby things I held onto are packed away in one of our bedroom boxes. Besides, we didn't have anything old-fashioned like this. Someone must have left it behind and it makes me think, not for the first time, about the people who lived here before us, the family who owned this house for so many years. I run my thumb over the soft wool and shiver. Something about the lone baby sock makes me uneasy, as though the house holds unfinished business. Hearing the soft pad of feet approaching, I tuck it quickly in my pocket.

'Mum, where are you?' It's Rose, sounding anxious.

'I'm here, love. I was looking for these.' I emerge from the darkness, holding out the bundle of sheets, Rose's unicorn duvet cover, Archie's Arsenal one, the faded Ikea double we haven't replaced since our first flat in Leyton, and the knives and forks.

Pushing the sock from my mind, I kiss Rose's head lightly. Things are going to be different here. We're going to start again, buy new, matching sheets and towels, new furniture, new cutlery. We'll make this place our own, decorate it from top to bottom. None of our friends will be able to believe it when they come to visit. They'll drive back to London wondering whether they should make the move themselves, once they've seen how many rooms, how much garden, how much view you can get for your money out here. Even Mum will be won over. And in the meantime, I'll just have to put a brave face on it. Forget the strange feelings, the discoveries, the people before us, the shapes in the dark. This is our new life. There's no going back.

After a makeshift dinner, the kids and I carry the sheets up the steep stairs, pausing at the top to admire the round window that exactly frames the bright moon outside. I ignore the crack and focus instead on the clear night sky, the stars that were never this visible from our London loft.

'This house is a bit spooky, Mummy,' Rose whispers as we push open the creaky wooden door that leads into her room at the back of the house. There's a window that overlooks the lawn, and Pete has pushed her bed below it, so she can see out through the warped panes. In one corner of the room is a small door, half my height, concealing a deep storage space we haven't found a use for yet, and she eyes it uncertainly. 'What *is* that?'

'It's a little cupboard,' I say lightly, sitting down on the bed and gathering her on my knee. She's tiny for six, still struggling to catch up after being so premature, and still my baby. 'Perfect for hide-and-seek, don't you think?' I smile, but Rose's eyes widen with alarm at the thought of crawling inside, and I can see I've said the wrong thing. 'It's going to look so much brighter and more familiar in the morning,' I whisper into her soft dark curls, her head tucked under my chin. I can hear Archie bouncing on his bed next door, eagerly chatting with Pete about plans to explore: the walks they'll take through the woods at the bottom of the garden, the treehouse they'll build together, when Pete gets the time.

'I liked our old house. That was bright, and familiar . . .' Rose says it wistfully, almost under her breath.

'We'll paint this room the same yellow as your old one, and you can get a new desk and anything else you want.' I'm casting around for other promises I can safely make, knowing exactly how Rose feels.

'I liked having Archie with me.' I look down and see tears starting to form.

'Maybe we can get a kitten to keep you company.' At this Rose's pale little face brightens instantly. She's been asking for a cat for years, but we were too worried about the busy roads, and her allergies. 'I'm sure we can find one that doesn't make you sneeze.'

'Really? Archie, Archie, guess what Mum just said!' Rose runs to Archie's bedroom, and I follow wearily, desperate now to get them tucked up in bed so we can collapse with a glass of wine.

I find the three of them piled on Archie's bed in his huge double-aspect room, overlooking the barn on one side, walk-in cupboard in one corner and the coveted sink in the other. Who are we, that this is only our second biggest bedroom?

'I hear we're setting up a menagerie.' Pete smiles at the kids, and looking at them, I suddenly feel it's all going to be okay. My attractive, only slightly greying husband, my two precious children, the most important people to me in the world, all together in our new home, the past behind us. We've made it through, intact. 'Rose tells me you're getting her a cat, and Archie reckons he's getting a dog. Maybe we should throw in a couple of pigs, some chickens. Really get this farm going.' I sit down and he puts an arm around me as I sink into the huddle.

'Oh, could we? Chickens! We could collect our own eggs in the mornings.' Rose's romantic countryside fantasies are getting out of hand now, and I kiss her on the head before heaving myself up from the bed.

'Come on, it's time to sleep. We'll talk about pets another day,' I say, leading her back into her room.

It isn't until Pete and I are alone again, having tucked in the kids, traipsed up and down those steep stairs three or four times with glasses of water, more cuddles, a few stern words, that we finally get a chance to take a breath. I sink next to him on the tatty yellow sofa that had dwarfed our old living room and barely makes a dent in our new one, handing him a beer and clinking my wine glass against his. 'Welcome to your new home.' I smile.

No point holding on to resentments about how quickly I had to give up everything we had back in London. I needed a clean break. I could see it was the only way, really. Now we've got to get on with it, even if I can feel a breeze circling my ankles and smell a musty scent, which, now I think about it, might be that little bootie I hid in my pocket. 'There's a fair amount to do,' I say to Pete as I stand up, putting my hands into my jeans to find the offending item, 'but I guess to begin with we just need to get everything . . .' I trail off. Pete is looking up at me, his skin pale, his eyes meeting mine for what I now realise is the first time in hours. I see a fear in them I haven't seen since that night in the summer, when he felt he'd let us down, hadn't been able to protect his family, couldn't do enough to keep us safe.

'Shit, Jess,' he says, running his hand through his hair and looking like he's going to be sick. 'What the hell have we done?'

Chapter Three

'Are you Archie's mum?' I look up with a jolt from my phone, where I've been scrolling through Instagram, trying to seem as though I might be busy, in demand. I'm waiting on the small stretch of playground outside the village school for the fourth time this week, fourteenth in total. This is the first time anyone has spoken to me.

'Oh yes, that's right. I'm Jess. We've moved in to the Maple House. We don't know anyone here at all!' I'm trying not to look too eager, but the woman is already backing away slightly, angling towards her group. I focus on her earrings to stop myself going on any more. Long silver drops that nestle in her bob.

'I'm Caroline, William's mum. I wondered if Archie would like to come to Will's party? It's next Saturday, at Super Bounce. We don't have any invitations left, but I'm sure we can squeeze one more in.' It's a small offering, and she looks as though she might already be regretting it, but I seize on it as though they're throwing a welcome do in our honour.

'We'd love to. What time is it? I'm not sure where Super Bounce is yet, but I'm sure we can make it along. It will be great to get to know the soft-play scene around here.' I attempt a laugh.

'It's drop off.' Is there a hint of pity in Caroline's smile? 'But you're welcome to stay, if you'd like . . .'

'Oh no, I've got Rose as well, so . . . It would just be good to know where they are. I haven't got a clue what there is to do with the kids around here.' I turn to the other mums, who are standing in a loose circle. Some smile weakly, others look away, as though I might try to invite myself to their houses any minute.

'So you're out in the Maple House . . .' one of them begins, and then trails off. A look passes between them that I can't quite identify.

'Yes, do you know it?'

'Of course – everyone knows the Maple House,' another mum joins in. 'It's so . . . big.' She looks up uncertainly, and I see Caroline frown. 'I'm sure it's fine when you get inside. But it's quite *looming*, isn't it?'

'Yes, quite the project, I'd imagine,' chips in another. 'We all had a nose around the online tour.'

I look at the concerned faces, feeling hot. Is that why people are always staring at me? Is our new home some kind of local in-joke?

'Yes, there's a lot to do.' I smile. 'But we've been so busy trying to get the children settled in, find out who their new friends are and everything. It's such a big move for them and . . . Sorry, I didn't catch any of your names?' I must stop acting as though this is a work social, but I've got no idea how else I'm ever going to get to know anyone around here.

I never had any problems making friends in Walthamstow. Arifa and I had connected on Archie and Tom's first day at nursery, sharing a laugh over the earnest motto printed on the board: *Make, Play, Create* . . . 'A mess,' Arifa had muttered.

31

'And then wash your hands afterwards, please,' I'd added with a smile, and that had been it: the start of an easy friendship that had gradually become a close one as our lives became intertwined. Becky had come along not long after, and the three of us had formed a tight bond. One I could still be part of, if I hadn't ruined everything.

But now we're here, and I can see how much I stand out in my bright pink coat. I've ditched the clashing teal scarf I used to wear with it, but I still feel like a focal point in a sea of black and blue parkas. I'm one of the few mums who doesn't come to school in full work-out gear, it seems, as though they're always on the way back from the gym or about to go for a run. And as for the dads – they're about as hands-on as Pete is these days, from the look of it.

'I'm Max's mum,' says one, adding 'Amy' as an afterthought.

The others all offer their names in turn – Julie, Kirsten, Sara – and then get back to the conversation they must have been having before Caroline invited me in.

'So, did you sign the flu form?' Amy asks Julie.

'No way.' Julie shakes her shiny hair. Despite wearing leggings and trainers, like most of these women, Julie has a full face of make-up and looks like she somehow had time to straighten her hair before pick up.

'Honestly, they're always trying to shove something up their nose, or in their arm,' Amy says.

'Well they're not getting their hands on Rory. I'd rather a bit of flu than loads of side effects.' There are nods, and I take my phone from my pocket, pretending to check for emails I haven't received. I'd signed the form last night without a moment's pause, just as I had done every year. Why on earth wouldn't you want your kids to be protected? But I don't want to get into an argument before I've even got to know anyone.

I'd never really been aware, all those days when I was at work, thinking wistfully of the kids and all the hours with them that I was missing out on, exactly what it was I was missing. Or avoiding. On my one day off a week, it had been such a treat to pick them up. They'd be beside themselves with excitement on a Friday to see my face at the window, to remember they weren't going to the childminder's or after-school club, that they'd have Mummy all to themselves. And I'd have the chance to catch up with the parents I'd known since their nursery days, who I'd bonded with gradually over the years at soft-play parties and summer fairs and school performances.

It hadn't occurred to me quite how quickly being there every day might become a grind. Or how soon the children would go from excited to pleased to indifferent, simply demanding a snack and starting to bicker immediately about whose turn it was to hold the remote control when we got home. And those idyllic afternoons in the playground opposite their old school, mums and dads relaxing on the grass while the kids made full use of the brand-new council-funded equipment? A distant memory. Here, there's no dawdling on the way home, chatting while the kids chase each other down the road. Instead it's straight into the car, home for a marathon stretch of TV before dinner and the eventual appearance of Pete – on the rare evenings he makes it back before they're asleep. I know we should get out more, get to know our new surroundings, but it's hard to muster enthusiasm for rural walks when the nights are drawing in, the air cold and damp, only eery, unfamiliar pathways, or looming woods to explore.

The mums have moved on to a conversation about some Year Six teacher I've never heard of, and then, to my relief, the classroom doors open and kids start streaming out.

33

'Here, put in your number.' Caroline hands me her phone. 'I'll text you the details for Will's party.'

I'm mumbling my thanks as Archie approaches, hands outstretched, rifling through my handbag for food before he's even said hello. 'Archie, wait a minute, I'm just in the middle of . . .' *attempting to make some friends*, I want to say, but the group has already dispersed and I find myself shepherding Archie and Rose to the car alone, again, trying not to notice the way everyone else seems to linger, making plans for the weekend.

'Who was that?' Archie wants to know as he climbs into the back seat.

'That was Will's mum. You know, in your class. He's invited you to his party next Saturday.'

'But I don't even like him. He told me London stinks. He said he's been down every street and they're all dirty.'

'That's ridiculous.' I catch Archie's eye in the rear-view mirror as I reverse away from the single-storey village school with a sense of relief. 'But you still need to make friends. We all do. So I think you should go.'

'But Dad and I are going to start planning the treehouse . . .'

'Archie, you're going to that party.'

'What about me? Have I been invited?' Rose looks ready to cry, her big grey eyes watering and her cheeks growing pink.

'I'm sorry, lovely, this one is for Archie. But we'll do something nice while he's there.'

'*She* can go. I don't even want to.' Archie scuffs his foot against the chair in front irritably, tossing his short brown hair and staring out of the window – my sociable child who doesn't want to make friends, sitting next to my shy one who seems desperate to. Had Archie been this difficult before

34

the move? Maybe it's an age thing. I know how quick I am to put every bad mood, every wobble, down to the trauma we've put them through, ripping them away from their old life, their friends, their home. Perhaps it's me experiencing the trauma, really. They're just helpless onlookers.

We've passed the pretty part of the village now, with the period houses, the traditional pub and small green, and we're driving through the drab stretch of Thirties and Sixties semis, the modern estate and then out into the winding country lanes, flat, featureless fields stretching out on either side. The sky is heavy, the drizzle forming a fine mist, and as we approach the turning for our house, the familiar knot starts to twist in my stomach. Even from the road it begins as I glimpse our ragged rooftop over the high hedges, the bare branches swaying either side. But it doesn't fully settle over me until we pull up and get out of the car. Back to the vast, run-down building we call home. And back to that feeling, the strange nagging that always comes over me – that something about this place is wrong.

Rose feels it too, I can tell. As soon as we get to the front door she huddles into me. She barely leaves my side in the daytime. At night, she's started waking up two or three times and crying out. Last night, I'd rushed in to find her standing at the window, new rosebud curtains opened wide, her face illuminated in the moonlight.

'There was a man out there, Mummy. He's come to take me away.'

'Come on, Rosie,' I'd soothed her, wrapping her in a hug and carrying her back to bed. 'There's no one out there, it's just the shadows of the trees.' But it had rattled me, and I'd found myself staring out into the darkness long after Pete had gone to bed.

Now we let ourselves into the dark hallway, and Archie disappears immediately into the living room, logging on to

Roblox on the iPad and joining his old school friends in cyberspace. He's been begging for an Xbox so he can talk to them online. We've resisted games consoles until now, in favour of Lego, football, long afternoons with school friends in the park. But now those are gone, I'm inclined to give in – anything to return some light to his eyes.

Rose follows me around the kitchen while I make them some toast and then drifts through to watch TV, leaving me staring at my own reflection in the kitchen window – my try-hard rainbow-striped jumper and messy blonde bob, grown out and tucked behind my ears – wondering how to fill the four and a half hours until Pete gets home.

I don't know what I'd imagined when I'd pictured myself looking after the children full-time. Crafts perhaps, reading together, board games, meaningful chats. I'd missed out on all those years as they were growing up, always feeling as though I rushed from one moment to the next – work, cycle home in time for after-school club pick-up, tea in the oven, quick bath, off to bed and repeat. In the early days, the children would cling to me, crying, whenever I dropped them at nursery, only compounding my guilt. As they got older, they complained bitterly about holiday schemes, boring babysitters, scrappy after-school clubs. So now I've finally given in, stopped trying to do it all, and where do I find myself? In the kitchen, preparing snacks, tidying up, making meals, clearing plates, all while refereeing screen time and squabbles. I feel more like a school dinner lady than the kind of artistic earth mother I'd pieced together from Instagram.

By the time Pete gets home, an hour later than promised again, the children have been fed, bathed, read with and put to bed – their spellings ticked off, their reading logs signed, glasses

36

of water fetched and night fears reassured. I've swept the kitchen, put on a stir fry and I'm finally sitting down with a glass of cheap white when I hear him pull up in the old Corsa we had to buy as a second car, once we realised I wouldn't be able to pick him up from the station at Manningtree every evening or manage without our Skoda during the day.

He walks in smelling of trains and smoke and London, and for a moment I can picture the day he's had, the hundreds of people he's brushed past, the dozens he's spoken to, the buildings, the noise, the energy. Then he takes off his jacket and closes the door behind him, and I'm returned to our depressing surroundings, the cracked tile worktop, the missing handles. I've scrubbed the kitchen for hours, but it still looks dirty. The windows rattle in the wind, making me startle and shiver at regular intervals. Pete creeps upstairs to kiss the children while they sleep, and then joins me in the kitchen, handing me a bottle of Chablis. He must think I can't see the relief on his face that he's missed all the work of bedtime, again.

'That's too expensive,' I say, eyeing the wine.

'I'm trying to keep you going,' he says into my neck, catching me round the waist, but I pull away and pick up our rapidly cooling noodles.

'What would keep me going is having you here.' I put the plates on the table. 'It's really hard doing all this by myself every night. You said you'd worked out the commute times, you were sure you'd be home earlier than this. What about all the promises of working from home?'

'It's not easy for me either, you know. I really miss them.' Pete sighs, as though the situation we find ourselves in is entirely out of his hands. As though he's been posted abroad and is bravely setting forth to provide for his brood.

'Well, you know what you can do about that.' I sit opposite him, unable to hide my frustration. If anything, when he gets home, it's amplified. Finally an audience, someone to witness my million small acts of martyrdom each day, to appreciate the sacrifices I've made.

After that first night in the house, and the almighty row that followed Pete's belated admission of regret, he's been keeping his feelings to himself. It had just been a freak-out, he said. He'd panicked about the cost of the building work, how we'd be able to pay for it all, what with the train fares and the second car and the parking costs and all the other little things we hadn't factored in. But a couple of days later, he was suddenly called back to work, the week we'd put aside to unpacking and getting ourselves settled cut short. Since then, he's been expected into the office every day, back late most nights. There's barely been time to discuss his fears about the size of the project we've embarked on, the money we'll have to spend on top of all the moving costs, especially now we don't have my salary coming in. The complete isolation he's only starting to acknowledge.

'It's that meeting with Graham tomorrow,' I remind him. 'Can you at least work from home so you can be here for that?' But I can see from the alarm in Pete's eyes that he's completely forgotten our appointment with the architect, and he starts to spout excuses that gather in pace and elaborate detail – an important meeting with a client, a new project that's more complex than anyone expected, the quarterly targets they risk missing if he doesn't pull it off, the promotion he's still hoping to secure.

It's so much harder, now that I'm not working, to tune into the vocabulary of office life. It all sounds so meaningless, so petty – the presenteeism, the infighting, the one-upmanship. I can remember how important it seemed at the time, but I can't *feel* it any more, even though it's only been a month or so. I nod and listen as Pete recounts the highs and lows of his day, thinking of how, if it wasn't for his countryside dreams, I'd still be cycling to the gallery, meeting donors, discussing campaigns, wearing earrings, buying new shoes in my lunch break that I'd actually have a reason to wear. I'd solve hundreds of small, manageable problems a week and still be home to tuck the kids into bed. His life has barely changed. He's still going to the agency, to Pret a Manger at lunch, for a pint after work on a Friday. I'm the one whose old life disappeared overnight; the contours of my personality, the person I was, seeming to dissolve into the dust around me.

Late into the night, I lie awake, listening to the wind brushing branches against the bedroom window. I've already been in to see Rose once this evening, when she cried out. She was sure she'd seen someone again. This time, I peered out with her, my heart pounding, trying to see what she described.

But there was no one there. And I'd tucked her back in, reassuring her that the man she saw in London wasn't coming to find us. That we were safe here. That Pete and I would protect her.

Back in bed, I lie awake, worrying about Rose. We'd all been so shaken up after the break-in – the kids hadn't wanted to sleep; I hadn't wanted to leave their sides – but somehow we'd settled back into our old routine. It's only now that we're at a safe distance from the scene of the trauma her fears have resurfaced, and she's started seeing the intruder again. I feel scared again, too. Haunted by visions of that big, broad figure framed in the doorway, Rose's terror, my helplessness. Conversations with the police afterwards about whether there was anyone who had any reason to harm us, any grudges, any debts. It didn't look like a standard burglary, they'd said, because he hadn't taken anything, hadn't even attempted to search for valuables. But Pete had interrupted him pretty quickly, we reasoned at the time. He didn't have a chance.

Now I wonder again whether that was true. Had there been something else he wanted? Some other reason he was there? The image that stays with me is that hand, large and powerful, curled around the edge of our front door. I picture him closing it behind him. It seems somehow too polite, too considered for a man on the run. What if it *was* someone we knew? But who could possibly want to harm us?

For some reason, my mind flits to the discovery I made in the utility room. That lone, stray baby sock, a keepsake perhaps, or worn years ago and long forgotten. The feeling I had that this house has a story to tell, one we've stumbled into, interrupted even. In the pull of sleep, I feel an unravelling, the connections waiting to be reknitted, brought back together. And then I hear a bang. Loud enough that my eyes spring open; I sit up in bed.

I've grown used to the nightly noises here, as though each room, each floorboard, has to creak itself back into place before the house can fully relax. But this is different. A crack that starts my heart racing immediately. I look at Pete, but he's sleeping soundly. I could wake him, but he'll only think I'm being hysterical again.

I slip out of the bedroom and move slowly down the hallway, towards the bright moon that shines through the rounded window-panes. Outside, trees are waving in the breeze, but there are no sudden movements. Nothing that could have produced such a startling sound. I pad downstairs and stare at the barn in the darkness through the kitchen window. 'Come on then,' I hiss under my breath. 'What do you want?'

I don't know who I think is out there. It couldn't be the intruder, not really. How would he find us out here? What about the weird guy who lived here before us? The one Pete told me about, unable to let go. Or some local kids, messing around. All I know is that it's someone. I'm not imagining it. My heart is racing; my fists are clenched. I'm almost tempted to go out there. To scream and shout into the darkness until this stranger comes out and reveals himself. But it's the middle of the night. If I wake the children, they'll be terrified.

I run myself a glass of water and creep back upstairs, hearing a whimper from Rose's room. As I walk in, I see immediately that the door to her strange, half-height cupboard has blown open in the wind. I feel my shoulders relax. That must have been what banged. Perhaps I am going mad, after all.

I cross the room, and I'm about to shut the cupboard door when I hear another little cry, this one coming from inside the opening. My heart starts pounding again. I crouch to my knees and peer in. It's Rose, curled up inside, sobbing quietly, her eyes closed.

I stifle a gasp. I hadn't even registered her empty bed. 'Rose, what are you doing in there?' I whisper, pulling at her arm. But she doesn't move; her eyes are closed and she's shaking her head a little, still asleep. 'Rose, darling, we need to get you out of there.' I edge in as far as I can and put a hand under each of her armpits, hauling her out. I pull her towards me, huddling her over my shoulder as I close the cupboard door and carry her to bed, feeling her sobs subside and her breathing calm. But mine is erratic. What on earth was she doing in there? I've never known her to sleepwalk.

I cuddle her on my knee and stroke her clammy forehead. 'It's okay, little one. You're safe now.'

'I don't like it here, Mummy,' she says in a voice that's surprisingly clear and coherent.

'What was that?' I'd heard all right, but I want to be sure.

41

'I don't like this house. The garden. It's safe in there.'

But her eyes are still closed, and as I hold her to my chest, and whisper to her that Mummy and Daddy are here, and she's perfectly safe, and she shouldn't go climbing into cupboards in the middle of the night, I feel her relax into sleep in my arms.

It's only as I lie her on the bed that I notice her little hand is clamped around something. A piece of fabric, greyish white. I tug it from her grip as she rolls onto her side and hold it up in the half-light. It looks like muslin. The kind we used when the children were small. Rose would hold on to one sometimes, dragging it around and sucking it, but we got rid of it all those years ago. And this one is old, dirty. It's probably been hanging around in that cupboard for years, and Rose was clinging to it for comfort, just as she had when she was a baby. The thought brings tears to my eyes.

Creeping back into our bedroom, I hide the muslin in the drawer where I put the baby sock. I hadn't told Pete about that discovery, and I know I won't tell him about this one either – or the noise that woke me, how I found our daughter cowering in her cupboard, clinging to someone else's old rag for comfort, sheltering from some unknown terror. There won't be time, for one thing. He'll be up and out when the kids and I are barely surfacing. But also, I can't imagine putting this heart-stopping moment into words he'd understand. He'd dismiss it, wouldn't be able to see how terrifying it was, to find our little girl gone from her bed, curled up in a confined space, crying. He'd think it's my anxieties rubbing off on her. That my weird behaviour is putting ideas into her head. And perhaps it is.

But as I climb into bed next to Pete, shivering and curling

up close to him, trying to capture some of his body heat, I can't escape the feeling that something happened in this house. Something bad. And that we won't be happy until we leave.

Chapter Four

It is a relief to be in daylight again. Pete at work. The children at school. Only responsible for my own mood, my own schedule. The unsettled feeling is still there. The house eerily quiet, every bang or creak a source of anxiety. But at least I don't have to put a brave face on – to pretend I feel at home, that I have a purpose, that I know what to do with myself in all this space.

I've set up my laptop in the living room, looking out of a corner window onto an overgrown patch of garden, on the opposite side of the house to the driveway and outbuildings, far away from the dark shadows they cast. In fact, I'm directly facing the problem weeds, which have died back now, reduced to dry, straw-coloured stalks – certainly nothing you'd expect to cost thousands of pounds. 'No idea where it came from,' Brian had said when he showed us around. 'It's usually not such a problem in this area.' Just our bad luck, then. One of the many issues that need to be resolved before we can make ourselves at home here.

Graham's late, and I know I should be researching weed removal, building contractors, planning processes, but instead

I scroll through the Facebook group for Archie's old class, seeing who's had a birthday and how they're getting on with their new teacher in Year Four. Then I find myself scanning the Twitter feeds of my ex-colleagues, clocking the build-up of excitement for the new exhibition, the progress of the fundraising project I helped to implement.

How I used to moan about the super-keen volunteers and smug curators. We were a small gallery, and the competition could be intense. I was convinced the bosses had overlooked my creativity, keeping me stuck in a low-paid fundraising role. I'd been storing up resentments for nearly a decade. But after only a matter of weeks away, and the fond send-off from the colleagues I'd seen most days for the majority of my thirties, I feel unexpectedly bereft and worthless.

Who am I without that job? I watch a small brown bird hop across the patchy lawn, looking as lost and forlorn as I feel. Without my career, my daily routine, any structure to my life. I open Instagram and scan through Becky's feed, and then Arifa's. A kids' party, a meet-up in our local park. Our *old* local park. They're careful to keep the children's faces out of the pictures, but I recognise some of them from their hair-cuts, distinctive coats, the mums gathered in the background, laughing. I feel a pang of jealousy, exclusion – and then I remember I had already been cut out of their lives anyway. Or I'd cut myself out, without even thinking about what I was doing. Though I must have known what would happen, really. That's what Arifa said.

I notice a heart appear in the top right-hand corner of the page and feel my pulse quicken. Maybe it's a message from one of my old friends, someone getting in touch to see how we're doing. But I see it's just a comment on one of my posts from yesterday. I'd put up a picture of some Art Nouveau wallpaper I'd been considering for the living room, and someone from a local gallery has suggested I come in and check out their paintings.

Nice wallpaper. You should pop in to #TheWhiteRoom if you're ever in Ipswich. We've got some great local landscapes for inspiration.

I click through to the gallery bio and scroll down the page. There is something interesting about the pictures, bright and eye-catching, layers of leaves and shadows, light and shade. Not right for the house, but maybe worth taking a look at when I venture into town.

I scroll through the recent pictures on my phone and pick out one of the children, taken from behind, at a distance, running through a field. Arifa doesn't follow me any more, but Becky does. Maybe she'll see it. And some of the other parents. My colleagues. I put on a filter and a caption – 'Rural life #kidsrunwild #countrybumpkins' – and post it to Instagram. I've got to at least maintain the illusion of having made the right decision.

I'm putting up another post – the copy of *The Yellow Wallpaper* by Charlotte Perkins Gillman that Mum sent me, next to a ceramic latte mug – when a loud knock almost lifts me from my seat. I race to the front door, trying to calm myself. I must project a sense of capability. Opening it wide, I give Graham a welcoming smile and lead him into the kitchen, searching through the cupboards for the cafetière.

It's the first time we've met, though he's seen the house, guided around and appointed by Pete, before he disappeared back into the world of important meetings and client drinks. Graham stoops through the kitchen doorway, tall and thin with a cloud of greying hair and an air of amused detachment. He's wearing thick cords and heavy boots, and his eyes rest on my skinny jeans and fluffy slippers. 'You've got your work cut out here,' he announces as I find mugs and milk, plunge the coffee and place two cups on the table, my hands shaking.

Already, I've grown unaccustomed to company, to small talk, retreated into myself in the silence. But I take a deep breath and try to look unfazed.

'We have, haven't we? But you come highly recommended, so . . .'

'Well, I haven't done much in these parts, but your husband seemed keen after he saw the Turners' place outside Cambridge.' I picture Rich and Amanda's barn conversion. The expanses of glass, the polished concrete, the reflective surfaces. That's never going to work here. But Pete looks up to Rich, who's a few rungs ahead of him at the firm. And Amanda works freelance as an interior designer, so she's been able to pull in all her contacts. They made the move to the countryside a few years before us, and are now fully ensconced with their teenagers, dog and Range Rover. If only we hadn't gone to Rich's fiftieth last summer, hadn't stayed over at a local B&B, a sun-drenched June weekend without the children, in an idyllic rural setting, perhaps we wouldn't be here now. Once Pete had seen another way of living, he wouldn't let up. It was the answer to the problem we had been going over and over for months. Now here we are, with the same architect, one county across, trying to recreate their life.

'Their place must have been a wreck to begin with,' I say, hopefully, as Graham's eye follows mine to the crack in the wall, running all the way up to the ceiling.

'Hm, it was more of a shell, I suppose. The problem you've got here is planning permission. Theirs was a barn, so there wasn't much red tape. But you're Grade II listed. As I'm sure Pete's told you, the council has to approve our plans. I doubt that conservatory was ever official, so you'll have no problems knocking that down, but the extension's going to have to get signed off, and well . . . we'll see.' He fiddles with the glasses in his shirt pocket impatiently. 'Now, the barn's a different story. You've got a lot more scope out there.' I nod, looking away. It's the house I'm desperate to get into shape, and I can't remember Pete ever conveying to me this level of doubt about our plans. Then again, we've had a lot on our minds, with the break-in, the speed of the move, all the loose ends to tie up in London.

'So, if you wouldn't mind showing me around the outbuildings.' Graham looks at me expectantly, as though this isn't the first time he's asked. I've been avoiding going into the barn and garage since we moved. I've told the children they're out of bounds – too many potential dangers among all the rubble and rubbish – and I've been following that rule myself. I'm busy enough with the house and garden, I've said to Pete whenever he's invited me to come and scope them out with him. I don't want to let on how much those buildings spook me. But Pete's obviously told Graham all about his dreams of a rental property empire, the bottle store for the boutique cider company he's convinced he's going to eventually develop from the run-down orchard round the back. Graham has already laid out the plans in front of me, talking me far too rapidly through everything he and Pete have agreed. There's a bedroom, a small living area and an en suite mapped out in the barn. In the garage, a storage area and yet another small living space. When will we get around to renovating the house we actually live in?

But now isn't the time for questions, so I lead Graham out to the barn. The door is unlocked, the padlock rusted off well before we moved in, and I push it open, stepping inside fully for the first time. It's a large space, derelict, with a musty, cloying scent and thick layers of dust across all the surfaces, the old work benches, the abandoned tools. In one corner is a large, dirty butler sink, which Graham points to, approvingly. 'Water source. So it doesn't have to be plumbed in.'

We step a little further into the gloom, and that's when I notice in the far corner an old beaten-up mattress and next to it, lying abandoned on the floor, a small hand mirror. Inching closer, I pick up the mirror, black-handled, the glass mottled with age and cracked in one corner, and on the back, scratches of dark green paint. I rotate it in my hand, watching a beam of light reflect from the window onto the mattress. It's only when I notice Graham studying me that I realise how oddly I'm behaving.

'It doesn't look that old, does it?' I gesture towards the mattress, prodding it with my foot. There's a fine layer of dust, but nothing like the coating on the work bench.

'You didn't bring it?' Graham asks.

'No. No one's been sleeping in here.' Why would we put a mattress in this horrible old building? We've got a massive house we can't even fill next door.

'I suppose it's been left here by the people who lived here before you.' Graham's already moving towards the door, ready to look at the garage.

'But the house has been empty for a while,' I say, 'and before that, it was rented out. So who would have stayed in here?' I think about the movements that have caught my eye from the house, the reflections against the small windows in the darkness, a cold dread running through me. Has someone been sleeping in our barn?

But then I shake my shoulders, an involuntary shudder. Who would sleep rough out here, miles from anywhere?

Graham's right, it must have been left behind, along with the mirror, which I slip into the pocket of my cardigan as I pull the barn door closed behind me.

Later, in bed, I tell Pete about the meeting, our discussions about the house, the barn, the garage, which was in no better state, but at least didn't have any nasty surprises. I drop in a mention of the mattress, trying to sound casual. 'It's just been left there; it doesn't even look that old. It almost seemed as if someone might have been staying out there.' But Pete just nods. He's tired. The rings around his eyes even darker than yesterday, the scent of beer on his breath from another client drink, keeping him in London late.

'Yeah, I've seen it. Someone probably dumped it out there when they didn't need it in the house any more.' He turns onto his back, ready to sleep.

'What about that guy, though, who sold us the house? You said he was a bit odd, didn't you? And he wasn't sure about moving on. What if he's still hanging around here? Sleeping rough out there?'

'Come on, Jess. We paid him good money for this house. He's not going to need to sleep in our barn. I know we had a scare in London, but we're safe here. You've got to stop imagining people are lurking around, that everyone's out to get you.'

I sigh and roll over. I've waited up to talk it all through with Pete, keeping myself awake with that book Mum gave me, about a woman confined to her home, convinced her wallpaper is moving in the moonlight. Probably not the right choice for now. I want to tell Pete about the mirror I found as well – delicate, antique, with scratched paint and cloudy glass. The one I've tucked into the drawer, along with the other objects I've found around the place, each of them unsettling in its own

50

way. But Pete's eyes are closing, and I know he'll only say I'm overreacting.

'It sounds like it'll be months before we get going on the house, anyway,' I say. 'I thought we were already underway with the planning permission. And I didn't realise you and Graham had agreed we'd do the barn first.'

'I'm sure I told you that,' Pete says sleepily. 'The sale went through so quickly, there wasn't time to apply for planning. It's going through now, but it makes sense to get started on the barn in the meantime, doesn't it? If we can get that done, we can put it up on Airbnb and make some money to put into the build.'

'Who's going to want to come and stay next to a falling-down wreck of a house?' I ask, leaning up on my elbow, feeling wide awake. 'And who's going to get it ready, and clean it, and let the renters in?'

'I thought you wanted a project, something to do with yourself now you're not working? Look, I really need to get some sleep, Jess. I've got to be up for the train in six hours.'

'What kind of a life is this?' I say it under my breath, but no answer comes. I thought the rental properties were a pipe dream, way down the line. That we'd get the house exactly how we wanted it first. I try to imagine having strangers to stay next door, while Pete's away all day and the children and I are knocking around here alone. I can already see my days filling up with menial tasks: bookings, cleaning, liaising with builders, with Graham.

What about the distance learning course we discussed me signing up to? Art history, to build up the skills I missed out on at university, get the qualifications I need to become a curator instead of a fundraiser. But the prospectus I sent off for never even turned up, and I can see now there's no way I'll manage to study on top of the build, the rental properties, the kids, with Pete never here. Besides, we're so far from any of the big galleries, and I'm not getting any younger. If we stay here, I'll miss my chance to make it as a curator altogether.

Watching Pete's shoulder rise and fall in the darkness, I feel a surge of frustration. Mum was right. I never should have given up my job, my income, my independence. I sit up in bed, but Pete doesn't stir. He's sleeping now.

Trying to make as little noise as possible, I fish under my bedside table. My hand feels for the cold solid weight. My second phone, the one Pete doesn't know about. The small oblong that represents some sort of freedom to me now.

I swore I wouldn't use it again. That I'd get rid of it as soon as I could do it safely, with no risk of discovery. But I feel a sudden urge to turn it on, just to know that there might be a way out of this situation. Another future, different to the one we've signed up to here.

I take the phone into the bathroom and lock the door behind me. Only then do I press the button, perching on the edge of the bath while I wait for it to illuminate, the logo bouncing merrily as the screen comes to life.

I haven't even allowed myself to turn it on since we moved. I've been so determined to put it all behind me. But with my desperation rising, I can't hold back any longer.

37 missed calls

29 messages

My fingers fumble for the off switch. I had no idea they would still be coming. What if the phone starts ringing right now, the noise echoing around this tiled room like a warning, waking Pete and the children? The thought terrifies me, and

I sit there, shivering in the darkness for a long time. What was I thinking?

Finally, I creep back to our bedroom, checking on Rose as I pass. She's in her bed now, sleeping, and as I get in next to Pete, I try to calm my breathing, relax my mind.

But all I can think about, all I can picture, is that blue Nokia. The secret button I could press. The lifeline that could one day get me out of here.

Chapter Five

It is a clear, crisp November afternoon. Cold light slants through the shop window as I stand, turning cards over in my hand, wondering which would possibly be appropriate for an eight-year-old boy. The one I'm holding has a rabbit perched on its hind legs, sniffing the air, ears high and pointed. It looks alert, scared really, the way its eyes roll and its nostrils, tiny pools of dark paint, flare. But at least it's a small animal. It could just about pass as cute.

I've come into Ipswich, desperate to escape the small village where, already, I'm on nodding terms with most of the locals. I've still only exchanged a few words at the school gates, but I'm pretty sure most of the villagers know us by now as the London couple mad enough to take on the crumbling Maple House. Every time I say the name, I'm aware of a telltale twitch, a barely perceptible adjustment in the face of the neighbour who has accosted me outside the shop, or by the post box, or as I'm escaping from the school. Something happened there, or something's wrong with it, beyond the obvious. I can never work out which it is.

But what bothers me nearly as much as those lingering

questions is the sense of being watched everywhere I go. I've taken my anonymity for granted, I realise now. I hadn't even been aware how important it was to me, to be able to operate independently of the judgements and observations of others, until it was too late. Wandering around the shopping streets in Ipswich on a sunny winter afternoon I felt I'd entered a new atmosphere, almost giddy with the sense of freedom.

I managed to find the small gallery, The White Room. The one I read about on Instagram. It's tucked away on one of the small lanes near the centre of town, selling hand-painted cards and a few artworks in the hundreds of pounds. They're paintings of the local area mostly, done with neat brushstrokes in bright colours – lots of foliage, rivers, trees that seem familiar. Similar to designs we displayed in the gallery in London. But something about these paintings jars. At the edge of each rural scene is an animal – rabbit, deer, mouse – with a look of fear in its eyes. As though something much darker is about to take place just outside the frame.

I recoil a little, turn back to the card in my hand, check my watch. It's two already. I need to get to school to pick up the kids. Will it do? William won't take a second glance in the rush of torn wrapping paper and sugary drinks. Archie's only making up numbers, anyway. Or it's an act of kindness towards the new kid who hardly speaks, his old confidence knocked out of him on his first day in this alien environment. I shudder involuntarily at the prospect of dropping him off, encouraging him to join this group of strangers. The effort it will take to summon up small talk, to shrug off the shock and disappointment of the last few weeks, to fend off the amused looks at any mention of our house. That's when I notice the shadow cast across me, the silhouette filtering the light.

'Very naive, those ones,' the voice says. I can't tell if it's approving or not and I look up uncertainly. 'I'm Eve Drake.' She points to the signature in the corner. 'It's one of mine.' The woman smiles and takes the card from my hand, holding it up to the light.

'It's lovely,' I say quickly.

'Hmm, I think that's probably not the word.' Eve laughs and looks at me, waiting for my response. She's around my age, or a few years older, short and petite, with dark, twinkly eyes and black hair, bobbed and shiny, a blunt fringe resting just above her eyelashes. Large silver hoops almost reach the shoulders of her black roll-neck, and her wide-legged trousers are cropped to reveal low-heeled, pointed boots. She looks like she should be running a boutique in Dalston or Brick Lane, not a tiny gallery in Ipswich.

'Well, lovely and a little unsettling, I suppose.' I smile. It feels odd to venture an opinion, after all these weeks of nodding and agreeing and trying to fit in. 'The rabbit looks a bit . . . uncertain. But the foliage reminds me of some of the paintings in the gallery where I used to work. In fact, I think we've got some of those trees in our garden.' I point to the edge of the card, at the leaves I now know belong to the English field maple, the tree that gave our house its name.

'Oh, really?' The way Eve studies me, I feel painfully aware of my unbrushed hair, my muddy trainers, the pink coat I've worn for too many seasons. 'Are you local?'

'Yes, sorry, I'm Jess. We've moved to a village nearby – my husband and two kids. Well it's not quite in the village. It's this big, old rambling place – the Maple House. You probably don't know it. But we've got lots of trees like that. And the way you've painted them makes me think of the Arts and Crafts style, like the wallpaper I posted on Instagram. Whoever runs your gallery account must have seen it. That's how I knew to come in. I haven't really seen any art, any galleries, since we left London, or met anyone who . . .' I trail off, blushing. I've allowed myself to go on far too long, come over too keen. But Eve just smiles.

'I know what you mean. It can be hard to find your crowd around here.'

'Yes, people are very nice, but . . .' I'm hoping Eve might rescue me, put into words what I'm trying to express, but she's looked away, tidying a pile of cards by the till. I wonder if it was her who saw my post, or if there's someone else who works here. It's so small, it seems unlikely. But whoever it is must send out those kinds of messages all the time, trying to get customers through the door. 'Anyway, there's a sprinkling of maples at the bottom of our garden, along the side of the stream. That's what the house is named after, you know. I'm sure it was lovely once, but there's so much to do to it, I'm feeling a bit overwhelmed.' I pause. 'Sorry, I'm going on. I should pay for this and get out of your way.' I flash what I hope is an apologetic smile.

'Let me put it through the till,' Eve says, her voice clear and unhurried as she takes the card and puts it in a paper bag. 'So, you used to work in a gallery?'

'Yes. Just a small one, in London.'

'Not *this* small, I'd imagine.' She gestures to the tiny box room, white walls covered in bright paintings. Are they all hers, I wonder. How does she keep afloat?

'No, and I'm not an artist, like you. I worked in fundraising. I wanted to . . . get into the more creative side, but I never got the break.'

'Well, London is a break in itself compared to somewhere like this. You're not from round here then?'

I shake my head. 'No, and neither is my husband. We picked it from a map really. On the right train line, lovely countryside, of course.' I gesture towards the paintings. 'But we don't know a soul. Or didn't. Well, still don't. Everyone seems to know us though, that's the weird thing. It's like our house is a local talking point, but I haven't worked out why.' I pull a face, and Eve smiles.

'It can be hard finding your feet in an area like this. I grew up here, but when I moved away and came back, it was as though I'd never lived here . . . It took me a long time to feel settled again. As much as I ever will.' I look down and notice her gripping the edge of the desk a little, her nails bitten down. I wonder where she'd moved to.

'Were you in London? Or somewhere else?' I quickly correct myself. *London isn't the centre of the universe,* I hear Pete reminding me. There are other places.

'Oh, all over the place.' She sweeps an arm in the air and begins stacking a set of cards by the till. 'Anyway, it was nice to meet you, Jess. Will you pop in again if you're passing by?'

I can't tell if it's a polite brush-off or a genuine invitation, but I smile anyway.

'I'd like that,' I say, turning to leave, and I mean it. For the first time in ages I feel understood, accepted, on a wavelength with someone. Eve's the first person I've met around here I could actually picture as a friend.

The children must pick up on my lightened mood, because on the way home from school we sing loudly along with the radio, even Archie joining in with the Little Mix song that's one of Rose's favourites. She asks me to turn it up, and once we're through the village I oblige, the lyrics blasting out as we wind down the thick-hedged narrow lanes. Approaching the house, I feel a sense of calm for once. Pete's right, I've got to get over this weird obsession I've developed. A house can't have bad energy. It's just a building, and one with a lot of potential. We're lucky to live here. I need to be patient. We'll get there in the end.

It's not until we've pulled up outside and I've switched off the engine that I hear the barking, frenzied and high-pitched. An animal nearby. A dog in distress.

I turn to the kids, Archie craning his neck to look for the source of the noise, Rose's eyes wide with alarm. 'What's that, Mummy, where's it coming from?'

'I don't know, lovely. Why don't you both stay in the car while I go and take a look? It sounds like a dog to me, but better to be sure.' I'm trying to keep my voice steady, though I feel a rising alarm at this unexpected intrusion into our land, our space. As I get out of the car, the barking gets louder. And along with it, shouting, a male voice, growling.

'Mummy?' Rose looks panicked now and even Archie's worried; I can tell by the way he tosses his hair. 'Where are you going?'

'I'm just going to find out where the noise is coming from, then I'll be back. Don't worry, Archie's with you. Here,' I say to Archie, 'take my phone. You can both play some games on it while you're waiting.' *And use it to call someone if I don't come back*. I'm aware of the thought flitting through my mind before I take myself in hand. There's bound to be a simple explanation for all this racket.

It's easy enough to follow the barks and whines, though I do so reluctantly, ducking behind the barn and dragging myself along its length, by the tall hedges and brambles that line the edge of our property. They're so overgrown in places that I have to scramble and pull my coat through the thorns, but gradually the noise gets louder – both of the injured animal and its owner, swearing and grunting to himself. Even so, I stiffen as I round the corner of the barn to find a man, bent double, half obscured by a large, ragged bush.

'Can I help?' I have to shout to be heard over the barking,

and the man springs backwards, dragging with him a large brown dog, a Doberman or something similar, blood pouring from its hind leg.

The man turns to me, nostrils flared and eyes bulging, a bead of bright red on his cheek where a thorn has scratched him. 'There you are!' An arm jabs in my direction. 'You should be more bloody careful. What are you thinking letting these bushes get like this? They need cutting back. Anything could get stuck in there.'

I'm shaking, taken aback by his outburst. So is the dog, whining, curled at his feet on the ground. But the man ignores the animal entirely, stretching to his full height, his long, hard face lined with anger, thinning hair, a tatty jacket over muddy trousers and boots. He can only be a couple of decades older than me and Pete, but he looks like he's from a different era. Hard-living, bloodshot eyes, his skin greasy and pallid against the crimson that blooms across his cheek. His voice is broad Suffolk, though he's spitting with rage, hardly able get his words out.

'It's been bad enough empty for so long, but there's no excuse now. This place is a bleeding dump. It needs taking in hand. What are you going to do about it?' He looks me up and down – my bleached hair, bright coat, designer trainers – and his lip curls.

'Excuse me, but you're on my property and I don't know who you are.' My voice comes out clearer than I'm expecting, my vowels ringing in the air.

'I'm your neighbour and this here's my dog, who's been injured on your "property",' he says the word in a mocking tone, still barely glancing in the direction of his animal, whose blood pools on the ground around his hind leg.

'But what's he doing here? Why are you walking your dog in our garden?' I can feel my hands shaking with adrenalin, the confrontation, but I'm determined to get to the bottom of this quickly, aware of the children waiting anxiously in the car. Part of me wants to go to them straight away and reassure them that's it's okay. Just our angry neighbour and his wounded dog. But I don't want them anywhere near this highly strung stranger, with his rough, swearing manner.

'I live over there.' He jerks a hand behind him. 'There's a lane other side of this hedge. We walk down it every day. Rex never comes in. Why would he?' Again the tone is accusatory.

'And how did you get in?'

'Through the hedge. I had to get Rex out, didn't I? Only he was stuck. I just managed to pull him free when you turned up.' As if remembering, he bends down to tend to his dog, pulling a large blue handkerchief out of a pocket and wrapping it around the wounded leg to stem the flow of blood. The dog is whimpering softly now, looking at me with wary eyes.

'Well, I'm sorry your dog's hurt himself, but I can't really see why it's my fault. You need to keep him out of other people's gardens.' It puts me on edge, how casual this man is about having torn through our hedge, lurking around our grounds when we're not here. Perhaps it's been empty so long the locals feel it's just common land to be walked across. Maybe that explains all the strange movements, the noises.

'But that's what I'm saying. I've lived back there for years. He's never come in before.' He wipes a hand roughly against his cheek, smearing the blood towards his ear. There's something in his eyes that makes me want to look away. A wild, darting energy that puts me on edge.

'Well, I can't explain it . . .' I turn towards the house. I need to get the children. Get rid of this man. But when I turn back, I see he's ducked into the bushes again.

'Keep an eye on him,' he growls over his shoulder as he disappears. I look down at the dog, uncertainly. Even injured, he seems like the kind of animal you don't want to be left alone with. But it's only a matter of moments before the man re-emerges, his hand dripping with blood and, at the end of it, a dismembered animal carcass. 'Here's your culprit,' he says, grimly, throwing it on the ground in front of his dog, who leans forward gingerly and starts to sniff and then tear at the glistening red meat with his pointed teeth, pinning the poor animal between his front paws and shaking his head this way and that, ripping the flesh from the bones.

'Oh, God.' I cover my face with my hand. 'That's disgusting. I suppose that's what your dog was looking for in the bushes. Another animal must have left it there.' I take a step back. 'Listen, I've got to get back, my children are in the car.' His eyes flick in the direction of the house and immediately I regret mentioning them at all. 'I'm Jess. We moved in a couple of months ago. We are going to sort out the garden, but we've got quite a lot to be getting on with in the house at the moment.'

The man ignores what I've said entirely. 'It's no animal that's left that there. That rabbit's been skinned, butchered.' His brow is furrowed, as if he's waiting for an explanation.

'What, you mean . . .'

'A human. Someone's put it there, as a trap, more an likely.'

'A trap for what? Who would do that?'

'Don't ask me.' He shrugs. 'Just watch out, I would. Seems an odd thing to turn up in your garden.' The way he looks at me then, his eyes glassy and bloodshot, makes me lift a hand to my throat.

'Okay,' I say, trying to ignore the question he's raised that sounds almost like a threat. 'Sorry about your dog, about Rex. I didn't get your name?'

'Trevor Martin. Live over there.' He gestures in the general direction of the small bungalow, set back from the road, that's the only house we've been able to spy in the vicinity of ours. I'd been wondering who lived in it. I'd heard the dog barking, but I'd imagined a friendly older couple. I'd even wondered a few times whether I should knock and introduce myself, since both houses are tucked away near each other, so far from anywhere else. Now I'm glad I didn't.

'Never had much to do with this place,' he adds, looking over my shoulder. 'Not with them lot.' And then he turns his back, yanking his dog by its collar. The dog picks up what remains of the bloody carcass in its mouth and limps along next to his owner, both of them disappearing into one of the bushes. I follow a few steps, open-mouthed. Sure enough, there's a gap wide enough for a person to slip through easily. I'd never even spotted it. Anyone could be getting in and out.

With a lurch, I remember the children. They'll be worried sick by now. I dash back to the car, trying to get a hold of myself before I reach them, so they don't see how spooked I am, how jittery. Thank God I didn't bring them with me. There's no way I'd get Rose to sleep in her bedroom once she'd come face to face with that man, his face bleeding, his injured dog – our nearest neighbour for miles around. And what did he mean about 'them lot'? As though even he thought there was something odd about the people who lived here before us.

Well, the children won't be meeting him at all, not if I can help it. I'll make sure they play in the other direction, by the woods and the stream, nowhere near that man's bungalow. The knowledge of his proximity makes me want to keep them close. To keep an eye on them at all times, though that's not quite the rural freedom we had in mind. Perhaps if I talk to Pete about blocking up the hedge, I'll be able to relax again.

One thing's for sure, if I find that man on our property again, I'm calling the police.

Chapter Six

'I know you don't want to go, but we've got to make an effort to settle in.' I try to catch Archie's eye in the rear-view mirror, but he's staring out of the window as the countryside flashes past outside, through a veil of rain.

'I'm sure it rains more here than anywhere else in the world,' Archie huffs from the back seat, resigned to his afternoon of enforced celebration. Rose is snivelling next to him because she *can't* go, which is equally annoying, though I try to keep my patience as I know from her night waking that her anxiety is only getting worse.

I take a deep breath and swing into a large industrial estate on the outskirts of Manningtree, scanning the buildings for signs of life. Everything looks shut, just like everywhere around here. But eventually we find an iron-clad building with a garish sign featuring clowns and juggling balls. 'Here we are!' I try to sound cheerful as we park the car and scuttle through the drizzle towards the windowless structure. At the entrance, we find William and his mum, along with all fifteen of the other children from Archie's class. He grips my hand tightly as Rose hangs off my other arm.

'Hiya!' I drag them both towards the group. 'We found it, eventually.'

I smile apologetically at Caroline; she has clearly been waiting for us to appear, while holding back a group of rowdy eight-year-olds.

'There you are! Archie, you go along over there and get your wrist band and . . . Oh dear, what's this? Are you feeling a bit left out?' Caroline looks down at Rose, who has buried her face in my coat.

'Don't worry, she'll be fine. We're off to explore a bit. Still getting to grips with where everything is.' I put my arm around Rose's shoulders.

'Are you sure? I mean, we're at full capacity, but you might be able to pay her in, if you really want to . . .' I follow her gaze to the café, where the group of mums I met in the play-ground are in a huddle, straining to hear each other over the yells and whoops, warming their hands on polystyrene cups. I couldn't feel less welcome – or less tempted.

'No, we're fine. Thanks, though. I'll be back at . . .'

'Four,' she confirms, barely hiding her relief. 'Or a bit earlier if you want to join in with the cake. Have a great afternoon.' She turns to leave before I can even murmur my thanks. It's not until I get back to the car that I realise we've forgotten to give them William's present and card. They're sitting on the back seat, next to where Archie had been strapped in. It's too late now. I'll have to hand them over when I pick him up. But maybe that's why she seemed so unfriendly. Or perhaps she just doesn't need any more friends. None of them do.

Was I this unwelcoming to newcomers before? I wonder as I drive back towards the house. Perhaps I was so wrapped up in my own friendships I didn't even notice the eager mums or dads who would have fallen on a friendly word or thoughtful invitation. But no, we weren't a group in the same way in Walthamstow. Almost everyone worked, drop-offs were hurried and brief – just as often a childminder or au pair as a parent. Not like here, where the same gang of mums turn up every morning and evening without fail. And now I'm one of them, though I certainly don't feel it.

Rose coughs and startles me. I forgot she was there, which is often the way when it's just the two of us. Archie's the one who makes the noise. It's only then that remember I promised her we'd set out and explore. But now we're nearly home, and I feel suddenly exhausted. The unremitting novelty is too much for me. Much as I dread going back to the house, at least we can take a break from new people, new places, the continual sensation of standing apart, being different, being wrong.

'Where are we going?' Rose asks. 'I thought we were finding a café?'

'We're nearly home, darling. Maybe we should go back and have a drink there?'

'But you said we were going to do something special . . .' The whine begins before I even finish my sentence.

'We could make some biscuits, or draw a picture?' I look at Rose in the mirror as she cowers in her car seat.

'I don't want to go home, Mummy.' She's even paler than usual, anxious. Is that fear in her eyes?

She didn't cope well with being left in the car outside the house for all that time the other day. When I'd got back, Archie was engrossed in *Minecraft* on my phone, but Rose was watching through the window for my return, tears streaming silently down her face. I'd explained to them that it was all fine, just a neighbour whose dog had got stuck in our hedge. Very friendly man, small-ish dog, I'd lied, saving the gory details about the carcass for Pete, later on that evening. But even once I'd described the full scene, he couldn't see the great drama. Our weird, aggressive neighbour finding a mysterious butchered animal carcass he'd claimed was planted in our garden. He was sure there was a simple explanation. Perhaps a fox had dragged it from a neighbour's bin. But that man's the only neighbour we know of, I'd pointed out. Well, maybe *he* put it there, came Pete's response, which only made me feel more anxious. Why would he lie? And if that was the case, what was he really doing there?

But that can't be what's spooking Rose, since she doesn't know the half of it. I must get to the bottom of what's got her so upset. Perhaps if I try to get her talking in another setting.

'How about we go to Ipswich?' The rain's cleared up for now at least. 'We won't have long, but there's a nice gallery I found with lots of pictures of animals. I think you'd like them. We could pop in there.'

This seems to please Rose, though having come up with the idea on a whim, I now realise I've got to turn up at the gallery again, only a few days after my last visit. I don't want to appear too keen, but I can't deny the draw of being around all that art again. The prospect of a conversation with someone I actually have something in common with, for once. Someone who knows nothing about our notorious house and the inhospitable community we've moved to.

Eve greets us as we enter the gallery without a flicker of surprise. 'Jess, how lovely to see you again. And what's your name? Hello, Rose.' She crouches down, easily reaching eye height with Rose, grabbing a handful of cards to flick through with her. 'These are all local animals. Bunnies I've seen playing in the fields. A little robin who likes to hop on my bird bath. And this is a badger who lives in the woods . . .' At this Rose looks startled.

'What, the woods behind my house? Do you know my house?' Rose looks at Eve, her grey eyes widening.

'No, I don't. Do you have woods behind your house? I bet there are badgers living there, and birds, and bunnies.'

I turn away to browse the pictures, trying not to picture the dismembered carcass, the glistening red flesh, the blue of the veins. I know I should leave Rose to develop social skills for herself, like the psychologist back in London was always suggesting. But hearing a sniff, I turn back to see her fiddling with her plaits defensively, Eve crouching closer again.

'Do you like your new house, Rose?' Eve asks gently, and Rose shakes her head. 'I suppose it's a big change from where you lived in London.'

'Yes, but it's not that. I like the country. And the bunnies. And the badgers.' Rose glances towards the cards. 'But I don't like that house. It's creepy.'

Eve nods, but I notice she doesn't say anything reassuring, as I would be quick to. Instead she listens as Rose opens up in a way she never usually does with strangers. 'There's all these big trees and bushes, and at night, my windows bang . . . I don't like going to sleep there. There's only one place I feel safe.' I look over sharply. Rose hasn't said any of this to me, or Pete. But I can see she's surprised herself, too. She turns away from Eve, rolling onto the outsides of her feet as she picks up a card and studies it.

'Well, I'm glad there's somewhere you can go,' Eve says gently. 'It's important to have a place you feel safe. And you can come here to look at the animals any time you like.'

Eve straightens up and I approach her. 'Sorry about Rose, she's got quite an active imagination,' I say softly, but she puts a finger to her lips.

'Would you like to choose one of the cards, Rose? I'd like to give one to you,' Eve says quietly, no trace of the false cheer or sing-song voice adults usually adopt around children they don't know well. 'You could keep it by your bed and look at it if you wake up feeling scared.'

Rose smiles at Eve. It's the happiest I've seen her in days. 'I'd like this one,' she says, holding up the badger. 'He can protect me.'

I look at it doubtfully. The animals in Eve's paintings are anything but comforting to my eye, and the badger looks particularly fierce. But it's Rose's choice.

Then Eve bends down and whispers in Rose's ear, so softly I can't make out a word of what she's saying. It must be something nice, though, since Rose giggles and looks quickly away.

'Thanks so much,' I say to Eve, realising that it's already time to collect Archie. 'We've got to dash. Sorry I didn't get a chance to . . .' Then I stop myself. Eve doesn't know how much I've been craving adult conversation, about anything other than rising damp or planning regulations. 'Anyway, this has been lovely for Rose. She really needed that.' I shepherd my withdrawn little daughter towards the door but Eve just shakes her head. I can see she doesn't want to talk about Rose in front of her. And I know I shouldn't – all the books and experts tell you not to, especially if your child is 'troubled'. But I find it hard to fight the urge to explain Rose's behaviour sometimes.

'It was lovely to meet you, Rose. And to see you again, Jess. I'd love to hear more about that gallery you worked in. Perhaps next time you drop by, if it's not too busy, we can pop for a quick coffee?' We both look around the small room. I haven't seen anyone come in so far. It seems likely we'll be able to find a quiet moment.

'That would be great,' I say as Eve and I swap numbers. And then, beaming down at Rose, with probably the first genuine smile she's seen on my face in days, I pull her hand. 'Come on, poppet. We'd better go and get Archie. See you soon then, Eve.'

Eve watches us leave, Rose's small hand in mine, and I turn the corner with a lightness I haven't felt in weeks.

'She was nice, Mummy. I liked her,' Rose says as I buckle her into her car seat, stroking the hair from her face.

'She was, wasn't she. Maybe we will make a friend around here after all.'

For the rest of the journey, Rose hums to herself softly, hugging the badger close to her chest with a secretive smile.

Chapter Seven

It's Saturday and I'm making pancakes in a vain attempt to revive our old, carefree routine. But Pete's hungover, back late from work drinks, and the children are subdued, a whole weekend stretching ahead of them without any playdates, activities, anywhere to go.

'What are we going to do then, Mum?' Archie asks, and I shrug, my back to him, busy trying to work the decrepit Aga.

'Why don't you ask Dad? You haven't seen him all week.' At the table, Pete groans and lifts his head from his phone. 'Can you put that away, Pete? We're about to eat.' It occurs to me that maybe he's started on the coke again. That would explain all the furtive texting, the epic hangovers. But that was one of the reasons for the move, to get away from all that, put some distance between him and the university crowd. Surely he wouldn't wait until he'd stranded me out here to revive his party-animal days?

'Hey, Dad, we could start building the treehouse, couldn't we?' Archie suggests, but Pete shoots him down instantly.

'I think there's enough building going on around here, mate.' He gestures out of the kitchen window to the barn, where

72

Keith and his team have already started clearing out the rubbish and replacing the floors.

'Not enough going on *inside* here,' I mutter as I transfer a plate of pancakes to the table, casting a look at the torn lino and cracked window. The repair to the front-door latch on moving day was the last bit of work we did on the house, and reinforcing the glass in the door panels; everything else is on hold until the planning application is through. We might be surrounded by rubble and drilling, but we're not seeing any of the benefit in here.

'We could go to that place again, with the nice pictures?' Rose says, pushing a pancake around on her plate.

'What place?' Pete finally slips his mobile into his pocket. Is that guilt on his face? What is he constantly looking at, anyway? I'm sure his phone addiction has been getting worse since we moved here. He thinks I don't notice the way he jumps every time a message arrives, that I can't see how quickly he shuts down the screen whenever I approach. Then again, maybe I'm just paranoid because of my own phone, my own secrets.

'Oh nowhere, just a gallery in Ipswich I took Rose to the other day.'

'There's a really kind lady there, she gave me a picture.'

'That *was* nice of her.' Pete looks at me, but I shrug.

'It was only a card. That badger, by Rose's bed. You probably haven't been in there to see it all week.' We could have moved out while he was in London and he wouldn't have noticed. He's barely here in daylight.

'Come on, Jess. It's not like I want to be trekking back and forth on the train the whole time. And it's not my fault work's got completely manic.'

'I know,' I say, not wanting to get into another argument. And aware that our entire livelihood now relies on him keeping

73

that job he's always at. 'How about we go for a walk? Get to know the fields around here. We might even spot some bunnies or badgers or something,' I add, for Rose's benefit.

'You do know badgers are pretty aggressive,' Pete says, and Rose turns to him, alarmed.

'Only if you get up close to them.' I shoot Pete a look. 'But they're quite scared of humans, I think. Maybe we'll spot one from a distance.' I smile at Rose. 'You could bring your sketch pad and draw some pictures of the animals we find.'

Ever since the afternoon at Eve's gallery, Rose has taken a newfound interest in drawing. I've discovered her more than once, perched by a window, attempting to capture a tree outside or the way the lawn slopes down to the stream, with the woods beyond. She hasn't woken as often, either. There have been no more repeats of the night in the cupboard.

Eventually, after various clothes are changed and snacks packed and Thermos flasks filled, we set out, wellies on and wrapped up against the greying winter day, Pete muttering to himself about everything that needs doing around the house, so that before it has even started, the walk feels like an endurance test, just one more thing to get through. For someone who was so keen to move to the countryside, Pete hasn't shown a particular enthusiasm for nature. He picks his way around muddy puddles while Rose and I stop to study brambles and spot birds and look out for signs of badgers.

But Pete has succeeded in arousing within Rose yet another fear, and before long we're struggling to convince her that she's not about to be attacked by small woodland animals, while Archie stalks through the bushes, snarling and hissing, pretending to be a wild badger on the loose. Shortly afterwards, the path we're following descends into a patch of nettles and all other concerns are drowned out by wailing, as both Rose and Archie are stung on parts of their bodies I hadn't even realised were exposed to the elements, while Pete rummages around for dock leaves and I try to reassure them that nature really isn't out to get them. Our country walk ends with us trudging through drizzle along the side of a narrow road in the general direction of our house, terrified that one of the children is about to be mown down by a speeding car.

The road takes us past Trevor Martin's run-down bungalow, and Rex comes bounding towards us, barking loudly and jumping up at the fence in a frenzy, seemingly fully recovered from his tangle in our hedges. Rose lets out a shriek and shields herself behind me, even Archie and Pete shrinking away from the long teeth and wide eyes, the snarl that lets us know not to come any closer.

'You said it was a small dog, Mum,' Archie says.

'I didn't want to scare you. But I'm sure he's very friendly when you get to know him.'

'Yeah, not sure I'm going to wait and find out.' Pete raises his eyebrows and we look towards the bungalow, windows obscured by net curtains and grimy with dirt. There's no sign of our unfriendly neighbour. And there's no suggestion he's about to come out and call his dog away, not that I'd want to come face to face with him again so soon again, anyway. We move quickly on, Rose covering her ears with her hands as we hurry past the house and over a stile into the neighbouring field.

As we approach the Maple House in silence, I try to picture it as it must have been when it was first built a hundred years ago, gleaming brick and sparkling windows, well-kept gardens and saplings, planted in anticipation. I imagine the family who lived there, sitting on the lawn out front, having a picnic, a mother, father and two small children, perhaps, dressed stiffly, formally, but happy – hopeful, their whole future stretching out in front of them.

What happened to that family? That house? How has it ended up like this, I wonder as I half drag Rose along by the hand, snivelling, her feet scuffing through the grass.

'Same family for years,' Pat from the pub had told me when she stopped me outside the village shop a few days back, the day after my confrontation with our neighbour. I almost asked her about this Trevor Martin. What she knew of him. But something made me hesitate. Perhaps I didn't want to know.

I had been caught off guard, anyway. Recognised, despite the fact we'd never had a conversation before. 'You're those ones moved into the Maple House, aren't you?' she'd asked, half smile, half sneer. 'It's a funny place, isn't it? Lovely when it was first built, so my mum said. But these days . . .' She sniffed, shifted her shopping from one hand to the other, laboriously, so that I wondered for a moment whether I should offer to help her with it, except that I hadn't actually made it into the shop myself, yet. I'd only popped by for some milk, a task that now necessitated a trip in the car. I made a mental note to drive further next time, away from the scrutiny.

'I'm sure it'll scrub up, though.' She nodded. 'Glad someone's taken it on, even if it's . . .' She stopped. Shifted her shopping again. 'Anyway, I suppose you're not *from* London, are you? Not originally.' She studied me, and for a moment I imagined the look on her face if I turned on my heel and walked away, as I'd liked to. It had started to rain. She pulled her anorak hood over her tightly wound curls.

'Yes, I am, born and bred.' I knew what they all thought of Londoners by now. Of the Riches and Amandas who sweep in with their city salaries to build glass extensions and invite their friends for legendary weekend-long parties. *We aren't those kinds of people*, I wanted to say. But I wouldn't give her the satisfaction. So what if we were? It was none of her business, anyway.

'I'd better be getting on. I've got the kids' tea to put on.' I smiled in what I hoped was a humble, endearing way. It was so unexpected, becoming a talked-about family. Moving into a house with a reputation, a focal point for the local community. If I'd known . . . well, I didn't allow that thought to take solid form. There were a lot of things I didn't know before we got ourselves into this situation.

'Yes, well . . . No place for children, I'd imagine.' Pat shook her head. I looked at her for a moment. What was she talking about? But she was backing away now, studying me closely, making mental notes, no doubt, to relay to the next villager she bumped into.

'They love it. So much nature, the walks, the fresh air,' I said brightly. 'Lovely to chat. Hope to see you again soon.' And I pushed through the shop door, a little bell tinkling, as if I wanted to attract even more attention towards myself.

Now, I stifle a bitter laugh. The nature, the walks . . . who are we trying to kid? Pat's right. This is no place for children.

We cut through the gap in the hedge and come out on the other side, beside the barn. No idyllic picnic spots here, only cobbles and abandoned junk. We're a fifty yards away, perhaps a little more, when I see a glint coming from between the trees at the bottom of the garden. A beam of light reflecting against moving glass – a phone, or watch. Then a rustling sound. I stop still, holding my breath.

'Who's there?' I shout, and then I turn to Pete. 'You must have heard that?' Both the kids turn to me, but Pete carries on walking. 'Pete! Stop for a minute.'

He turns and eyes me wearily. 'What is it?' he asks and my certainty evaporates. Seeing the bags under his eyes, his shoulders slumped, I decide to leave it. It's getting dark, we're all tired. We need to get inside.

'Oh, nothing. Don't worry about it.'

But Rose is spooked, and she grips my hand even tighter as we approach the house. The second time I hear it, the noise is much louder and closer at hand. Without thinking I shake Rose off and break into a sprint, running down the length of the garden towards the woods. I'm determined to find out who is skulking around.

I'm breathless by the time I reach the end of the lawn, and I spin around, ready to catch someone snooping from behind the trees, or darting into a bush. Our weird neighbour, perhaps. Or the man who sold us the house, back to check on his property. Maybe even the intruder from London, lurking in the bushes. His dark hair, his thick hand.

But everything is quiet now. All I can hear is my own heavy breathing, the faint trickle of the stream, the distant cry of birds. Pete catches up with me, Archie and Rose in tow, all of them pale-faced. But it's not the house they're scared of, or these woods, I realise with a jolt. It's me. I'm the one who's behaving oddly. There's something wrong with me.

'I was sure I heard something,' I pant, pushing my hair back from my face and taking a deep breath. 'Sorry, it was probably just a bird or something.' Rose is sniffing. She huddles into Pete.

'Come on you two,' he says gently. 'Let's get inside, get these wet boots off, make some hot chocolate.' He looks at me with a cold expression, as if it's me who's ruining everything. As if it's my fault we're here, in the wild, unknown countryside around our ramshackle house, instead of enjoying a short walk around the reservoir and returning to our warm terrace, the reassuring presence of neighbours either side.

I linger outside, waiting until my breathing slows. Once I hear the back door click shut, I pull the phone from my pocket. Not the iPhone Pete knows about, that's in the backpack he's carrying, but the Nokia, the secret phone I always keep close, in case he ever found it. I switch it on and the screen ignites:

41 missed calls

32 messages.

They're still coming and, for a moment, my thumb hovers over the button. I don't know what I want, really. Reassurance. An escape route. But I know this isn't the answer. Not really. That's why I had to stop taking the calls, replying to the messages. That's why I need to get rid of this phone.

I'm about to switch it off and tuck it away again when I hear a crack and then a low rustle, as though someone is adjusting their footing. Someone very close at hand. I gasp, thrust the phone in my pocket and run for the house, adrenalin pumping through my body. As I reach the back door, I turn. Maybe it was an owl, or a fox, even a badger. Perhaps I've never given animals their due, city girl that I am, and they really do have a presence that feels palpable, almost human.

I turn and jump back, startled, suddenly aware of Rose's face pressed against the window, her small frame illuminated by the light of the kitchen behind her, watching me anxiously.

What if it is me? I'm losing my mind out here. Seeing and hearing things other people can't hear. Feeling a presence that doesn't exist.

I take one last look at the bushes, and then I retreat inside, ready to comfort my children. To convince my husband that I'm still on the right side of sanity. To hold together our fragile family against all the odds for a little longer.

Chapter Eight

It's freezing in this house. The kind of cold that seems to seep up through cracks in the floorboards, rising like a fog through the downstairs rooms, chilling me to my core. I can see my own breath as I make my way up to our bedroom, lugging a basket of damp washing, the creak of the stairs my only company. The kids are at school, Pete at work. I'm alone again, except for the noise of the builders in the barn, banging and sawing and shouting as though they own the place.

They seem much more at home here than I do, Keith and his team. There are four of them, although they come and go. One is younger, skinny arms and a smattering of spots. Two look around my age, though one has receding hair and a pub belly. And then there's Keith, who must be near retirement. I do know the others' names – George, James, Harry. But I haven't quite worked out who's who.

They're friendly enough to my face. Deferential. They ask me what I want from time to time, but Keith has taken to calling Pete on his mobile for any of the bigger decisions. I hear them laughing, sometimes, after I've offered them tea or moved something out of their way. I'm a joke to them, I'm sure, in my ripped jeans and designer trainers, my straggly bleached hair. 'You'll never guess who's bought the Maple House,' they probably say to their wives when they get home, laughing about how clueless we are, how out of place. The wives might know me from the school playground. They'll have seen me standing on my own, looking for my withdrawn children among the rowdy after-school crowd.

The builders make me feel like a stranger in my own home, even more than I do already, and I consider with a heaviness how long they'll be here, all told. By the time we've done the outbuildings, and Graham's got the planning permission through, they'll get started on the main house and we'll be living around them for months. The best part of a year, probably. Yet again, I wonder if I've got the stamina for this. Whether we'd be better off calling it quits. What if the trade-off we've made is too great?

I survey the basket of damp washing. Sinking onto our bed for a moment, I picture the gallery in London. It's half ten. Perhaps I'd be making tea. Carrying it back to my desk in the back office. Having a chat with Lydia about the weekend, which kid's party we'd been to, who we'd had round for Sunday lunch. It's impossible to imagine it all still going on, now I'm here, looking out at the white sky, bare branches, a lone bird circling overhead. They'll be having the staff Christmas drinks soon. What would happen if I went back and said it had all been a mistake – could I have my job back?

I consider calling Becky, but I promised I wouldn't. A clean break, that's what we agreed. And I definitely can't call Arifa. There's Mum, of course – I've hardly spoken to her in weeks. But I don't want to talk to her when I'm in this state. She'll hear immediately how desperate I'm feeling. And she won't rest until she's tried to make things better. She'll want to bust me out of here. To her, my happiness is more important than Pete's, or even the kids'. It's a comforting idea. But one I need to nip in the bud. That way, madness lies.

An hour later, I'm wandering through Ipswich, feeling the weight lift once again, the panic subside. Perhaps we could move here, I consider idly. Downsize into a small, manageable house, where I could be anonymous again, find a local job, even some friends. Somewhere modern, no work required. Near a football team for Archie.

But I know it's impossible, for now at least. We'll never sell the Maple House before we've done it up. No one else would be foolish enough to even approach the trap we've fallen into. We're stuck there, goldfish in a bowl, the locals watching in amusement.

The bell on the gallery door rings loudly as I enter with a nervous wave, muttering something about passing through the area.

'Shall we get that coffee?' Eve asks, smiling widely. I hadn't noticed how perfect her teeth are. Even pearls, framed by red lipstick. She's the only other person I've met around here who isn't afraid to stand out. To let her personality shine through in her bright lips, chic blazer, her lightning-bolt earrings.

'I haven't had a single customer all morning,' she announces cheerfully as she flips the *Open* sign to *Closed* and lets us out into the bustle of the street.

We take seats opposite each other in Blend, a small café a few doors down, and Eve orders a bowl of soup: 'Might as well grab some lunch,' she says, her nose wrinkling with that infectious smile, so that I find myself ordering the same, leek and potato, without even glancing at the menu.

'It must be hard, being new.' She pushes her hair behind both ears and clasps her hands. 'What with your kids to think about, and so much to do on the house.'

'It really is.' I smile, though I feel tears prick behind my eyelids. 'I didn't realise I'd already bored you with the renovation dramas.'

'Well, you gave that impression . . .' Eve brushes her fringe from her face and it falls back in a neat row just below her eyebrows. I tug my fingers through my grown-out layers, thinking that I must find out where she gets her hair done.

'Yeah, we've got a team of builders working on the barn at the moment, so it's constant noise, questions, music blaring. Though at least I don't feel so alone . . .' I trail off, worried I've made myself sound too needy, but Eve nods, her round eyes wide with understanding. 'It's just, we were so established in London. We had our social group, a small house we'd done up, the kids were settled at school, and now . . .'

'You're in the arse-end of nowhere, no friends, no job, nowhere to be,' Eve says as I brush away a tear. 'It'll get better, honestly. It always feels like this when you move to a new area.'

'I know, I'm sorry . . . It's been a really difficult month or so – year, actually – and I've felt so on my own with it all.'

'Look, no apologies, okay?' Eve gives me a mock frown as the soup is delivered to our table. 'We've all been there. It's a nightmare arriving somewhere new, plus you've got a young family to think about.'

'Thank you.' I sniff, taking a spoonful of warm soup and feeling for the first time in weeks as though all might not be lost. 'It just felt like the move was the final straw, you know? I got a bit . . . cut off from my friends in London.

Things all went a bit wrong and . . .' I feel a sudden, reckless urge to tell Eve the whole story, to unburden myself after all these months, to someone with nothing invested in the situation. But then I remember I barely know this woman. I don't want to drive her away before we've even made friends. 'Anyway, our house got broken into and after that it was obvious it was time to call it a day. Only I hadn't expected to feel so adrift when we got here. It's been so much harder than I expected for us all to settle in. I wanted to say thank you, actually. You were so good with Rose the other day. You really made her day, her week even. Do you have children?'

Eve shakes her head quickly, in a way that makes it clear I shouldn't ask any more. 'Rose is a lovely girl,' she says. 'She's got real spirit in her, you can tell, but she's obviously struggling . . .'

'She is. Always has been. She has a hard time of it. She was very premature, it left her with allergies and asthma, and she's always been very shy. Then there was the break-in and, well, she didn't cope with it brilliantly. Her brother Archie doesn't help – always talking over her and pushing her to one side. Anyway, sorry, other people's kids must be the last thing you're interested in. I'd love to know more about your art. How did you get into it?'

'You know, the usual.' Eve shrugs. 'Art school, a few group shows and then nothing . . . Went into publishing for a while, photography, marketing. Obviously I never dreamed I'd end up back here in Ipswich, selling greetings cards.'

'They're hardly greetings cards. They're beautiful. Most people would kill to have a talent like yours. I know I would.' Suddenly everything in the café seems loud and clattering and I concentrate on my soup, embarrassed to have revealed my own creative shortcomings, my admiration. I'm being a fangirl again, as Pete would put it. He's always teased me about how quickly I gravitate towards anyone even vaguely arty, desperate to prove myself, even though I studied media and stumbled into fundraising for the gallery. Now here I am again, doing the same thing in a new setting. But Eve seems genuinely moved. I think there might even be tears in her eyes.

'Thanks, Jess. You don't know how much I needed to hear that.' She sips her coffee thoughtfully for a moment. 'You never trained artistically then?'

'No, no real talent for it, unfortunately. I used to love going to galleries with my mum growing up, though. We were in Hackney, so it was just a bus ride to the National, the Tate, the Portrait Gallery. Mum would find a corner and mark papers, while I wandered around the exhibitions for hours at a time. She was a teacher and I was her only child. She wanted me to grow up among culture.'

'You don't know how lucky you were.'

'I know, right? Everyone always goes on about how awful it is for kids to grow up in big cities, but if I hadn't been in London, I'd never have seen all that art, and I might not have ended up working in a gallery myself. I was planning to go back and study art history, try to get into curating. But then . . .'

'You ended up here?' Eve looks around at the small pine-panelled café, the amateur sketches on the wall.

'I know. I did everything I said I'd never do. Escaped to the country – gave up on all that.'

'And how are you getting on with the house now? Are you feeling more at home?'

'If anything, I'm feeling less at home than ever. We had no idea what we were taking on,' I admit and then, unsure whether to go further, I add: 'And there's something about the place that doesn't feel right.'

'What do you mean?' Eve gestures to the waiter for another coffee.

'There's just this feeling I get. That we're being watched. That someone might be hanging around. I know it sounds mad.' I look up, hardly believing I've said this out loud to the one person I thought might actually be a friend around here.

'It doesn't sound mad,' Eve says, quietly, as the waiter clears our empty bowls and sets down another cup. I wait until he's left us alone before I go further, lowering my voice.

'It's just these little things that keep happening . . . things turning up. Like the other day, I came home to find this creepy guy who lives nearby crawling around in our bushes. Apparently his dog had found a butchered rabbit that he reckoned had been left there as a trap. I mean, who would do that? And then a few days later, we got back from a walk and I was sure there was someone lurking at the bottom of the garden . . .'

'Let me guess,' Eve cuts in, her eyes bright with intrigue, 'the neighbour?'

'Well, no. Maybe . . . I don't know who it was. That's the point. When I got down there, I couldn't see anyone. But I was absolutely *sure* there was someone. Part of me wonders whether it's the old owner. Pete said he was a bit of a weirdo, and people do get attached to their houses, don't they?'

'I guess so.' Eve nods. 'Although it sounds like it's more likely to be the neighbour, if you've already found him hanging around once.'

'True . . . I don't know.' I shiver, imagining that man stalking around in our trees. 'I'm so not the kind of person who usually feels like this, so it's totally thrown me. I'm sure Pete thinks I'm losing it. I think he's worried I'm turning into my mum. She's always believed in spirits and that kind of thing. And the kids look almost scared of me sometimes. It's like I don't know myself any more. Like I'm going crazy.' I stop and take a deep breath, accept the waiter's offer of another coffee.

'It doesn't sound crazy,' Eve says, eventually, after it's been delivered. 'It sounds upsetting, for you. Especially if Pete isn't taking it seriously.'

'Well, he's got a lot on. He's commuting now, so he's always at the office, or on the train.'

'And let me guess, it was his idea to move to the country? A better life for you all, no doubt.'

'Exactly. But now he's never home, and when he is he's exhausted. He seems to be working later and later each day.'

'They always do,' Eve says. 'And then you're left doing everything – not just the cleaning, the washing, the meals, but the planning . . .'

'. . . the cooking, the food shop, organising playdates, overseeing the builders.' I shrug.

'The emotional labour.' Eve nods sagely.

'It sounds like you know the score?' I'm waiting to see whether she's got more to say on the topic, her own absent husband to complain about, but she just smiles.

'So what about this presence? Has anyone else felt it?' she asks.

'I think Rose does, but I don't want to freak her out by asking her. And Mum definitely did, but I can't talk to her about it. She's already worried as hell about me. Maybe if you came over you could see what you think?' I can see I've got carried away now. Eve's looking away, gesturing for the bill. I've come on too strong – or too strange. 'I mean, I'd love to invite you round for a coffee. You could take a look round the house, see if you've got any inspiration for the decor, with your artistic eye. I'm feeling totally overwhelmed by the whole thing. If it was up to me, we'd pack up our things and move to the nearest hotel tomorrow.'

'I'd love to.' Eve turns back to me, the sympathy in her eyes making me realise just how manic I must seem.

'Sorry, I'm not usually like this. It's like that story, *The Yellow Wallpaper*. You know? My house is driving me mad.' I grimace to convey my hysteria. But as soon as the words are out, I realise I'm doing that thing Pete says I always do – assuming everyone has the same frame of reference as me. That we all grew up in east London with a lefty English teacher mum, spouting feminist politics and handing out improving literature. 'Sometimes you have to adapt to the people around you,' he'd lectured me only the other day, when I was moaning again about the cliquey school mums and their impenetrable conversations. 'You can't expect everyone to have the same interests as you. Just because people's lives are different out here, that doesn't mean they're boring, or they don't have anything to say for themselves. Anyway, you're only catching up in the playground, not holding forth in a gallery.'

At the time it had stung. I had been making an effort after all, trying to smile and be friendly and tone down my opinions. But I knew there was a grain of truth in what he said. I had packed up a fair few prejudices and preconceptions with all our boxes and furniture – convinced I'd never meet anyone I really clicked with out here. And now here I am with the one potential friend I've encountered so far, alienating her with talk of madness and nineteenth-century literature.

Eve chats with the eager young waitress who brings over our bill as we each pay our share. It's not until we're alone again either side of the table, ready to take our leave, that I realise she's even registered my obscure reference point, that she's already on the same page, perhaps even one step ahead of me.

'It's not the house that drives the woman mad in that story,' Eve says as she stands up and pushes back her chair, flashing me a knowing smile, 'it's her husband.'

Chapter Nine

'Were you in Ipswich again the other day?' Pete's slouched on the sofa, scrolling through his phone, while I try to restore some post-bedtime order in the dingy living room, packing away Archie's Lego and piling up Rose's drawings.

'Yes, why?'

'Nothing, it's just come up on the joint account. Blend in Ipswich, so I wondered what that was.'

'I had a bowl of soup in Ipswich. Is that okay? I'll ask your permission next time if you want?'

There was so much I hadn't thought through about giving up work, but being answerable to Pete for my finances was something I hadn't even registered as a potential problem. After all, I'd never earned much, and now I'm saving us the cost of childcare, plus being around for the kids. What I hadn't considered was that my small income had been mine to spend how I wanted, after my monthly payment into our joint account. Now I have no money of my own, no independence, no privacy.

'It's fine, it's only you didn't mention it. I thought it's the kind of thing you'd tell me, if you went out for lunch in town. Were you on your own?' Pete looks up at me now, and I feel the old guilt twisting in my stomach. Though I've got nothing to feel guilty for this time.

'No, I was having lunch with a friend: Eve. The one from the gallery. Who gave Rose that picture.'

'Oh, the weird badger lady.' Pete smiles, but it's a weary, half-hearted attempt at humour. 'So are you two BFFs now? I wondered why she was giving Rose presents.'

'No, we're not. I barely know her. But she's friendly, which is more than I can say for the mums around here. And I like her. She's coming round for coffee next week, if that's all right with you? Or would you like me to run my engagements by you first, even though you're never here?' I hate the sound of myself these days. Hate how quickly all our conversations turn into rows, how the resentment rises to the surface every time.

'Come on, Jess. I'm just making conversation. You're quite hard to talk to these days, you know.'

'So the best way you've found is to go through my receipts and quiz me on them? I bought a loaf of bread and two pints of milk in the Co-op yesterday too, in case that causes any alarm.'

'For God's sake, Jess. Listen to yourself. I'm not the enemy. And there *are* people around here who'd like to make friends. George says his wife Sara sees you in the playground sometimes but you're in and out so quickly it's quite hard to grab you. They've invited us round for Christmas drinks on Saturday. I've said we'll go.'

I roll my eyes. The thought of drinks with George the builder and his wife fills me with dread. Probably some of the other mums will be there, too. The ones I've taken to avoiding at all costs. 'Fine,' I say, though I know I'm making a face. 'I have tried with those women, you know. I've got nothing in common with them. And they never make an effort.' I slump down on the sofa next to Pete.

'Maybe you seem quite intimidating to them,' Pete suggests. 'You could try to fit in a bit more. Talk about the things they're interested in.'

'What like planning permissions and parking permits?' I turn to look at him. 'And do you want me to buy a parka and take up running? Why did you even marry me, Pete, if you wanted this kind of life with these kinds of people?'

'Come on, Jess. They're not "these kinds of people", they're just people. You don't know them yet. And one of the things I love about you, one of the reasons I married you, is that you always had so much fun, got on so well with everyone, you were the life of the party.'

'That was before we had kids. Most people calm down their partying a bit once that happens . . .' I give him a meaningful look. I don't want to get back into the old rows about his late nights, the lost evenings he had when the children were young. Archie had come along sooner than we'd expected, and Pete had gone through some kind of crisis in the early years, suddenly desperate to let off steam, start DJing again, reconnect with the hard-living university crowd. But we'd come through all that now. And the move was meant to signal a shift in priorities for both of us. I had my own demons to escape, after all.

'And I have changed my ways, haven't I?' Pete takes my hand in his. 'All I'm saying is that it'd be nice to make a few friends around here, feel like part of a group again. I don't know what's happened in the last year or so, what went on between you and Arifa and Becky, but you don't seem yourself these days. Something's up. You can talk to me about it, you know.'

I look away, thinking how much I'd love to go back in time, edit the past, reconnect with the old Pete, the old me, when the children were younger – bring us back together in our old life, before this move felt like the only option. Then my eye catches on a crack in one of the small windowpanes to the front of the house that I'm sure wasn't there before. And I remember that it's already too late. 'There's nothing up. It's just this house, I don't feel like myself here. I don't feel settled. Safe.'

Pete shifts away from me again, with a sigh. 'There's nothing wrong with this house, Jess. You've got fixated on it. I know I freaked out when we first moved in, but that was about all the work, the financial side of things. We're perfectly safe here. We'll settle in, make friends. It's an old building. It needs modernising. Brightening up. And then it'll be an amazing place to live, to bring up the kids.'

I nod, exhausted, and astonished that Pete can overlook the reality we're confronted with to such a degree – that none of us is happy, the kids and I hate it, and he's never here. But I know it's no use going over it all again, so I tell him I'm going to bed. I'll check on Rose on the way. She's taken to wandering again in the night. Twice this week I've found her in her cupboard and had to coax her out. Pete knows about it now. But as I predicted, he thinks it's a phase. She's freaked out at the moment, he'd said, giving me a fixed look that was very easy to read: *you're freaking her out.*

I get ready for bed as quickly as I can, hoping that I can have the lights off and my eyes closed before Pete's had the chance to lock up downstairs. I don't want to speak to him again tonight. I don't want him to reassure me that it's all going to be okay and we're going to get through this together. The words are hollow. I've heard them too many times now. I know that he's saying them to himself, really, not to me.

The evening of the Christmas drinks begins in high spirits. I feel unexpectedly excited to be preparing myself for a night

94

out after all this time, sitting at the dressing table in our bedroom fixing in my long drop earrings, red lipstick, cat-flick eyeliner. Even Archie and Rose are cautiously optimistic about a party in the village – the potential for unlimited fizzy drinks and unsupervised gaming. I can hear Pete singing in the shower as I dig out my bright green velvet dress from the back of the wardrobe. I remember wearing it last Christmas, to drinks at Becky's house – all the compliments I got on the sequinned shoulders, the low back. Back then I'd paired it with my vintage cowboy boots and felt dressy but cool, drinking mulled wine from mugs and sneaking into the garden for a cheeky cigarette with Arifa and Miles. Now I think about it, that was the night everything started to go wrong. The beginning of the end of all that.

But I throw back my shoulders. Take a deep breath. I'm not going to think about any of it tonight. I'm going to have some fun for once. I pull out heels and black tights, a small, sequinned clutch bag. I'm shimmying into the dress when Pete walks in, a towel wrapped around his waist. 'Wow, you look great.' I give him a twirl. 'Do you think it's going to be that kind of evening, though?'

I stop still, study his expression. He looks apprehensive. 'What do you mean? I wore it last Christmas, you didn't complain then.'

'But, things might be different here, more casual . . . Maybe since it's our first event, it's worth testing the water . . .' He tails off when he sees my face. I'd wanted to look nice, to feel confident, even sexy again, for once. To remind Pete how we used to be together, how we could be again. But now I feel ridiculous. I start to pull at the shoulder of the dress as he puts his arms around me. 'Ignore me, I'm sorry.' He buries his face in my neck, inhales my perfume. 'You smell great. You look great.' He holds me at arm's length. 'I'm a lucky man. Sorry, I'm feeling nervous myself.' He smiles, and just about saves himself, before clocking the glass of wine I've poured myself, next to my make-up bag on the dressing table. 'I suppose I'm driving then?'

'Well, it's only one. But I can't get through tonight without a drink. And you're the one who wanted to move to an area where you can't even book a taxi this close to Christmas.'

'It's fine, I'll drive,' Pete says, hands raised, making amends. 'And keep the dress on.' He puts his arms around me. 'Let's try to have a good time, shall we?'

By the time we're approaching the estate at the far end of the village, I'm having second thoughts about my outfit, too. Nothing about us fits in around here. At our place we've struggled to achieve anything approaching festivity, our small locally sourced tree dwarfed in the large bay, the exterior walls as dark and crumbling as ever. Here, all the houses are newly decorated and dripping with fairy lights, tall trees twinkling in their windows. The children gasp enviously as we pull up outside George and Sara's house to find a miniature Santa with a full complement of reindeer marching across the front lawn.

Standing on the doorstep, listening to the sound of Slade and deep laughter, I'm tempted to go home and change. But Pete's already rung the bell, and before I know it we've been welcomed in by Sara, in a sparkly jumper and reindeer antlers. Sara's kids, Leo and Molly, whisk our two straight upstairs to watch a Christmas film, Rose shooting me a panicked look over her shoulder.

'Come through,' Sara says, accepting the bottle we've brought and taking our coats. 'Wow, Jess, that's an amazing dress. You've put us all to shame!' She's smiling kindly, but I feel a wave of humiliation as I look around. The white and beige living room is lined with men in jeans and shirts, bottles of beer in hand or propped on spotless surfaces. In the brightly lit kitchen beyond, a group of women circle a kitchen island in glittery tops and jeans, one or two wearing festive headgear, not a dress in sight.

'We're shoes off, actually,' Sara says, and I slip out of my heels, following her across the deep white carpet, waving hello to George and Harry.

George claps his arm around Pete and begins introductions, but I feel awkward, my smile tight. I'm used to George's presence in the barn, to him shouting to Keith or Harry about some piece of equipment, or a joke I can't catch. Seeing him in his own house, all of them together with other dads from school, their wives in the room next door, deep in conversation, makes me realise how much they must already know about me, about us, about how we live. They've probably watched me tapping away at my laptop. They've seen the mess in our house. Heard the kids fighting, crying, me shouting at them to behave. What must they have told their wives? What has already gone around the village?

I follow Sara into the kitchen, grabbing a glass of Prosecco from a tray and wondering how long it will be before Rose comes to find me and I can justifiably excuse myself. It used to feel like a drag the way she was always breaking up parties. Now I can't wait for the interruption.

'How are you settling in?' Sara asks as I join the group of seven women gathered around the granite worktop, who have all fallen silent at my arrival. 'George says the barn's coming along. Jess has moved in to the Maple House,' she announces to the group, though I recognise a couple of them from the school already.

'Oh, you know, we're getting there.' I smile, tugging at my too-short dress. There's a spotlight shining directly into

97

my eyes. 'I'm sure you don't want to hear about all the boring building work, you must get enough of that at home.' There's polite laughter, but I wince inwardly. Most of these women are here because their husbands work together on building sites. I've put my foot in it already. 'I mean, not that building work is boring. But it's *so* slow, isn't it? . . . And dusty.'

'Oh, the dust is a nightmare,' a blonde woman agrees quickly, helping me out. 'Especially when there are children running around the place. You've got two, haven't you?'

'That's right, Archie and Rose.'

'Year Four and Year One,' a brown-haired mum chips in, impressively quickly. 'I think your Rose is in my Milly's class.'

'Oh yes.' I nod, trying to look as though I recognise her.

'I'm Julie,' she reminds me.

'Are you at home with them, then?' the blonde mum asks.

'I am . . . at the moment,' I add. 'I used to work in a gallery. But I had to quit that when we moved. I'm planning to retrain.'

'It must be so nice to spend some time with the children,' Sara says, offering me a plate of sausage rolls. Nobody asks about the gallery, which is unusual. People are normally interested in that.

'Oh yes, I guess – although it's only now that I realise what they mean about absence making the heart fonder.' It was an attempt at humour, but the smiles are mostly uncomfortable.

'I suppose it takes a while for them to get used to you being there again?' suggests Caroline, Will's mum, who has a pair of mistletoe deely boppers perched on her glossy hair. 'Were they quite attached to their nanny? I've heard that happens.'

'We didn't have a nanny, just childminders. But Rose has always been quite clingy.' I knock back a mouthful of fizz, willing my needy daughter to interrupt us right now.

'It's all to do with early attachment, I think.' A red-headed

98

woman I recognise as Max's mum, Amy, nods sympathetically. 'But we all do what we have to, don't we? I've always said to Dean how lucky we are that I don't *need* to work. We might have to forgo a few expensive holidays, but it's worth it to be there for the important moments, don't you think?' She smiles, and I can see that she is trying to be nice, to make me feel better.

'I know what you mean,' agrees Caroline. 'Sometimes I think they only need us *more* as they get older, don't you?'

The other women nod reassuringly. It's clear they feel sorry for me. They think I was trapped in my career. Or that I've made all the wrong choices, and it's only now that I've come to my senses. I hear Pete laugh loudly next door and wonder whether he would agree with them.

'I just want to give the kids the best start in life. I want Rose to know she can do anything she wants to – any job she wants to.'

'Of course,' says Julie. 'That's what we all want. That's why we make sacrifices.'

So that your daughters can make sacrifices for their daughters? I don't say it. But in the awkward silence that follows, I drain my glass and top it up. There's only one way to get through this.

'How are the kids settling in?' Sara asks. She's got a strand of blonde hair stuck to her lipstick but no one has said anything. I want to pick it off, like Arifa or Becky would have done for me, before laughing and starting on the elaborate cocktails, the dancing, the karaoke. Instead we stand awkwardly, sipping fizz around a kitchen island, waiting for the ordeal to be over.

'They're okay, thanks. It's quite a change for them, but they're dealing with it really well.' I'm nearly at the bottom of my second glass now. I can't keep this going much longer.

'It must be weird, all the way out there on your own.' Julie shivers dramatically.

'Well, not quite on our own. We've got a neighbour. I don't know if any of you know of him, Trevor Martin – lives in that bungalow?'

'Oh him.' Caroline pulls a face. 'Yeah, I'd keep away, if you know what I mean?' There's nervous laughter and I'm about to ask what she's talking about when Julie cuts back in.

'It must be a bit creepy, though, what with everything that happened in the house. But you wouldn't have told the children about that, would you?' She gives me a strange look.

'What do you mean?'

'It's only that . . . my Milly said Rose saw something out of her bedroom window. And now all the children have been going on about how Rose saw a ghost. But I was sure you wouldn't be filling their heads with that nonsense.'

'What nonsense?' I ask, sharply this time. The room falls silent again. Two women who had broken away into a conversation turn back to join us. They're all looking at one another. 'What happened at the house?'

'The little boy, who died,' Julie says in a tone that suggests she can't believe I'm even asking the question. I put my glass down on the worktop and steady my hands against the cool granite. That spotlight is so hot. I feel dizzy, sick, as though the make-up is slipping down my face.

'What little boy?' My voice comes out very low and quiet. I don't want to know. I don't want to hear it.

'The little boy who lived there. A long time ago, now. He drowned in that stream. We thought you must have known. Everyone does.' Julie turns to the group, and the other women nod their heads, sharing glances, looking away. I'm sure they must all be able to hear the thump of my heartbeat.

100

'So that's why no one can believe we bought the house. It's not just the state it's in . . .' I'm thinking aloud, both hands supporting me now as I take it all in. The noises, the movements, the sense of being watched, the negative energy. It couldn't be . . . I don't believe in all that.

'Well, there have been stories . . . about sightings and curses and everything,' Sara says, as though reading my mind, 'but no one believes that any more.'

'It's just, how *did* he die, though?' Julie asks the group. 'I mean, everyone said he drowned, but how can you be sure when he was just found like that? Nobody knows what really happened, do they?'

'Is that why you said to keep away from Trevor Martin?' I ask Caroline. My heart feels like it's slowed right down, like the blood might have stopped pumping around my body. I feel sick.

'No,' Sara cuts in, frowning at the other women. 'Those were just silly rumours. And it was all years ago, honestly. I don't know why we're making such a big deal of it.' She laughs lightly and puts a cold hand on my bare shoulder, making me jump. 'I said I was sure you wouldn't have told Rose about it.'

'Of course I wouldn't.' I look around at the faces – concerned, sympathetic, just a little bit intrigued, excited even. So they *have* all been talking about me. 'I didn't have a clue. But even if I did, that's the last thing I'd tell my six-year-old daughter. And not only because she might spread it around her class.' I lean back against the worktop. 'It's not the kind of thing they put on the estate agent notes, is it? And no one has actually come out and told us what it is about the house that makes it so fascinating. We didn't realise it was the local house of horrors.' I look up and see that everyone has turned to the door, where Rose is standing, tears welling in her eyes.

'There you are, Mummy,' she says, coming to stand by me and putting her hand in mine. 'What's a "house of horrors"?' she whispers, loud enough for the other women to hear.

'It's nothing, darling.' I pick her up, let her wrap her legs around me and carry her out of the room towards Pete, who is laughing again at something one of the men is saying.

'We've got to leave,' I say quietly. 'Rose is scared.'

Pete looks from Rose's face to mine, pulling us into the corner for a moment.

'Are you, Rose?' Pete asks her but she doesn't respond. She's buried her head in my shoulder. 'Who's really scared?' Pete frowns at me. 'Rose or you?'

'Pete, I'm leaving. You can come if you like, or you and Archie can stay and get a lift with someone. But Rose needs to get home.'

'Obviously we all need to leave together.' Pete looks over my shoulder to where the other women are huddled in the kitchen. 'What happened in there?'

I shrug. I'll tell him about it later, not in front of Rose. I've barely even allowed myself to think about the story they told me, the little boy who drowned. The rumours about our creepy neighbour. I'm still reeling from the judgement that surrounded me, the weeks of whispering that must have led up to this moment. The idea that we might be spreading scary stories about our house among the local children. That moving here has somehow tainted us, set us apart.

It's not until later, with both the children asleep and Pete's back turned towards me in bed following our terse conversation, that I'm able to run through it all in my mind. Pete's managed to convince me it's my imagination. That the trauma of what happened in London is making me see things, hear things. That I've become paranoid, jumping at every shadow, every loud noise.

But what if the negative energy I've felt is connected to something that happened here? Are we really safe – are the children? Is there some terrible legacy we somehow became caught up in when we bought the house?

I think about Rose, the terror on her face those nights when I've come in to find her standing at the window, sobbing, alone. The fear that drove her into her cupboard, the only place she feels safe. Can she sense something – even see something – when she looks out to the garden?

It's late now, and I know I've allowed my irrational brain to take over. I'd never have believed back in London that I'd be buying into all of this – the ghost stories, the hauntings, the weird movements around the house, the local bogeyman. But now? I don't know any more. I can't think what to make of it, and the more Pete denies it all, the more confused I feel.

I know who I want to call, but there's too much water under the bridge now. Too many details I've kept hidden, too many secrets I haven't shared. Besides, I'm scared she'll confirm my worst fears. She'll take it as evidence she was right all along.

The last person I can talk to about any of this is my mum.

Chapter Ten

'I don't even believe in ghosts, do you? I mean, not in the woo-woo white figures in the hallway kind of way. I suppose I've always had a feeling that people don't just disappear completely when they die, that maybe their energy lives on, or something. But I've never bought into apparitions or seances or anything like that . . .' I trail off, realising I've been talking non-stop since we arrived. Eve is sitting opposite me, nodding, holding a cup of tea in both hands, but I can see she's taken aback. And who can blame her? This must sound so strange to someone looking in from the outside.

I'd been planning to invite her to the house this time, to get a second opinion on our plans for the extension. But after everything Caroline and Julie said, I thought another meeting in Ipswich would be better. I couldn't exactly tell Eve the whole thing in a text message. And it would be too weird to reveal the story of a long-lost child, tragically drowned at the age of six, sitting in the exact spot where it had happened. So I suggested we meet in Blend again. Only now I'm regretting it – there are too many people, taking a break from Christmas shopping. I have to raise my voice to be heard over them.

'As if I'd be scaring my own children with stories about ghosts in their new home. How was I supposed to know there'd been an accident in the house? It's not something estate agents usually think to mention, is it? It didn't come up in any of the Google searches.'

In fact, as soon as Sara told me more details in the school playground, I did find the story online. A little boy, Jack Millington, found drowned in the grounds of his family home near Ipswich. There was only one report, on one of those websites that shows clippings from old newspapers, and the name of the house wasn't included, which is why it hadn't come up before. Accidental death. There was no mention of our creepy neighbour, no suggestion of anyone else being involved. That must have been local gossip that came along later. Jack had been playing alone at the end of the garden. 'By the time his family found him, he'd been lying face down in the river for too long. They couldn't revive him,' I tell Eve. 'They carried on living there for a while afterwards, so Sara told me. But eventually it got too much and they moved on. The house was rented out for years, then left empty for a while . . . and now it's ours.' I pull a face.

I don't tell Eve about the picture I found and printed out. Not of the boy, or his family, but of the house as it was then. A colour shot, taken in the summer when the pink roses were in bloom and all the woodwork newly painted. It had been published a few years after the accident, when another tragedy had befallen the family; but even though it was taken in sad circumstances, the picture had given me a little chink of hope. It helped, somehow, seeing how the house had looked once, and how it might be again – grand, well kept, the warm redbrick welcoming, homely even.

'Funny how these things can happen nearby and you never even hear about it,' Eve says.

'Why would you, though? There must be sad stories you

105

can tell about most houses if you look back far enough. I suppose that's why it's odd. It happened nearly forty years ago, for God's sake. Why's everyone still interested? Why are they still throwing accusations around about our weird neighbour? And why do they think I'd be terrifying my children with all that?'

Eve shakes her head. 'And did Pete stand up for you at the party?' She sips her tea. 'It sounds like you needed some support.'

'Pete? He couldn't get us out of there quickly enough. He was so embarrassed, with Rose crying and everyone staring at us. Even later, when I told him the full story, he thought I was overreacting. He's not spooked. He thinks it's just local gossip, and that I've got a problem fitting in.'

'That's hardly surprising, is it? This was his dream, wasn't it? He's uprooted you from everything you know, your job, your mum, your friends, and landed you in the middle of nowhere. What does he expect?'

'Exactly!' I splutter my coffee and slam down my cup in the excitement of being seen, being understood. Of course, Eve doesn't know how much I needed to leave London, too. But I'm not going to get into that now. 'I mean, I did agree to the move. But I'd never have gone for somewhere so big, so remote, if he hadn't been so sold on the idea of rural living. And I suppose I have always had a bit of trouble finding my feet in new situations. I worry I don't know as much as everyone around me, that I'm always catching up – that's how I felt at the gallery. Now here I am in a completely different crowd, getting it all wrong again.'

'I'm sure you're not.' Eve gestures for the bill. 'What are you doing for Christmas?' she asks as I fish for my wallet.

'We're staying at the house.' I look up from my big red

106

tote where I'm rifling through a jumble of gloves and note-books and children's sweet wrappers. 'It's been planned for months, almost since before we moved in. Mum's coming to stay – she's on her own – and we'd imagined a few cosy days tucked up together, long walks, roaring fires. Before we found all this out, obviously. And realised what a state the house was in. It's quite hard to imagine anywhere *less* cosy at the moment . . .' I must stop talking. What is it about Eve that brings it out in me? Her intent, careful way of listening, perhaps. That spark in her eyes that lights up at any amusing story, but also gives the impression she's always one step ahead in her mind. I'm desperate to impress her.

'Oh yes, didn't you say you were going to have me round?' Eve remonstrates with a twinkly smile, and my anxiety eases again. Perhaps she's not trying to shake me off, after all. 'I never forget an invitation.' She laughs, tucking some loose hair behind one ear as she reaches for her purse, though I insist on paying for us both. It was my idea to meet this time.

'Absolutely. Next week's busy with Christmas and every-thing, but how about early January, once the kids are back at school? I'd love to show you around, get your take on it all.'

'Perfect.' Eve shoulders her small, sleek handbag and we wander back down the road.

It's not until I'm leaving her at the gallery that it occurs to me I didn't think to ask where she's spending Christmas. I've been so caught up in discussing my own problems and plans, I haven't even managed to find out where she lives yet, or who with. She could be spending Christmas alone for all I know. In fact, now I think about it, I can easily imagine she will be.

There's a sadness in Eve, a brittleness, beneath her easy confidence, and for a moment I consider inviting her to spend

107

Christmas Day with us, in our new home, rather than all alone, as I picture her to be. But then I see Pete's face, Mum's confusion. The embarrassment of putting Eve on the spot. I turn to give her a wave, and she smiles cheerfully. She probably does have plans. I'm sure I've imagined it all.

'Oh, Jess,' Eve calls, as I'm about to turn the corner, 'it's got a name: that feeling you were describing earlier – of always feeling like you're in the wrong place, never really fitting in. It's called "imposter syndrome".'

And then the bell jangles as she opens the gallery door, and she's gone.

Chapter Eleven

Mum's uncomfortable from the moment she arrives. She's always tense around Pete, anyway. He thinks she doesn't like men, but it's not as simple as that. There's a certain kind of man she's always avoided – traditional, alpha – and it's been clear since the beginning that she sees Pete as one of those. I've always stood up for him, especially when there's so much she doesn't know about our relationship, but these days I feel less inclined to. It's like Eve said – he's changed my life beyond recognition and he expects me to just get on with it. Suppress who I really am. Fall into some traditional role, while his life carries on unchanged.

For the first twenty-four hours I tell myself that's why Mum's acting weirdly. She thinks I've turned into some surrendered wife, with my baskets of washing and ferrying the kids around, wrapping presents, serving meals. Pete's still working on Christmas Eve, and Mum watches, quietly, as I skivvy about the place, trying to create some semblance of a festive scene in our wreck of a house – the small Christmas tree leaning slightly against the cracked windowpane, the red cloth thrown over the table in the draughty kitchen. She doesn't offer to help; that's not her style. Instead, she stands outside, smoking, her watery eyes on me through the warped window-pane. Or sits in the corner, wrapped in three layers of thick jumpers, clutching mug after mug of black coffee.

By Christmas morning, it's clear there's something else the matter. As the children open their presents, throwing aside mountains of wrapping and squealing over extravagant gifts bought in a vain attempt to improve their suddenly empty lives – an Xbox for Archie, a digital camera for Rose – Mum can barely raise a smile. She's perched on the edge of our old armchair, dressing gown tied tightly against the draught in the bay window, shivering. She waits until after lunch to tell me she's planning to leave.

'I need to get back, love,' she says, her voice low, cigarette hovering by her face. I've come out to join her while Archie and Pete battle aliens in the living room and Rose poses her dolls for a series of arty shots.

'What do you mean? You can't leave on Christmas Day. I know it's cold, but we're doing our best to warm it up. And maybe it's not as festive as it could be – things will be much better next year, when we've done up the house and made everything nice. But you can't go back on your own to the flat.'

'I'm happy enough on my own. I'm used to it.' Mum drops her cigarette and grinds it under her foot.

'But the kids will be so upset. And *I* don't want you to leave, either. I miss you. I've barely seen you since the move. I want us to spend some time together.' I can hear a pleading tone in my voice that I don't like, but I feel abandoned, like a child myself again.

'Maybe you could come and visit me? In a few weeks, once the school holidays are over.' Mum won't catch my eye. She's never been overly demonstrative, like some mothers, but even she isn't usually so cold. So closed off to me.

110

'Don't you care how I'm doing at all? It's been really hard for me, moving here. I know it's tough for you, too; I know we left you on your own, but don't punish me by withdrawing. I need you more than ever now.' I feel a tear roll down my cheek, and Mum puts her arms around me. It feels so good to be held. It brings home to me how little physical contact there is between me and Pete these days. It's not just that he's out all the time – even when he's here, we've started to avoid each other: we sit apart, sleep on opposite sides of the bed. I snuggle in to Mum's thin arms and feel her shoulder grow wet as more tears slip out. It's such a relief after all these weeks to admit out loud that this isn't working.

'We had to leave, Mum. We couldn't have stayed in London the way things were. But now, somehow, it's even worse. And I don't know what to do. We're both so unhappy. The kids haven't settled. Pete's never here. I don't fit in.'

'You need to leave.' Mum says it so firmly that I stop mid-sob and look up at her face. Her mouth is set. She's shaking slightly.

'Mum, we can't come back to London and slot into our old lives. That's not going to work. This was a new beginning for us.' I try to find her eyes, but she's looking into the distance. Does she mean leave Pete? Is she telling me my marriage has failed? She should know, having been through her own break-up all those years ago when I was only tiny. But Dad was a drunk. Unreliable, never there. Mum always said she had no choice. Surely things between me and Pete haven't come to that.

'What about the children?' I ask quietly, an admission that the thought has crossed my mind more than once these past few months. Only I don't know where we'd go, what we'd do. But when Mum turns to me, I realise I've misunderstood her entirely.

'This is no place for Rose and Archie.' She's shaking her head, trying to pull away from me, but I've got her by the arm. I won't let her walk away.

'What do you mean, Mum? What are you talking about?' But even as I ask her, I know. I haven't said a word about the little boy, the river, the broken family, the local whispering. I didn't want to ruin Christmas. To give her more reason to hate this place. But I didn't need to. Mum has a bad feeling about the house, and it's got nothing to do with the state it's in.

'There's negative energy here, Jess. You must be able to feel it?' Mum's gripping my hand now. In the past, I would have shut her down at this point. I've never wanted to hear her nonsense about auras and energy. The feelings she gets about a place or a person that can't be explained or ignored. 'But where's the proof?' I'd ask her when she took against a wayward school friend, or our pushy landlord. 'Maybe you just don't like him?' It was another one of the differences between us – my rebellion, as she probably saw it. To reject her spirituality, her self-reliance, her refusal to conform. Now here I am, married, with two kids, two cars, a house in the country – and finally ready to listen.

'I can.' I nod. 'I get that feeling all the time. That there's something wrong with the house. That we shouldn't be here. There's something about this place, it drains my energy, my happiness, things keep going wrong.' I think of the leak that sprung in the outside drain only yesterday. The new crack in the living-room window, the strange objects that keep turning up, the noises, the knotweed. My mind turns to what the other mums told me – the rumours about our neighbour. A cold feeling runs through me. What if what Mum's sensing is a premonition? That we need to get away. That the children aren't safe. 'But what can we do?' I ask her, feeling panicky, trapped. 'No one will buy it from us in this state.'

'Can't you rent somewhere nearby, while you do it up? Then sell it as soon as you can?'

'We can't afford to, not without my salary coming in, and with Pete's train fares, all the money going on the build. We're only just managing at the moment. We need to start letting out the outbuildings so we've got some more money coming in.'

Mum looks towards the barn with a shudder. I'm readying myself to tell her about the mattress I found, the broken mirror, Rose's night waking, the hiding place she's discovered in her bedroom cupboard – perhaps even the boy who died here – but Pete's head appears through the back door.

'There you are. What are you doing out here in the cold?' He looks at us, a question in his eyes as he rubs his hands together, and we snap apart abruptly, as though we've been doing something forbidden. His smile fades. 'We were wondering where you'd got to. The kids are getting hungry.'

I sigh and turn to go in, hearing Mum tut audibly under her breath. It didn't occur to Pete to warm up some leftovers himself, of course. He never used to be like this, I want to say to Mum. It's only since I gave up work, since he became the breadwinner. But there's no time, she's already standing in the doorway. She turns to me with a pinched expression, her hair in strings from the damp air, the layered jumpers dwarfing her so that she looks like a small child, vulnerable somehow.

'I'll stay tonight, but then I have to go, okay? We'll work something out. I'm not leaving you here like this. We'll find a way out.' She says these last few words under her breath, and I can't be sure exactly what she's getting at – the house, Pete, our financial situation – maybe all of it.

I want to feel reassured, but Mum doesn't know the half of it. The house with a haunted past, the local gossip, the creepy man in the bungalow. There's no way we'll get rid of this place. Not in this state, anyway. No local would buy it, and any out-of-towners would have ruled it out when it was on the market before. We're stuck here, haemorrhaging money, and feeling more desperate by the day. There is no way out.

Chapter Twelve

I'm bent double in the patch of garden outside the kitchen door, wrestling with the weeds that are threatening to invade the house now. It's a clear, bright day, though I can see my breath as I heave with every ounce of energy I have left. We haven't even begun to tackle the knotweed yet, but now that the children are back at school, and Pete's at work, I'm desperate to take this house in hand. I've got to make a start on the garden. We can't live like this any more.

My task would be so much easier if only I could find the secateurs I left in the greenhouse. They're an old pair we inherited with the house, worn black handles with flecks of green paint, though the blades are still sharp, still usable. God knows how long they'd been lying out there, but now they've disappeared, just when I need them.

Like everything else, the greenhouse is almost at the point of collapse: the panes of glass cloudy and cracked, the door hanging open slightly on its hinge. I have a clear memory of going in there the last time I attempted to tackle the garden, before Christmas, and leaving the secateurs with the trowel and fork Pete bought in his early enthusiasm after the move, back when he imagined himself awake and present in daylight hours. But when I went out to find them this morning, they were nowhere to be seen. The trowel and fork are still there. It doesn't make any sense.

I've texted Pete, but he swears he hasn't touched them, so unless one of the children has developed an unexpected horticultural streak, they've disappeared, like so many other things around this house. An image appears, unbidden, of our neighbour pushing open that creaking door, eyes darting, alighting on the first object he comes to. Then my mind flits again. I picture the blades gripped in the hand that scared me before. The man who shattered the peace in our last home, the faceless figure who still haunts me at night. Why did I leave a sharp object lying around with no lock on the greenhouse door, so near to my children? What was I thinking?

I dig the fork into the ground. A sting of pain shoots up my arm. Looking down, I see that my hand is bleeding. I've caught it hard with one of the prongs. I lift the graze to my mouth and suck the blood away, the warm metallic tang mingling with the taste of soil, sweat. What is going on with me? In a matter of months since we moved here, I've unravelled, become someone I don't even recognise. Someone obsessive, so caught up in horrific daydreams, visions, that she injures herself, in fear, in anger. I've got to get a hold of myself. The kids are at school. They're safe. There's nobody here except me and the builders.

And then I look up and see that I'm wrong. There is someone else here. How long has she been watching me?

'Jess?' Eve is peering over the gate, clearly on tiptoes, trying to get my attention.

'Eve, you're early!' I say, quickly rubbing my injured hand on the back of my jeans and then shoving it in my pocket as I lift the latch to let her in. And then I smile, to show I

116

don't mind that she's caught me off guard, even though I'm standing here with my hair matted, mud covering my oldest clothes.

'Oh, sorry – I thought you said eleven.' Eve checks her watch. Her bob is glossy and newly trimmed, her large sunglasses giving her the air of an off-duty actress.

'I did, but . . .' I look at the old clock in the kitchen, the one we haven't got around to taking down since we moved in, and which currently reads just after 10 a.m. 'Oh, great. Another thing that's broken.'

'Sorry, I tried the front door, but no one answered, and I thought maybe with all the work going on in the barn you couldn't hear, so I came round the back and . . . what an amazing space.' She spins around, having picked her way down the path in shiny Chelsea boots, a large bunch of lilies in hand. She stops, takes a deep breath and turns to me. 'You're so far from anywhere here, aren't you?'

'Oh yes.' I grimace. 'Nobody can hear me scream!' It's meant as a joke, but as soon as the words come out they sound odd, and Eve gives me an awkward half-smile, turning to the house and pacing up and down the patio, examining the window frames, the door, the brickwork, the vines climbing around the conservatory. Eventually, she joins me where I'm clearing up my garden tools. She stoops down to the flower bed and runs her fingers through the soil.

'You could make an amazing kitchen garden out here, with herbs and lavender and fragrant shrubs.' I look at her, trying not to show my surprise. I didn't have Eve down as a gardener. 'And that lawn just needs a good weeding and a mow, doesn't it?' She stands up again, handing me the flowers she's brought, smiling brightly. 'Now, are you going to show me around this famous house?'

Suddenly I feel foolish, on the back foot. I'd planned to

get myself showered and dressed before Eve arrived, get the coffee ready in my stoneware pot, arrange the cakes I picked up in the village, before I lost all that time searching for those stupid secateurs. I was looking to impress her, I suppose, to prove that I could continue with some semblance of my usual style, even in these unlikely surroundings. But I wanted her to sympathise, too. To see the house as I do – as Mum does. To recognise it for what it is: an unmanageable project. Maybe even to pick up on the sense that there's something wrong with this place that no amount of renovation can fix.

Mum's reaction over Christmas had felt like vindication of a kind – that I wasn't imagining things, wasn't going mad. Now Eve's here, and she doesn't see it at all. In fact, she seems to be humouring me, the way Pete does – or used to, before he lost patience entirely. I follow her around the house in stunned silence as she darts from room to room, enthusing about the brickwork, the round windows, the rotting parquet, the panelling, the beams.

'Please tell me you're not going to *modernise*,' she says when we end up in the living room, pronouncing the word with a shudder. I laugh lightly, though of course that is absolutely our intention.

'Well, we plan to keep some of the features, but I'd love it to feel lighter, more airy. Definitely cleaner.' I run my finger along the broken stained glass in the window, showing her a grimy streak.

'Yes, but there's so much you can do sympathetically. Without changing the look of the place, the feel, everything that makes it so unique.' She turns away from me, captivated by something else she's seen. 'Jess, look at this.' She beckons me over to the corner where she's peeled back a patch of lining paper to reveal a long stripe of vivid green leaf-patterned wallpaper. 'Hasn't it got that classic William Morris feel? It would look so stylish if you restored it. Just think of how you could breathe life back into this place.'

My first instinct is defensive. Why hadn't I spotted that wallpaper, and who said Eve could rip off our lining paper? What gives her the right to march around the place, pointing out to me the original features of my own house? But then I see her eyes, shining with excitement, and I feel terrible. We're so lucky to have this huge, beautiful old house that someone like Eve would kill for. She probably lives in that tiny flat above the gallery, I realise with a jolt. She's never talked about anywhere else, after all. It makes sense. And here I am complaining to her about feeling overwhelmed by all these rooms, by everything there is to do here. Boring her with problems that I can see now, in her presence, aren't really problems at all, but challenges to be overcome.

We could make this house into something really special, I realise as I watch Eve stroke the wall, run her hand along the fireplace, bend down and inspect the brickwork. All it needs is a bit of creativity, inspiration, imagination. I've become so caught up in all the silly stories, the irrational fears, the local gossip, that I've lost sight of what made me want to live here in the first place. The unique features, the classic design – all the elements that Pete and Graham have been planning to strip back, knock down, open up.

'You know, there's something else I spotted,' Eve says, taking my hand and leading me back through the hall and into the kitchen. 'Look at this.' She tugs at the corner of the lino, where it's ripped, and pulls the hole slightly larger. 'The original flagstones! Imagine how beautiful they'd be if you polished them up.'

Eve's excitement is contagious, her admiration for the

house only making me realise just how wrong-headed all our plans have been so far. 'Well, we were planning a hardwood floor,' I say, tentatively. 'Once we've knocked down the conservatory, the floor was going to run right through the kitchen and into a new glass extension . . .'

'Oh God, no. Tell me you're joking.' Eve looks at me with mock horror, but I can see the genuine distaste in her eyes. We've turned up from out of town and we're determined to ruin one of the local treasures. We should have bought a new build, or land that could be developed on.

'Well, we've got to get it through planning, anyway. And it's not looking too promising . . .'

'Why on earth would you need an extension?' Eve opens the conservatory door and the smell of damp envelops us. 'Surely this house is big enough for the four of you?'

'You'd think so, wouldn't you? Pete's obsessed with having the biggest house possible. But you're right, we don't need the space.'

'Far better to knock down the conservatory and restore the doors that would have been here originally, with little panes and scalloped wood. Look, like this.' Eve takes out her phone and types in a search, showing me a picture of tall French doors, painted white, full of small panes of glass, just like our windows.

I see instantly that she's right. The doors would look fantastic, opening the room up to light but entirely in keeping with their surroundings, with the house, framing the greenery outside in a way that would be both classic and contemporary. I turn to Eve, impressed by the way she can tell, in a single visit, exactly what this house needs. But she's turned away, distracted by something she's seen through the window.

'Will you show me the work they're doing out there?' Eve asks, looking over at the barn, and I put down the coffee pot and cups I've been gathering and follow her out of the back door, caught up once again in the exhilaration of seeing this place, its potential, the way Eve sees it.

'You've worked wonders out here,' she says to George, who has left off his hammering at our arrival. I usually leave them to it, these days. I've given up offering them tea as they always refuse. Since the Christmas drinks, we mostly ignore each other, which seems to be the approach the school mums have adopted as well. Now I drop off and run, darting into the house on my return and logging onto my computer. That's where I do most of my living these days, lurking on Twitter or Facebook or Instagram, checking out Becky's and Arifa's feeds, and posting shots of my own. Little pictures that illustrate a lifestyle I'm not even remotely experiencing. A coffee and a classic novel, artfully arranged on a side table. A close-up of the engraving on our mantlepiece, cropping out the cracked surround and the layers upon layers of dirt no amount of scrubbing will shift.

'It's not bad.' George nods towards the interior of the barn, which I haven't entered in weeks. We walk in together now, Eve and I, to a bright, white, high-ceilinged open-plan living area, a doorway leading into a small shower-room and, next to it, a bedroom. I can hardly believe the progress they've made, and Eve's obviously impressed, though she didn't see the state it was in before.

'Very modern,' she says. 'And check out that view.' I join her at the window and find myself looking straight into our kitchen. I can see our red kettle through the cracked pane, and beyond it, the table with two cups and the coffee pot.

'Hardly,' I say, a shiver running through me. 'Anyone staying here would be able to watch us having breakfast. Pete didn't think about that, did he?'

'No, I mean the garden, the trees.' Eve directs my gaze away from the house, but I can't help returning to it. It's an unsettling feeling, observing our home from inside another living space. I try to imagine strangers having a holiday in here, while we're carrying on our day-to-day lives next door. How it would feel to be watched, overlooked.

'Well, I think you don't know how lucky you are,' Eve says as we cross the garden back to the house. 'Those are only your *out*buildings. Imagine what's it's going to be like when this whole place is done.'

'That's the problem, I suppose. I haven't been able to imagine it. It doesn't feel like we'll ever get it done. They've nearly finished out there, but they can't even get started on the house until it's all gone through planning. And we won't get any bookings for the barn while there's a massive build going on at the back of the house, will we?'

We sit down opposite each other at the kitchen table, and Eve is silent for a moment while I pour out the coffee. Then she looks at me, a smile forming at the corners of her lips. 'So forget the extension. You said yourself, you've got more than enough space, and you love the original style. This house is a design classic, a piece of English heritage right here, waiting to be rediscovered. Restore it to how it was and you'll be able to have paying guests in no time. Just think of all the money you'll save.'

Eve puts it so simply, I can't believe Pete and I haven't even considered this as a solution. Listening to her talk, I feel as though the clouds are slowly parting, the fog in my brain clearing a little. Could it really be that simple? A quick renovation job, get the outhouses rented out and some money coming in, so that Pete might even be able to work less, and I could retrain, get a new job, make more local friends.

Why hadn't we thought of it? We'd come here for a new beginning and somehow got caught up in this negative spiral of things we couldn't change, couldn't achieve, would never get done.

What if we really could move things on that quickly? We might even start to feel at home here.

'You're right.' I smile at Eve and look out to the garden, where the winter sun has flooded the lawn with a bright, piercing light. Seeing the house through Eve's eyes, anything seems possible.

'So your friend thinks we should change all our plans for the house and now you're happy?' Pete is determined to misunderstand me. We're sitting on the sofa, side by side, a house-moving programme on low, attempting to discuss our future.

'It just hadn't occurred to me, until she suggested it, that maybe we don't need to wait for it all to go through the planning department. What if we scaled back our plans? We could still make the place look great, but we could get it done quicker, more cheaply, get things moving. Come on, surely you can see we can't go on like this?'

Pete sits up, picks up the remote, switches off the TV. 'Of course I can see that. We can't carry on with *you* like this. Manic, up and down. In tears one minute, ecstatic the next. I don't know what I'm going to find when I get home. None of us do. The kids are so tense, they barely speak in your presence. People around here avoid you. I know you're not yourself, but I don't know what to do about it.' I can see the frustration in his furrowed brow, but I can't process what I'm hearing. Why can't he see that it's not me – it's the house that has made us all like this?

'Come on, Pete. The kids don't talk because they're miserable. They hate their school, they don't fit in. Archie doesn't have any friends. Rose isn't sleeping. She's creeped out by this place. We all are. The only one who doesn't feel it is you, because you're never here!' I can hear my voice rising, but I can't help it.

'I'm never here because I'm always working, Jess. To pay for everything, since you decided to leave work.'

'I *had* to leave work. We couldn't both commute. It wouldn't be fair on the kids. You know that.' I sit forward, feeling the anger rise.

'Yes, and you hated your job. You were desperate to quit. But I thought you were going to retrain, get some freelance work. You don't know how stressful it is being the only one earning any money. We're on a knife-edge. If I lose my job, we'll be completely stuck, with no way of paying for the build.'

'But I can't retrain,' I cry. 'I can't do anything because of this bloody house. I've got to be here overseeing it all, picking up the kids and driving them around. Can't you see? If we could get the build done quickly, then we'd be able to get some money coming in again.'

Pete's thinking it over, his hands on either side of his head, tugging at his hair. 'It's all costing so much more than I thought. I don't know how we're going to manage.'

'But that's what Eve's saying. We could get it done more quickly, cheaper. We could get people staying here sooner.'

'Who is this Eve, anyway? Why does she care so much about our house?'

'She doesn't! Not really. She's just my friend. The only one I've got around here. And she was trying to help. It was an off-the-cuff suggestion. But it makes sense, doesn't it? We're never going to get that modern extension past the planners. This is a listed building. A famous one at that, if you speak to any of the neighbours. Or infamous. They're not going to let us change it. So we might as well get on with what we *can* do and make it liveable. So we can sell it or live in it . . . and get on with our lives.' I turn to Pete, but he sinks back on the sofa. He looks exhausted.

'I don't want to move again.' He says it quietly, to the ceiling. 'I want us to stay . . .'

He might as well add the final word. We both know what it is, though neither of us will say it out loud. *Together*. Would we survive another move? If we leave this house, it might not be as a family.

I rest my head on Pete's shoulder. 'Why don't we go for lunch with Eve?' I say gently. 'Honestly, when you hear what she's got to say, you'll get it. She's got so much vision for this place. She really was a breath of fresh air when she came here today.'

Pete grunts and I look up. He's on his phone. He's retreated to the place where I can't reach him. Where he can lose himself in football results and political infighting and work gossip, or whatever he looks at. That old suspicion twitches in my mind again. Why *is* he always glued to that thing? Is there something I don't know about, or some*one*? But I know it's paranoia on my part. Or my own guilty conscience.

'I could book a table at The Rising Sun.' I look at the side of his head, watching his eyes flick as his thumb scrolls. 'It's not far from Ipswich. How about Saturday?'

Pete turns to me for a moment, his eyes searching my face and then he goes blank again.

'Okay. Whatever you think.'

And I know that's the best I'll get out of him on my own. I need Eve's enthusiasm, her insight, the certainty she projects that banishes every doubt from your mind.

Chapter Thirteen

The Rising Sun is packed, pub lunches being one of the only things to do in this part of the world. I asked for a quiet table, but we're surrounded by raucous laughter, squabbling children, crying babies. Next to the locals, we must look like a family beamed down from space. Ghostly faced, quiet children and Pete, whose wince suggests that the noise might be causing him physical pain, after his usual Friday night after-work session.

I'm the only one of us pleased to be here. Despite the dark brass-adorned walls and low-beamed ceilings, I feel brighter than I have done in weeks, longer probably. Finally, a way forward, if only Eve can persuade Pete to abandon our plans. Rose is excited to see Eve again, too, although I'm not sure she'll stand the sensory overload of being in this pub for too much longer, and Eve is already half an hour late.

It's the first time I've known her not to be punctual and it surprises me. She'd seemed eager to join us for lunch when I rang and had understood the importance of the task ahead of her – to support me as I try to persuade Pete to forget the ambitious extension. But now I'm wondering if she's had a better offer, if I've driven my family out to a pub in the middle of nowhere for nothing.

We get a first round of drinks and I'm about to relent and order the children some food when Eve bursts through the door, full of apologies, but looking unusually tired and dishevelled. Her hair is dull, tied back. She's wearing a plain black T-shirt and no jewellery, no make-up. I feel somehow disappointed. Not that I expected her to go to extra effort, but right now she's about as far as possible from the stylish, artistic force of nature I've described to Pete.

'I'm so sorry,' she says, slumping into a seat and turning to Rose. 'Hello, darling, how are you?'

Rose shies away a little, perhaps wary of the difference in Eve's appearance, her breathlessness and general air of disarray.

'This is Pete, Archie – this is Eve.' I'm expecting her to flash one of her winning smiles, but she's staring at her menu and orders a gin and tonic as soon as the waitress appears. Pete looks up in surprise, or approval perhaps, and orders a pint in turn.

'Hair of the dog,' he says to Eve, meeting her eye for the first time, and I'm reminded of that other side to him – cheeky, flirtatious even. One I've barely seen since we left London. He's probably been saving it for his work colleagues and clients, on those legendary nights out.

'God, tell me about it.' She rolls her eyes, and I order a Diet Coke, realising it will be me who drives us home. I've got no idea how Eve will get back if she starts drinking now.

'Big night last night?' I'm trying not to sound disapproving, but here I am, with my two children, and two adults who are getting stuck in before lunch.

'Oh you know, long story. I'll tell you later.' She looks towards the children and raises her eyebrows. I smile, trying to adjust to this new Eve, who drinks spirits in the daytime and has intriguing secrets.

Eve and Pete quickly fall into a conversation about the house: the financial value of preserving its distinctive features; the mistake so many people make when they renovate, turning beautiful homes into empty shells that quickly fall out of fashion – though we'd never fall into that trap, naturally. Pete's charmed, I can see. He listens, nodding and basking in Eve's undivided attention. She asks about his work, commiserates about the long commute – she used to do it, too, it turns out, though she's never mentioned that to me. She's so petite, she tucks herself neatly at the end of the banquette Pete's sitting on, with Archie on his other side. Rose and I are opposite, eating quietly and listening, each waiting until it's our turn.

But that time doesn't come. Eve is taking her role seriously here. I prepared her – told her how resistant Pete would be, how wedded he is to the idea of a cool, minimal living space, just like his friends Rich and Amanda. I'd asked her to help me. But somehow this doesn't feel like the two-pronged attack I'd envisaged. It feels like a first date that the kids and I have accidentally gatecrashed.

'Jess tells me you're a painter. Would you ever consider doing the house?' Pete asks, three pints down, his cheeks flushed, as the children order their desserts and I ask for the bill.

'What, just emulsion, or do you want the woodwork done as well?' Eve's eyes twinkle as she watches Pete cotton on to her joke. They share a laugh, and an image flits into my mind of her tucked under his arm, how neatly she'd fit, their dark heads together. Why am I thinking like this?

'No, I mean, we could commission you – to do a painting of the house.' Pete turns to me and I give him a look. What's he thinking? We don't have the money to commission artwork right now.

But Pete's warming to his idea. 'It could go in the hallway. A big canvas. That would be really grand, wouldn't it?'

'Pete, we're months away. Maybe more than a year,' I point out. 'Even if we don't do the conservatory, it's going to take a long time to repair every last windowpane and splintered shutter, all the brickwork, the pointing . . . We don't want a painting of the house in the state it's in.' I'm desperate to get away now from this hot, noisy pub, the children restlessly playing with our phones, Pete and Eve settled in for an afternoon session.

'Why don't I paint it as it's going to look?' Eve suggests. 'You could describe it to me exactly as you see it, and I'll bring it to life on the canvas. Then the architect, the builders, they'll have something to work from. And you'll have a keepsake for the rest of your lives.'

Pete turns to her, his eyes lighting up for the first time in weeks. 'That's a brilliant idea. We can sit down together and map out the whole house, how we want it to be. Maybe not so modern as we thought – you're probably right about that. But fresh and classic at the same time.' He turns to me, enthused about the house for the first time in months, and I smile, despite myself. I wanted this – I asked Eve to help me persuade Pete. And she has. He's changed his mind. Almost as quickly as I did. So why do I feel uneasy?

'Well, if you're sure, Jess. Why don't you both think about it?' Eve says, catching my eye for what seems like the first time in the best part of an hour, one eyebrow raised. A reminder of our agreement.

And I can't help but smile, though my eyes dart towards Pete. He's totally oblivious, already discussing the idea of another, smaller, canvas for the barn, which he's now convinced will be fully booked by next summer, just as soon as the exterior of our house is done.

'I think we'd better be going.' I look at the kids, who have slumped, their faces lit blue by technology. I can't wait for this afternoon to be over. I need a chance to think in peace. But as we leave the pub, I notice Eve stagger a little and I glance at Pete, who is also half-cut, though safe in the knowledge that I'll be driving.

'Eve, are you sure you're okay to drive?' I ask.

Eve looks up from where she's rummaging in her bag. 'Hm, well – I could always order a taxi and come back and get the car tomorrow.' She fishes out her phone.

'No, don't worry,' I say. 'We'll drive you home.' I still don't know where Eve lives. I'd be interested to see her place, to find out if my hunch is right and she is sleeping above the gallery.

'Or better still, why don't you come to ours?' Pete suggests. 'It's not far, and we could talk through some of the plans; you could even do some sketches. I've got a lovely bottle of red just waiting to be opened.'

'Well, you've probably got things to be getting on with?' Eve turns to me. I hesitate, weary of Pete's 'all back to mine' tendencies. I could really do with some quiet. I want my next conversation with Eve to be in private, without Pete and his puppyish enthusiasm.

'Oh please, Mummy. I can show you my bedroom and where I've put my badger picture.' Rose smiles and slips her little hand into Eve's. Pete and I exchange a look. This never happens. I can't remember Rose ever volunteering physical contact outside of our family.

'C'mon, Mum, I want to get back. I'm playing *Roblox* with Milo at five.' Archie kicks his foot against the ground, impatient to return to his online world, populated with his old friends.

'Absolutely, come back with us. It will be lovely.' I say,

aware that I've got no choice. 'We've got some cheese, and wine – as Pete says. I'm sure I can rustle something up for supper.'

'Honestly, don't worry, I couldn't eat another thing,' says Eve, who picked at a Ploughman's in between three G&Ts. 'I can squeeze in the back with the children, if you're sure it's no bother?'

'We'd love to have you.' Pete opens the car door with a flourish. 'Your chariot awaits.'

Archie rolls his eyes at me, and I stifle a giggle. But I can't remember the last time Pete even bothered to make a dad joke, so perhaps it's not such a bad thing to be taking Eve home with us.

As I drive, listening to Eve and the children singing along to Billie Eilish in the back seat, I reason with myself. She's my only friend around here, and she's won over my terrified daughter, charmed my grumpy husband – even Archie seemed surprised at lunch by her impressive knowledge of Xbox games. So what's my problem?

I catch Pete grinning as he watches them in the rear-view mirror, and he meets my eye with a searching look. Is there a chance I might just snap out of my gloom? Is it possible we could remember what it was we enjoyed about each other's company?

I smile at him. I'm determined to relax when we get home. I'll have a glass of wine, join in with the jokes, the singing. I'll get caught up in Pete's excitement, in Eve's, in the possibilities the house seems to present when she's there. She can crash in the spare room, and then I'll drive her back to get her car in the morning. By the end of the weekend, our friendship will be cemented. Perhaps Eve is just what this family needs.

Chapter Fourteen

The queue snakes all the way back past the outdoor seating department and nearly towards children's furniture. We're standing, with our trolley piled high, the kids hanging off the handles, complaining.

'Can't we have an ice cream, or a hot dog? We don't all need to stand here, do we?' Archie whines.

'Yes, we do,' Pete snaps. 'None of us wanted to come to Ikea, but we're here now, so we'll wait together.'

'I could take them to . . .' I stop as Pete scowls at me. He thinks this is all my fault. That I was the one who suggested this whole thing. But he was barely conscious by the end of the evening, and the way I remember it, the enthusiasm was all his.

Pete and Eve must have had a couple of bottles of red already by the time the children were in bed, and while I was upstairs running baths and brushing teeth and reading stories, they were evidently busy discussing everything from shutter design to fanlights and door colours. By the time I joined them, Eve had made pages of notes, peppered with sketches and annotations. I tried not to feel annoyed as I settled myself next to Pete on the sofa, pouring myself a glass of wine and snuggling a little closer to him than I'd usually sit, if I'm honest. But I wanted to present a united front. To make it clear that I was a part of this decision-making team, even if it didn't seem like it. I wasn't just a silent partner.

Eve had made herself at home, her tiny feet stretched out in front of her on the other sofa, toes pointed towards the fire, wrapped in one of the blankets I always leave lying around to protect against the damp air and persistent draughts. She looked small and angular in the firelight, shadows falling across her high cheekbones as she sketched a mantlepiece somewhat similar to the one Pete was in the process of describing, though with a few flourishes of her own.

I needed to wrest back control of the situation, and I was casting around for a distraction when I remembered Eve's secrecy earlier in the day.

'So what was going on that you couldn't say in front of the children?' I asked, interrupting an eager discussion about wood carving and varnishes. It must have sounded abrupt, because both Eve and Pete turned to look at me, Pete frowning slightly as Eve shifted a little and patted down her blanket. She looked into the crackling fire with a sigh, and then put down her pad and pencil and seemed to let her shoulders fall, her body sag.

'Oh, that. I'd decided not to tell you. It seems too much to burden you both with, really, but I had some bad news last night.' To my relatively sober ear, Eve's tone sounded surprisingly steady. I looked at Pete, propping his head with his hand. He'd clearly had the lion's share of the wine.

'Oh no,' he slurred. 'Is everything okay?'

'Not really.' Eve looked away for a moment. 'I've gone bankrupt. I'm going to lose everything – the gallery, my home. I don't know what to do.'

'My God, Eve. You never let on.' I sat forward, hands clasped, wondering how to respond. 'Here we are boring on about our renovations and you've got all this going on. Why didn't you say?' It was all so sudden. She'd never mentioned money troubles before, not even when she'd come for coffee earlier in the week. But that must have been why she'd arrived at the pub late, and dishevelled. No wonder she'd hit the booze at lunchtime.

'I know, I'm sorry. I thought about cancelling today, but then I decided I could do with the company. I just need to work a few things out. I'm sure it will be okay.' She put her head in her hands then, and Pete and I exchanged pained looks in silence. What could we do?

'I mean, you must have seen that the gallery was pretty empty?' Eve turned to me, and I nodded, not knowing what to say. 'I stopped breaking even and, well, that place is my whole life. I live above it. I don't have anywhere to go.'

I remember sitting down next to her and putting an arm around her, making comforting noises, stroking her shoulder. But in my memory, it was Pete who made the offer, not me.

'Why don't you stay with us?'

At the time, in the warm glow of the fire, with a row of empty wine bottles and a friend in need, it seemed the obvious solution. We had a converted barn, practically ready to move into. We couldn't let it out until we'd made the main house presentable, anyway. And I could do with the company. It was definitely Pete who'd said that.

'Jess is lonely as hell out here all on her own all day. It would do her good to have someone around. Anyway, where better to start on the painting, the commission?'

He'd smiled then, and Eve had looked at us in disbelief. Like we were angels sent from on high. And it was true, really. We'd offered her a bed, paid work. We hadn't discussed a fee yet, surely she wouldn't charge us much, but it was something for her to focus on while she picked up the pieces of her life, dismantled the gallery, put all her paintings into storage and packed up her belongings.

She hadn't wanted me to come and collect them with her. She didn't want anyone setting foot above that shop, she said. Too many memories. And so she turned up three days later, with four boxes and a holdall. She's officially moving in later today, arriving with the last of her stuff once we've bought everything we need to kit out the barn for her arrival. She's ready to pitch in and help with anything she can around the house, by way of thanks. She even offered to pay us rent. Just a token amount. But how could we accept her money when she has nothing?

So here we are, buying furniture for the barn in a rush, so that Eve has everything she needs. We'll be able to use it all for the paying guests, too, as I keep reminding Pete. Anything we buy for the barn now is preparation for when we sign up with Airbnb. The arrangement with Eve is only temporary, I find myself reassuring him, even though I'm sure, almost sure, it was his idea in the first place.

But now Pete's back at work and feeling the pressure again, he seems to have forgotten all about last weekend – the boozy lunch, the hours of excited discussion about the house, the sketches, the plans. He's twisted it all around so that it's me who invited my new friend to come and stay with us. Who convinced him to call Graham and cancel the extension plans. To get the builders started on the house, now that they've finally finished the barn. In his mind, the whole thing has been my doing. And perhaps I did start the wheels in motion when I arranged that lunch. But my modest plan to get things moving with the house seems to have snowballed into a whole new project, a new lodger, a new dynamic.

We have the usual moment of panic that we won't get everything in the boot, followed by a silent drive home and hours spent reading instructions, fiddling with screw bits, swearing over missing parts. The kids collapse in the corner of the barn with their iPads, while Pete and I shift the new furniture into place, hastily wiping away sawdust from where the builders have only just finished the laminate flooring, polishing up the small kitchen and shower-room.

By the time night falls around us, the newly converted barn is gleaming, fresh, furnished with a double bed, armchair, a small table and chairs. Gone are the tatty mattress, the cracked sink, the cobwebs, the eery corners of darkness that terrified me when we first arrived. Now it's all pine and bright lights, modern, minimal. It's perhaps not as stylish as if we'd had more time. It's certainly missing a few personal touches. But to my eyes it represents everything the Maple House isn't, and I allow myself to imagine for a few moments locking myself away from that house, from Pete, from the kids and their moods, their needs. I picture myself stepping into the brand-new shower and washing away all memory of the past few months, the gloom, the dust, the ghosts of unhappy families who have lived here before us. Afterwards, I'd sink into the bed, alone, and close my eyes. Drift off into a deep, peaceful, uninterrupted sleep . . .

It's a knock at the window that shakes me from my fantasy, and I gasp as Eve's face appears from the darkness, her nose red from the cold.

'What is it?' Pete asks wearily from where he's fixing up a blind. He's used to my moments of panic by now, my edginess, the way I never seem to relax here, how I'm always on high alert. The children don't even look up from their screens.

'It's only Eve,' I say, lightly, my heart returning to its normal speed as I open the door, letting her in, along with a gust of cold air and a powerful blast of spices.

'Here, take these.' Eve thrusts two large brown paper bags into my arms and returns for the rest of her belongings, while I unpack an Indian takeaway onto the new table. But there aren't enough chairs for the five of us, and we haven't bought enough cutlery or crockery, so we troop over to the Maple House, leaving behind the warmth and light of the newly fitted-out barn, with its underfloor heating and specially positioned spotlights.

We settle around the table, my eyes adjusting to the gloom of our kitchen, the draught circling our ankles as I dish out small portions of curry for the children that I know they'll just push around their plates before rejecting outright.

'Sorry, I should have called ahead, checked if this is what you wanted.' Eve looks from Rose, who is trying to smile eagerly despite her obvious recoil from the food in front of her, to Archie, who is already wrinkling his nose in protest.

'No, it's great, thanks. We hadn't eaten. We were so busy on the barn I'd forgotten all about dinner. It would probably have just been nuggets and chips, so this is perfect.' I smile and turn to Pete, who is already tearing a naan bread in half.

'Yeah, most of the takeaways won't deliver out here, so this is a real treat.' He grins at Eve between mouthfuls, his good humour returning with the first sips of Kingfisher she's brought to accompany the meal.

'I didn't mean to make you change your plans. It was a spur-of-the-moment thing. The least I can do,' Eve says, and it's only then that I remember the reason she's really here. The bankruptcy. How can she afford a takeaway for five on a whim? Also, who turns up at someone's house with a meal, unannounced? What if I had already cooked?

But I'm being churlish, really. We were hungry, we needed food, Eve provided it. Besides it's only right that we eat together to mark her first night with us. I'm sure we'll soon settle into a routine; she'll find a rhythm of her own in the barn, her own meals and visitors, a different schedule to ours. And it's only for a few weeks anyway, until she gets back on her feet.

I suppose I hadn't been expecting the air of celebration, perhaps that's it. The drinking session that goes on into the night while I put the children to bed, comfort Rose through her nightly anxieties, lock up, clean up after the meal. Once I've finished stacking the dishwasher, wiping the residue of oily sauces and sweeping the popadom crumbs, I hover in the living-room doorway for a moment. Pete's put on some music, and he and Eve are talking about the house again, Eve with her sketch pad on her knee. She's describing something to him in a low voice I can't quite make out and then he leans over to take a closer look at a drawing she's done, both of them laughing and settling back on the sofa again, relaxed, like they've known each other for years.

There's something different about Pete. I see it instantly in the creases around his eyes, the way he tips his head back slightly, the smile that takes up his whole face – the one I remember from Melissa's party, all those years ago. I'd watched him that night, laughing with friends, downing tequila shots, his dark eyes twinkling at a girl hanging around the edges of his group. I knew who he was, heard about his reputation, a different girlfriend every few weeks. But he hadn't noticed me until it was nearly time to leave. It was that stage of a house party when people start casting around, weighing up their options. I was standing against the wall where I'd been for most of the night, waiting, in my suede coat with the fake fur trim, for Vicky to stop flirting and get in a taxi.

'That's quite a style statement,' a voice had said in my ear, and I'd turned to find Pete running his hand along my collar.

'At least I won't get cold while I endure the eternity it takes for this party to be over.' I probably rolled my eyes. I'd had enough that evening. I barely knew anyone – they were all maths and geography types. I'd been hoping Oscar might be there. I'd recently bleached my hair for the first time and invested in a new coat, a denim skirt. I thought I might finally catch his eye. He was an art student, a sculptor, while I was just a wannabe, studying media and hanging around with people who had the creativity I could only dream of. But none of the art crowd had showed and I was desperate to leave. Pete was only trying his luck, I guessed, one last roll of the dice before he gave up and went home. But I was getting the full treatment – the gleaming white teeth, glinting eyes – what I came to realise was the legendary charm.

It had worked on me that night. Back in his room, he'd asked for a critique of his decor, laughing with me as I took apart the *Reservoir Dogs* poster, the lava lamp, the obligatory Edward Hopper. Everything was up for grabs with him, back then. He projected an easy confidence to the outside world, but in private he was full of doubt, genuine, trusting – more than ready to open himself up to ridicule, guidance, affection. And I, who had always pined after arty types just out of my reach, shrouded in mystery, surrounded by admirers, found I couldn't resist this good-looking, easy-going business student.

Pete hung on my every word, laughed at my jokes, pulled me towards the bed at every opportunity as though he couldn't ever get enough of me. I took his wardrobe in hand, picked out more stylish shirts, helped him buy his first pair of designer trainers – the ones that became his trademark. And he made me mixtapes, a new one every few weeks, each unique, tailored to me, to our lives together – all our favourite dance tunes, acoustic numbers, Sixties' classics, the songs we listened to together in my room in halls, and then in the flat I shared with friends, and then in the place we rented together in London. He had an ear for it. Knew exactly when to speed things up and when slow them down, how to create a mood, moving eventually onto playlists, DJ sets, creating the soundtrack to our life together.

It's why his friends always wanted him on the decks at a party; and I'd watch him up there, the girls lining up to request tunes, but it was me he looked over to with a secret smile. I was the one he went home with as the sun came up. I was the one he proposed to, had children with, sooner than either of us expected. That was when the party was suddenly over. Pete gave up on his dreams of breaking into the recording industry, took a job in advertising sales. I cut back my hours at the gallery. Together we made it work, just about. But Pete's mates still wanted him to DJ at the weekends, and then there were the work events as he rose up through the ranks at the agency. I'd seen my friends on the odd week night too, when Pete made it home. But it was the time together as a couple – drinking, talking, listening to music – that seemed to fall away. We both started to feel neglected; I know I did. Everyone wants to think they're desired, needed, more than anyone else in the world. We'd grown up together, but gradually we'd been growing apart. It was that distance between us that nearly broke us in London. I should have realised moving out here would be the final straw.

I hardly recognise the look Pete's giving Eve now. The song he's playing for her, acoustic guitar, a female vocalist I haven't heard before. Eve's cheeks are flushed; she's tucked her hair behind her ear on one side, and she's glancing up from her sketch pad every now and then, through those long, dark eyelashes. Pete isn't looking at her, I can see that. His eyes are fixed on anything else – her drawing, the ceiling, the label on his beer bottle that he's picking at intermittently – the only sign that he isn't completely at ease, that he knows there's something wrong with this scene.

I stand there a little longer, breathing softly, in the doorway behind the sofa, so that they aren't aware of my presence. I just can't see how to fit myself into this picture. I could walk in, join them, sit on the sofa opposite and ask what they're talking about. I can already imagine them sitting up straighter, both starting to talk at once, moving only slightly apart, but it would be enough. I don't want to witness that transformation. I don't want to interrupt this scene, as much as I know I should. Eve is my friend, she's come to stay with me; Pete's the one who doesn't want her here. Or that's how it had seemed until this evening. Now, I'm not so sure.

I pull the door to a little and turn, quietly walking upstairs alone.

Chapter Fifteen

'Well, I'm glad you're not on your own all day. I've been worried about you.' Mum's striding along beside me through the small stretch of patchy grass that passes for a park near her house in Hackney. Beyond us, a group of boys around Archie's age are kicking a ball, their breath emerging in clouds as they shout to one another in the cold air. Mum puffs her own cloud of cigarette smoke as we stop and watch one of the boys score a goal, before they all pile on top of each other. It could be Archie's class at his old school, if I narrow my eyes, and I imagine how jealous he'd be if he saw them all, gathering spontaneously for a kickabout, no parents in sight, no need for a lift or an endless exchange of text messages to arrange. He'd barely believe this other world still exists, back in his small, well-organised, homogenous countryside bubble.

That's partly why I haven't brought the children with me today. I don't want to remind them both of what they're missing, just one borough across from all their childhood friends, the house they grew up in, the school they know so well. And after what happened at Christmas, I need to talk to Mum alone. It's a Saturday, so Pete's got the children, but as soon as I mentioned my trip to London, he remembered some work he's got to catch up on, so Eve's offered to help out as well, to 'show them a good time'. And I'm sure she will. Too good, probably. She's already got into the habit of indulging Archie in long gaming sessions, listening patiently as he shows her around elaborate virtual worlds and instructs her on how to protect them from invaders. When she's not playing with Archie, she's drawing or reading with Rose – they've become so lost in *The Enchanted Wood* that, last night, Rose requested her bedtime story from Eve. I tried not to overreact. After all, it was a one-off and Eve's only staying with us for a few weeks. But since Archie began reading to himself in the evenings, that's been our nightly ritual – Rose and I tuck ourselves up together in her bed and I read her stories from my childhood, revelling in the weight of her soft head on my shoulder, her warm breath against my ear. It's one of the few moments I get to really slow down and connect with her, and I'd been saving up my favourite Enid Blytons.

Eve has so much more time for the children though, without all the cleaning and washing and cooking to do. Without the builders to manage. Now that they've begun knocking down the conservatory, it's all I can do to stay on top of the dust, scrubbing the floors every afternoon so that we don't tread it through the entire house. We moved the TV and Xbox to the front half of the living room, but that hasn't stopped the children decamping to the barn after school most days, to watch TV there, away from the noise. And then Eve drifts back over with them in time for dinner, so of course I have to cater for her, too. Only a few weeks into our new arrangement and she's eating with the family most nights – even with Pete, who suddenly seems able to get home earlier than usual.

'Yes, it is nice to have someone else around, in the daytime, I suppose,' I say to Mum, aware of the caveat, even if she isn't.

'I didn't like the thought of you spending all that time shut away on your own in that place.' Mum shudders at the memory of the house. 'Have you thought any more about what we discussed? About getting away from there?'

'Not really.' I kick my toe against the hard ground. 'I just don't see how we can.' There's no way I can describe to Mum how much things have moved on in the few weeks since her visit. I can barely remember the fear that had dominated Christmas, the feeling of being watched, haunted even; Rose's night waking, her terror. She's stopped all that now, since Eve arrived. She says she feels safer. I don't find her standing at the window looking out at the lawn in the darkness any more. And I don't find myself doing that, either. Instead, my eyes are drawn to the barn. To the lights in Eve's windows, through her open blinds and into the bright, pristine living area. She's put up some of her paintings; large, abstract, colourful canvases. Sometimes, as Pete and I sit side by side on the tatty sofa binge-watching Netflix, I hear music drifting across the night air – Billie Holiday or Ella Fitzgerald, songs I remember Mum listening to when I was growing up. I picture Eve painting or reading or doing something solitary and enriching, creative. Not compromising on an evening's viewing, just so you can sit in silence, under the guise of spending quality time together.

I'm sure Pete's as aware of her presence as I am on those long evenings, but he never mentions her, and neither do I. Even when she's not in the house with us – laughing, sketching, singing, playing with the children – she's an unspoken presence. She's always out there, bringing life and colour and music to the barn. Much more vivid, and perhaps even more unsettling, than the presence Mum sensed during her visit.

'I don't know why you had to leave London anyway.' Mum grinds her cigarette underfoot. 'Or why you have to be so far from everything. You've got someone paying you rent now.

144

Couldn't you use that money to move out while you get the house done up and put on the market?'

'Eve's not exactly paying rent.' I turn away, focusing on the boys, celebrating a goal with some elaborate victory dance I recognise from one of Archie's computer games.

'Why not? Who is she, anyway? You said you met her at the gallery – is she a friend from work?'

I pause, wondering how to explain. It's all happened so quickly. 'She's an artist. We met at *her* gallery, in Ipswich. We hit it off, became friends, and then she was made bankrupt, she lost everything. So we're helping her out, until she gets back on her feet.'

I can feel Mum's eyes on me as we turn back towards the flat. 'Back on her feet? How's she going to do that?'

'I'm not completely sure.' I've started to wonder that myself. She seems to be doing a lot of sketching of the house, offering plenty of advice about what should go where, how various features should be restored. She's been doing her own painting, too, I assume. But I can't quite see where the money is going to come from that will allow her to move out again. 'I think Pete's going to talk to her about it. I've asked him to.'

'And how does he feel about all this?'

We're nearly at the flat, and I have a sudden urge to confide in Mum. I need to talk to someone. 'At first, he was really reluctant to let her stay with us, even though he was the one who invited her. But now she's here, he seems to really enjoy her company. The kids do, too. Everyone loves her.'

'Pete invited her?' Mum asks slowly. 'But I thought she was your friend?' We're climbing the stairs to her first-floor flat, the ones I traipsed up so many times after school, heavy rucksack on one shoulder, trying to ignore the gloom of the hallway and the pile of post on the doormat that no one ever sorted through. It's a Victorian conversion, small rooms, thin

145

walls. Mum has lived in this house for so many decades, she's stopped registering how dirty and noisy it is. As she lets me in, I can hardly believe how small it seems to me now. It's only since I've moved away that I notice the thick grime on the windowpanes, the way the frames rattle as the number 30 rolls past, the incessant bark of the neighbour's dog.

'Yes, he felt sorry for her, I think.' I push aside a pile of papers and books so that I can perch on Mum's green sofa. Now I'm here, I remember instantly why I was so keen for space, for views, for light and airy minimalism.

'And how about you? Do you like having her around?'

'She's great,' I say, as if to convince myself, as much as Mum. 'You'd like her. She's artistic and interesting and a feminist. She listens to Billie Holiday.'

'Can't be so bad.' Mum looks up to a shelf and pulls down a CD. 'So what's in it for Pete?' She raises her eyebrows at me over her glasses. 'Why does he want this ball-breaking feminist friend of yours hanging around?'

'Come on, Mum. I know Pete's quite . . . traditional. But he's kind. And he loves you.' At this, Mum raises her eyebrows even further. 'Anyway, she's not a ball-breaker. They get on. He likes having her around. I do, too.'

'Well, just keep your eye on it. You don't want her getting too comfortable. You need to be making money from that barn, don't you?' I can see from her face she thinks there's more to this arrangement than meets the eye. She's never trusted Pete, not really. She thinks he's just like Dad; that all men are, deep down. I wouldn't know, since Dad disappeared from my life all those years ago, and she's never shown the slightest interest in helping me find him. But I don't raise that now.

'It's only for a little while, and the kids love her. At least I've got someone to talk to. Aside from Pete,' I add as an afterthought. She doesn't know how things have broken down between us. And she doesn't know why.

'It doesn't matter what I think, anyway. All that matters is that you're okay. I'm still not happy about you staying in that house, but I'm glad you have a friend, someone to confide in. You need an ally out there.'

I sit on the train home, watching as the grey buildings turn to fields, and then to rain-sodden smudges, rolling that word over in my head. *Ally.* Mum's right – I do need an ally. But is that what Eve is to me? That's how it seemed when we first met, but already alliances have shifted. I walk into a room where she and Pete are together and I feel a disturbance in the air, as though I've changed the atmosphere, interrupted something, however subtle. Even when she's with the children, I feel like an unwanted addition. An annoying parental witness to their games and confidences. It could just be my paranoia, of course. I'm sure that's what Pete would say. But I can't help worrying away at it in my mind. All this time I've spent trying to bring our family back together – the move, distancing ourselves from our old friends, starting again in a new environment – and now I've unwittingly introduced a wild card to the household that's thrown us all off course.

I reach into my bag and rummage around for my phone. My hand lands instantly on my iPhone, but that's not the one I'm searching for. It's the old Nokia I want to check. Just to look at it. Not to make any calls, though I can't say I didn't consider it as I was leaving Mum's. How easy it would be to reconnect, to see how the land lies, to have another option. But now I can't find it, and I realise in my panic that I must have left it at home. I never leave the house without it. I'm always so worried that Pete might find it. I can't believe I've been so careless.

I sit back and try to calm myself. Pete will have been busy

147

with the kids all day, or 'working'. Anyway, he wouldn't think to rummage around in my bedside cupboard. He's got more obvious distractions.

Trudging from the train at Manningtree with the other passengers, heads down, anoraks pulled over suits, shoulders bent against heavy laptop rucksacks, I try to imagine how it's been for Pete all these months, adjusting to that journey twice a day, returning to a family near collapse, children subdued, a wife on the edge. It's been hard for him, too. Harder than I've acknowledged. He probably hates the house as much as I do, but he has to keep it to himself. He knows he can't add to my worries.

As I drive home, wipers at full speed, peering out into the darkness of the country lanes, I resolve to go easier on him from now on. I need to cut him some slack. Perhaps we could even pop out for a quick drink when I get back, since Eve is at the house. We could spend a bit of time alone at The Stag, catching up, like we used to.

I pass the neighbouring bungalow, all but one of the lights off, the dog jumping menacingly towards the fence, alerted by my headlights. I need to show Pete how it's been for me, alone in the house every day with the kids, surrounded by nothing but fields, woods, this weird man our only neighbour. And I need to try and understand what he's been through, too. We need to come back together. We should use Eve's stay to our advantage, make the most of the babysitting while we've got it.

But as I pull into our driveway, lights gleaming from every room in the house, I see instantly that's not going to happen. I switch off the engine and kill the headlights, sitting alone in the darkness of the car, watching the scene through the window, as though observing someone else's family.

Pete's taking a pizza from the oven, laughing as he turns

to the table, facing Eve and the kids, who are dancing around the kitchen. Pete turns back to the fridge and takes out two bottles of beer, flipping the lids on both and handing one to Eve. They clink the bottles together and smile, Rose clinging to Pete's leg and Archie actually holding Eve's hand as she twirls him under her arm.

I feel a physical pain in my chest, a stinging sensation that makes it hard to breathe. It's not just being shut out, though the alienation is running through every part of me. It's how happy they look, without me around to dampen the joy. Even Rose is smiling, her face shining as Pete swings her into the air, the pizza congealing on the table.

'Sit down and eat, it's getting cold,' I hear myself saying. That's what I'd be doing if I was inside. Trying to marshal the fun, returning order to the situation, insisting that everyone stop enjoying themselves this instant. That's what Pete's always saying: that I can't relax, can't live in the moment any more; I'm always planning the next meal, the next outing, preparing for the next tantrum. 'Somebody's got to,' I'd snap, feeling it was my motherly duty to keep the show on the road. But what if he's been right all along? I wasn't like this in London, when I'd come in from work to find the kids already fed by the childminder. I've lost myself to the routine, the drudgery. I'm making life miserable for us all.

The pizza's getting cold and that's fine. They all sit down and eat it eventually, presumably once the song's ended, the one that's got them all so joyful and breathless. Even the kitchen seems more inviting, from this perspective, the orange glow from the pendant light reflecting on the tiled worktops. All this time, I've felt like an intruder in that house, unwanted, observed. I've moved from room to room, imagining unseen eyes watching from outside. But now I'm the one outside, watching, and I've forgotten all about my fears of the impenetrable darkness, the shapes that might be lurking in the shadows. All I can see is brightness and warmth, a family who are talking and smiling and eating without a thought for what lies beyond those walls. Because they do look like a family, the four of them. A happier one than we usually are, with my nightly school-day interrogations, Pete's monosyllabic accounts of his journey and the children desperate to get back to their screens as soon as possible.

I know I should get out of the car, go inside, throw off my dark mood and join in with the festivities. But I can't will my body to move. I feel hunger gnaw at my stomach and remember that I haven't eaten since the single slice of cheese on toast that passes for lunch at Mum's place. The cold is setting into my fingers and toes. But I feel trapped, unable to tear my eyes away from the window, desperate to put off the inevitable moment when I'm forced to witness the change in mood brought about by my return.

Eventually they finish eating and move through to the living room, all four of them settling on the sofa to watch something together, like we used to in London but never seem to now. I've got to move. I can't stay here forever, suspended in time. Wind howls past the car. I hear my phone vibrate.

It's getting late. Where are you? Px

Pete's put his phone back down and has an arm around Archie. Rose is snuggled into Eve on the other side; I can tell from the way their heads rest together over the back of the sofa. I slam the car door and approach the house slowly. Pete looks up as I walk through the hallway into the living room.

'There you are.' He smiles, relaxed. 'I was about to send out a search party.'

'Mummy!' Rose cries, but she doesn't move from her seat.

'Did you have fun with your mum?' Eve asks, sitting up a little. 'The children have been as good as gold.'

'I did. Thanks so much for looking after them,' I say, but everyone has already turned back to the screen, where Paddington is hanging onto the back of a train, the kids utterly immersed in the drama.

'We saved you some pizza,' Pete says without looking at me. 'It's in the oven. We started watching this before dinner. It's nearly finished.'

'We said the kids could stay up and watch the end while they waited for you,' Eve adds, and it's the *we* that echoes around my head as I sit alone in the kitchen, barely able to swallow down the shards of hard pizza.

Eve comes in, opens the fridge and pours a glass of white wine, handing it to me. 'You look like you could do with this. Long day?' She pours a glass for herself and then stands beside me while I eat. In the window, we're reflected against the darkness, her raven bob and my bleached, straggly mess. Smudges of mascara where I wiped away tears in the car. I'm still wearing my London clothes – an orange blouse, skinny jeans, asymmetrical earrings. Eve, in a slouchy oatmeal cashmere cardigan and sheepskin slippers, looks like the one who's at home in this country-style kitchen, not me. Pete appears in the doorway, dark like Eve, a few chest hairs visible from where his shirt is open one button lower than usual.

'The film's finished.' He turns to me expectantly. This is where I swoop in with my military-style operation, washing and brushing and reading and cuddling, but I don't move. Does he expect me to do it because I always do? Or does it just suit him to see it that way? Much easier to declare yourself useless and open another beer.

Eve looks from Pete to me. 'Why don't you put your feet

up? Have the night off. I'll run the bath and read the kids a story. I'd like to.' She smiles, and I wonder again why she's never had children herself. She'd be a natural.

'Are you sure?' I'm reluctant to cede control, but I'm also exhausted. And I'm aware that Pete and I could do with the time to reconnect. I'm about to suggest he pours himself a glass of wine, too, but Pete turns to leave the room with Eve.

'I'll help. I know where everything is.' And he follows her up the stairs, the children coming in to give me a quick kiss before bed.

'I missed you, Rosie.' I smooth down the fine hair that has escaped from her scrunchie. 'Did you have a good day?'

'It's been so fun, Mummy. We played in the garden with Eve, and then we found this secret door inside the cupboard in my bedroom that leads through to Archie's room. You can actually crawl through it. It's like the wardrobe to Narnia . . . only you end up in Archie's room!' Rose laughs, but I can't join in. I don't want to begrudge her this happiness, but I can't help it.

'I'm glad you enjoyed yourself, Rosie. I'll have to take you with me next time, though. Granny really missed you. She's very lonely without us down the road, like we used to be.'

Rose's face falls immediately. Tears fill her little round eyes. 'I miss Granny, too.' She rubs her nose. 'I don't want her to feel sad.' She huddles into me, and I feel instantly terrible. The cruelty of making your sensitive child feel guilty just to pierce her little bubble of joy.

'Come on, don't be sad. I'll come up and read you some *Milly-Molly-Mandy*.' It's the book she used to read over and over with Mum, and I know it will comfort her. But Rose turns and runs to the door.

'No, Mummy, Eve says we've got to let you rest. You've had a long day. You're having the night off.' She stands in

152

the doorway, blows me a kiss, and then I hear her little feet pad upstairs. The floor creaks and there's the sound of running water, doors opening and closing. It goes on for what feels like hours as I sit and sink my glass of wine, and then another. I wait for the cries, for Rose's nightly anxieties, so that I'm called to her bedside to sing away her fears. But all I hear is murmuring and the odd muffled laugh. I watch myself in the window with pity, and then disgust. When did I get like this? Why do I want my children to be unhappy? Maybe Pete's right: I just want to bring everyone down to my own level of misery.

Or maybe it's Mum who's right, and I'm being shut out. I need to keep an eye out. All this time, I've been worried that it's me who is on the verge of tearing the family apart, with my erratic behaviour, my moods, my inconsistencies. I never stopped to think that the danger might come from somewhere else entirely. That I might be the one left picking up the pieces.

Chapter Sixteen

It's nearly time for school pickup and I'm rushing around the kitchen, trying to clean the grime off the windows and mop the floors when Eve appears at the back door.

'There's a leak,' she announces breathlessly. 'A burst pipe round the side of the house. I spotted it from my window.' She leads me out, and I watch, dismayed, as water streams down the side of the brickwork and pools in the gutter below.

I don't understand it. It's been cold, but this is the third pipe that's burst in so many weeks, and that's only the beginning. Last week three tiles fell off the roof, one of the kitchen windows is leaking, and the knotweed doesn't seem to be dying back, even though we started the treatment for it weeks ago.

I can't decide whether to scream or cry. Rich and Amanda are coming for dinner tonight. Pete invited them, along with Graham, so that we can show the place off, discuss our plans, get another perspective. I begged him to wait until the house is more presentable, but, as Pete pointed out, that could be a while. And in the meantime, we need to get Graham back onside.

He's been difficult to pin down since we cancelled the extension. Pete thinks he's sulking, that he feels he's been duped into taking on a project that's beneath him, now that we've abandoned the more ambitious aspects of the build. He wants to talk Graham into sticking with us, ask him to draw up scaled-back plans for the kitchen and the boot room. For the bottle store he's planning to erect in the garage.

It's all about saving face, really. Graham did Rich's grand conversion, so he's got to do ours, too, even if it's not so grand any more. And even if we can't afford it, especially with all the last-minute repairs we're having to pay out for at the moment. When Pete got wind that Rich had Graham over for dinner recently, he decided we'd have him round, too. Butter him up, Pete says. Convince him we can still get this place looking fantastic.

I'm halfway through a tricky salmon en croute recipe, and now this – another burst pipe, another call to the plumber, plus the children to collect from school. Eve must be able to see I'm on the edge, because she offers to pick them up while I get the pipe sorted.

I pause, thinking fast. It's the second time Eve's gone to the school this week. What will the other mums say if my 'friend' is back at the gates again? But then according to Archie, she never gets out of the car anyway. He collects Rose and they come out together to find her parked down the road. I have to hand it to her, really. If only I'd thought of that.

'I'll take the kids to a café afterwards,' she offers. 'Keep them out of your way until the plumber's been.' I look at her for a moment. It's strange, really. She came across as so confident, so self-assured when we first met, but she clearly feels awkward about our arrangement, about what other people might make of our mysterious lodger who seems to be staying with us for an indefinite length of time.

That's an argument that's come up between me and Pete more than once in the last few weeks. 'How much longer is she going to be here?' I hissed after another late-night drinking session last weekend. Somehow it's Pete who's defending her position now, urging me to go easy on her, give her a bit more time. Of course, I'd never say anything to Eve's face. We're still maintaining the facade of our friendship. But deep down, I know she can see what's going on, what her continued presence is doing to my family.

'Are you sure?' I'm desperate not to take her up on her offer, but I've got no choice. I can't leave the pipe leaking. And someone needs to be on time for the kids.

I watch Eve's red Mini retreat down the driveway, the phone to my ear, cursing myself. I must get myself more organised. Must keep on top of things, so that I don't keep giving her the opportunity to swoop in and rescue me. But how could I possibly foresee all the many ways this house will take its revenge on me?

Four hours later and the kitchen, at least, is transformed. Andy has fixed the pipe, the surfaces are as clean as they can be, the table laid, the smell of golden pastry filling the room. I stand by the oven, taking a gulp of wine, already one glass down. I've been drinking more in the two months since Eve moved in. She's joined us most evenings since my visit to Mum's, though I never allow myself to knock back as much as she and Pete do. We sit around and chat, or watch something on TV, glasses in hand. I always think she'll excuse herself at some opportune moment. That she'll understand our need for time alone. But clearly her need not to be alone looms larger in her mind. And so she whiles away the evenings, often sketching as we lose ourselves in the latest TV series, interrupting us every now and then with a question about coving or skirting boards or paint colours.

We still haven't seen the great commission. She's kept the painting entirely to herself in the barn. I've managed to get the odd glimpse of her sketches, over her shoulder, but there hasn't yet been a grand unveiling of her vision for our house. I've given up asking myself why she's the one to be making a record of all our decisions, our adjustments, the decorations we have planned. Pete offered her the job, and she accepted, that's how he sees it. But I thought it would be a matter of days, maybe a week or two. Not two months spent perfecting line drawings and sketching out every last detail. I've lost interest in the process, to be honest. It's only going to be an artist's impression of what we're envisaging. Not a precise representation. But to Pete, the painting seems to have become a talisman, a central focus, bringing together all our dreams for the future of this house.

The children are in bed now. Pete's up there singing Rose one last bedtime song. That's one improvement since Eve came to stay – he's been keener to take part in family life again, perhaps aware of how it appears to an outsider's eye if he sits downstairs every evening while his wife does all the work. Only Eve's not around to witness his paternal devotion on this occasion, since she's taken herself off to the barn for once. It's a relief to have the house to ourselves. It would have been nice if it was an evening Pete and I could actually spend alone together. But at least we'll be able to present a united front to Rich and Amanda, and discuss the house with Graham without interruption, without a third opinion asserting itself as it so often does these days.

'All settled.' Pete walks in, surprising me with a kiss on the cheek, an unexpected show of affection. 'You look nice.'

'Thanks.' I smile and brush myself down. I've brought out one of the old dresses I used to wear to gallery events. A bright blue shift with geometric patterns. I don't want to let the side down in front of Amanda and Rich, after all. Pete's changed into a dark floral shirt, his best jeans, hair slicked back, a new woody aftershave lingering in the air. 'You look nice too.' I kiss him back, enjoying the feeling of his arms wrapped around me for once.

'Where's Eve, then?' Pete asks, turning towards the barn. 'Everyone will be here soon.'

'She's at her place.' I pull away. 'I didn't invite her, did you? She's never met Rich and Amanda – and she doesn't want to spend all evening talking shop with Graham.'

'Yes, she does.' Pete looks at me, confused. 'She's the one who's been doing all the drawings. And she's staying with us, of course she's going to join us. You didn't think we'd keep her hidden away in the barn, did you?'

'She's a lodger, Pete, not a family friend. She doesn't have to join in with everything we do.' I open the oven door to check on the pastry and then slam it shut again. 'Besides I haven't cooked for her. I haven't laid her a place.' I gesture towards the table, to the five place settings, five glasses. 'This is *our* house. She's only painting it – she doesn't need to have a say in everything.'

'She *is* your friend, that's why she's here. And she knows what she's talking about. She's artistic, that's what you told me. She was the one who convinced us to scrap the extension. So I just assumed she'd have some useful input into the rest of the plans. And that you'd want her to meet Rich and Amanda. I invited her days ago.'

'But you didn't say anything to me. And she didn't either. What's going on here, Pete? Why are the two of you making plans behind my back?' My voice is rising, but I can't stop it. Eve *was* my friend, my confidante, before I invited her into this house. Now, I don't know what she is to me.

'I didn't think it would be a big deal! What *is* going on here, Jess? You've been acting so weirdly since she arrived.'

'This isn't about *me*, it's about *her* and . . .' I catch sight

158

of the expression on Pete's face and stop, turning towards the back door, where Eve has appeared, dressed head to toe in black: a sleek cocktail dress, black tights, heels. She looks classy, understated, calm. I have no idea how long she's been standing there.

'Sorry, I'm interrupting.' She turns to leave, but Pete ushers her in, grabbing a plate and an extra knife and fork.

'We were just setting the table, weren't we, Jess?'

'Yes, that's right. You're just in time.' I force a smile and take off my apron.

'That's an amazing dress, Jess. I wish I had the nerve to pull off a look like that.' Eve takes a glass from the table and fills it from the bottle of white that's open in the fridge, while I marvel once again at how quickly she's made herself at home.

'You look great,' I say before Pete gets the chance. I turn my back to check the oven and take a deep breath, trying to calm my anger.

'Very chic,' Pete adds disloyally, to my ears, and I glance at him sharply. But he's busy getting out nibbles and more glasses, and then he goes to answer the knock at the door and suddenly the house is full of voices – Amanda's high-pitched laugh, Rich's deep rumble, Pete's eager guffaw.

'Jess, how *are* you?' Amanda sweeps into the kitchen, bearing two bottles of wine and making the room seem instantly smaller, shabbier, more run-down. She's even taller than I remember, and more striking, in heels and a grey silk jumpsuit, her long brown hair swept up, and silver earrings swinging forward as she wraps her arms around me and then holds me at arm's length. 'This place is a-mazing.'

'You're too kind,' I say, accepting the wine. 'Maybe one day it will be a patch on yours. It's a total mess at the moment.

Amanda and Rich have this fantastic barn conversion near Cambridge,' I tell Eve. 'Graham did the work on it. That's how we found him. We were so lucky he was able to fit us in.' I smile at Amanda and notice Eve raise an eyebrow. She and Graham haven't had much direct communication, but he certainly hasn't been thrilled by the changes she's brought about so far.

'Lovely to meet you,' Eve says. 'I hear you're an interior designer. You must relish the sight of a blank slate like this.' She runs a hand along the cracked worktop, and I look at her, confused. Eve seems to be enthralled by every last rotten beam in this place, she can't possibly see it as a blank slate, really. And how did she know about Amanda's line of work, anyway? How long has Pete been preparing her for this evening?

'Oh, I wouldn't call it that.' Amanda's eyes scan the low-ceilinged room, her forehead wrinkling only slightly. 'Although there's plenty you could do to open this up, with some bifolds, an extension, maybe a light well . . .'

'Yes, I hear your barn's all glass and exposed concrete. It sounds breathtaking,' Eve gushes. Has Pete been showing her photographs or something? And is she testing Amanda? I can't work out what she's playing at.

'Eve's been staying in our barn for a few weeks,' I interject, to explain her presence. 'She's an artist – and she has plenty of opinions of her own about what we should do with this place.' I laugh lightly and pour the drinks: a sparkling water for Amanda, who's driving, and a glass of red for Rich, who swaggers over, collar up and greying hair spiked, his radar for a single woman undiminished. Who knows what goes on behind closed doors, but in public, Amanda only ever seems amused and gently exasperated by her husband, ever the laddish rogue, even in his fifties.

160

'Jess, looking lovely as ever. That's quite the outfit.' He gives me a kiss on the cheek, eyebrows raised. 'And this must be the legendary Eve.' He turns and takes both her hands in his. 'Pete's told me all about *you*.'

Pete moves over to join us. 'Honestly, Rich, what are you like?' He rests his arm on my shoulder. 'Eve's a friend of Jess's,' he explains to Amanda. 'She's been staying here, helping Jess with the builders and everything.'

I turn sharply, extricating myself from Pete. Helping me with the builders? What's he talking about? But there's a knock at the door and moments later Pete's showing in Graham, empty-handed and underdressed in brown cords and a checked shirt.

'Sorry, I thought this was more of a working dinner, or I would have come prepared,' Graham says as Rich pumps his hand and Amanda leans in for a kiss. Pete introduces him to Eve formally, though they've met before. Is he trying to set the two of them up? I briefly wonder. Do we even know if Graham's married? There's a strange glint in Pete's eyes. He seems nervous, excited even.

Graham sets a folder of papers on the table and sits himself down, accepting a glass of water. 'Driving,' he says gruffly. He has an air of impatience. He wants to get down to business, but first Pete insists on a tour. I excuse myself – there's so much to do in the kitchen, but also I can't bear to be present as Amanda comes up with new and creative euphemisms to describe each shabby room she's greeted with. It's not that I don't like her – we've had some fun nights at parties, she's good for a laugh. But I've always felt in awe of her legendary taste, her glamour, her self-possession. And I'm painfully aware this house will never match up to the minimalist chic of their barn conversion, no matter how much Pete might try to convince himself otherwise.

I haven't anticipated, however, that Eve might choose to join the tour rather than stay to help me in the kitchen, and so I somehow find myself alone, slaving over a hot stove, while Pete and Eve show our guests around our new home. By the time they return, I'm red-faced and put out, sleeves rolled up, apron back on. I watch as they all seat themselves around the table and start picking at the caviar blinis I've laid out in place of a starter.

'Jess, take that thing off and come and join us.' Amanda pushes her chair back as I take a seat beside her. 'I want to hear all about the move, how you're settling in. Such a shame, what happened in London, but really it was the push you needed, wasn't it?' She tops up my glass. 'Eve was just telling me how the children are thriving with all this fresh air and countryside to run around in.'

'Well . . .' I begin, put out to discover that Eve's already managed to make her opinions known, 'Archie's okay, but Rose has been struggling to adjust.' I lean towards Amanda. 'Obviously Eve's only known her a few months, but she's definitely withdrawn since the move.'

'Oh, I didn't realise. I thought you two were old friends.' Amanda looks from me to Eve, and as I start to explain about the gallery, the new friendship, Eve jumps in.

'You know what it's like.' She smiles. 'Sometimes you just click. Jess and I were both struggling to find like-minded people around here – arty, cultured, switched on. And we found that in each other.'

'That's so important.' Amanda nods earnestly. 'I know when we moved to Cambridgeshire it took a long time to find our people, but we did eventually. And if anything, that bond's even stronger than it was back in the city, because we know we're in it for the long term. We've found our forever home.' She glances at Rich, who's ruddy-faced, draining his glass of red as he bends Graham's ear about their state-of-the-art drainage system.

'We're so lucky Jess met Eve when she did,' Pete says, joining our conversation, and I flash a tight smile, taking a gulp of wine. 'It's been so good for her to have a friend around here. And one with such an artistic eye.' He turns to Eve. 'In fact, Eve's got something she wants to show us all,' he announces as I exchange a glance with Amanda.

There's a look of recognition in her eyes, pity even, and I feel suddenly hot, exposed. This is so far from the evening I'd imagined: a relaxed dinner, the chance to have a gossip with Amanda, for Pete and I to share a few jokes with another couple, enjoy each other's company for once, get back in Graham's good books. Now Eve is pushing back her chair and excusing herself from the table. She's halfway towards the back door when I realise what's about to happen.

It hits me with a cold, hard thud. They've chosen this moment to unveil Eve's painting of the house. Pete has invited our friends, our architect, to present to them a future version of our home that I haven't even seen. A fait accompli. Either they think I don't have an opinion, or they don't care if I do. I can hardly believe it, except with a glance at Eve's face, I can.

There's a glint of triumph in her eyes as she returns from the barn. She looks flushed, excited, like Pete does. Has he seen the painting yet? Or will it be new to him, too? There's no way of finding out without revealing to our guests that I'm as clueless as they are about the plans for my own property.

Eve carries in a large canvas, resting it, face away from us, against the kitchen units as she carefully closes the back door. And then she picks it up, slowly, tenderly, and spins it around. I feel as though there should be a drum roll. Instead, everyone falls silent.

There it is, the Maple House, in full colour, every last detail – the window frames, the shutters, the door knob, the herringbone path. The front door is open and inside you can make out our parquet floor, restored to its former glory, the wood panelling stripped back and varnished. A new fireplace in the hallway. Eve has thought of everything.

I can see her hands trembling as she holds the canvas. She's anxious for our opinion. And it's a good painting, I can't deny it. But there's something odd that I can't put my finger on. Something old-fashioned, unsettling, strangely familiar. Something wrong.

'I love it,' Pete says, looking not at the painting but at Eve. She smiles, blushes, rests it lightly back on the floor, propped against the work surface, saying nothing. She's waiting to hear from the rest of us, from me. But I can't speak. Blood is rushing past my ears. I feel like I'm going to be sick. It's not just the painting, it's the whole situation. Being forced to admire something, in public, in a way that will commit me to that vision. Forced to make a pronouncement, with no room for manoeuvre.

'It's a lovely painting,' Amanda says, haltingly, filling the silence. 'Have you done it as a present, Eve?'

'It was a commission,' Pete explains. 'We asked Eve to paint the house as we want it to be.'

'It's very traditional,' Rich says. 'Is that what you want?'

'It's not that different to how it is now, is it?' asks Amanda.

'No, it isn't.' Graham pushes his chair back. 'So I'm not really sure what you need me for.'

'What do you mean?' Pete turns to him. 'You're here to make this vision a reality.'

'This isn't architecture, this is restoration. You don't need me for a renovation job like this.'

'It's true, Graham is kind of a big-projects man,' Rich joins in, pulling rank on Pete.

I'm aware I still haven't spoken, but I don't know what to say. I can't stop staring at the picture. Trying to work out what it is that's putting me on edge, beyond the obvious – the sense of being manipulated, overridden, ignored.

'It's good,' I say eventually. 'I like it . . .'

'But?' Eve asks. In her eyes, a challenge. *Go on then*, she's saying. *Do your worst.*

And that's when I realise I can smell burning. The en croute. It should have come out ages ago. I run to the Aga, swearing under my breath. Another thing ruined. Another disaster.

I fling open the door and make a grab for the baking tray, trying to get it out before the pastry gets any blacker. It takes a second before the jangle of pain makes it from my hands to my brain and then I gasp, dropping the tray on the floor with a clatter.

Eve rushes to my side with the oven gloves I've forgotten and tries to pick up the tray before it burns a hole through the lino, but I will not let her be the one to salvage this situation. Not again. I grab a tea towel and wrestle the baking tray from her, determined to deal with this myself, for once.

'Enough!' I hear myself shout. 'I can do it. I'll sort it.'

For a moment, the tray is in my hands. There's a chance to rescue the evening, to restore order. Nothing has been spilled, nobody hurt. And then it slips from the tea towel, the hot tray hitting Eve on the arm as its contents flip onto her dress and across the canvas. She falls back as though I've pushed her. The fish and burnt pastry scatter across the floor, the scalding juices running down Eve's arm as she cowers on the floor, whimpering.

The room is silent. Everyone looks at me, Pete's eyes widened in alarm. Eve, wincing in pain, is helped to her feet by Graham, while Amanda dashes to the freezer for ice to press against her scalded arm and Pete runs her a glass of water. Everyone seems to have forgotten that I have burns, too. That I'm also in shock.

'Are you okay?' Graham asks Eve as Amanda sits her on a chair and presses a towel full of ice against her skin.

'I'm all right. What about the canvas though, is it ruined?'

Pete rushes to the painting, dabbing at it with kitchen towel.

'Don't!' Eve cries. 'Don't touch it. Leave it to me, honestly.' She struggles to her feet, holding the ice against her arm, and approaches the painting. I'm still at the sink, running my stinging hands under ice-cold water, alone. I watch her bend down and inspect the painting, Pete at her side. Still, no one has asked how I am.

'I think I'd better call it a night.' Graham eyes the burnt food on the floor and the two of them, crouched next to each other, studying the canvas.

'Yes, we should probably leave you to it.' Amanda joins me at the sink. 'Will you be all right?' She glances at my hands, red and welting up, but I can hear in her tone that she doesn't mean my injuries. 'Thanks so much for inviting us.' I turn to meet her eyes, but she looks away, kisses me lightly on the cheek. 'Let's speak,' she whispers in my ear. 'Call me, okay?'

She and Rich make their goodbyes, Pete getting up to see them and Graham out, but still he hasn't looked at me, hasn't spoken to me. Eve mutters something about changing her dress and lets herself out of the back door. I'm on my hands and knees, scooping up chunks of salmon and burnt pastry when Pete comes back into the kitchen.

'Jess, what the hell was that?' he asks in a low, urgent voice. 'What is going on with you?'

'What's going on with *you*?' I demand, getting to my feet. 'What was all that about?' I gesture at the painting. 'The grand reveal without even talking to me about it first?'

'It was meant to be a surprise. We thought . . .'

'*You* thought. You and Eve. And you can't see what the problem is?'

'Honestly, Jess, you're twisting things. You're not yourself. What must Rich and Amanda be thinking? And Graham? That's the last we'll see of him, no doubt. I'm sure he thinks there's something weird going on here. They all must do, now.'

'You're damn right there's something weird going on here . . .' I break off, distracted by the painting again. What is it? I can't put my finger on it. I move towards it again, drawn to it, this perfect replica of the house I'm standing in. Pete watches me as I examine the windows. Is it something about the effect Eve's used that has created the appearance of shadows? Figures looming, outlined in the darkness.

But that's not what's unsettling me. Not really. There's something truly uncanny about it. It's so similar to the house as we saw it on the first day we came here. Well, the first day I came here, in the sunshine, feeling hopeful. Except this house looks brand new, almost more familiar. I stare at it, mesmerised. And then, an image flashes into my mind and I remember where I've seen it before.

I turn, leaving Pete in the kitchen, and race up to our bedroom, to the picture I printed off the internet just before Christmas, after Sara and her friends had bombarded me with stories about drownings and ghosts and the dark history of our house. It was a photo of the Maple House as it was then, accompanying a news story, and as I rifle through my bedside drawer, I almost hope I'm not right about this. It would be too weird.

But as I take the colour printout from the drawer, I see immediately that it's exactly the same, down to the shade of green on the door, the colour of the roses twisting up around

167

the frame, long dead now, but brought back to life in Eve's painting.

I walk downstairs, holding the picture in front of me as I enter the kitchen. Eve has returned, in jeans and a long-sleeved jumper, covering her burns. She's crouched by the cooker, helping Pete to clear up. But I'm not interested in them, it's the painting I want to see.

I hold the picture next to it, my eyes flicking between the two, back and forth. It's not an exact replica. She hasn't just copied the photograph. There are differences. In Eve's painting, the door is open. And so are the shutters, which are all closed in the photo. But the colour is the same on the shutters and the door, and the chimney stacks are identical, the brickwork, the window frames. All altered from how they are now, but all the same in Eve's painting as they were when the picture was taken.

'Why did you bother?' I demand. 'Why spend all that time on a painting when there's already a picture of the house exactly like it online? Was it the money? Were you having a laugh at our expense?'

Eve comes to stand next to me, snatching the article from my hand and studying it. 'I've never seen this picture before.' Her face is blanched; she looks surprised – it's probably the humiliation of getting caught out.

'Let me see that.' Pete takes the picture from Eve and studies it. 'But we don't want the house to look exactly like it used to, anyway. You knew we wanted to do something different, original.' He frowns. 'I don't understand . . .'

'It's not *exactly* the same.' Eve grabs the picture back. 'There are similarities, but that's only to be expected. Anyone with an eye for design can see how the windows should be, the doors, the shutters. And anyway, this *is* how you wanted it.' She turns to Pete. 'All those conversations, the sketches, all

168

my time locked away in the barn . . . this has taken me months. And you clearly hate it.'

She appears to be on the verge of tears, and Pete moves towards her in a way that looks instinctive, before he stops himself. Remembers I'm there.

'We don't hate it, do we, Jess?' Pete turns to me, indicating with his eyes that it's my job to smooth this over, to reassure my friend. But I've lost the will to make everything all right now. And she's not my friend. If I hadn't been sure before, I worked that much out this evening.

'It doesn't matter what I think.' I take the picture from Eve and fold it into my palm, for safekeeping. 'If it did, you'd have shown me the painting, the plans, before you presented them to Graham, to our friends.'

'It was meant to be a surprise,' Eve says.

'Yes, Pete mentioned that already.'

Eve moves towards the canvas. 'I'll take this back to the barn. I can see it's not what you wanted, and it's damaged now, anyway.' She winces as she stoops to pick it up.

'No, Eve, not after your injury.' Pete looks at me for a moment, as if remembering the scene by the oven earlier, my anger. I haven't forgotten. My hands are still throbbing. 'I'll bring this to the barn. And then I'll tidy up down here. You go and have a lie down, Jess. You've had a lot to drink, haven't you?'

I prickle at the suggestion that the events of the evening have been down to my alcohol consumption. It's barely nine p.m., but I can't deny that I'm longing to get upstairs with an ice pack and close my eyes. Try to forget everything that's happened, at least for a few hours.

Up in our room, I fold up my directional dress. What was I thinking? I smear burn cream on my hands and then lie myself

169

down carefully, clutching the ice pack between my palms, trying to ease the throbbing. As my eyes close, I imagine the house as Eve painted it, as it is in the picture I printed out. The gleaming redbrick, the neat pathway, the restored stained glass and pale blue window frames. It's not that I don't like it, it's just not what we planned. We were going to modernise. Keep the classic touches, but with a contemporary twist. The vision Eve created is like stepping into the past.

I think of the wallpaper she uncovered above the fireplace. The flagstones under the kitchen lino. Eve seems to have an instinct for how the house was. Or how it should be, perhaps. She seems to understand it better than I ever could. And my family, too, at the moment – Archie's moods, Rose's fears, Pete's needs. I can't compete any more. I've become an interloper in my own home. The feeling of defeat, of surrender, washes over me. I could just lie here and watch while she takes over my house, my family.

That's what she wants, I'm sure of it now. I picture her watching me in the gallery that day, sizing me up, with my husband and children. The big house. Everything she lacked. All that time I felt sorry for her, too polite to pry into her solitary life, her loneliness. Perhaps if I'd asked more at the beginning, I'd have worked it all out. I'd have seen the warning signs before I invited her into my home. But now it's too late. They can't see it – Pete, Rose, Archie – they think she's lovely and kind and selfless. They won't realise the truth until it's too late.

Or maybe I'm being paranoid, and she really does want to help us. That's what I tell myself as I will myself to sleep. It's all an overreaction. I'll be able to see that in the morning. And in a few weeks, she'll be gone. We can get on with our lives. Patch up the painting, hang it in the barn as a historical artefact and get on with our own plans for the house.

I must drift off eventually, because when I wake, the room is dark and still. I sit up and register the empty place beside me in bed. What time is it? Can Pete still be cleaning up downstairs? I listen for noises, but there are none. I check the clock on his bedside table. It's after midnight. Hours since I went to bed.

I get up, open our bedroom door and let myself quietly into the hallway. I hear a sigh from Rose's room, but the house falls silent again. I creep to the end of the hallway and peer down the stairs. There's no movement in the house. Could Pete have fallen asleep on the sofa, in front of the TV? I should go down and get him. He'll wake up freezing in the night.

Then I look out through the rounded window and see the lights on in the barn. I open the glass a crack and hear the jazz softly on the night air. The blinds are drawn for once, so I can't see what's going on in there, but I know, instantly, the certainty running through me like a blade. I close the window, run back to our bed and pull the covers over my head, burying my face in my pillow.

I can't believe he's betrayed me. It's only what I deserve. But that doesn't make the pain any less.

I must shut off something, because when I wake, the room is dark, but still lit up, and there's an empty place beside me in bed. What time is it...? Peter will be collecting the thingummy. Listen to ... but more, because I check the clock on the bedside table. It reads ... midnight, since I went to bed.

I get up, open our bedroom door, and tiptoe quietly into the hallway and bring a light from the ... room. But the house falls silent again. I creep to the end of the hallway and peer down the stairs ... there's something ... wrong. Some should know if there's a burglar in the house. But on the thought, my brother-in-law, I think I should go down and get him. He'll wake up, reaching in the night.

Then I look out through the frosted window and see the lights on in the barn below. I'll ... to the car, and then the fare ... into the night again. The blinds are down, but the woman's voice... see what's going on in there. I creep to reach the curtains running through the house, and I can't see the window, but back to console I and pull the covers over me, and I rest the weight of my head on my pillow.

I can't believe he has brought me here. I only want to leave, but that doesn't make things right now here.

PART TWO

Eve

Chapter Seventeen

SOLD.

I have to pull over before I veer off the road. It hits me like a punch, winding me, breathless. I turn into the drive and sit with my head on the steering wheel, my eyes closed, willing the sign to be gone when I look again. But there it is, the white-on-red lettering. It might as well read *THE END*.

Turning off the engine, I listen to the silence – intense, all the more blissful because I know what will follow. Removal vans, owners, tenants, diggers maybe. Who knows what fate awaits the Maple House.

I suppose I always knew this moment would come. But not so soon. I'd been clinging to the hope that I'd find a way to stop the sale. I had to. And now this . . .

I pull out my phone and jab a finger on the shortcut to the property listing. *Sold*. There's that word again. Not even *Under Offer*, with its hint of possibility. It can only be twenty-four hours since I last checked. What the hell happened? There hasn't been any middle ground – yesterday it was *For Sale*, today it's *Sold*.

'I'm afraid we aren't able to arrange any more viewings

unless you're a serious buyer.' That's what the uptight bitch at the estate agent had said when I'd last called, a month ago.

'But I am a serious buyer. I'm just getting my finances together.'

'Then get back to us when you have a mortgage in place. Thank you, goodbye.' The line had gone dead, and I'd slammed my phone against the kitchen work surface in anger. I run my finger over the cracked screen I still haven't been able to afford to replace since.

It had been such a thrill, being shown around inside the house after all those months prowling around the outside. The first time it was Brian, who'd let me take my time, lingering in the kitchen, which had barely changed since I was small, and waiting patiently while I wandered around the upstairs rooms, inhaling that rich, woody scent that took me straight back to childhood, running my hand along every window frame and doorway, checking the cupboard in my old room to make sure everything was intact, imprinting that view from the window in my mind – the garden, the trees, the stream.

The next time it had been Alison, who'd whisked me through each room with a brisk monologue. The third time, she was full of sighs and snippy remarks about mortgage lenders and valuation costs. And then that final visit, when I knew it was never going to happen. After Carl left and Dom stopped answering my calls. I'd managed to sweet-talk Brian into taking me one last time. I turned on the charm, smiling up at him through my fringe, asking him to wait downstairs while I paced around the house, taking pictures on my phone, tears falling on the screen as I checked them over to make sure I'd caught just the right angle, the exact slant of light.

Who knew when I'd be back inside these rooms again? Someone was bound to buy the house eventually, and the bastards at the estate agent had started screening my calls, just like Dom does. Nobody understands what this house means to me.

Taking the keys had been a spur-of-the-moment decision. Opportunistic. They had tumbled from Brian's trouser pocket onto the grass as he bent forward to open his car door, his arms full of viewing notes. I spotted them, glinting in the sunlight, and put my foot over them immediately. All I had to do was stand casually for a while, encourage him to go ahead. I just needed to make a call before I got back in my car, I said. I watched him pull up the narrow drive before I dared bend down and retrieve them. But now I had what I needed. I could enter the Maple House whenever I wanted. I could spend as much time in there as I liked, reacquainting myself with every last corner of the place before it was taken from me forever.

I had to pick my moments, of course. I didn't want to risk running into one of the agents showing around another potential buyer. But there didn't seem to be many of those, thankfully. Not since my knotweed discovery. The house even went off the market for a few weeks, and I barely slept for days, waiting for the moment Dom would return my calls and tell me he'd had a change of heart. But then the listing went up again online, the *For Sale* sign erected once more at the end of the drive. It felt almost more painful the second time, even harder to accept.

Still, I held out hope. And still I continued my early-morning and evening visits, parking my car up the neighbouring lane and cutting through the gap in the thick hedge. Creeping around the back of the barn, picking my way carefully across the worst of the broken piping and shards of glass.

The damages had been minor, at first. The odd chip to a small windowpane, with a stone or rock. I might crumble away a bit of brick if I could, but not enough that anyone would notice, unless they knew the house as well as I did. The drains were easy to snap in places, they were so old anyway. But the knotweed was a masterstroke. It came to me late one night, in those desperate early months when the house first went on the market, once I realised Dom was determined to sell, and that Carl and I would never be able to afford it. An outline of a memory, half-buried, but sharpening into focus as I drifted towards sleep. Dad, pointing out a patch of weeds growing on the river bank not far from our house, when I can only have been five or six – Japanese knotweed, he'd said. The name stuck with me because it was so exotic, so unlikely in our very English patch of countryside. And because he seemed so anxious about this harmless looking leafy plant. That it might spread uncontrollably, past the boundary to our property. That it might grow out of control.

When I looked it up online the next morning, I realised quite what a gift that moment of inspiration had been. If that plant really had been knotweed, if it was still there, I could easily replant a small cutting in the garden and it would soon take hold. What better way to put off potential buyers than an invasive weed that threatens the foundations of the house? It didn't take long to find it, a short walk from the house. There it was, all along the river bank, a perfect match with the picture on my phone. And digging up a small section was a matter of moments – not so much that I couldn't get it removed, once I got hold of what was rightfully mine. Just enough to cause the estate agents pause.

I'd made sure to point it out on my first visit with Brian. After I'd had all the time I needed in the house, he'd taken me on a tour of the garden. 'Isn't that Japanese knotweed?' I'd asked, all wide-eyed innocence, and I swear I saw the fake tan drain from his face before my eyes. 'I don't think so . . . Let me take a picture . . . We've got experts we can check with . . . I'm sure it isn't that.'

He couldn't get me out of there fast enough. I was right, of course. And by the time Alison showed me around two weeks later, she was already practised on the spiel – nothing to worry about, easily treated, we just need to mention it to potential buyers.

I'd nodded, furrowing my brow. 'That's going to put a lot of people off, isn't it?' I distinctly remember the little wink she gave me then. 'Well, that's where you can pick up your bargains!' That was before she chalked me up as a time-waster. Back when she still believed I was a serious buyer.

And I would have been, if I could have afforded it. But even after the asking price plummeted, in the wake of the knotweed discovery, it was still way out of my reach. And Carl had run out of patience by then. He said it wasn't healthy. That I was 'fixated' on the house – I needed to move on. But he knew as well as I did that this place should rightfully be ours. I shouldn't have to pay for it at all, for Christ's sake. If Dad had known what Dom would do, he'd never have left him in charge. It was our house, our family home. My only chance now of owning a place of my own.

But it's too late. I pull my car down the lane, park up and make my way carefully to the side of the house, my head darting left and right, making sure no one is approaching from the road. There it is again. The *Sold* sign. I steady myself for a moment, a hand against the cold, crumbling brick.

Then, slipping the key from my pocket, I dash to the front porch, rattle the latch a little and I'm in. I pull the door closed behind me. Inside, I take a deep breath, inhaling the familiar scent of the old hall, possibly for the last time. Tears fill my eyes as I look up at the landing. Slowly, I climb the stairs towards my favourite spot in the house.

How many evenings did I spend sitting here on that window seat with Mum, the circular panes of glass shining red and

179

orange and yellow against her milky-white skin, her eyes puffy from another day indoors? Dom and I would each nestle under an arm while she sang us the song that still haunts me now, the one I can never listen to – 'Scarborough Fair', with its minor key and its haunting melody, the question left hanging in the air. *Parsley, Sage, Rosemary and Thyme* – all herbs that Mum grew in her kitchen garden, the one I started tending once she retreated inside. The one I'm desperate to bring back to life. What would I give to sit one more time in that window seat? But it's gone now. Rotted away. Just another feature of this beautiful old house, of our family, lost to time.

I gaze out across the lawn to the trickle of stream. But I won't let my eyes rest there, won't allow myself to dwell on it, like Mum did. This house could be a place of joy and happiness, too. Turning towards the front bedroom, with its once grand fireplace and sloping roof, I picture us scuttling in on Christmas morning, stockings in our arms, piling into one big bed together, Mum and Dad smiling, moving up to make space. On summer mornings, Mum would lie with her eyes closed while I read aloud to her, the sunshine falling on her upturned face. In the winter, we'd snuggle up while she told us stories about her own childhood in the Maple House, the adventures she had in the woods, us children basking in the warmth and closeness before dashing through the cold night to our own beds.

It could be like that again, this house, full of life and noise and light. It just needs the right owner, the right family to bring out the best in these old rooms. Someone who knows exactly where everything should go, what it should look like, how it should be revived. Someone who can keep it in the family that built it.

I walk back down the broad wooden stairs, which used to be a dark, gleaming mahogany, but are now coated with chipped white paint, a beige runner blanketing their grandeur. The hallway panelling has been painted too, but that can easily be stripped back. So can the woodwork in the drawing room, where the original maple-print wallpaper has been papered over, just waiting to be uncovered.

I know I should be going now. I need to get back and open the gallery. If Carl walks past and sees it closed, he'll be on the phone straight away, asking how much longer I'm planning to flog that particular dead horse. But I can't resist taking one final look. What if this is the last time? I need to make sure everything is in place.

In the drawing room, I've left a small toy, a tiny soldier, tucked away in a gap in the floorboards. One of the hundreds of green figures that used to be lined up in rows in here, ready for battle. In my bedroom upstairs, a muslin I've hung onto over the years. In the pantry, a tiny bootee. It's where Mum used to do the washing. I'd sit in the corner and watch her sometimes, bent over, humming gently to herself. I want to leave a trace in every room, so that this house doesn't ever forget the people who lived here before, even if everyone else has.

Finally, I move towards the front door, pulling it open and standing on the threshold. Rain is falling in sheets across the front garden and I pause, allowing the memories, the sadness, to wash over me. In a moment, I will step outside and lock the door, shut away all the tiny fragments contained inside that make a life, a family, a home. Today we have pictures, reams and reams of them stored away on phones and laptops, videos, jaunty slideshows with jangling music, memories on tap. But what's left of my childhood is in here, in the scents, the spaces where furniture once stood, the words written on walls inside cupboards, the traces left by a touch, the molecules settled in the dust. These are the only remnants of the family I lost.

181

I wipe impatiently at a tear, and I'm turning to close the door behind me when I hear the rumble of an engine. I stand still, waiting for it to pass. But it doesn't. Instead, it gets louder, a flash of silver at the corner of my eye as I dart back inside the house. There's a car. Pulling down the driveway. I have to get away.

But I can't leave by the front door now, so I turn and run towards the back, my hands shaking as I find the key. The sound of a car door slamming, and then another. Is it the estate agent? It couldn't be the buyers already, could it? Whoever it is, I can't let them find me. How would I explain myself? What would I say?

Finally, the right key, smaller, brass. I push it into the back door and fling it open, making sure to shut it again behind me before I flee down the path. It's only then, as I approach the barn, that I remember the front door. I didn't hear the click. Did I pull it closed? It's too late now.

I slip inside the barn as a panicked voice cuts through the air. 'The door's open. It wasn't locked!'

I pick my way around the rubble and debris, trying to regain control of my breathing, steady my legs. How can I have been so careless? And what about the back door, did I lock that properly? At the window, I crouch down and peek out. I can just see them, standing at the front of the house, a tall couple, the woman fair and slim, with a long, thin face, in a rainbow-striped top and skinny jeans, her hair pulled back. The man darker, attractive, collar up, talking urgently.

They haven't seen me. I duck a little further down, but they're not looking in the direction of the barn, which is partly shielded from view when you're standing by the front door, anyway. I should know, I've played enough games of hide-and-seek around here. And blind man's terror, as Dom called it. They're studying the door frame, the handle, back

182

to the frame again. I can't hear what they're saying any more, but I can see that they're hesitant to go in, and I smile to myself, despite my panic at how close I was to being found. I had no idea they would be arriving today, but I've succeeded in making them feel like outsiders already. I've alienated them from the house they've bought, before they've even moved in.

I keep thinking they'll be followed by vans, more people, children, a dog. But it's just the two of them – anxious, faces drawn, like clueless city folk on a day trip gone wrong, nervous, ridiculous. They won't last two months. It might not even take them that long to realise the magnitude of the mistake they've made. And by the time they do, this place will be even harder to sell – no one will want to take it off their hands when they've owned it for such a short time. They'll know there must be an issue – something serious. And there is, of course: the knotweed. But that's not the only problem they're going to face. Not if I've got anything to do with it. By the time I've finished with this house, the only person prepared to buy it will be someone with a deep attachment, limited funds perhaps, but endless patience and imagination.

They've gone inside now, the pale couple with their worried faces. I imagine them walking around my home with critical eyes, focusing on every flaw, every fracture. They won't see the beauty of the place as it was. They won't be able to restore it like I could – in fact, they probably want to knock it all down and start again. That's what these rich couples do when they buy a house in the country: they bulldoze its charm and replace it with concrete and glass. I've seen it plenty of times on those TV shows. Well, I won't stand by and watch that happen to the Maple House.

183

I almost can't tear myself away, but it's time to leave now, while they're still inside and I can creep off unseen, on foot, find my car and roll quietly down the lane and back to safety. I tiptoe towards the barn door, holding my breath as I let myself out, making sure to close the door behind me. I dash to the garage, and I'm about to make a break for the thick hedges by the driveway when I hear the back door open and voices again.

'. . . rental property . . .' It's those words that reach me from the back of the house, along with the sound of footsteps. I dart into the garage, to the shadows behind the door, grateful for the dark clouds that loom menacingly overhead. Are they planning to rent the house out? Is this some kind of business venture? I peer out through the crack behind the door, watching as they open the barn latch and creak the door open wide. But the woman just stands there, not moving.

'Don't you feel like we're being watched? Like there's someone else here?' Her voice is high, shrill.

I spring back instinctively, and then stop myself still, holding my breath, watching the man walk into the barn while she stays outside, eyes darting, features tensed. Will they come into the garage next? I pull a little further behind the door, trying not to make a sound, and peer out again. The woman is still outside. For a moment, I think she's caught my eye through the crack. She knows I'm here. But then she turns and dashes back to the house, followed by her husband, muttering to himself as he runs through the rain.

I wait until I'm sure they're back inside, gasping for breath, afraid to move. I took such a risk. Came so close to being caught. But I feel strangely exhilarated, too. A surge of energy jolts through my arms and legs, making me want to jump on the spot, to run, to throw my hands in the air and dance around. All this time I've been poised here, coiled, ready to bolt at any moment, but I've survived the first encounter. I'm flooded with relief, but also elation, power – the hold I have over this couple, who don't know that I'm here, yet who sense it, somehow.

I wasn't seen, wasn't detected, but my presence was *felt* in some indefinable way. That woman knows someone is watching them, even if she doesn't yet know who, or why. She is aware, deep down, that this house belongs to someone else. Perhaps she can even feel the weight of the secrets that are buried here.

I push open the garage door, convinced they must be safely inside by now. Then I see, with a jolt, that the car has gone. Turning, I catch a glint of silver at the end of the drive. They've already beaten a retreat, hopefully unsettled by the little changes, the clues, the breakages they won't have noticed before. The lurking presence that I know the woman, at least, can sense. I've driven them away, for now at least. It's only a matter of time before they leave for good.

Chapter Eighteen

It's the last thing I expect: that she will just walk into the gallery in broad daylight and strike up a conversation. That she'll respond the very next day to my casual invitation on Instagram. But that's what she does, and I can tell instantly from her eager smile, her nervous chatter, quite how hungry she is for company, for approval, to make a connection.

Jess Masters. That's her name. It didn't take me long to find out. The postman didn't hesitate when I stopped him at the top of the driveway the morning after the move, before he'd even made it to the house. My sister had just moved in, I explained. I'd take the post with me on my way in, save him the walk. He'd handed over two letters with a leery wink. He was of that age, fifty-something, watery-eyed – the kind of man I seem to attract these days, at least a decade older than me. As though I've moved into a different realm with the crow's feet around my eyes. I remember hoping he didn't have a long memory. But he must see hundreds of people every day. He surely doesn't care who lives where, as long as the letters arrive safely.

Only this time they didn't. I darted back down the lane and into my car, tearing them open immediately. A water bill and a university prospectus. Disappointing. But at least I was able to look up their names on my phone. Jess and Peter Masters. Nothing online for him – the name was too common – but for her, there was an Instagram profile picture I recognised straight away. Blonde, pretty in a worn-out way, light blue eyes, a little younger than me, hair a bit wispy and wild. She was more made up than when I'd seen her the day before, on moving day, but it was definitely her. In this picture she wore big earrings and thick black eyeliner. Her bio listed her as working in an east London gallery. Below it were arty shots of books and lattes and soft furnishings and sunlight through flowers.

Since then, I've been checking the page obsessively. Who is this woman living in my house, who's clearly researching Arts and Crafts design, posting pictures of gaudy bird-print wallpaper and tacky gilded pineapples that I can instantly see will be all wrong for the house? This woman who shared a close-up of the view through a single stained-glass window-pane that I recognised instantly, like a blow to the chest, the early-morning orange light slanting across the dew-beaded lawn. Who puts up image after image of her new country-based life of leisure – striped socks resting on a table behind a mug of herbal tea, a robin perched on one of the old maples in the garden, a book resting open on a table next to a pair of garish blue reading glasses. *The Yellow Wallpaper* by Charlotte Perkins Gillman. I'd never heard of it, but I found myself browsing for it in the bookshop near the gallery, desperate to get a better sense of the person who has stolen my home.

It's an odd choice of book for a photo opportunity, I realised once I'd read it. More of a cry for help than an aspirational reading recommendation. But then, that's all it was, I'm sure:

an artfully placed paperback. Because it's all for show with Jess, it hasn't taken me long to realise that.

I've always detested social media. Why would you want to share all your private thoughts and opinions online, even if you aren't worried about people catching up with you, piecing together stories from your past, making connections you don't want to be made? Besides, who could care less if I've had a nice latte, or put up another piece in the gallery? I have a page for The White Room, of course. All businesses have to these days. But no one ever visits it, and I barely remember to post on it. It's the account I used when I lay the breadcrumbs for Jess to follow – a little appreciative comment on her hideous wallpaper choices, an invitation for her to visit the gallery. But I didn't expect her to take me up on it so quickly.

I thought it would take much longer to tempt her in, enough time for me to plan my next move. I didn't anticipate quite how desperate she would be, although perhaps I should have. The Jess I've been watching couldn't be further from the version she creates online. Her posts don't show her walking aimlessly from room to room, hair tied back messily and deep purple bags under her eyes. They don't recount the arguments that go on late into the night or the afternoons spent bent over her laptop, face contorted in anger or misery or frustration. The husband and the children don't look much happier. The girl always seems to be crying or staring out of the window. The boy disappears up to his room as soon as they get home from school.

Sometimes, as I sit freezing in the barn, thick coat and scarf wrapped tightly around me, watching silently through the cracked windowpane, I feel almost sorry for them in their grinding, everyday misery. And then I remember: this is my house, they have no business here. The unhappier they are, the sooner they'll leave.

I intended to cut back on the visits after they moved in. I didn't want to get caught, after all. But I couldn't resist a quick check, just to see how many of my little destructive acts they'd got around to repairing, how many small but unmistakable changes they'd already made to the house. And then, once I realised they weren't making any progress at all, were barely getting through each day by the look of it, I couldn't help making the odd adjustment – the relocation of a flower pot, a tiny crack here, a barely noticeable rearrangement there. The animal remains, the carcasses carefully placed to attract the local wildlife, were an ingenious idea. Perfect to lure in foxes and badgers, and any other creature that might help to unsettle the family, infuriate them, make them feel out of control of their surroundings. It's addictive, the little thrill of destruction, confusion. And the sense of power, of subterfuge, watching the frustration cloud Jess's face as she discovers yet another problem with the house they've bought.

Some days I go first thing in the morning, long before the gallery needs opening, before anyone is awake, and creep into the barn, waiting impatiently on the old mattress I dragged under the window months ago, until I see the first signs of movement. I slip Mum's mirror from my handbag, the one I always carry with me, which once had beautiful maple leaves hand-painted on the back but now only scratches of green paint, and I have some fun with the early morning sunbeams. The odd reflection, bouncing back at the house, making the little girl pause at her bedroom window and look out. That was until I couldn't find the mirror any more. I must have dropped it somewhere, and its absence stings. Just another little part of my mother taken from me.

Jess is jumpier in the evenings, though, when a flash from my camera phone or a stone skidding across the patio can bring her straight to the window, her eyes scanning the darkness, her features pinched, forehead low. The women of the house are much more aware of their surroundings than the men. The preoccupied husband and skinny son barely look up from their devices. I could appear at the window waving my arms and they wouldn't even register. The females, on the other hand, are most definitely spooked.

And since I established the pattern, it's become irresistible. Every evening, I vow to stay away the following day. I'm terrified I'll get caught – by Jess and Pete, or even worse, by old Trevor next door. I'd do anything not to run into him again. But each morning, I find myself drawn back to the house. The opportunity to snoop on this new family, these cuckoos in my nest, their depressing daily routine, the anxiety and unease I can bring – it's like a drug I can't give up.

The Instagram post was a shot in the dark though. I never imagined Jess would make it so easy for me. And when she first appears in the doorway, I panic. I shrink into the corner of the shop, unable to catch my breath. Has she come to confront me? Has she spotted me, lurking in the shadows around her house? Does she know I've been watching them for weeks now?

But as she browses the shelves, looking nervously around in her bright pink coat and chunky trainers, trendy reading glasses poised on her head, blonde hair fraying at the ends, I realise she hasn't even seen me. She's engrossed in the pictures, studying them closely. It must be my invitation that piqued her interest after all. Perhaps she even likes what she sees – one of those rare customers drawn into the gallery by genuine interest, rather than someone in need of a last-minute birthday card.

The prospect makes my heart beat a little faster, makes me forget for a moment all my resentments, my anger. No one comes into the gallery any more. Not since the last downturn. Local art is the last thing on most people's minds. If you can call it art, really, and not just a hobby, a bit of dabbling. Who am I trying to kid, attempting to keep a gallery going on the strength of a few birthday-card sales? Not my accountant, that's for sure. Or the bank. Or Carl – he could never understand why I couldn't enjoy it for what it was. A passion, rather than a serious career.

But his shop had been lying empty, so he could hardly argue when I wanted to turn it into a business, even one that didn't make much money. That was when we were still together. Now he wants it back, and I know my days here are numbered.

Shuddering, I push the financial worries from my mind for the moment. Those are for the night-time hours, when I pace the flat upstairs, trying to work out my next step, my next move, what I can possibly do to get out of this hole. For now, I need to concentrate on making the right impression – making the most of the opportunity that has dropped right into my lap. Or walked straight in through my open door.

Jess is hovering by a rack of cards. Of course. Not interested in the art, after all. But I need to make my move, so I approach, tell her the paintings are mine, try to drop in an arty sounding word: 'naive'.

'It's lovely,' she says, turning to me with a card in her hand, and as she catches my eye, I see instantly how desperate she is for my approval. I have the upper hand. I don't need to try too hard. In fact, the less I say, the more readily she'll come to me.

They're not lovely. Nobody who looks closely at my work would ever call it that. Dark. Bleak. Angry. Those were the words thrown around at art college, before I decided I'd heard enough. Before Carl came to my rescue. Even now, with my hard edges supposedly rounded by a long marriage, my youthful rebellion far behind me, my paintings are still cold and inhospitable. I can see that, without my husband having to point it out during our long, bitter arguments. Ex-husband. Estranged. Whatever he wants to call it.

But Jess clearly doesn't have an artistic eye – that much is apparent from her Instagram feed. She's babbling now, talking about my house as though it's her own – my garden, my trees, my stream. Complaining about how much there is to do, without a second thought for whether other people might have problems of their own, worries slightly more pressing than a renovation project. She's entirely unaware how spoilt she sounds, with her husband and children and her big house, and I find myself imagining the gratification of introducing this sheltered, self-involved intruder to some real-world anxieties.

But I know I need to keep my cool, so I take a deep breath and watch the shoppers walk slowly by outside, not one of them stopping to even look in the window.

'Let me put it through the till.' My voice comes out steadier than I'm expecting. 'So, you used to work in a gallery?' As if I haven't seen the name-dropping online, all the smug tweets and Instagram posts. I nod and sympathise and tell her a little about myself, just enough to get her interested, to keep her guessing, before inviting her to come again.

It's a gamble. I could have tried to get her number, or given her mine, but I don't want to scare her off. She knows where I am now. I'll have to rely on her being interested enough to come back again. Somehow I know that she will.

It's the girl who gets to me. Her hesitant smile, the anxiety in her eyes, the soft halo of baby hair that frames her face.

She reminds me of Jack, in the early days, when he wouldn't stop crying, never seemed to take a breath. I still find it hard to be around young children. I'm not expecting Eve to bring her daughter in, but as soon as she's in front of me, in the gallery, I see his face, feeling that sharp pain, the sting in my chest.

I don't want to stare, but I can't turn away. For a moment, I worry Jess will think I'm behaving strangely, following her little girl around my shop. But I realise soon enough that she's just relieved. Someone prepared to take an interest in her needy daughter. She's one of those mums who can't leave well enough alone – always fussing and meddling, as though the child is just an extension of her own neuroses, her own issues. She can't leave Rose's side for a minute, can't help but intervene, even when I'm trying to get her talking. She wants to speak for her, wants to steal the words from her mouth. She's surprised by how Rose opens up to me, I can tell. But there's no secret to it with children – you just have to listen instead of talk, you have to ask questions and be genuinely interested in the answer. I want to get the measure of Rose, but Jess's hovering, overanxious presence is making my hackles rise. *I'll show you a child with real problems*, I want to say. Not some pampered city kid who needs a bit of fresh air and freedom.

Rose does seem spooked when it comes to the house, though. 'It's creepy,' she says, her lip wobbling and tears forming in her eyes, and it's all I can do to suppress a smile, despite myself. Whatever I'm doing, it's worked. I'd rather there was another way. But at this point, I'll take any opportunity I can. I'll tear apart another family, if it means I can reunite mine.

Jess and her daughter are close, I can see that. But that doesn't mean it will always be that way. I, of all people, know that much. And if things start to deteriorate between them while they're living in the Maple House, then surely that will help to hasten Jess's departure. It's instinctive, my desire to win Rose over. But I can already see how it will form a part of my wider plan, even as it takes shape. To scale back my secret visits and come out into the open. To befriend Jess, to infiltrate her family, to become a part of her life in plain sight.

When I offer Rose a card, she chooses the badger immediately. Jack always loved badgers, too. And that picture is important to me. Not just because of the association with him. Something about the frightened look in the badger's eyes takes me back to a moment in childhood; an injured animal, Dom holding a rock. Did he hurt it? Or put it out of its misery? I can't remember any more. It's one of those moments that has faded around the edges, only that single solid picture, that freeze-frame from the past, remaining.

I hand the card to Rose and bend down to whisper in her ear.

'He's a special friend, that badger. He lives in the woods behind your house, and he'll look out for you, protect you. I'll tell you more about him the next time I see you, okay?'

Rose nods, smiling. I want to keep her waiting: for our next encounter, for the truth about the badger. Not that I'll tell her the real truth. She can never know that I used to live in her house, used to sleep in her bedroom, used to hide in her cupboard, used to roam around her woods. There's no way a girl of her age could keep that a secret from her parents – even an intelligent, sensitive girl. But I'll think of something. I've always been imaginative.

This time I give Jess my number and take hers in return, watching Rose walk away, clutching the postcard close to her chest. That Jess's daughter will prop one of my paintings next to her bed at night, look at it as her little eyes close, perhaps even see it in her dreams, gives me an unexpected thrill. A tiny part of me returning to the house that is rightfully mine. I think of that badger as my Trojan horse. He's got in there first, but it won't be long before I follow.

Chapter Nineteen

She won't stop talking about him. Not his name. But the story. She keeps going over and over it. Taunting me, torturing me. She must see I can't bear to hear it.

We're in Blend again. The first time I met Jess here, it was just the usual chit-chat. Lonely, friendless, disappointing husband, stalled career. I made the right sympathetic noises and nodded as though I believed she really knew what misery was, as though her tales of woe were anything but privileged, mindless whingeing.

There was a shaky moment when I thought I'd let slip that I knew about the work on the barn. And another when she told me she was sure someone was snooping around the house – she even replayed our close encounter in the garden the week before, when I'd been lurking in the woods and she'd nearly discovered me. But she's convinced it's old Trevor Martin, and I was happy to encourage her in that delusion. She even mentioned the 'weirdo' they bought the house from, and how she wondered whether he was still hanging around. I was sure she must have sensed how my breathing quickened, seen the way my hand clenched my cup. But I realised soon enough that Jess doesn't take notice of anything beyond the end of her nose. She certainly isn't the slightest bit interested in my feelings, or my life. If she was, she might not be falling so easily into my trap.

More than anything, she likes the *idea* of me. An artistic friend, a painter and gallery owner, who went to art school and has heard of *The Yellow Wallpaper*. Someone she can tell her friends in London about. Proof that we're not all country yokels out here. She doesn't need to know that I found out about her strange little book from her Instagram feed. That my art was only ever amateur and destined for greetings cards. That the gallery is on the verge of closing down.

It had gone well, that first little meet-up. She'd even invited me round for coffee, asked for my advice on interiors. Afterwards, I felt excited. One step closer to getting back inside my home. But now she's talking about my Jack, incessantly, as though he's some kind of curiosity, a local freak show. Not a beautiful little boy who lived and died and has never been forgotten.

How would she like it if someone talked about her precious Rose like that? Or Archie? If they fell victim to a terrible accident and became nothing more than the source of local gossip? She's an only child, she told me that last time, so she can't even imagine what it's like to lose a little brother. To be haunted by the loss. Then to hear him talked about as a source of intrigue, a horror story passed around, whispered from house to house. Still brought up at Christmas drinks in housing estates.

It's one of the reasons I left the area for so long. And why I'm desperate to keep as far away as possible from anyone who might know the house, my family. I can't stand the thought that I might hear Jack talked about, even in passing. That someone might recognise me, might know our story. And now I've got even more reason to keep a low profile – in case one of the locals blows my cover to Jess. So here I am, sitting opposite the intruder who has taken over my family home, listening to her discuss my brother's death as though it's just another spat with the neighbours. As though some ridiculous ghost story might be the thing that drives a wedge between her and the other mums, and not the fact that she obviously looks at them with open disdain, these country housewives who couldn't possibly measure up to the trendy set she hung out with in east London.

It's so pathetic. Listening to her ramble on, I don't know who I despise more: the local gossips dining out on my brother's tragedy, or this stuck-up Londoner who feels person-ally slighted by their tales, as though what went on in that house is all about her. As though *everything* is about her.

I'm taken aback to discover he's even still talked about, to be honest. It's gratifying, in one way, that he hasn't been forgotten. That none of us have, this tragic local family. But listening to Jess tell Jack's story again, I feel as though a layer of my skin has been ripped straight off. As though she must be able to see my heart thumping, my muscles twitching, the blood pumping faster through my veins. To see how painful this is to the touch.

Of course she doesn't sense a thing. She's too wrapped up in her own drama, her cheeks flushed, talking faster than she can think. It's the ghostly element she's hung up on. Not the fact of the horrific tragedy that happened in her house, the family pulled apart. Not thinking about how that little boy must have felt in his final moments, or the raw howl that came from the back door moments later. Or the months and years of grief, anger, blame, regrets.

Those are the real ghosts in that house. Do I believe he's still there? Jess wants to know. I've fallen quiet. I can't speak, can't hear for the pounding in my ears. Luckily she fills the silence with her own thoughts on the matter. Like her, I don't believe in ghosts. And yet . . . I feel closer to Jack when I'm at the Maple House. It's only there that I can fully picture his face, hear his voice again, high, like the calling of the birds in the trees, feel his soft hand in mine as we search through the garden for Dom, for our strange older brother who we can already see is different to the other children at our village school.

Jack was two years younger than me, so young when he died, but we understood each other like Dom and I never had. We were the same: dark hair, green eyes, frail, petite. Not big and clumsy like Dom. Not slow, or impressionable. Jack was quick, bright, lively as the brook bubbling through our garden. Perhaps that's why it was his favourite place. The spot where you could always find him during games of hide-and-seek, or fishing with long branches, or building a fort from leaves and sticks.

So yes, I do believe he's still there, in one sense. I feel his presence in that shady, secluded spot at the end of the garden. I can talk to him there. That's just one reason why I need to be back in my own home, back where my memories take shape once more, where I can fall through a trap door to my childhood and feel truly alive again, not cushioned in a thick blanket of forgetting.

It's only since Carl and I moved back to the area, since I started visiting the Maple House again, that I realised how much of myself I'd been suppressing, how unhappy I'd been for so long. It was spending time at the house that made me start painting again, allowed me to rediscover the passion I'd inherited from my mother, recapturing moments from my childhood in tiny fragments of the countryside – dappled sunlight through a tree, a badger's wild eye, the flare of a rabbit's nostrils.

But it was the house that drove a wedge between me and Carl, eventually. I was consumed, he said. Lost in the past. I needed to concentrate on what we had now, not what went on in my childhood.

He could never understand, not really. All that time I'd been playing the long game. Waiting for Dad to hand the house down to us. I knew Dom wouldn't want anything to do with it. He's always on the move, never settled, a perennial loner, first in the army, then labouring, or truck driving, or whatever he's doing now. And Dad's other kids out in California weren't interested in some crumbling old Suffolk country house. No, it's been me keeping an eye on it, making sure the tenants were looking after it, since Dad was so far away. But of course they couldn't care less, and Dad seemed to have given the letting company free rein to modernise as they saw fit. I could see it falling to ruin as I peered in from the outside, but I was powerless to do anything.

When Dom told me about Dad's cancer, I was sad, naturally, but pragmatic. I was prepared to share the house with Dom, to buy him out eventually, once Carl and I had saved enough. It had never even crossed my mind that Dad might leave the house to Dom and not me.

'Dad knew you wanted nothing to do with him,' Dom had shouted during one of our bitter phone calls, in the early days after we heard the news that he'd died. 'He probably thought the last thing you'd want was more memories of our childhood. More unhappiness. And why *do* you want it so much? Why torture yourself?' It was exactly the same question Carl had been asking me, although he at least understood why I was angry.

'Dom should give you half of what he makes on the house,' Carl had argued. 'It's rightfully yours.' That was after we heard he was putting the house straight on the market; that he wasn't even entertaining the thought of keeping hold of our family home, the one our grandfather built and passed on to his only daughter. The one we grew up in, that had been allowed to fall into disrepair when Dad moved away with his New Age wife and their stuck-up kids – when he decided to forget all about his old life, his first family.

'I just want to be done with it, once and for all,' Dom barked, during our final phone call. That was before he stopped answering completely. 'With the house, the past, all of it.' I must have rung him hundreds of times since then, left God knows how many messages, texts, but he never replies. How can I convince him to reconsider if he won't even speak to me? How could he leave me without a home, or a share of Dad's money?

For Carl, that's all it was about: the money. He could never understand what the house meant to me. Why it mattered so much to be back where Jack died, and where, before that, I had spent the only truly carefree years of my life. He couldn't see how important it was to keep it in the family. Or how happy we could be there, together. My jaw clenches as I remember our final argument. The one that pushed us over the edge, into former lovers, estranged, whatever he wants to call it. I can feel myself shaking my head, even as I try to focus on Jess's face, to listen to what she's saying.

I'm aware that Jess has fallen silent, and I'm probably expected to respond to her latest conspiracy theory about the neighbours, or the house, but instead I change the subject. I can't stand to hear any more about Jack, to think about him now. And Jess is always more than happy to lay into Pete, so I bring the conversation around to

201

him again. I'm intrigued to meet this absentee parent, the vacant man I see drifting from room to room, barely looking beyond the small screen in front of his face. Jess is so caught up in her own problems, she hasn't even thought to ask about my marital set-up. Instead she babbles on about feeling out of place, like she doesn't know anything about anything. A rare moment of self-awareness.

Before we leave, she bores me with their Christmas plans, in that casual manner of people who have living parents, loving home lives, support systems in place. As though this joyful family celebration is just one more thing they deserve, are automatically entitled to, yet can barely make it through, regardless. Meanwhile I find myself having to practically beg to be invited into my own family home.

'Didn't you say you were going to have me round?' I force myself to remind her, not wanting to miss my opportunity. I try to keep my tone light, desperate not to reveal how much I have riding on this. But Jess blithely pushes the arrangement back to mid-January, as though I won't be counting the days until I'm back inside.

'Perfect,' I say, a mixture of pride and frustration flushing my cheeks. Ridiculously grateful to be allowed inside the house my grandfather built. To the house where, by rights, I should be setting up my own cosy family Christmas.

I can still picture the elaborate twelve-foot tree we used to have in the hallway. The large, hand-knitted stockings hung over the fire. My parents, grandparents, brothers all gathered around the grand walnut table in the dining room. It's like a scene from a film, when I think of it now. From someone else's life. I can hardly believe it was real any more.

But it was, and it will be again. We can recreate that, even if it is on a smaller scale. Just as soon as I can get rid of these interlopers, who have taken over my home, who think they are its rightful owners. These imposters, that's the word. Pretending to fit into our house, our lives. I feel it so strongly, I have the urge to say it out loud, so that Jess can hear. So that she knows what I really think.

'It's called "imposter syndrome",' I shout out to her, down the road. So that the word rings in her ears as a warning to them all. They don't have long to get out. And if they refuse, I'll be forced to find a way to make them leave.

Chapter Twenty

I approach the Maple House on one of those clear, crisp January mornings when the air tastes sugary sweet, the weak light filtered through the sunglasses I've put on to mask my emotions. I am coming home. Even the fact that I have to knock on the door doesn't dampen my mood today. It won't be long until I'm letting myself in again. I just need to be patient.

But there's no answer. I knock again, pulling out my phone to check the arrangement we made. I definitely wrote down 11 a.m. Could I have got the wrong day? Or has Jess forgotten? It would be typical, really. She couldn't care less about my time, the other plans I might have. And she has no idea how significant this day is to me.

After the third knock, I decide to try around the back. I can hear shouts and drilling, the blare of a radio that tells me the builders are at work in the barn. Poking my head around the side of the house, I scan their faces to make sure I don't recognise any of them. When I'm satisfied I don't know them from my past, I carry on around the side of the house, giving them a cheery wave.

Craning my head over the gate, I hear myself gasp. I feel dizzy, as though I might faint. Bent down in the kitchen garden is a blonde woman, long hair hanging over her face, concentrating on the plants with a ferocity I haven't witnessed since I last saw my own fair-haired mother crouched in the same position. She's even wearing the kind of jeans Mum wore for gardening, though my mother would never have been caught in a lime-green sweatshirt or pink trainers. Even so, I'm taken aback. It's a few moments before I regain enough composure to call out Jess's name.

When I do, I can see that she's been caught unawares, too. A darkness clouds her face. She stands up and comes to let me in looking wild, bedraggled, sucking blood from a cut on her hand. As she greets me, she checks the clock, making some excuse about the time. But it's her next comment that throws me off course – 'Nobody can hear me scream!' For a moment, I wonder if my cover is blown, if she knows why I'm really here. If she feels the threat that my presence represents. But then I realise it's a half-hearted attempt at humour. Another sign of her discomfort in this place.

I don't know how to process this version of Jess. She's so much less confident, more reticent when she's on her home turf. She watches moodily as I tour the garden, staking claim to my territory, so familiar to me and yet clearly so alien to her. This is working out even better than I dared hope. I can call the shots here, that's more than obvious. I hold all the cards, all the power.

As I return to where Jess is hunched over, tidying up her tools, I'm aware that this is a make-or-break moment. It might be too late for the barn, but this is my chance to convince Jess to replant the kitchen garden, repoint the brickwork, replace the door frames and windowpanes. I lead her inside the house, through the kitchen and into the living room, the familiar sweet scent of musty wood threatening to overwhelm me. I feel tears prick my eyes, but I distract myself by examining the panelling, the walls, the fireplaces and flooring, anything to keep my mouth busy while I try to think.

I can't decide how far to go. Should I show Jess the wallpaper, or would that overplay my hand? I don't want to arouse her suspicions, make her wonder how I know. But then I remember that she's shown herself to be completely incurious about my feelings, my motivations, so far. And when she says those dreaded words – 'lighter, more airy' – I realise there's no time to lose.

'Look at this.' I carefully roll back a small patch of magnolia lining paper to reveal the old maple leaf design my mother restored back in the early days, when they took over the house from my grandparents and polished up its classic features. It was fashionable then, the dark green, intricate design. Not like now, with all these featureless, whitewashed walls and echoing empty spaces. 'Just think of how you could breathe life back into this place,' I say, feeling the goosebumps rise on my neck as I swallow the conviction that it should be me doing the breathing, the decorating, the restoring.

But an idea that has only gradually been forming in my mind solidifies, as I continue my tour around the house to the kitchen, where I peel the lino back to reveal the deep grey of the original flagstones. Back in the early days, before the house was sold, I thought I could drive potential buyers away with a few well-placed damages, an infestation of destructive weeds. Even since Jess and Pete moved in, my main tactic has been to spook them, to grind them down with unexpected noises and breakages. But what if I can persuade Jess and Pete to renovate the house exactly how I want it, and then claim it back? I'm still waiting for my copy of Dad's will to come through. I need to buy time while I work out how to contest it. In the meantime, they can be getting it into just the right shape, ready for me to inherit – or if I really must, to buy it back from them.

I'm so caught up in my thoughts I barely hear what Jess is saying, until a single word cuts through to me: 'extension'. I spin around. This is exactly what I've been dreading. I know I need to tread lightly; I can't be seen to have too much skin in this game. But I also know how much Jess values appearances, approval, how strong is her desire to be cool. So I appeal to her taste, her vanity, her sense of humour. 'Oh God, no. Tell me you're joking!'

What I don't convey is the visceral anger that runs through me, my fists clenched at the idea that this beautiful old house could be improved by an architect, a wall of glass, a vast extension. That a family of four might need any more space than they already have here, when I'm currently living in a single room above my estranged husband's shop. I grip the rough wood of the rotting frame between the kitchen and the conservatory and picture how the doors used to be. Before I can stop myself, I'm describing to Jess the little glass panes and scalloped wood, pulling out my phone to show her a picture. I need to get a grip on myself. I can't let her see the emotion in my face, the way my hands shake when I let go of the door frame.

I need to get outside, so I ask Jess to take me to the barn. The last time I was in there was before Christmas, before the padlock appeared and I stopped my nightly visits. Now it's bright and white and featureless. All the games we played in there, the dens and hiding places we found, the area Dad set aside for his tools and projects that Grandad had used before him – all of it gone, wiped away, never to be seen again. And that's only the beginning. Just imagine what damage they'll wreak to the main house, every inch of it designed and built by Grandad and his friends. The magical home of my childhood destroyed, lost forever.

That's if I don't manage to stop them, don't get to them before it's too late. There's no hope for the barn now, but I can still save the house. I *will* save the house. I owe it to Mum, to Grandad, to Jack, even to Dad. I won't let them all down, like Dom has. Besides, I need a stable home if I'm going to get anywhere with the court case, if I'm going to win Carl back.

The one focal point of the barn is now the large, newly glazed window, with its clear view straight into Jess and Pete's kitchen. My plan is only just beginning to form, but it's growing in scope and ambition at every turn, so perfect I can barely suppress my excitement as I stand beside Jess, looking into the house.

I need somewhere to live while I research my claim to the inheritance. To persuade Jess to knock down the conservatory that was built for the rental market, and restore the house to how it once was. I need to get away from the gallery, from all other distractions. Where better to stay and watch the old house emerge from the wreck of the new?

Chapter Twenty-One

It's my last evening in the studio and I survey the row of bottles by the kitchen bin, my lip curling in disgust. This move is going to be a new beginning. I need to keep a clear head if I'm going to pull off my plans. And this can't fail. It's my last chance. Once I get back into the Maple House, I'm not going to be the one who leaves.

As soon as I'd arrived in the pub for lunch with Jess's family, I realised the whole plan hinged on Pete. I'd made sure I looked dishevelled enough that I might have had some bad news, but that didn't stop him from eyeing me up immediately. And he'd scrubbed up surprisingly well – newly shaved in a smart checked shirt, hair slicked back. From a distance, through the barn window, he looked pretty average – tall, stocky, clipped hair. But close up, his heavy brow made way for deep blue eyes; his stubble removed to reveal smooth, sharp cheekbones. Seeing them together at the table, not four isolated figures drifting around a crumbling house but a well-turned-out family unit, made me feel suddenly reckless, destructive. I realised I might be able to have more fun than I thought.

The flirting had gone on well into the evening, right in front of Jess, who was increasingly tight-lipped. And who could blame her? I don't think I'd be too happy if my husband welcomed a complete stranger to stay in my barn conversion. But that's what Pete did, surprising me by falling straight into the trap I'd laid for Jess. I thought she'd be the one to offer the invitation, but it was Pete who jumped in. The commission for a painting was his idea, too.

At first it had seemed like an unwanted distraction. But it didn't take long to realise what a strong position that painting could put me in, how influential it could make me. I could produce a scale model of how the house used to look and use it to influence their plans – all from the comfort of the barn they've offered me rent-free while I get back on my feet. I could hardly believe my luck.

Since then, Jess has been offering to help me move my belongings, but there's no way I'm going to let her see how I've been living all these months. If she walked into this small studio, with the filthy hob, the tea-stained sink, the tatty, blue sofabed, the rows of empties it would be game over. She'd know immediately there was more to my situation than I've been letting on. So I told her I'd see her at the house. I've already dropped off a few boxes. I've only got two more bags of things to take with me tonight. Just some clothes, my paints, a few canvases that haven't gone into storage.

But first I've got to get rid of all the bottles and takeaway cartons that have been collecting up for weeks. The evidence of my nightly routine, which I've been too embarrassed to dispose of. I bag them up and take one last look around the poky room. How could Carl have lived here all those years, back when he was starting out? Before I forced him to find somewhere with enough space to hang both our clothes, brush our teeth without standing in the shower, where we could sneeze without startling each other.

How could *I* have lived here all these months? I hear him throw back at me with that snarl I see so often now. How could things have fallen apart between us to the point where it was me who had to move out, leaving him our rented three-bed, while I shacked up in the tiny room above his old shop? It had been empty for years while his business took off, moving us to Bristol, then Exeter, then York – always another market to conquer, another gaggle of bored mums eager to invest in his bespoke photography products, the T-shirts and place mats and jigsaws and oversized canvases, all emblazoned with the faces of their darling offspring in terrifying close-up, priceless mementos to last a lifetime, as the marketing went. And now it will be empty again. I lug everything down to the gallery, which looks naked in the slanting street light, rectangles of dust marking where the paintings once hung, packaged up now in a container, waiting to be sold online. Some hope of that.

I take the rubbish to the recycling bin by the pub on the corner. I should have done it days ago, but it feels safer under the cover of darkness. And Carl is coming round to pick up the keys any minute. I need to create some semblance of a functioning existence.

On my way back to the gallery, I order a takeaway on a whim. A final banquet for me and Carl. He'll want this to be over quickly, I know. He doesn't like to get caught in conversation these days. It always descends into argument and he doesn't have the energy for it, he says. But perhaps if the food arrives while he's here, he'll be tempted to stay, have one of the beers I've bought to take to Jess and Pete's. I could even let him in on my plan, although he's bound to talk me out of it. Better to wait until the house is empty again, when I've been able to get it back, and then surprise him with my good fortune. *Our* good fortune. I've got to take things slowly.

As I round the corner, I see Carl standing on the doorstep, shoulders slumped, hunched over his phone, forehead scrunched in a frown. Where is she? he's clearly wondering. He looks tired, his face baggy, hair messy and unbrushed. Unrecognisable as the stylish young man I met that misty day in Ipswich, back for the holidays after my first term at art college in London, his black peacoat and dark jeans a stark contrast to all the long-haired, baggy-trousered students.

I'd escaped Grandma's miserable bungalow for the afternoon, wandering aimlessly around town until the last bus, and I spotted Carl by the marina, camera in hand, taking shot after shot of the water, the sky, a bird in flight. I'd perched on a bench by the waterfront waiting until he reached me, large sunglasses obscuring most of my face in the winter sun. He'd asked me to take them off and I'd laughed, taken aback by his confidence, his utter absorption in his task, so that he didn't even think twice about photographing me without my permission. But I didn't mind. I was flattered. I felt seen, by his camera – recorded, made beautiful. Once he finished, we'd gone to the pub and I'd missed the last bus anyway. He drove me home that night – he had a car, a job, a place of his own. He wasn't going to waste his time going to college, he told me. Like me, his parents weren't around to support him. But unlike me, he was taking matters into his own hands. He was going to start his own business. He wouldn't be waiting around for someone else's handouts.

Within six months, I'd dropped out of college and moved in with him, convinced I was wasting my time with those art school losers. Grandma was moving into sheltered accommodation anyway, and Dom was off working on a building site. Dad was long gone by then. So Carl became my family, my world. Within the year, I was designing his marketing material, helping out with customers in his tiny Ipswich studio-slash-shop, any dreams of painting, exhibiting, travelling long extinguished.

At the time, I'd been content to be back near the Maple House, surrounded by the countryside I grew up in. But when Carl outgrew the Ipswich shop and rented out bigger premises in Bristol, I followed without question. It was a wrench to leave Suffolk. I had to give up my secretive walks, the rambles I went on around my family home whenever I could sneak off in Carl's Citroën. But they had begun to depress me anyway, as I watched a series of careless renters rampage through the house, damaging wood panelling with picture hooks and posters, allowing the gardens to grow wild. Back then, I had no idea how much worse it would get.

I watch Carl punch my number into his phone and then turn in surprise as he hears it ringing right next to him.

'There you are,' I say softly, keys in my hand, ready to open the front door and let us both in. 'Do you want to come up for a bit?'

There's a flash of anger in Carl's eyes. 'Are you joking? I'm busy, Eve, you know that. I've got to get back.' He shoots me a look and my stomach lurches. But I don't want to think about that, not now.

'Come on.' I try to smile, but there's something about his aggression, the way his hands are shaking, that makes me take a step back, towards the door. 'I'm getting an Indian delivered. You could join me?' My voice is faltering now. I've misjudged the mood, again.

'Just give me the keys and I'll be gone. If you want to talk to me, come over to the house. Stop avoiding it. You can't run away forever, you know. This isn't just about Jack . . .' He holds my

213

eye but I turn away. I'm not ready. Not until I've got everything set up exactly how I want it. Then I'll go round and we can have it out. I'll be able to show that I've got the house, the life we've always wanted. That we can be a family the way we've always wanted to be.

I'd kept the faith for so long that one day Dad and I would be reconciled. Dom would convince him to visit and we'd put all those harsh words behind us. He'd see how much the Maple House still meant to me, and offer to let me and Carl move in. There would be plenty of room for studios for both of us in the barn, with its high ceiling and slanted light, and we could raise a family in the old house, happy and carefree, like mine had been, in the beginning at least. I would be able to start a new life among the memories and spirits that had been the most vivid and constant companions throughout my life.

But Carl had grown tired of all that years ago. As his business took off, and we moved from place to place, he'd become increasingly preoccupied, leaving me to deal with all the negative pregnancy tests and fruitless doctors' appointments alone. And then eventually, after years of growing the business, increasing our outgoings, struggling to keep on top of all the orders and postage and marketing and sales, along came Snappy Snaps and Prontaprint and all the other online services that sucked the air from any competition, and left us back in Ipswich, downsized, Carl running operations from the garage of a rented three-bed, me struggling to revive what was left of my artistic career.

We were so close to getting our hands on the Maple House by then. Surely it was only a matter of time before Dad succumbed to his illness and Dom and I came to inherit, I'd say to Carl. Not that I wished him dead, not quite. He might have abandoned us, ignored us, cut us out of his life, but I still cared enough to feel upset when Dom told me he'd died. To cry the tears I never allowed myself when he first left us behind for his new life in America, when I was only fourteen.

It was the news about his will that pushed me over the edge – that pushed our marriage to the brink. It was all I was clinging onto by then, the hope of inheriting the house. I couldn't see a future without it, living in a soulless rented semi, trying to keep a small shop going with the odd birthday card sale. It was only at the Maple House that I felt alive again. That's where I did my best painting, on an old folding stool hidden away at the bottom of the garden, among the trees we'd climbed as children. All this time I'd been waiting, patiently, and then not-so-patiently, until it was our turn to live there. And now that wasn't going to happen. Carl couldn't understand why I was so distraught. Wouldn't. He could never be bothered to see things my way. He was too caught up in the unravelling drama of his failing business. We were both drinking too much. I still am.

'Fine, have it your way.' I put the keys in his hand and sniff, shivering slightly in the cold evening. I should have put on a coat, but it would have spoiled the effect of the tight dress I've put on to impress him, the red lipstick he used to love. Not that it's made any difference. Carl is immune now to whatever attracted him to me all those years ago. We've been through too much together. I only bring him misery, that's what he said.

'Why are you moving out, anyway? What are you going to do now?' Carl asks, one eye on his Nissan, which is parked on a double yellow up the road. I shrug and look down at the bags I've pulled to the front door.

'A friend invited me to stay for a while. I knew you wanted me out of the gallery, so I thought it'd be better that way.'

'A friend?' He looks at me, and for a moment my stomach

flips. He still cares, he wants me back. But then he scowls at his phone again. 'I've got to go. Look, you're right. I need to let out the shop, I need the money. But you can stay in the spare room at home if you need to. We can keep out of each other's way.'

I shake my head. It would be too painful, trying to pretend that nothing has changed. 'I know when I'm not wanted,' I say, watching the delivery driver pull up with the big bag of curries I ordered for our reconciliation meal. 'I've got some plans to put in place, and then I'll be in touch. Things will be different.' I thank the driver, take the bag, hand him a tip.

'How can you afford that?' Carl demands, nodding at the food cooling in my arms.

'It's none of your business now. That's what you wanted, wasn't it? I'm out of your way. I can do my thing and you can do yours?' I grab my bags and the food and throw them into the back of my Mini. 'I told you, I'm going to get things sorted and then we can talk, properly. Once I know where I'm going to be.'

'Are you sure this is what you want?' Carl's eyes search my face for a moment. And then he shakes his head, turns away, muttering to himself. I get in the car and slam the door, watching him walk down the street and safely out of view before I bend my head over the steering wheel and allow the sobs to convulse my body.

Is my plan going to work? I straighten up with a shudder and examine the mess I've made of my face in the rear-view mirror. If I can win back the house and reunite my family, this will all have been worth it, I remind myself, wiping the mascara from under my eyes.

Then I take a deep breath and apply another layer of lipstick. I want to arrive in style, after all. And as I approach the familiar lanes, the stresses of my encounter with Carl recede. I'm in celebratory mood all of a sudden. One step closer to the endgame.

I see as soon as I arrive with the takeaway and beer that Jess is annoyed. Her little darlings don't like spicy food and no doubt she had other plans – something familiar with oven chips, an early night with a cup of tea, me tucked safely away in my barn, far from her and Pete and their sexless marriage. I watch her face flinching as I hand out cartons of jalfrezi and bhuna, the oil spilling on the surface of their kitchen table, and then chink my Kingfisher against Pete's.

Jess feels like I'm taking over, I can tell. And she's right. I am. The sooner she realises that, the better.

Chapter Twenty-Two

Jess has gone to London to see her mum. I'm not sure I'd leave my husband and my lodger alone together, given the way we've been behaving, but she's nothing if not trusting – or naive. Luckily for her, it's the children I'm interested in now, not Pete.

I've already got him eating out of my hand. All it took was a bit of flattery, a few late nights, understanding looks, sympathy on tap. We'd linger after Jess had gone to bed, sketching and chatting. It was deadly boring – Pete's work dramas, some other bloke's competitive account handling, his superior extension. Sometimes we'd discuss his plans for the house, though I'm keen to keep those vague. I don't want him getting too many ideas, when it's my vision I'm capturing on the page really, not his.

Archie and Rose are more of a challenge, though. It's not just that they're uncertain about this stranger who's taken up residence in their barn. They're also much more set in their ways when it comes to the house. Archie's determined to build a treehouse in Jack's tree, the one he always used to climb, overlooking the stream, in the exact spot where I've planned a bench, so I can sit and watch and think for as long as I like, once the house is mine again.

I need to work on them while Jess is away, and I can see my opportunity waiting right through my perfectly positioned window. Having served up a couple of toasted sandwiches, Pete has deposited the children in front of the TV in the living room and is slumped at the kitchen table, his phone in hand, typing furiously with his thumbs. If I didn't know better, I'd say he was having an affair, the amount of time he spends looking at that thing. But having observed him and Jess at close quarters, seen how twitchy he is around her, how tentative he is with me, I'd guess he doesn't have the nerve. Maybe he's in some trouble at work. Or debt, or something. Whatever, it leaves me with the perfect chance to make up ground with the children. I said to Jess I'd show them a good time. It's been weeks since I began playing *Rocket League* with Archie, giving drawing lessons to Rose, inviting her to look through the canvases I brought to the barn, but they're still holding back. They haven't started to see things my way yet. It's time to make sure they do.

I pull on a long cardigan and walk across to the house. It's always freezing in there. Jess and Pete haven't worked out how to get the heat from the Aga to spread around the rooms, and I'm not about to show them. The more uncomfortable they are the better. The barn's been kitted out with underfloor heating, and no doubt they're intending that kind of modernisation in the main house. That's just one of the many plans I need to knock on the head with my detailed scale painting. Once they see how the original parquet could look polished up, the kitchen flagstones buffed to perfection, there's no way they'll consider ripping them all out to make way for heating pipes and engineered flooring. This is how I reassure myself, anyway. It's also why I need to time my plan to perfection.

219

Too soon, and they'll leave me with more work than I can afford to do myself. Too late, and they'll have damaged the house beyond repair.

The children look up from the screen as I appear outside the French windows at the back of the living room, waving, with a finger to my lips. Rose unbolts the door, her eyes round and questioning.

'Hello, Eve.' Her eyes flick from me to the living-room door as she lets me in. 'What are you doing?'

'I thought we could have a game,' I whisper. 'Shall we play hide-and-seek? Come on, Archie, turn that thing off!' I try to keep my voice sing-song, but they must pick up on an edge to it because they look anxious.

'What's going on?' Archie slouches reluctantly over, as though I've interrupted something vital he can barely take his eyes off. 'What are you doing out there?'

'Come on, put your shoes on and we can have a game!' I smile at them both brightly. 'The trees down there are brilliant for hiding in.' I point to the end of the garden, by the stream.

'How d'you know?' Archie asks, and I correct myself quickly.

'Well, they look it, don't they? Come on, let's go.'

They both slip on shoes and join me outside, looking around them.

'Shouldn't we tell Daddy where we're going?'

'He won't mind.' I pull them by the hands. 'Besides, that's part of the fun!' They seem to catch some of my enthusiasm as we run together across the dewy lawn to that part of the garden, half-hidden from the house, where the trees thicken and the stream babbles and the magic begins to take hold. I'm panting now, and the children look up at me, their eyes giving away tentative excitement at this unexpected adventure. I cover my eyes with my hands, counting breathlessly, slowly, to twenty. One, two, three . . . My head's spinning from the sudden exertion, my mind swirling between the present moment and the countless other times I've stood in this spot, counting, that old anticipation bubbling up inside me.

Jack was always so good at hiding. He'd learned from the best, after all. All those little spots I'd shown him, the thickest trees, the tallest bushes, secretive cupboards and hidey-holes. I can almost hear his laughter as I count – a little choked – mingled with fear. But that was what Jack enjoyed – the excitement of the chase, teetering on the edge of safety, always pushing the boundaries. We both did in those days. But he was the one who paid the price.

I'm lost in the past, so caught up in memories that when I open my eyes I forget for a moment what I'm meant to be doing. Finding Archie and Rose, of course. But also demonstrating to them how beautiful, how perfect this corner of the woods already is. How easy it would be to break the spell of this place with some half-baked construction, an unnecessary blight on the landscape. How much fun you can have here without anything needing to be built or altered.

I'm helping them to relive with me the wonder of this place. I want them to feel it, even though I know they won't be staying here. Perhaps *because* I know they won't be staying here. I want them to remember it, to be haunted by it, to carry it with them as they go through their lives, as I have. To know what happened here, and how it shaped me. Never to forget.

I look up to the branches of Jack's tree, but they haven't thought to hide up there. Children today are too cautious for that. They'd never dream of climbing that high without parental permission. Too risk-averse. Or perhaps just enough.

I find them easily – flashes of Rose's purple jumper and Archie's

221

red hoodie behind two slim trees. They're hoping to be found, no doubt. None of the wildness of our childhood games, the thrill of getting yourself so lost, you might never make your way back again. The enchantment of discovering another world, without adults, without rules, without limits. That was the world Jack and I had inhabited – always nudging each other on, competitive in our acts of daring. Perhaps if we'd let Dom in, things might have been different. But he was too lumbering, too slow, too much part of the other, adult, world.

'Now it's my turn to hide!' I run deep into the woods, finding the old willow we'd always bury ourselves in, its branches reaching so far down you could easily never be found. I can hear the children darting this way and that, searching, calling out my name. I feel a shiver of satisfaction as I hear their shouts become increasingly uneasy, and eventually frantic.

'Eve, come out!' Rose cries. 'Where are you? Eve?'

'Yeah, Eve, it's not funny any more,' Archie joins in. 'Show us where you are.'

I could stay in here for hours, until it gets dark and the children are crying, terrified. I could tease them, toy with them – make them understand that the world isn't how they think it is, that sometimes people just disappear, never to return, and there's nothing you can do about it. Shatter the illusion of safety, security that Jess has worked so hard to create for them. But I know they'll give up and fetch Pete any minute. So finally I emerge from between the branches, my arms thrown wide, a smile on my face. The children run to me. Rose has tears in her eyes.

'Where were you? We couldn't find you?' She throws her arms around me.

'Come on, that's the whole point of the game, isn't it?' I laugh, and with wary eyes on me, both the children join in, giggling, though Rose clings to my hand.

'Shall we play again?' Archie's eyes are glittering. He's got a taste for it now, the unknown. And I nod, seizing my moment.

'Isn't it wonderful out here?' I spin around, exhilarated. 'So much space, so much freedom. You don't want your dad down here, building some little kiddie's den, do you? Wouldn't it be more fun to create your own world, explore, adventure, escape from all that—'

'Rose! Archie!' Pete's voice reaches us from the house, hoarse, panicked. 'Where are you?'

'Dad!' Archie shouts before I can continue. Before I can tell whether anything I've said has cut through. 'Dad, we're over here!' Archie runs out from the trees onto the lawn, in sight of the house once more. Pete looks over as Rose and I emerge behind him, and breaks into a run, reaching us in moments.

'God, you scared me, disappearing off like that. What were you up to?' Pete turns to them both, visibly relieved, but angry, too. 'And making Eve come out and find you when she's got better things to do. She's busy, you know. She can't go running around looking for you two.'

'But—' Pete grabs Rose by the arm, cutting her off.

'Come inside now. No more silliness.'

He takes Archie's arm too and begins marching them up the garden, but I don't want to be cast in this role. Part of Pete's adult world. I want the children to know I'm on their side.

'Pete,' I call, after a beat, my voice soft, trying to calm him, 'we were playing hide-and-seek. Just having a bit of fun.'

'Yeah, Dad.' Archie breaks away from him and turns to me. 'It was Eve's idea.'

'There's so much to do out here.' I turn, flinging my arms out wide. 'I didn't like to see them slumped in front of the TV all day.' Pete catches my eye anxiously, chastened, perhaps

223

calculating what I might say to Jess, what I might report back.

'Oh, yes, of course.' He lets go of the children, breaks into a smile, laughing lightly at himself. 'Sorry, I totally over-reacted there. I was just scared when you weren't there. You slipped out without me even noticing, and then I searched all over the house and I couldn't find you . . . But you're right, of course. There's loads to do out here.' He looks around at the towering trees, overgrown bushes, creeping ivy, as if for the first time. 'You guys should carry on playing, if you want to . . .'

But the children shake their heads. The spell has been broken now, the excitement evaporated; my little disappearing act has left them jittery. It's starting to drizzle. 'No, Daddy.' Rose pulls away. 'I want to go inside now.'

She walks into the house, head bowed, and Pete moves to go after her but I put a hand on his arm. 'Let me,' I say softly, and leave him and Archie standing on the lawn looking at one another, while I follow Rose through the French windows and up the stairs to her bedroom.

I find her lying face down on her rose-print duvet, kicking her legs against the mattress, head turned towards the wall. Kneeling beside the bed, I run my fingers through her soft curls, her skull so tiny and fragile beneath my cold hand.

'What is it, Rose? Are you okay?'

'I don't like that bit of the garden and I don't like hide-and-seek. I want Mummy,' she sniffles, her voice muffled against the pillow.

'Why don't you like it?'

She turns her head sharply. When she looks at me, it's as though through the eyes of someone much older, who has seen more than she can ever express.

'Things move. It's creepy.' She holds my eye. Does she know? Have the children at school told her?

'Mummy will be home soon. Do you remember you told me there was one place you felt safe? What place was that?' I already know, of course. I guessed the moment she said it in the gallery, the first time we met. This used to be my room. I know there's a place no child could resist.

Rose points to the small door, tucked into the corner of her room, my room. She moves across to it uncertainly, unsure whether to let me into her private world, and then she gives it a tug. Inside the small opening are two cushions, a torch, a stack of books, a diary left open.

'Wow! You've made a proper little den for yourself in here, haven't you?'

Rose nods, she looks over her shoulder and then tiptoes to her bedroom door and pushes it closed. 'Don't tell Mummy and Daddy. They don't like me going in there.'

'Of course not. You need somewhere that's just for you. I won't give away your secret hiding place.' She shuffles inside and I crawl in after her, leaving the door open. I never did like enclosed spaces. That was Jack's thing, not mine. 'It's cosy in here, isn't it?' I smile, but Rose's face is sombre. She hands me the torch, and I shine it around the walls, looking for the spot next to the other door, where Jack and I wrote our initials. But the writing isn't there, and neither is the other door – the one that led from my cupboard into Jack's room. It's so long since I've been in here, I hadn't even noticed that someone has blocked it up and covered it over.

'Look,' I say to Rose, 'there's a line there. It looks like there used to be another door, doesn't it?' She shuffles closer and runs her finger along where the door once was. I knock against it and hear the hollow ring of wood, in contrast to the solid wall around the edges. It's only papered over, not bricked up.

'Let me check out the other side.' I back out of the small door.

'That's Archie's room. Maybe the door leads to the cupboard in Archie's room!' Rose exclaims, brightening now.

I pick my way across cars and Lego until I reach Archie's cupboard. The little door is papered over on this side, too. I knock three times and a knock comes back.

'It is! It goes to Archie's room!' I can hear Rose's excitement through the wall and then her footsteps in the hall. 'Daddy, Archie, come quickly! We've got something to show you!'

The unveiling of the hidden door takes on its own momentum after that. I don't have to persuade anyone; Rose does the job for me. And Pete, perhaps guilty after losing his temper in the garden, agrees straight away to cut through the wallpaper in Archie's cupboard and reveal the outline of the small door I remember so clearly from my childhood. It doesn't take much scraping to get off most of the lining paper. But the door is locked, the key nowhere to be found.

The children start whining, disappointed. Pete's searching for a paperclip to try and pick the lock when, from nowhere, a feeling takes hold. A memory at the edge of my consciousness, an idea that seems to have its roots way back in a past I can barely lay claim on. The time before.

'Daddyyyy,' Rose complains, 'there's got to be a way to get through it. Then me and Archie will have a secret passageway.'

'I wonder why they put it there in the first place?' Pete eyes it suspiciously. I know, of course. Grandad built it that way for my mother, as a secret tunnel from her room. But I keep that to myself.

I'm already on my way into Rose's room. I shuffle inside the cupboard again and start tapping on floorboards, trying to find the loose one that Jack and I used as our hiding place all those years ago. I'd forgotten all about it until this moment, and when I find it and wriggle the rotting board loose, I have to stifle a cry. It's not just the key that's inside: there's Jack's small blue teddy, the one he was always parachuting down the stairs, or launching off tree branches, or snaking through the long grass. It's still intact, only a little tatty after all these years hidden under the floor.

'Ewwww!' I hear Archie's voice in my ear, his breath on the back of my neck. He's craning over me to see inside the little chamber I've revealed. It makes me jump, startles me out of my memories, sends us both flying backwards. 'Ow. Eve, what're you doing? Dad, there's some disgusting old toy in there. It stinks like it's been buried there for years.'

'Let me see.' Pete pushes past me into the small space. 'Don't touch it. I'll throw it away. Who knows where it's been.'

'No,' I say, too quickly, all three of them looking at me in surprise. 'No, don't throw it. I can patch it up, clean it. You might like to play with it.' I soften my tone. I've got no intention of letting either of them lay their hands on it again, ever. 'And, look, what do you think this is?' I hold out the rusted brass key on my open palm, and there's such excitement, everyone forgets the teddy immediately. I push it deep into the pocket of my cardigan and follow them into Archie's room, standing back to watch the grand opening, all the while running my thumb over the soft, worn bear. Who would have known, Jack? That one day I'd be here watching our old hiding place get rediscovered by a new family, explored by a new brother and sister, who both have so much to lose, just like you and I did. But don't worry, I won't let them get too comfortable in here. It'll be ours again before too long. I'll bury Teddy back in his hiding place, where no one will disturb him.

There's a loud scrape and then Pete flies backwards, the door flinging open in front of him.

'Loooook! It's like the wardrobe to Narnia!' Rose crawls through and calls behind her. 'Only on the other side it's my bedroom. Come through, Archie. You can visit me any time!'

Even Archie has thrown off his usual state of disdain at the discovery of a secret door in his bedroom. 'It's sick!' I hear him say as he crawls through behind Rose.

'I can't believe you found that key.' Pete turns to me, but I'm relieved to see there isn't a hint of suspicion on his face, only amazement.

'Thank you so much, Eve!' Rose crawls back out and flings herself on me.

'Yeah, thanks, Eve. This house is cooler than I thought!' Archie joins her and they both hug me, Pete smiling at me over the tops of their heads. I smile back, but I want them to leave me alone. I want to spend time in these rooms. I want to run my hands over every contour of that cupboard, smell the stale air that Jack once breathed, find the initials we carved, small and discreet so that Mum and Dad wouldn't see them. I don't want to be enveloped by these awkward, needy children, their inability to thrive in these surroundings written on every part of their pale, skinny bodies.

'Wait till Mummy gets home and sees what we've found.' Rose turns to Pete, who picks her up in his arms.

'Oh yes, I wonder where she's got to. Well, we'd better get on with dinner. And I think this discovery calls for a celebration. How about pizza?'

'Yesssss!' cries Rose.

'Best. Day. Ever!' Archie shouts, and they pound down the

stairs, leaving me alone in the bedroom, with just enough time to bury Teddy safely away again. 'Don't worry,' I whisper softly, sure that no one in the kitchen can hear me over the music they're playing, the cries of excitement. 'You're safe in here now.' As I push the loose board back over his tiny body, a memory comes back to me, as if from nowhere. I must be around eight. Hunched in exactly this position, burying Teddy for the first time, tears falling and soaking his worn tummy, the noise of crying, wailing even, rising from the floor below. My knees are scraped raw against the hard wood of the cupboard floor, my skirt hitched up, my hair hasn't been brushed for days – in my stomach, a hollow emptiness. A sickness that is spreading through me and threatens to eat me from the inside.

How had I forgotten Teddy was in here? That it was me who had buried him under these floorboards, in our special place? Perhaps I sensed already then that my days in this house were numbered, that it would be a long time before I was back here again. I wanted to keep a part of Jack safe, where he belonged. Where we both belonged.

I can hear the children calling my name now, telling me dinner is ready. Reluctantly, I back out of the cupboard and close the door behind me, tucking the key in my pocket and taking a deep breath before I go downstairs to join in the singing and dancing, the exuberance that seems to have been unleashed in their mother's absence, allowing myself a smile as I imagine how it will seem when Jess gets home.

Not long after, I watch her car pull up in the darkness outside, but Pete doesn't notice. He's too busy spinning the kids around in turn, twirling me under his arm, grinning with a breathless energy I haven't seen in him before. I turn away quickly, so she doesn't know I've seen her, sitting outside in the darkness, alone, watching. Shut out of her own home, looking in from the outside, just as I have been for years. But not any more; I know that now. When the time comes, Jess will be the one to leave. Not me.

Chapter Twenty-Three

The painting is nearly ready. I lift the sheet from the canvas propped in the corner of my barn room and study it with a frown. It's not my most accomplished work. Mum would have done a better job. She was the real artist. I could never live up to her talent, no matter how hard I tried. To begin with, in the sunlit days of early childhood, she'd encouraged me. I felt like I could do anything then, be anything, if I set my mind to it. But later, when the light had gone from her eyes, I could see my work as it actually was – dull, lifeless, a pale imitation of reality. It might have been enough to get me into art school, but it was never a patch on the paintings she dashed off, untrained, in her spare evenings. The ones that had hung around the walls of our childhood home, shipped off to storage and lost now, forever.

Looking at my latest work through her eyes, I can see that I've failed to capture the essence of the house somehow. Its magic has eluded me. But then, I don't want to make it too appealing. It's the details I care about. And I've been checking those obsessively against the childhood photo in the inner pocket of my suitcase. I have to get every last shutter and blind just right. I'll know when it's all finished if something is even slightly off, any little thing out of place. It's got to be perfect for when I show Dom. When I remind him of how the house used to be – and what it could be again. If only he'll help me buy it from these desperate sellers. The ones who can't wait to be rid of it.

That's an element of the plan that still needs work. Winning Pete over to my way of thinking has been so straightforward, I've forgotten to focus on the other person who needs my attention: Dom. I've got to find a way to break through to him, get him speaking to me again. Present him with a development he can't ignore.

I've become so caught up in the strange dynamic of this family, I've let the other aspects slip from my sight. But it's addictive, somehow. Those little wins that are so easy to achieve – listening to Archie, rather than turning a back when he gets in a mood, sitting with Rose and drawing or gluing or whatever it is she wants to do until she opens up about the fears and visions that plague her in the night. It's so clear to anyone with even the slightest empathy what every member of this family needs, but Jess is too wrapped up in her own worries to care about anyone else's.

My eye is caught by the family scene in the kitchen, four stony faces around the breakfast table, shovelling down Weetabix, hair messy, each lost in their own world. Pete will be taking the children to school any minute on his way to work; Jess will be alone in the house again, half wishing I'd drop in to alleviate her unending boredom and half dreading it too, no doubt. But I've got other plans for her today. I've another little renovation in mind.

Jess pushes her chair back from the table and sleepwalks to the sink, rinsing the dish, bending to stack it in the dishwasher. She glances, briefly, in my direction but I've been expecting she will and so I've stepped back from the window. She's always staring at the barn, watching furtively through my windows, as if I don't know what she's doing. Then again, I can't talk. I'm watching her, too. The difference is, I know everything there is to know about her life, and she knows nothing about mine. Not the first thing.

Pete and the children exchange looks while Jess's back is turned. They're trying to assess her mood, what they can risk saying today, what they can get away with. She's half out of that family already. Removing her from the situation would be all too easy.

It's Pete's turn to come to the sink by the window now and throw a glance in my direction. But this time, I let him catch a glimpse of me before I turn away, as if embarrassed, shy. He laps up my attention like a starving dog. I can't quite work out how far to take it. Part of me wants to let him act on his desires, let the guilt consume him like a slow flame. I might even enjoy it, having a hold over Jess that I can tantalisingly reveal at just the right moment. But I don't want things to run away with themselves. Everything at the right moment. All in good time.

Take the painting, for example. I was all but finished with it last month, but I've been waiting for my opportunity, for when the grand unveiling will make the maximum impact. When Pete invited me to dinner with Graham and their friends, I realised I had found my moment. I keep thinking surely Jess will invite me, too. She wouldn't cut me out like that, would she? But the closer it's got, the more certain I've become. Her mood has changed. She's had enough of me being around. She's going to throw me out soon, I can feel it. And then my advantage will be gone. My opportunity over.

233

So I invited Pete to the barn, allowed him just the briefest glimpse of the painting, let him feel he was part of my plan. I suggested that we reveal it at the dinner – the one Jess still hasn't mentioned to me – and Pete's eyes shone with excitement. I couldn't tell whether it was for the painting, the house, or for me, for our secret assignation. Whatever, he was on board with my plan. The stage was set. Now to mess with Jess's head a little, before her big night.

I leave it a few hours, until Jess is in full flow with her preparations for the evening, and then I take my opportunity to slide around the back of the house and up the stepladder that's stashed there. It's the same pipe I damaged last time, only further along. There's already a little crack, so I bang on that, lengthening it until I see water start to seep through. It won't be long until it's gushing and I can alert Jess to the problem. It will be the last thing she needs when she's getting ready for a dinner party. I know exactly how she'll spin out – just as she has after all the other little damages I've inflicted. And I'll be able to smooth things over, help her out yet again. She'll be in my debt, as usual.

Picking up the children will keep me out of the house long enough to avoid the plumber, in case he's local and recognises me from childhood. And it's easy enough to make sure I don't see anyone at the school gates. I'll wait in the car and get the children to come to me. Then we can hide out at the graveyard again, back to the spot they seem to love so much.

I discovered their enthusiasm for it by accident, one afternoon after school when it was pouring with rain. We were looking for somewhere to while away a couple of hours. They don't ever voice it, but I know they're as desperate as I am to avoid their mother now, in her misery, her paranoia, her fits of anger. It's unspoken, but we always find an excuse for a little diversion. This time it was to the old church in the village, tucked away down a narrow lane, behind all the houses. No one ever goes there except the older congregation, on a Sunday. Midweek, it's the perfect place to lurk – dark and gloomy, the graveyard thrown into shadow by the looming church, all Gothic arches and miniature turrets.

My grandparents would take us to church some Sundays, but the last time we were there as a family was for Jack's funeral. Possibly the last time we went anywhere as a family; a silent, broken unit of four, by then, the absence among us overshadowing everything.

I've been back whenever I've been in the area. I spent hours by Jack's grave as a sullen teenager, escaping the stifling heat and boredom of Grandma's house – the bungalow she and Grandad had moved to in the village when they handed the Maple House over to their daughter and her growing family. When Dad left and the house got rented out, it was to the bungalow that Dom and I were dispatched. Grandad was dead by then and Grandma like a shadow, moving quietly around the house, barely speaking. Jack's grave felt like a sanctuary in those years. A place I could go to sit alone and remember the old days, when we were a family of five, full of laughter and noise and light.

The first time I took the children to the graveyard, we huddled in the covered archway at the entrance. The lychgate, I told them. I only knew the name of it from Jack's funeral, from the vicar's nervous chatter as he tried to distract these ghostly faced, traumatised children whose parents had chosen to travel separately to their brother's funeral. I can see the vicar's face now, round spectacles, a hairy mole on his cheek rising and falling with every word.

'It's also known as the corpse gate,' he'd told us as we stood in the small covered gateway, a rickety wooden roof sheltering us from the drizzle as we waited for the adults to join us. 'It's where they used to rest the bodies before they were buried . . .' He'd tailed off at the sight of our horrified faces, as we imagined the body of our own small brother, who I'd last seen lying face down, water rushing around his tiny frame.

The corpse gate. I consider telling Rose and Archie that name, passing on the baton of this knowledge that I was given too young. But I don't want them repeating it to Jess, arousing her suspicion. This is our secret place; I've already made that clear.

The lychgate had been patched up over the years, the wood replaced, so that it was a decent shelter from the driving rain. And as the shower subsided that first day in the graveyard, the children had started to explore. Rose and I toured the gravestones, reading the names and dates, imagining together the lives of the people below ground, the families they left behind, while Archie spun around with a stick, fighting imaginary assailants.

'Archie, be careful!' I'd shouted as he nearly caught my eye with one of his branches, so that I barely heard Rose the first time.

'Look at this one,' Rose called again, and before I'd even turned around, I knew the exact spot where she would be standing, could instantly picture the stone, the inscription I'd read so many times before. 'It's small. Does that mean it's for a child?'

'Jack Millington,' Archie read out, coming to join us. 'He was only four when he died.'

'That's sad,' said Rose. 'I wonder how old he'd be today.'

'Forty-three,' I'd said, without even thinking. 'If you add it on, you can work it out.' My voice sounded harsh. Archie turned to me with a frown.

236

'It's creepy here.' He shuddered, and I thought – not for the first time – what an insensitive, unobservant little boy he truly was.

We've visited twice since then and, this time, Rose gravitates straight to the grave. I hang back. There's something eerie about the way she's drawn to Jack. Almost as if she knows, though of course she couldn't. Somehow, after all the years I've spent alone on that very spot, I can't force myself to stand there in company. I don't want to risk giving anything away. Or letting my head turn even slightly to the right, to the other grave I can never bear to visit, or even to look at.

I rest on the bench in the gateway while the children run around. I'm sure Jess would be horrified if she knew this is where we come after school. But they seem happy enough, and I feel calm for once, the same way I do at the end of the garden. As though through proximity I can make my peace with Jack's memory, silence those voices that have kept me awake at night for so many years.

By the time we get back to the house, the pipe has been fixed and Jess has created some kind of order in the kitchen. The children go to watch TV, and I retreat to the barn. I need to get everything just so – make sure the painting is ready to be seen, make sure I'm in the right state to present it.

I know that Jess will put on one of those garish outfits that look totally incongruous in the Suffolk countryside, so I decide to go for understated chic. The little black number I used to wear for Carl's work functions and a pair of heels. I feel ridiculous teetering across to the house, but it seems important to project a certain calm and class, in contrast to Jess's chaos and barely concealed insecurity.

237

Walking into the kitchen, I see her bent over by the Aga, dirty apron wrapped around a short dress in clashing shades of blue. Her tights are yet another shade, purple almost, as though dressing like a children's TV presenter might make her appear more interesting than everyone else. To begin with, it seemed like an affectation, her unlikely sense of style – now I know it's more like armour. But I compliment her, all the same, and help myself to a glass of wine, aware of Jess's glare as I stride confidently around her kitchen. I can't help it. It's too easy to score points, especially when Pete's eyes are following my every move. If I can just push them to breaking point, nudge them over the brink they're already teetering on, then Jess will leave with the children and they'll surely put the house on the market. All I need to do now is allow the evening to unfold as I planned – as Pete and I planned, together.

He'd agreed to keep the big reveal a secret. Hadn't even needed persuading – Jess loves surprises apparently. Only a husband as clueless as Pete would think this is the kind of surprise his wife would enjoy. I take a deep breath and hang back as the guests arrive. I don't need to make an impression on these people, in fact it's better if I don't. And they're the kind of company I'd usually do anything to avoid, loud and self-satisfied, the man clearly a prolific shagger, the woman overcompensating with clouds of perfume and a ridiculous jumpsuit.

I've already heard all about their barn conversion, and it doesn't take long for Amanda to start using those classic buzzwords – 'bifolds', 'extension', 'light well'. As we tour the house, without Jess, who's playing the martyr in the kitchen, Amanda ticks off 'open plan', 'eco-flooring' and 'ergonomic design' – it's like renovation bingo. Graham knows the jargon too, though he seems just as nonplussed by this company as

I am. Mostly, I keep quiet and smile inwardly, anticipating the shock they all have to come.

Pete begins the build-up as we're all seated at the table, before we've even eaten. He's so excited he obviously can't wait any longer, and neither can I. It's time to show Jess who's really in charge around here. This is my moment, and as I return from the barn with the canvas, I find I'm trembling so much I can barely hold it. I lean back against the kitchen unit, coiled like a serpent, waiting to see how events will unfold.

Pete starts gushing immediately, Amanda and Rich both respond in a more muted way, but Jess doesn't say a word. Her face is white, nostrils flared. She's staring at the picture, but she doesn't speak. It's Graham who's the first to take offence, with his ridiculous architect's pride. And then Jess dashes towards the oven. Typical that her incompetence, her general air of chaos, should interrupt the dramatic moment I've planned so carefully.

She springs back, swearing, almost hissing, as the tray clatters to the floor. I immediately spot my opportunity to sweep in, but Jess lashes out – her confidence chipped away day by day, week by week. The others couldn't possibly know, but as far as she's concerned this is clearly the final straw. This is where the unspoken rivalry between us reaches its logical endpoint. And it's all happened in front of her friends, her architect, her husband.

The gasp I let out is genuine, the hot juice from the pan a jolting shock. But the pain passes quickly, much more so than I'm going to let on. After all, I'm drawing sympathy all round. I couldn't have planned this any more perfectly if I'd tried.

To the assembled crowd, Jess looks like a lunatic. All her frustration, her humiliation, taken out on an innocent friend.

There are so many witnesses to Jess's disintegration, her break-down. 'It's hardly surprising,' they'll say when they hear about the split, the house move. 'She seemed pretty on edge that night, didn't she?'

The painting is damaged, too. Though it's superficial, I can see that straight away. But I'm not about to smooth things over. I'm more than happy to play the victim, accepting ice, comfort, sympathy.

The evening ends there. The dinner is ruined, there's nothing to eat, but also we can't sit back at the table and pretend nothing's happened. Pretend that one of our hosts hasn't just unravelled in front of a room full of guests. And so we melt away. I head off to the barn to change out of my dirty clothes, leaving the painting in the kitchen. I want Jess to get a proper look at it. To see exactly how her house renovations are going to pan out.

When I get back to the kitchen, Pete's on his hands and knees, sweeping up the mess.

'I'm so sorry,' he says as I crouch beside him. 'Jess isn't herself at the moment. I don't know what's got into her.'

'It's not your fault.' I lay a hand on his shoulder, and he turns away quickly, concentrating on scooping up flakes of pastry from the tiles. 'I'm just sorry she doesn't like the painting. I only wanted to recreate what you wanted. What you *both* wanted.'

Pete looks at me intently. 'Please, don't apologise. You've put so much work into that picture, so much of your time, your energy. It's beautiful. Honestly it is. And I—' Pete breaks off, springs away from me as we hear footsteps on the stairs. We're side by side as Jess stalks in with a strange expression on her face.

'Why did you bother?' She's standing in front of my picture, a piece of paper in her hand, thrust forward. She's looking

240

from one to the other and back again as though she's possessed. 'Was it the money? Were you having a laugh at our expense?'

I take the paper from her hand and my stomach plummets. On it is a reproduction of my photo. The one I've kept tucked away all these years. The one I used to paint the Maple House.

It must have been in the papers around the time Jack died. It had never even occurred to me it might be out there still, available for anyone to see.

I can see that my hand is shaking, my face must give away my shock. But I try to calm my voice. 'I've never seen this picture before,' I say. It's the most I can get out without giving myself away.

It's only then that I unfold the paper and see the headline below, reproduced from an old newspaper, years ago.

Doomed Family Hit by Tragedy Again

Mother of boy who died in tragic accident at home found dead . . .

I can't read any more through the tears that fill my eyes, and then Pete snatches it from me. 'Let me see that.' But like Jess, his focus isn't on the tragedy described in the article. He doesn't care what happened in this house, whose lives were ruined. For him, this is all about their pathetic renovation job, their doomed country retreat.

It's such a shock, seeing my mother's story laid out in this dispassionate way after so many years. But I've got to hold it together. When Pete looks at me, I can see the betrayal in his eyes. He thinks it's a stitch-up, that I've cheated. And I have, but not just for ease, to save time. This is how I want

241

the house to be. How it *has* to be. How it was designed by my grandfather and maintained by my mother. This is the house she died in, for God's sake. The one I found her in, too late to make any difference.

She'd taken too many sleeping pills. The doctor said even if we'd got to her sooner, it would have been no good. And I would never have thought to look in Jack's room, anyway. I'd searched the house from top to bottom when I got home from school. I knew she couldn't be out – she never left the house by that point. But Jack's room was the last one I tried, and I wouldn't even have considered checking in his little cupboard, the one connected to my room, if I hadn't seen the door slightly ajar on his side. Everything goes black from that point. My stomach is churning. I think I might be sick. I still can't picture the moment I found her, though I know it was me – Dad had been out at work; Dom's school bus got back later than mine.

Instead, my mind flits to another memory, the one that assailed me when I found Jack's teddy with the children. Me as a girl, hunched over in that same cupboard, sobbing. I'd assumed I was eight at the time, that I was caught in the midst of grief after Jack's death. But what if it had been two years later, if it was Mum I was grieving for? Or both of them. What if that was the last time I went in that cupboard? Before it was sealed up on Jack's side for good.

It's funny how memory works. For years, just tiny fragments have been available to me. The rest sunken to the bottom of a deep pool, only to rise whenever I'm back in this house. It's since I've been inside again that I've been able to remember the good times, before Jack died, when mother still loved me. Before that affection, that care, was withdrawn for good – taking with it the girl I was, the woman I could have been.

It's only in this house that I can connect to that girl again, that I have any hope of recovering that happiness, that peace. Of course, Dad abandoned us, too, but by then the damage had been done. Neither Dom nor I would ever be the same again. And I had vowed to myself on that grim Saturday when we left the Maple House for the last time, as I watched Dad lock up, his face grey and hollow, ready to deposit us down the road with our grandparents without a backwards glance, that one day I would come back. I would restore the house, and cherish it and breathe life into it again, just as Mum had.

It feels so personal, so intimate to see the window frames she painted by hand, printed out from the internet and smudged under Pete's thumb. I can picture her now as I lay on my tummy on the front lawn, inspecting ants, making a daisy chain, kicking my legs behind me. She had spent that whole hot summer, it seemed, repainting those frames, slowly, patiently, lovingly – the same duck egg her own mother had painted years before her. The same colour I intend to repaint, as soon as I'm able.

This house was the only thing that kept Mum going after Jack died. The endless patching up, repairing, repainting. She could have been a real artist, but she was never allowed to develop her talent, and so she threw herself into this place, as though it could consume all her sadness, could make her whole again. As though anything could.

We'd sit, Dom and I, either side of her on the window seat, looking out through the stained glass onto the garden, the trees, the stream where it happened. That's how I picture her now, lit up with soft yellow, pink, blue light as the sun sets, tears running down her cheeks. How sad she would be, how devastated to see her father's house reduced as it is now, the splitting wood, the peeling frames, the damp and mildew. To see the Knight family home reduced to this rotten shell. Abandoned by the husband she trusted to continue her family legacy. The husband who deserted her children, too.

I feel my tears threaten to spill out, and I know I have to control this train of thought. I have to use it to my advantage. I can't lose my grip on the situation when I'm so close. And I need to get that picture back, get my mother's story back. I can't have them both pawing at her legacy in this way.

'It's not *exactly* the same.' I'm aware I sound snappy, defensive, and I can see Pete wants to comfort me, but feels he can't. Jess snatches back the piece of paper – my family, my house – and folds it away, as though it belongs to her.

Pete offers to carry the canvas back to the barn for me, but I know what he really wants. To be alone with me. To debrief on the evening's events. To be reassured that it was Jess at fault, not him, not me.

All I want is to be left with my memories. I want to lie awake all night, as I have most nights since I came back to the house, and replay the happy moments, the times when she held me in her arms, or swung me around in the garden, lifted me to put the angel on the Christmas tree, stroked my forehead when I couldn't sleep and sang one of the soft lullabies I will always associate with her. *Alas my love you do me wrong . . .* Before the sadness came and consumed the light in her eyes.

But as Pete gently props up the canvas and checks that the door is locked, pulling the curtains across my large windows, I can see that I have him exactly where I want him. Where he wants to be. And to miss this opportunity would be madness, self-sabotage. Pete's angry with Jess, he's frustrated, he wants support, understanding. He wants an escape from it all.

244

I blink away my tears and turn to face him, a smile forming on my lips. That's what I can offer him: an escape from his marriage, his family. An escape from this house that isn't rightfully his anyway. That will never be his family's home.

PART THREE

Jess

Chapter Twenty-Four

It is twenty-four hours since Pete left. I'm standing by the circular window, looking out to the garden, the March afternoon bright and fresh, new leaves glistening on the trees after a brief shower, the grass a vivid, dewy green. I can see what Eve meant now about building a window seat up here. It's the perfect place to sit and gaze out on the newly blossoming garden, to curl up with a book and feel the weak sunshine on my winter-pale face. From the roughness of the wall under the window, it almost seems as though there was something there, once. Another one of Eve's intuitions.

We went along with some of her suggestions in the end. I agreed to the fanlight, the restoration of the kitchen flagstones and parquet floor, the stripping back of the wood panelling – I originally wanted to repaint it a bright white, but I can see that the mahogany has its own charm. I'm even tempted to give way on the window seat, now. But I'm tearing down that old-fashioned wallpaper she seems so attached to. There's no way we're painting all the outdoor woodwork that sickly blue she used in her painting. And we're closing up the creepy cupboard in Rose's room. There's no reason for the children to be crawling in to see each other anyway, and it's giving out a terrible smell. I've told George to board it up on both sides.

Rose spends less and less time in her room these days, anyway. This morning she and Archie are down at the end of the garden again. They stayed out there while it rained. It's the Easter holidays, but I've hardly seen them all week. They're always off outdoors; usually I find out Eve's been with them, too. Whenever I ask what they've been up to, I get the same answer: playing. But after they return from hours among the trees, by the stream, in the woods, Rose is often in a strange mood. Her eyes dart, she's flighty, hard to calm down. I've tried taking her upstairs alone, to find out what's really going on in these long, involved games, but she says the same thing every time. It's make-believe. There's nothing to tell.

I peer through the cracked windowpane. I can't even see them now. They're hidden among the thick branches and wild undergrowth, and for a moment, I feel my heart constrict. I know I wanted them to have an outdoor, independent childhood, but how do I know that they're safe? I think of that strange neighbour snooping around our garden. What if he came across them? I remind myself that Eve is probably there, but that doesn't make me feel any better. I can hardly tell them they're not allowed to spend time with our lodger, but somehow her presence in their games makes me more uneasy, not less.

It has suited me, to some degree, having Eve around the past week or so. I've been so busy overseeing the building work, wiping down surfaces, sweeping piles of dust, moving boxes around and coping with the never-ending noise, the banging and drilling and sawing and shunting. Some days I've felt like I want to run down to the end of the garden, too, only I can't. I'm needed here. And I have a feeling I wouldn't be welcome, anyway.

It's not just the children who have been behaving strangely around me. Eve and I have been avoiding each other since the night with Rich and Amanda, and Pete's hardly been here. He's up and out early in the morning, and he's started working late again. When he is at home, he and Eve take pains to keep away from each other. If she walks in to a room, he finds an excuse to leave. If she even comes up in conversation, he changes the subject.

I honestly can't tell whether they're deflecting attention from what's going on between them, or if they had a falling out that night, and they're not speaking any more. Whenever I've brought it up with Pete, he says I'm imagining things. There's nothing to tell: they had a long chat, he came to bed – just like every other evening they've spent together. But I know I'm not imagining the strange atmosphere, how oddly they're behaving around each other, or how shifty Pete is with me these days. In my more paranoid moments, I wonder whether they've found a way to meet up away from the house – when Pete's supposed to be working and Eve's out at one of her many viewings.

That's one thing that's changed since the fall out that night – Pete's told Eve she needs to find somewhere else to live. He wants me to talk to her about it, too. This has gone on long enough, he says. We need to start renting out the barn. I know he's been worried about money – he sits up late some nights poring over our accounts, trying to work out how we're going to pay for all the renovations. And he knows I've wanted Eve to leave for ages. But I can't help wondering what's prompted his sudden change of heart. A few weeks ago, he was urging me to give her more time. Now, he suddenly wants her gone. Is it so that they can have more privacy, with her tucked away somewhere else? Or because he can't live with what he's done?

The theories and conspiracies run over and over in my mind. Perhaps because of my own guilty conscience, or the fact that I have a secret now, too. It was Mum who gave me the idea first. 'Why not have a look at a few properties?' she'd suggested over the phone one evening. 'Dip your toe back in the water.'

In the desperate days after that dinner, when I'd broken down so spectacularly, revealing to a carefully selected crowd of our friends just how bad things had become, it had seemed like some kind of solution. I clearly couldn't go on living here, like this. The house is driving me mad, or this situation is. Either way, something's got to give. And so Mum had made an appointment for me with a Tottenham estate agent. 'It's cheaper there,' she'd said. 'You'd get more for your money, if you really have lost as much as you say on that house.'

I'd gone along to humour her. To see how it would feel to be back in London, so near to Mum's house and only a short drive from where we used to live. I'd told Pete that Mum and I had theatre tickets, I'd be staying overnight. It was only one weekend, to test the water. But the minute the estate agent led me into a small, dark terraced house, moments from a main road, directly opposite a scruffy park, I had known instantly, unquestionably, that it was where I wanted to be. The countryside retreat was someone else's dream: Pete's dream, one that belonged to other couples, other families, but not to me. This was where I belonged. Not this particular house, which would surely be snapped up long before we'd manage to decorate and sell the Maple House. But a house like this, in an area like this, surrounded by noise and people and chatter and life. This is where my children and I should

252

be. And if Pete didn't agree then, well . . . I hadn't got that far.

That was last weekend, and I'd resolved to speak to Pete as soon as I got back. But when I arrived from the train station, he'd been full of the news of his last-minute work trip. He doesn't usually travel for business, but this is something to do with a potential promotion, a chance to impress some new clients, get back onside with Rich. After my performance when they came to visit, I could hardly say no. And Pete's desperate for a pay rise, to get more money coming in. It all came about quite suddenly. He was asked to step in when someone else pulled out, apparently. He went yesterday, a Friday, which struck me as odd. He'll only be in Sheffield a few nights, but for some reason it's left me feeling even more vulnerable. Out here on my own with just the children. And Eve. I'd feel happier if she wasn't here. Something about her presence has started to make me feel really unnerved.

I move away from the window to begin the task of sorting through the drawers in our bedroom. The builders are starting work up here next week, so we're moving into the spare room. But at the back of my mind is the thought that if I pack thoroughly now, I can kill two birds with one stone – we'll be all ready for our next move when the time comes. Because I know it will, now. We can't stay here.

I start on Pete's side, since he's away – emptying his drawers, his half of the wardrobe, his bedside table. As I sweep my hand wearily one last time across the back of the drawer on Pete's side of the bed, double-checking for any stray pens or coins, my finger snags on something cold. I pull it out slowly. A delicate silver chain with a tiny leaf at the end. I turn it over in my hand. Had Pete been planning to give me a present? But he knows I only ever wear gold. Could it be Rose's, a birthday gift she's forgotten about that has somehow ended up in Pete's bedside table?

I hear the back door slam and check my watch. Dinner time already, and I've barely started on the packing. I turn and dash downstairs, the children will be hungry and I haven't even begun making the casserole I'd planned. It will have to be pizza again. I walk into the kitchen, clutching a pile of assorted junk I've found in our room, old drawings, felt pens, a joke book, and on top of the pile, the mystery necklace.

'That's pretty.' Rose moves towards the pile, holding the necklace up to the window and watching it glint in the sunlight.

'Isn't it? I thought it might be . . .'

'That's where it got to!' Eve says, following the children in through the back door. 'I've been looking for that everywhere.' She snatches up the necklace from where Rose is dangling it and runs a thumb over the smooth silver. 'Where did you find it?' she asks Rose.

'It was Mummy who found it.'

'Oh, thank you, Jess.' Eve turns to me. 'Where was it?' There's a strange expression on her face. Surely she doesn't think I stole her jewellery? I want to ask her how it ended up in Pete's drawer, but I can't. Not in front of the children.

'Oh, it was in one of these drawers.' I point to the kitchen units. 'Someone must have found it and stashed it away.' I turn away, busying myself in the freezer looking for pizzas, my fingers clenched around the handle.

What was Eve's necklace doing by Pete's side of the bed? When could she have been in our room? I think of last weekend when I was at Mum's. Pete said Eve had kept out of his way the whole time. But that's surely the only explanation – that

254

she was in our room, with Pete. How else could it have got there?

I'm still running over it all in my mind when Eve excuses herself for the evening, and as the children and I sit in silence over dinner, my fury only builds. What have those two been getting up to in our house, with our children only yards away? It's bad enough visiting her in the barn, but how could Pete do this to me in our own home?

After we've eaten, the kids go to watch TV and I try Pete's phone. I'm determined to quiz him while I'm still feeling angry, certain – before the doubts set in again and he's able to twist my words, making me feel as though I'm imagining the whole thing, as if I'm losing my mind. But he doesn't answer, and so I decide to corner Rose after her bath. She won't be able to help telling me the truth about what really went on that weekend – whether Eve came into the house, and for how long. I've just got to wait until I can get her on her own.

But Rose is in a funny mood again this evening. After I've washed all the garden dirt off her, I get her into her pyjamas and we cuddle up on her bed. I'm hoping she'll at least open up to me about what she's been up to with Eve all day, out in the garden and later in the barn, locked away together while I carried on packing in the bedroom. But all she'll tell me was that they were painting and playing.

'All day? That's all you were doing?'

'Yes, Mummy.' There's a note of impatience in her voice. I feel so much more distant from her these days, as though there's a whole other dimension of her inner life that I have no access to – her mind has another room, and only Eve has the key. 'Eve *likes* playing. She doesn't have other things to do all the time. She's not interested in all that grown-up stuff.'

Rose looks up at me through her dark eyelashes, and I feel a twinge of guilt. When's the last time I played a game with her? Sat in her room and gave voices to her dolls, like I used to. Even got out one of the board games we kept piled up in a corner of our old living room, which are still packed away in boxes. Rose is right – I've become consumed by this house, by all the work it needs, by the misery it causes me. I've got to find a way back to the person I was.

Next door, I can hear Archie kicking the wall rhythmically as he reads a comic. I resolve to put aside time for both of them, together and apart, like I used to. Just as soon as this build is underway.

'Rosie, how would you like it if we went away somewhere, just the two of us, for a night?' I tuck a wet curl behind her ear and try to ignore the look of alarm that passes across her face.

'What, without Daddy, or Archie. Or Eve?'

'Yes, without Daddy and Archie. They can spend the weekend doing something fun together, too. And Eve isn't part of our family. She's going to be moving away soon.'

'What? Eve can't move out, Mummy. She lives in the barn.'

'No, darling.' I take a deep breath. 'Eve is staying in the barn for a little while. She doesn't live with us. She can't stay here forever.'

'Why not?' Rose demands.

'Because families live together, sweetie, not friends.'

'You lived with your friends before you lived with Daddy. You've told me before. Eve is my friend. I want her to live with us. And she wants to live here, too. This is the only place in the world she feels at home. She told me that.'

'Did she now? And what else did she tell you?' I'm trying to keep the anger from my voice, but I can't help thinking of Eve snuggling up with Rose in the chair we bought for our barn, plotting how she can entangle herself in our lives even further. It was a masterstroke, I see now, getting my children onside, as well as my husband.

'She said she loves me like I was her own daughter,' Rose says quietly.

'But you're not her daughter, Rose. You're my daughter. Mine and Daddy's.' I'm gripping her shoulders now, and I try to relax my arms into a hug instead, but Rose pulls away, backing into a corner on her bed.

'I'm your daughter, but I'm Eve's friend. Her special friend. And in our world, friends live together.'

'Which world is that? What are you talking about?' I'm using the wrong voice. I can see Rose's face shut down; she's not going to tell me any more unless I calm myself, soften my tone. I change tack for a moment. 'Rose, when I was at Granny's last weekend, did Eve come into the house?'

Rose studies me, her little eyes narrowing. I feel terrible. I don't want to put her in this position, stuck between two parents who barely speak to each other, and a lodger who has long outstayed her welcome. 'I can't remember,' she says softly, climbing underneath her covers and resting her head on the pillow, ready to sleep. I stroke her hair and decide to leave it for another day. It's not fair to put her under this pressure, not when she's already been through so much.

'Don't worry, darling, it's nothing to do with you, anyway. Let's talk about it another day.'

I give her a kiss and then tuck Archie in, too, returning downstairs to lock up before finishing the packing.

On my way back up, I stop for a moment on the landing to look out into the night. I think of the fears I had when we first got here – that intruder with his big, thick hand. The strange man who owned our house. The creepy neighbour lurking in the shadows. Somehow those have receded over recent weeks, only to be replaced by another, more visceral fear. That of the woman we've invited into our home, and what her presence might do to our family. The light leaking from around the edges of her blind is more terrifying to me now than anything the darkness might conceal.

I move to my side of the bedroom, packing away my clothes, my books, the contents of my bedside table. And then I get down on my knees and push my hand underneath to retrieve my second phone. I haven't looked at it in weeks. But when I reach around, it isn't there.

My stomach turns over. I thrust my shaking hand further under, feeling beneath the cupboard, under the bed, in the gap between the floorboard and the wall, though it couldn't possibly have fallen down there, it's too narrow, there wouldn't be room. I get my head down to floor level and shine a light from my other phone, but all I can see are a few pens, some tissues, a stray hairband gathering dust.

Panicking, I sit back on the bed, trying to remember when I last took it out. But it must have been last month, at least. I've been trying to wean myself off it, taking it out less and less. It's all in the past now, after all. I'd been planning to get rid of it, to throw it into some bushes or a river somewhere. To put the whole thing behind me.

But now the phone has gone. It's been taken. Could it have been one of the children who found it during a game of hide-and-seek and gave it to Pete? Or could he have come across it and discovered some way to open it? Perhaps that's why he's gone away. To give him time to think. The only alternative seems so much worse, somehow. That it was Eve who discovered the phone and she's holding on to it as insurance, as evidence, as some kind of blackmail.

The image comes back to me of Rose cowering on her bed, her face blank as I asked her whether Eve stayed in the house, the note of doubt, of hesitation, in her answer. It stays with me as I get ready for bed and try to fall asleep, to dismiss my worries about the phone, the necklace, about everything. But they won't be ignored, and neither will the flickering, jangling, jolting feeling in my chest that something is deeply, inescapably wrong.

Chapter Twenty-Five

Pete's not answering his phone. I must have called him four or five times yesterday, after my discovery on Saturday night, and it's been many more this morning, since the builders arrived. They bombarded me with a stream of questions as soon as I got back from dropping the children at school – where do we want the light switches, will the en suite door open in or out, what height do we want this 'window seat'? This from Keith, a note of doubt in his voice. We hadn't mentioned a window seat before. Where had that come from? he's clearly wondering. But somehow, without my noticing, Eve has let herself in through the back and followed us upstairs, and she's answering Keith's questions smoothly, without hesitation. Switches in their existing positions, en suite door opening out, window seat resting just below the curve of the window frame. It would be a relief, if I wasn't already desperate to keep her as far as possible from the builders, from the house, from my family.

I barely slept last night. I've had only the briefest contact with Pete since he left. Just a couple of text messages explaining that his connection is patchy, and I've got nothing to worry about. Since when did a major city like Sheffield have bad mobile coverage? And how can I believe anything he tells me any more? He claims he has no idea how Eve's necklace got into his drawer. Obviously I didn't mention my missing phone, but when I said I was worried about Rose, that she was acting strangely, he replied telling me to keep the children close.

It's only now, as I stand at our bedroom window watching Eve walk back to the barn that I remember the text, and a feeling of panic grips my stomach. I pick up my phone and scroll back to find it.

Keep the children close. Look after them for me xxx

What did he mean by that? They have to go to school, obviously. I can't keep them close all day. When it had arrived, just after eleven last night, I'd rolled over in bed, read it, and turned to go back to sleep. I'd slept deeply for a couple of hours and then lay awake from 2 a.m. with the events of the day playing over in my mind. In many ways it had been a normal Sunday – Eve and Rose playing yet another secretive game in the garden, Archie's withdrawal to his room, me distracted by the packing, endless packing, and cleaning, clearing, preparing for the builders. I'd poked my head around Archie's door a couple of times to check on him, ask if he knew where Rose was, what she was up to. But he'd only shrugged, headphones on, eyes still on the screen of his tablet. At the time, I'd been preoccupied. I just needed to clear out the airing cupboard and move some boxes up to the loft and then I'd have a chance to sit down with him and have a proper chat. But that moment never came, and when I thought back to the look on his face, there was something closed, worried, withdrawn about the way he was hunched on his beanbag in the corner of his room.

Rose, by contrast, had been animated last night. She was full of stories about this other world she and Eve had discovered in the woods, Maple Land, or something. Apparently it was a world Eve had discovered with her younger brother when she was growing up nearby, one only the two of them had been able to see. But now Rose can see it, too, and she couldn't stop talking about the magical creatures who live there, the adventures they would have together – how they were going to see this brother of Eve's, to make things right again, to rescue him from danger.

I made a mental note to talk to Eve once the children were in bed. Have a word about allowing Rose's imagination to run away with her. But by the time I got downstairs, a wave of exhaustion came over me, so extreme I could barely move. I made some toast and sat at the kitchen table, my eyes on the barn, where the blinds were drawn, as is usual now. I can't look in to see what Eve's doing any more. But then, I suppose it means she can't see us, either.

I still hadn't brought up the question of when she would move out. But it wasn't the moment. I didn't have the energy, with the builders arriving in the morning. And Pete would be back soon. We could talk to her together; it would be better that way.

Now, rereading Pete's text, I pick up on the warning it represents. *Keep the children close.* What does he know? As soon as school has finished, I'll bring them home and we'll play together, just me and the kids. We'll finally unpack those games. We'll spend the afternoon and evening, the three of us, away from Eve, and I'll tuck them into bed and get an early night myself. We'll all sleep, and when we wake tomorrow morning, Pete will be on his way home and all this will be over.

Well, not all of it. The builders, already banging and drilling in the bathroom next door, will be here for weeks, months even. But now that I have a backup plan in mind, a smaller city house, a return to the place we know, I feel calmer again. If only I can persuade Pete.

I walk downstairs, trying not to breathe in the dust already billowing down the hallway. As I pass the front door, I spot the postman approaching and open up to accept the letters, mostly for Pete. More to add to the pile that is amassing in his absence – he's been getting a lot more post than I'd ever noticed before.

'Lovely morning,' the postman says cheerily. 'How's your sister, by the way? Haven't seen her since you moved in. Very nice lady, she was.' He gives me a wink, and I frown.

'I don't have a sister. You must be thinking of someone else.' I smile politely, ready to push the door closed, but the confusion on his face makes me pause.

'Sure that's who she said she was.' He shakes his head. 'Oh well, have a nice day.'

I say goodbye and watch him walk down the driveway towards his van, parked up at the end, wondering where he got that idea from. Maybe he was thinking of another house, another sister. But there aren't many houses around here that look like ours. There aren't many other houses full stop. I stand on the doorstep and take a deep breath of the clear morning air, feeling the weak rays of spring sunshine on my face. For some reason, a conversation I had with Sara in the school playground a few days ago comes back to me. She'd been trying to get the measure of Eve, I think. To work out where she fits in to our family scene.

'Is she from the area?' she'd asked. 'It's just, there's something familiar about her. I saw her waiting in her car outside school the other day, and I could swear I know her from somewhere.'

'You've probably been into her gallery in Ipswich,' I'd said at the time. 'It's closed up now, but it used to be in the shopping lanes.'

'That must be it.' Sara had nodded, but she didn't look convinced. She seemed preoccupied. The matter clearly wasn't closed in her mind. I don't know why I think of it now. But I feel an uneasiness I can't put my finger on.

I try Pete's number as I make a cup of tea, but there's no answer. Then I hear Eve's car pull away down the drive. Off to another viewing, probably. We don't tend to discuss our plans much any more.

I call Pete again. I just want to hear his voice. Want him to reassure me that the children will be okay. That we'll be all right. That nothing is going on between him and Eve, and once she moves out, and the house is finished, we'll finally have the fresh start we've been talking about for so long now.

But it goes to voicemail, over and over throughout the morning. By lunchtime, I've been staring at the screen of my phone for so long that when it suddenly comes to life with an incoming call, I jump back, startled. But no name comes up. It's not a number I recognise. Could Pete be calling from someone else's phone?

'Hello.' My voice sounds high-pitched, unfamiliar.

'Is this Jessica Masters?' My stomach lurches. It's the school, something's happened to one of the children.

'Yes. Who's this?'

'My name's Dominic Millington. I think you know my younger sister, Evelyn.' His voice is halting, slow, with a local twang.

'Evelyn?' My mind is racing, it takes me a moment to catch up. 'Oh, Eve. Yes, she's staying with us at the moment.'

'Yes, I thought so. It's just . . . could we meet? I need to talk to you about something.'

'Where do you want to meet? When? Can you not just tell me over the phone?' My brain has frozen, my body tensed.

It's as though all the anxiety, all the worry of the past few weeks has been building up to this moment.

'It would be better if we could talk face to face. I've had a few messages from your husband but I can't get through to him. And I don't think this can wait.'

'My husband,' I repeat. 'Pete?'

'Yes, that's right. He wanted to talk to me. He didn't say what it was about, but I think I can guess.'

'What?' I'm practically shouting now, with impatience, but also to be heard above the banging upstairs. 'What is it about?'

'I'm in Ipswich. I'm staying in the Travelodge. There's a bar nearby on the quay. It's called The Waterfront; you can meet me there.'

'A bar?' I check my watch. It's just after 1 p.m. 'Look, I don't know what this is about, but I can't go to a bar in Ipswich. I've got builders in, children to collect from school . . . Couldn't you come here? I can give you the address.'

'I can't come to the house. I don't want to see Evelyn.'

'She's not here . . .' I say impatiently. She might have gone into town herself. We're more likely to bump into her there, I want to say, but he cuts in.

'I need to talk to you in private. It's important.' Something about his urgent, hollow tone gets through to me. This is Eve's brother. He says it's important. It could be information that will help us get Eve to move out, to extricate her from our lives. Maybe that's why Pete's been trying to get hold of him.

'Okay, I'll meet you there in half an hour. But I can't stay long. I've got to pick up my children.'

'It won't take long. I'll see you there.'

I hang up and immediately dial Pete. No answer, again. I leave him a message, explaining what just happened, and then race around in a panic, finding my bag, purse, car keys, phone. I don't want to go and meet this man on my own. But I don't see what choice I've got. I need to find out what's going on.

Chapter Twenty-Six

The traffic into Ipswich is terrible. The Easter holiday road-works have collided with the first day back at school, and I inch into town, watching the minutes tick past on the dash-board clock. By the time I park and reach the quayside, I'm nearly half an hour late. I scan along for The Waterfront bar, and spot its flashy neon sign, incongruous in the early after-noon sunshine. I know Dominic will be waiting inside, but before I can go in, I need to call someone. Arrange for the kids to be picked up. I'll never make it back in time.

I don't want to ask Eve, not now, so I scroll through my phone for Sara's number, explain that I've got stuck in traffic. Would she mind taking the children home with her for an hour? It's no problem at all, she tells me, her voice light and cheery, and I feel a slight easing in my shoulders. I resolve to make more of an effort with Sara in the future. I'll repay the favour sometime, try to find some common ground with her and the other mums, at least for the rest of the time we're here. I've been too quick to judge them, I can see that now. And it will help the children settle, if they get invited round to play with friends more often. Help smooth the transition once Eve moves out.

But as I hang up from Sara, I see that Eve is calling. My instinct is to reject the call, but what if something's happened – with the builders, or with the children?

'Hi, Eve, is everything okay?'

'Yes, fine. It's just, I'm at home and I saw your car isn't here. I thought maybe you were stuck somewhere. Do you need me to pick up the children?'

The word 'home' jumps out at me. The sooner Eve moves on, the better. 'Oh thank you, that's kind, but it's fine. Sara's going to collect them and take them back to hers for a bit.'

There's a pause at the other end. 'Sara?' Another pause. 'Are you sure?'

'Yes, why?'

'It's just . . . I didn't think the two of you were particularly friendly these days. And I thought Archie and Rose would probably rather be in their own space than hanging around with kids they don't really know. It's no problem for me to get them.'

'Oh, they'll be fine. I'll only be an hour.'

'Where are you?' The directness of the question throws me. I clear my throat, look around.

'Um, I'm in town. In Ipswich. Meeting a friend.'

'What, one of the mums from school?' There's a note of doubt in Eve's tone. She knows I don't have any friends here.

'Oh, no. Someone who's come to visit from London . . . An old friend . . . Arifa.' Why did I say her name?

'Okay.' Eve sounds unconvinced. 'If you're sure you don't want me to get them.'

I can hear from Eve's tone that she's put out. It's a further rejection, a betrayal. Now I won't even let her look after the children she's grown so close to over the weeks. But I don't trust her, especially after Pete's text. I hang up and check my phone, but there are no missed calls from him. No responses to my many messages.

Then I turn to The Waterfront bar, the anxiety prickling at my neck and shoulders. The sooner I get this conversation over, the sooner I can get back to the kids, to our home, to safety.

For a moment I stop outside the bar, about to go in and meet a total stranger, a man who told me he's Eve's older brother. I've heard about a younger brother, from Rose, but Eve's never mentioned an older brother before. How do I know he's telling the truth? How can I be sure he is who he says he is? What the hell am I doing?

I think about calling Eve back, putting her on the spot, double-checking his story. But I've just made up a lie. I can't tell her I'm sneaking around behind her back, meeting up with a brother who claims he doesn't want to see her.

I make one last panicky call to Pete. Leave a message on his answerphone, telling him what I'm about to do. And then I put my phone back in my bag and walk through the double doors and into the darkness of the bar.

It's a cavernous room, probably loud and rowdy by night, but for now empty, just one or two lone men drinking at the bar, and a couple of young women, early twenties, chatting at a table in the window. There's a man on his own in the far corner and, as I walk in, he looks up. I can just about make out his face – untidy beard, low brow, dark eyes fixed steadily on me, mouth clenched, clutching a pint in one hand. I approach warily.

He's big. Surely too big to be related to Eve. Tall, a mass of dark hairs on his forearms, sprouting from his shirt. The

269

hair on his head is dark, too, greying, flecks of white in his thick eyebrows. His expression is grim, unsmiling.

'Are you Jess?'

'Yes.' I clutch my pink coat around me, self-conscious as I survey his wax jacket, cords, heavy boots. But he's the one who looks out of place in this waterfront bar, not me. He shifts his long legs to one side, uncomfortably, allowing me to join him in his booth.

'It's table service.' He motions for the barman, spotty-faced, barely out of his teens, ordering himself another pint and a sparkling water for me.

'I'm driving,' I explain. As if I need an excuse in the middle of a Monday afternoon, meeting a man I don't know, at his request.

'I'm sorry if this seems odd,' he says slowly, his voice thick Suffolk, tailing off at the end of his sentences. 'I wouldn't have got in touch, but your husband sounded worried in his message and I didn't like to think of you getting caught up in it all.'

'Caught up in what?' A queasy feeling in my stomach tells me I don't want to know. Don't want to hear what he's got to say at all.

'In the house, the family, the money, all of it.' He takes a swig and slams his pint on the table. The frustration in his brow suggests he thinks I should know exactly what he's talking about. But I've got no idea.

'Which house? My house?'

'Yes.' He sighs heavily. 'The Maple House. You bought it, didn't you? You and Peter.'

I nod, waiting for him to continue.

'Well, it's my house. Our house.' He stares into his pint, avoiding my eye.

'What do you mean *your* house?'

'Mine and Eve's. It should be, anyway. We grew up in it. It was our dad's. When he died, we thought . . . well, Eve thought, we'd inherit. She'd been banking on it, really. Waiting for it. For years.'

'What, waiting for your dad to die?' I turn to Dominic, feeling a tightness take hold in my temples. All this time, all the conversations we've had, all the time Eve's been staying with us, she's never once told us it was her house. She used to live in it. She grew up in it. It doesn't make any sense.

'Well, waiting to inherit. I should have got in touch sooner. But I had no idea . . . Didn't know what she was going to do.'

'What do you mean, what she was going to do?'

'You know, hangin' around. Making a nuisance of herself. Moving in.' He's shaking his head now, muttering to himself. 'She never did know when to leave well enough alone. Never could move on from it all. Wouldn't let any of us move on.'

'So when I met her, when I told her all about the house, when I showed her around . . . she already knew? She knew the house?' I'm thinking aloud now. Trying to process what he's saying. 'All those little things she found. The wallpaper, the window seat, the hidden door. She knew where they were because she grew up there . . .' I can hardly believe I hadn't realised. But why would I? Why would you do that – pretend you didn't know your childhood home, tell so many lies, so many little lies? 'I . . . I don't understand.'

'I inherited, you see. Not Eve, in the end. And she was furious, so angry. Especially when she realised I was going to sell. She became bitter, obsessed. She couldn't leave it alone. She would have done anything to get back into the house.'

'So it was you who showed Pete around the house?' I'm still piecing it together. This man I've come to meet in a bar, alone, is the 'odd' guy Pete told me about. The one I've imagined creeping around my garden. Who has haunted my dreams ever

271

since. 'You had second thoughts, you took it off the market. But then you sold it to us.' Dominic nods, warily. 'And Eve tricked her way back in because she couldn't bear to leave. She'd lived there all her childhood . . .' I pick up my drink and wrap my hands around the glass, feeling the coldness of the iced water in my hot palms. What on earth has been going on?

'Well, not all her childhood. Not after Jack died.'

I look up sharply, nearly dropping the glass.

'Jack?' The boy in the river. The ghost.

'Yes, Jack.' Dominic turns away, staring towards the floor where his long legs are extended. 'Our younger brother. He died. And then Mum died, and it was all over. We moved out. We never went back.' He's rocking now, his foot jiggling. Something isn't right here.

'I'm so sorry. I knew about the little boy who drowned, but I didn't realise he was your brother. Eve's brother.' I want to get out of here, now. I want to get home to the children. I want Pete to be with me. I don't want to be dealing with all this on my own. Dominic mutters something bitterly, but I can't make out what he's saying.

'What was that?' My hand is on my phone in my bag.

'He didn't drown,' he says gruffly.

'How did he die, then?' I ask and Dominic looks up with such fierce anger in his eyes, I recoil. A ringing starts up in my ears.

'She pushed him. They were in the tree and she pushed him. It was one of their games. This world they had. Maple Land. She wouldn't let me join in, but I used to watch them. I'd hide in the bushes. She could boss him around, get him to do whatever she wanted. She didn't want me getting involved and spoiling their fun. But then he was getting older, he wanted to have his say. And he was always Mother's favourite.' His jiggling has amplified now; he's jolting back

272

and forth. 'She knew that as much as I did. It didn't bother me. I was used to being ignored. But Evelyn was the golden child until Jack came along, and then she had to get used to being second best.'

'So she pushed him on purpose, out of the tree?' I feel like the room is spinning. I think about Maple Land, Rose – they were going to rescue Eve's brother, she said.

He nods, looking down. 'I saw her, from the bushes where I was hid. Maybe she didn't really mean to hurt him. Who knows? But by the time she scrambled down and turned his poor little body over, she knew what she'd done. I watched her drag him into the river and leave him face down.'

'And she never told your parents what had happened? And you didn't either?' My mind has slowed down to a single point: that image of the boy face down in the water; Eve's knowledge of what she had done.

'It all happened so fast. Mother was running into the garden, screaming. Evelyn said she'd lost sight of him and then found him there. By the time I came out from where I was hiding, they had their story.' He scratches at his neck angrily. 'They blamed her anyway. She was in charge of him and she let him drown. I couldn't come out and make it worse for everyone. It would have killed Mother if she knew what Evelyn did.'

'So the only person who knows what really happened that day is you?'

He nods. 'Me. And Evelyn.'

'Did you ever tell her you saw her?' I ask. Dominic shakes his head.

'I couldn't. I didn't know what she'd do.' He looks up, and I see genuine fear in his eyes. 'She always had a way of twisting things around. I was no match for her. Anyway, she got her punishment, right enough. We all did.'

'What do you mean?'

'Mother. She killed herself. Couldn't live with what had happened. And that's when Dad really turned on Eve. Wouldn't have her in the house, couldn't live with her, he said. We were sent to our grandparents, and he moved away. Went off to America with his new family . . .' He breaks off, takes a deep breath. 'I couldn't believe it when Evelyn said she'd been expecting to inherit the house after all that time. She hadn't spoken to Dad in years. He'd never forgiven her for taking her eyes off Jack that day, for what it did to Mum – and he didn't even know the half of it.' He's shaking now, his hands trembling. 'I didn't say anything, to him. Never told anyone. But I had to tell you.' He turns to face me. 'I need you to know what she's capable of, with her living with you – with your children.'

I sit up straight, as if coming out of a trance. I pull out the phone I've been clutching and check the time. How long have I been sitting here, listening to this? All while that woman – that liar, who deceived me so easily, so completely, is in my barn, with access to my house, and my children. That woman who killed her own brother. Who inspires such hatred, such fear, in her surviving brother, a grown man. I've got to get back. To collect Archie and Rose and keep them away from her. Keep them in my sight at all times until she leaves.

But I don't have any reception.

'I've got to go outside. I need to make sure my children have been collected from school,' I say to Dominic, watching his eyes widen in alarm. 'Don't worry, I won't tell Eve anything you've said.'

'That's not what I'm worried about. Where are they?' he asks. 'Where's Eve?' He stands up, but I'm already running outside, thinking of Rose's face last night, the excitement in her eyes, all this talk of another world, the games they've been playing. This world that Eve made up with her brother

274

before she killed him. What has Eve been up to? What has she been doing with them?

I stand outside, waiting for the phone to reconnect, a high-pitched buzzing in my ears. I just want to get through to Sara, hear the children chatting in the background, know that everyone's safe. And then get out of here, go home, put my arms around the children, send Eve to the barn and then get her away from our lives for good. Once she knows what I know, she won't want to hang around.

Finally I see some bars of reception and immediately a message flashes up, three missed calls, all from Sara's number. A text arrives, and then another:

Hi, Jess, I went to get the kids but Eve had already collected them. Did you know she was doing that? The teacher said they didn't seem worried. Sx

Hi, Jess, just checking in again to make sure you've got hold of Eve and the kids. Sx

I dial Sara's number, holding my breath, my heart pounding.

'Oh Jess, there you are. I was getting worried! Have you tracked down the kids?' Sara sounds anxious. 'I'm so sorry I didn't get to them in time, but I wasn't late. I was just grabbing Leo and Martha first.'

'No, I haven't got hold of Eve yet.' I'm trying to keep the panic from my voice. 'Do you know where she took them?'

'No, the teacher didn't say. But she said she'd picked them up before, so she didn't think it was a problem. And the kids seemed to be fine with it. Jess, is everything okay?'

'I don't know. I need to get hold of Eve.'

I hang up the phone and dial Eve's number, but the call disconnects immediately. I try again. Again the same click

275

and then silence. I try the house landline. It's just a low, monotonous tone. It's disconnected, too. Something is seriously wrong.

I call Keith, but he says they knocked off early to finish up another job. There was no one home when they left. They'll be back first thing in the morning. Or I think that's what he's saying. I hang up halfway through, in my rush to call Pete. And then to try Eve, again, when Pete doesn't answer.

I'm calling Eve for a fourth time when Dominic comes out of the bar, blinking into the daylight, holding his phone in his hand.

'I've had a missed call from Evelyn, a message.' His face looks even more panicked than before. 'She knows I'm with you. I went to see Carl this morning; he told her I'm in the area. Somehow she's worked out we're meeting up.'

'Who's Carl?' I ask, frantically pressing Eve's number, over and over. But I don't have time to wait for a response. 'I can't get through to her. She's not answering. Her phone's disconnected. She's got my children.' I repeat helplessly. 'She's got my children. I've got to get home.'

I'm shaking. Dominic takes hold of my shoulders. 'How long has she been with them?' he asks.

I look at my watch. 'An hour or so.' How far could she have got? Or maybe they're at home and her phone's out of battery. But why is the landline disconnected? She knows I'm with her brother. The realisation filters through to me as if on a time delay. She knows that I know.

'You check the gallery; I'll check her place in Ipswich,' Dominic says quickly. With authority.

'What place in Ipswich? Shouldn't I go home? That's where they're most likely to be, isn't it?'

'We're here now, we might as well check the places she could be nearby, and then meet back at the house. You try the gallery. There are a few places I can try. The graveyard . . .'

'Graveyard? What graveyard?'

'Where Jack's buried. She's obsessed with it, always going there. But first I'll try Carl's place. Then I'll see you at the house.'

'Who's Carl?' I ask again, my head swimming with all the information I've already had to take in.

'Her husband,' Dominic shouts from over his shoulder, but he's broken into a run, and I start running too, towards my car. I've got to find Archie and Rose.

Chapter Twenty-Seven

'Let me get this straight. You're telling me your children are with a friend. She picked them up from school. They've been gone around an hour, and they could be at home. But you can't get through to her?'

I'm sitting in the car, near the gallery, trying to calm my breathing and sound like a reasonable, sane person to the police officer.

'That's right. I was . . . busy with the builders. And then I went out. But I didn't ask her to pick them up. I asked another friend. And now I'm really worried because I can't get through to her, and I don't know where she's taken them.'

'But she collected them from school?'

'Yes, I rang the school. She definitely collected them.'

'And she's picked them up from school more than once?' The officer is trying to sound patient, I can tell. But she thinks I'm a time-waster. An overanxious mum.

'Yes, lots of times.'

'And she's always brought them home safely?' An audible sigh at the other end of the line. Is that the flicking of paper I can hear?

'Yes. But I didn't ask her to get them this time. And I don't know where she's taken them.'

'Has she taken them other places before?'

'Yes.'

'Where has she taken them in the past?'

'I don't know,' I admit. 'I've never asked. A café probably, but then she's always brought them home, so . . .'

'And where does she live? Could she have taken them to her house?'

'She's staying with us at the moment, although she used to live in Ipswich, so she could have taken them to her old house.' That's where Dominic has gone to look. He said he had a few other places he could try, too. A graveyard. Why would she take them to a graveyard?

'Does she have a place of work? Any family? Could she have taken them to visit someone?'

'No work. She used to run a gallery, but I've checked there and it's empty. Locked up. She's got a husband. I'm not sure where he lives, but her brother is checking there.'

'And where does her brother live?' It's then that I realise I didn't even ask Dominic where he had travelled from, where he's living now, what he does with himself, beyond keeping an eye on his younger sister.

'I . . . I'm not sure.'

'Hmm, since this "friend" has collected your children lots of times before and there's never been any incident, and since you haven't yet arrived home to check whether they are in fact at your house, I would suggest you return home and call us if you have any further problems.'

'But the landline is cut off. That seems odd, doesn't it?' I can hear how I sound – panicky, irrational. But I know something is wrong. This woman doesn't know Eve. Doesn't know what she's capable of.

'You did say you've got builders in, didn't you? So there could be a simple explanation. And you've got your mobile, so you can call us from that if you need us.' Her tone is patronising, infuriating.

'So that's it? You're not going to send anyone?' I can hear my voice rising in anger. It's the powerlessness – just like last time we needed the police. They failed us then, too.

'As far as I can tell, there hasn't been a crime committed here. If I were you, I'd ask your friend a few questions when you do get hold of her. That way you won't get into this situation again.'

'Well, thank you for your time,' I bark, suddenly desperate to get off the phone and back on the road.

'Not a problem, let us know if you have any further issues.'

And then she's gone, and I'm pulling out onto the road and driving faster than is strictly legal in my desperation to get back to my children, to hold them close to me, to never let them out of my sight again.

As I pull up to the house, the first thing I notice is the darkness, the silence. The sky has turned grey and overcast, but it's not just that, every light is out. There isn't a sound, beyond the rustle of the trees and a lone bird, hooting in the distance. It doesn't look like anyone's home, but I fling open the car door and run to the house, fumbling for my keys. I've got to be sure.

The creak of the front door sounds louder today. I call out for the children and then stop in the hallway and listen. No noise, except the drip of the tap upstairs. The dust from the builders is still heavy in the air. Where are Rose and Archie? Where has Eve taken them?

I turn to put on the hallway lights and pick up the landline, but it's dead. So I pull out my mobile and press Dominic's number. Maybe he's already found them. He could be on his way back with them right now. Just around the corner. They'll be in my arms any moment.

But I'm in one of the black spots. I never get any reception in the hallway, or the kitchen. So I move through to the back door. I ring again. This time, it's Dominic's phone that's disconnected, his ringtone a low hum. What the hell is going on here?

I run to the barn. Maybe they're in there, with Eve. But the barn is dark, the door locked. I search through my bag for the spare key, but when I open the door there's no one there. The air is still, Eve's citrus scent lingering. It's so tidy, so spotless, in here – almost like it isn't lived in at all. But then, Eve barely has anything to her name. All she turned up with were a few bags of clothes.

I turn off the light again, close the door behind me. Maybe she's taken them to a café and her phone's run out of batteries. Or she's got no reception. I try her number again. Then I remember, and I feel my heart constrict: she knows I met Dominic. She knows I know. Where has she taken my children? What does she want from us?

I've got two missed calls, three messages, but they're all from Sara, and there's nothing I can tell her yet. I try Pete, cursing him under my breath when the call goes straight to voicemail. Why did all this have to happen while he's away? Suddenly my brain makes a leap, or it tries to. Why *has* all this happened while he's away? Why has he been calling Dominic when he hasn't called me? What did he want to talk to him about?

None of it makes any sense. My thoughts speed up, my mind making connections wildly, randomly. Pete away. Eve disappeared. The children gone. An image appears of the four of them – Pete, Eve, Archie and Rose – in our car, driving into the darkness, music on, laughing, singing.

For a moment, I think my legs will give way, but I manage to steady myself on the door frame.

I go back into the house.

Chapter Twenty-Eight

Why am I creeping around my own darkened rooms? Up the stairs, into the bathroom, half-removed now, our bedroom full of dust. The sky is a moody grey and I'm about to check the children's bedrooms when I pause, on the landing, a movement catching my eye outside, among the trees. I look out. That feeling again – the one I grew so used to when we first moved here. The awareness of something living, breathing, just beyond my line of vision. Something lurking in the shadows, waiting.

I should run downstairs and out into the garden shouting. *Archie, Rose, Rose, Archie.* Their names are running over and over in my mind. Their soft, pillowy cheeks. Rose's dark curls. Archie's fuzzy halo of hair. The desire to feel them in my arms – to lift them, to hold them – makes me weak. I will sacrifice anything, do anything, just to find them safe. It's only been two hours since they were at school. They must be nearby. They can't have got far.

Should I call the officer back now? Something tells me to wait. Not to shout. Not to make any sudden movements. I walk slowly out into the garden, down the lawn, back towards the place where this all began. This dark family story in which we have somehow found ourselves entangled, the decades of misery, loss, anger, and regret.

It isn't until I'm nearing the stream that I see the shape shift in the darkness of the trees. I can hear breathing, the presence of another human. I know who it is. But where are my children?

Eve takes a step backwards, turns around to face me, her eyes glistening.

'This is where it happened.' She looks up at the branches of the large maple and then back to me, studying my face. 'But you know that now.'

'Where are Archie and Rose?' My voice sounds louder, hoarser, than I expected. I dig my nails into the palms of my hands. My instincts tell me to tread carefully.

'Dom told you, didn't he? He told you his twisted version of events.' Her nostrils flare, her eyes wide, small frame tensed.

I take another step towards her. 'Are they out here? Hiding somewhere?' I look around in the shadows of the trees for shapes, movements.

'He's only jealous, you know. Bitter. He always has been. Nobody wanted him, the slow, lumbering fool. We used to joke that he was a changeling, from someone else's family.'

'Rose, Archie,' I call softly. 'Mummy's here. You can come out now.'

'He thinks I don't know the lies he's been spreading about me. Thinks I didn't see him lurking in those bushes. But I saw. I know what he told my parents – how he poisoned Dad against me. Made sure he'd be the only one to inherit. He'd get the house all to himself.'

'Where are they?' I demand. 'Why did you collect them when I told you Sara was getting them? What have you done with them?'

284

'We need to talk, Jess. I need to tell you a few things about myself. Things you've never even bothered to ask.'

'I already know. And as far as I'm concerned, that's your family business. I'm not getting involved. I just want you to tell me where my children are, and then we can forget all about it.'

'Forget all about it! You want to forget that a little boy, my brother, died on this very spot?' She points to the ground, soft and muddy from the rain earlier. 'That would suit you, wouldn't it? Well, I can't forget. Ever. And that's why I need to be here. Need to live here. To be close to him. That's why you and your *pathetic* husband and children need to leave.'

'What do you think – that you can drive us away? That we'll just give you our house? Where are we supposed to live?'

'Sell me the house. I'll take it in the state it's in. You don't want to live here anyway, do you? You're desperate to get it off your hands.'

A picture forms in my mind of the four of us – me, Pete and the children – back in London, in a house like the one I looked around, like our old house, small and warm and cosy. Surrounded by friends, neighbours, a community. But Eve can't give us that.

'You could never afford this house. If you could, you'd have bought it when Dominic put it on the market. You'd have given him the money and we wouldn't even be here. We'd never have met you.' A blissful thought: that we could be somewhere else now, this house never even a feature of our lives. But we are here. And my children aren't. 'Where are the kids, Eve?' I say it more urgently now. 'Where are Rose and Archie?'

'How much is the house worth now? With the rooms torn apart and the crumbling bricks, the knotweed running rampant

285

through the garden. That was a nice touch, wasn't it? I thought there'd be no one stupid enough to take on the house in this state. I didn't reckon on you and Pete.'

I've been wildly scanning the trees, the bushes, looking for any sign of my children, but Eve has caught my attention now. I spin back and look at her, the strange smile on her face, the flash of amusement in her eyes.

'What? Did you . . . did you plant the knotweed? Is it you who's been breaking things? You're the one who's been sneaking around the house? I knew I wasn't imagining it!'

'Oh, Jess, it's taken you a while to catch on, hasn't it?' Eve laughs lightly. 'I suppose that's why you and Pete were duped into buying this house in the first place. Nobody else was clueless enough to make an offer.'

'But why go to those lengths? Why not just speak to your brother, get him to sell it to you? Why get us involved at all?'

'Because I couldn't afford it! And Dom wouldn't give it to me, even my half. Even though I deserve it. Even though it's rightfully mine! He hasn't replied to my calls. He won't respond to my messages. Doesn't want to share with his sister, with anyone. But now you've flushed him out.' Her mouth contorts into a twisted, crooked smile. 'I don't know how you did it, but he's finally turned up, just when he's needed. And *he's* got the money. All we've got to do is convince him, and he'll buy it back from you. You can get out of here. I'll have a home again.'

'Look, *he* contacted me, not the other way around. And we can talk about the house, Dominic, all of this. But first tell me where the children are. Tell them to come out. Once I've seen they're safe, we can work all this out.' I can hear the desperation in my voice, and Eve can too. She looks over her shoulder and for a moment I think she's going to call to them, but then she rolls her eyes and turns back to me.

286

'No, Jess. We need to keep the children out of the way for now . . . to *focus* your mind. We need to work a few things out.'

I feel in my pocket for my phone. I need to call the police. Tell them this is a kidnap, or a hostage situation, or something. Eve knows where my children are but she won't tell me. I don't have any way to make her. I turn back to the house.

'Where do you think you're going?' Eve asks calmly.

'I'm going to look for the children.' I'm holding my phone close to my body, feeling with my thumb to unlock it.

'No, you're not.' Something in Eve's tone makes me stop still. 'They're not here. You'll never find them without my help.'

Suddenly she's beside me, and before I know it she's grabbed hold of my arm. She wrestles the phone from my hand and throws it towards the stream. I hear it land with a splash. I'm aware I am shouting, the blood draining from my face, tears forming in my eyes. I run to the stream and feel around with my hand. When I find my phone, the screen is blank, the light flickering. I press the button over and over. The phone is dead.

'Eve, what the hell are you doing? What do you want from me? Where are the children? Where are my children?' I'm screaming now, and Eve grabs hold of my wrist tightly, giving my arm a sharp jolt.

'You need to calm down, Jess. That's always been your problem, hasn't it? You flap, you panic, you're so easily riled up . . . so easily caught in the moment.' She says this last part in a strange tone, and I turn to look at her. 'Oh yes, I know all about the affair. Your friend's husband no less. The other phone you still keep. He's really not over you, is he, Miles?' She shakes her head slowly. 'I suppose it spices things up when you're a depressed housewife who spends all day chasing

287

around after her kids. That you're still getting messages; that someone's desperate for you. That's why you keep it, isn't it? You've been thinking about replying, reigniting things. But I suppose Arifa had a thing or two to say about it when she found out. Betrayed by her best friend . . .'

I shrink back, staring at Eve, hardly able to believe what I'm hearing, how it all sounds coming from her mouth.

'It was you! You took my phone! How did you get into it?'

'It's not hard to break into a phone these days. Take it to the right shop and it's a matter of moments.'

'And how did you know about Arifa, about everything? You haven't spoken to them, have you? You haven't returned the calls?' I think again about that day when Arifa found my messages on Miles's phone and confronted me. The cold fury, the shouting. They had only gone back a few months, the texts between Miles and me. Just since Christmas, after that party. It was one drunken night. I'd been feeling so neglected by Pete for so long – and suspicious, with all the time he spent on his phone and out of the house. I'd become convinced he was having an affair. Not so different to now, with Eve. Only back then I had admirers of my own.

Miles was tall, blonde, confident, attentive. I'd always pretended not to notice his lingering looks, but that night he offered to walk me home. Pete and Arifa were stuck into the karaoke, and I could barely focus my eyes, I'd drunk so much. Pete hardly looked up when I said I was leaving, but Miles did. He'd had enough himself, he said. Though not too much to come in to mine for a nightcap.

He made the first move, but I didn't resist. We knew Pete and Arifa wouldn't be back for hours. It was all over before I'd even thought about the consequences, but afterwards, I was horrified. I'd been so caught up in the moment, the pleasure, feeling attractive, desired again, I'd betrayed my husband and one of my closest friends. I wanted to forget all about it, but Miles wouldn't leave me alone. He'd wanted this for years, he said. He even gave me a second phone, to receive his messages. I'd tried to give it back to him, but he wouldn't accept it. He just wanted to be there for me, he said. In case I changed my mind. He kept saying we should run away together: that things weren't working with Arifa; that I wasn't really happy with Pete.

And he was right about that. When Pete wasn't at work, or out, he was on his phone, or we were arguing about moving out of London. Pete said it was the only way we could manage financially in the long term, the only way to be a real family. But Miles was convinced it was a terrible idea – like me, he was a Londoner born and bred, a journalist who thrived on the buzz of the city. He kept talking about moving somewhere together, smaller, more central – Shoreditch, Stoke Newington. We could share custody, he said, we'd work it all out. I knew it was a terrible idea. I could never leave Pete, never break up our family. But every now and then, in my lowest moments, I'd give in and reply to Miles, tell him I needed time to think about it all.

By the time Arifa found our messages, Pete and I had already starting looking at houses in the countryside. Miles was getting obsessive, and I could see that moving out of London was the only way to really cut things off with him. Then Pete got fixated on the Maple House, and we were broken into. So I promised Arifa we'd make an offer. We'd leave London, and I'd never contact them again, if only she wouldn't tell Pete.

Once Arifa had time to process it all, she realised she didn't want to break up her family, either. So she said she wouldn't speak to Pete, as long as we cut off all ties. I agreed I wouldn't contact Becky, either, and eventually she gave up on me. But that didn't stop Miles from calling. And yes, I had been tempted at my weakest moments, by the thought of that flat in Shoreditch, especially when we'd first moved here, but I never once called back.

'There's nothing going on between me and Miles,' I insist. 'You didn't tell Pete, did you? Is that why he's gone away? Is that why he isn't answering my calls?'

'Relax. I haven't said anything to Pete . . . yet. Let's just see how things pan out, shall we?'

'Anyway, what have you been doing, right in front of me?' I spit back. 'What's been going on between the two of you? Why was your necklace in his drawer?'

'Oh, that?' Eve laughs bitterly. 'I put it there. Back when I thought the best way to get you out of here was to drive you apart. But you're so self-involved you didn't even notice. And I realised eventually that you don't really care what Pete does, anyway. Whereas poor old Pete, he could never hurt you. Never go through with it. That's what he said when I had my hand down his trousers that night in the barn. He pushed me away. Said that you and his children were the most important things in his life, and that he'd never do anything to jeopardise that, and blah-blah-blah . . .' Eve twists her mouth, disgusted. 'That's when it clicked, when I finally I realised . . . the only way to really get to you was to get to Rose and Archie.' She looks at me, a triumphant glint in her eye. 'So here I am – I know about your affair, I've got your children. You can have them back when you agree to leave the house. To give it to me and leave forever.'

'Eve, this is completely mad.' I pull away from her, turning to the house. I've got to get to a working phone. 'If you tell me where the children are, then I will— I'll speak to Pete, Dominic, we'll make some arrangement. I promise. But I can't hand the house over to you this minute, can I? Just tell me where they are.' I break into a run, back towards the house, towards my car. 'Rose, Archie! Where are you?'

I picture them, hiding, frightened, wanting to come out and find me, but not able to. Or maybe they're not even here at all. Maybe she's got them somewhere else. The graveyard Dominic was talking about. But he was trying there. Where is he? Where are my children? She wouldn't do anything to hurt them, would she? If she's done anything to them, I'll kill her. I feel it suddenly, the strength of my anger frightening me.

I'm hysterical now. Standing in the kitchen and shouting their names one last time before I grab my bag and run out to the car. Drive to safety, to a phone, to someone who can help me.

Except that then I hear the door click behind me, and I turn around to find Eve standing calmly with my bag, my keys next to her by the sink, a knife from the chopping block in one hand, a pile of papers in the other.

Chapter Twenty-Nine

I freeze, mid-scream, all the breath sucked from me. What the hell is Eve planning to do? She isn't actually going to hurt me, is she? What about the children – where are they? Where are they?

'Eve, this is crazy, what the hell is going on?'

'I asked my solicitor to draft some documents. It won't take long. You just sign the house over to me. And then you leave. Simple.'

'But Pete isn't here.'

'He will be.' She looks at me, calmly, as I sink into a chair, tears running down my cheeks.

'I just want to see my children.' I can feel my breath getting erratic. I don't care any more. I don't care about the house. She can take it. She can have everything. We'll start again. All I need is my babies.

I picture little Rose, her eyes red, crying, Archie holding her hand. At least they're together, wherever they are. 'What have you done to them?' I ask, my voice hoarse. 'Eve, you need to tell me what you've done.'

I see a movement outside the back door, the slightest shift in the light. And then a face. Dominic. He's here. But does he have Rose and Archie? My eyes dart towards him, but I don't want to make any sudden movements. I don't want Eve to know we're not alone.

He must have tried the front door and found it locked. Now I can see he's turning the back door handle, but that's locked too. Eve has trapped me in here. I meet Dominic's eyes through the window, over Eve's shoulder. I widen them. *She's got a knife*, I'm trying to convey. But how? I don't want him blundering in here and making the situation worse.

I hear a sharp crack and then the tinkle of falling glass. The back door flings open, and Dominic's large body fills the frame.

'Dom, there you are!' Eve cries.

'What the hell are you doing?' Dominic growls. He's frozen to the spot. He's looking at the knife, but he won't catch my eye. There's something shifty in his face. Something's going on here. Is he in on it?

'The children,' I cry. 'Did you find the children?'

Dominic shakes his head, but still he won't look at me. He's watching his sister. 'Where are they, Eve? Don't do this to another family.' His fists are clenched; he's inching towards her.

'Another family? What are you talking about?' Eve demands.

'Don't tear another family apart like you did ours. What has Jess ever done to you? What have her children done? It doesn't need to come to this.'

'Well, it wouldn't have come to this if you'd listened to me after Dad died. If you'd returned my calls, answered my emails. But no, you thought you'd pocket all the money and disappear. Not a thought for your younger sister and what she might need.'

'You wouldn't leave me alone.' Dom's shaking. 'You never

293

let up. You never have when there's something you want. Don't hear from you in years and then Dad dies and I can't move for calls and messages.'

'But why did he leave it all to *you*?' Eve screams, stabbing the knife into the table, making us both jump. I take a step towards the front door. Could I smash my way out at the front like Dominic did at the back? All I need to do is get away and call the police. I don't trust them, either of them. I need to find the children. 'Why you and not me? This house is ours, mine. You don't even want it.'

'Why *would* I want it?' Dominic roars back. 'This is the house where Jack died. Where Mum died. There's nothing but sadness in this place. You're mad if you want to spend another minute here.'

'Mad?' Eve says sourly. 'And here I was thinking you were the one who wasn't all there.'

'That's enough! I won't hear you say that again, not any more. That's all lies you told to make it seem as though I was the one who made things up, when it was you, all you. You know I saw you push him.'

Eve turns to Dominic, slowly, removing the knife from the wood and pointing it towards him.

'And you wonder why I never contacted you, why I kept away for so many years? When you've been spreading this *poison* about me through the family. When you turned our own father against me until he disowned me, wrote me out of the will, left me penniless.'

'You know you did it, Eve. I saw you drag him from the tree. I saw you leave him in the stream.' Dom sits down, his face white. Eve sits down too, puts the knife down. I inch closer to the door.

'I did move him, but I didn't push him,' Eve says, her voice quiet now, eyes on her hands. 'We were playing a game; he'd edged along the branch too far. I was worried it would snap.

I reached out to grab him, but he backed away from me. That's when he fell . . .' She takes a deep breath. 'I knew I'd get the blame if they found him like that, so I pulled him to the stream. But I got the blame anyway. Nobody could ever look at me again, least of all Mum.'

I can't tell any more if she's telling the truth, if Dominic believes her. Or if it's just another manipulation, another lie. But all that's important now is finding Rose and Archie, and I'm nearly at the door, trying not to make a sound, to leave them caught up in the past, in all their misery.

'I didn't tell a soul,' Dominic's saying. 'I never have, until . . .' He looks at me. But he must see from the alarm in my eyes that I don't want any attention. He turns back to Eve. 'Anyway, it wasn't Dad's fault you're penniless. You and Carl, you can't blame this all on him . . .'

I've reached the door now, and that's when I remember. Reinforced glass. When we moved in, we reinforced it. I thought we were trying to stop people getting in. I never thought I'd be the one trying to get out.

I feel the panic starting to cloud my vision; the room is starting to spin. I've got to take control here somehow. I've got to get through to Eve.

'ENOUGH!' I scream. 'I can't listen to any more of this. *Where* are my children? Tell me where they are and I'll leave this house, leave you both alone. I never want to see either of you again!'

'It's not that simple though, is it?' Eve turns to me. 'We need to get something in writing, otherwise who's to say what you'll do?'

'Eve, what the hell are you talking about?' Dominic asks.

'The house, Dom. Jess and Pete don't want this place. They're desperate to leave, as I've been telling you in my messages for months. If you give me my half of the money,

I'll buy them out, and you can both be shot of me. You'll never hear from me again.'

Dominic looks at her, blinking. He's trying to work out what she means.

'So you're telling me you've taken her kids, so that she'll give you the house?' He looks aghast, his mouth slack. So he isn't in on it then. I lean against the door frame, feeling like I'm about to faint. 'Have you done something to them? If you've hurt them, I'll . . . I'll . . .'

'You'll what, Dom? What will you do?'

'Are you mad, Eve?' He springs up, towering over her. 'How's all this going to look when you go to court?'

Eve gets to her feet so quickly her sleeve catches the knife and it clatters to the floor, narrowly missing Dom's foot.

'What did you say?' she demands.

'Carl told me all about it. The custody battle. I didn't realise your Jack was living with him.'

'Don't bring Jack into this,' Eve hisses, her eyes narrowed.

'Jack? What are you talking about?' I'm totally lost now, tears running down my face, desperate.

'Eve's Jack. Her son – he's fifteen, now. A big, strapping lad. Living with Carl in Ipswich. She's trying to win back custody, aren't you, Eve?'

'How can you have a son?' I turn to Eve. 'You never mentioned him, or your husband. You never told us anything . . .'

'You never asked!' Eve cries. 'You couldn't care less about anyone except yourself, and your precious family. You don't *care* if there's another family who should be living here.' Eve's shaking now. She sits down again. Her shoulders sag. 'I should be living with my son, here, right now. But he won't speak to me, won't see me, since Carl and I split up. And it was all

296

because of this house, Dad's will, Dom selling it. Look what it did to me, to my marriage . . .'

'You can't blame Dad for that. Or me.' Dominic slams his hand against the table. 'You drove Carl away! You've been obsessed, that's what he said. He reckons coming back here has been the final straw, but Jack's been struggling with you for years. Carl thinks you don't know how to show love because of what happened with our parents, with our brother. I mean, what did you think would happen, giving him that name? How was he ever going to live up to it?'

All colour has drained from Eve's face. 'He wasn't. He didn't . . .' she admits. 'He's nothing like Jack . . . He reminds me of you, actually.' She looks up at Dom. 'He wants to join the army, just like you did. He's got none of Jack's spark, his spirit. But I *did* show him love.' She bangs her own fist on the table. 'I do love him.'

'Then how can you have left him with Carl, then? Why don't you ever see him?'

'He won't see me! I didn't *want* to leave him with Carl, but I didn't have anywhere to go. I need a permanent house, a stable living environment, my *family* home . . . There's no way the judge would give Carl full custody if I was living here. And Carl would come around, too, eventually. We could be a family again, like we were before everything fell apart. We could live here, together. Keep the house in the family for another generation. This is his birthright too, you know.'

'None of that's going to happen if Jess goes to the police and tells them you've taken her children. What are you thinking?' Dominic shouts.

'Yes!' I cry. 'How could you do this to me when you've got children of your own? How would you feel if someone took your son?'

'Someone *has* taken my son! His father has taken him. For

297

his own good, they said. I wasn't a stable influence. Couldn't provide the loving home he needed. But if I move in here, I can get him back. Get my life back, my family. That was always my plan. Only you came along, with your architect, and your renovations, and your children . . .'

'If you tell me where they are, if they're safe, if they're unharmed, then we'll talk okay? We can work this all out.' I'm talking calmly, now. I've dried my tears. Something about Eve's unhinged state tells me this is the only way to get through to her.

She looks at me. Her face goes slack, the light extinguished from her eyes.

'Oh for God's sake, your children are fine. They're in the cupboard upstairs. In Jack's old room.'

'You locked them in there? Like you used to with our little brother?' Dom stares at her, his hands shaking. 'Where Mum was found? That's sick, Eve. What's wrong with you?'

'Mum only wanted to be close to Jack,' Eve says. 'And Jack *asked* me to lock him in there. It was a game we played. He enjoyed it.'

'He didn't enjoy it all those times you left him in there for hours on end while Mum and Dad were busy. It was always me who freed him. You never saw how upset he was. What's wrong with you? What happened to you to make you so cruel? So jealous of a defenceless little boy . . .'

I don't hear the rest. I'm already flying out of the kitchen and up the stairs, two at a time, running into Rose's bedroom and collapsing in front of the cupboard, sobbing. I tug at the door, but it's locked. It's locked.

'Rose, Archie, it's Mummy! I'm here, you're okay. I'll get you out of there in no time.'

'Mum!' Archie shouts. 'Mum.' And then more muffled

words, but I can't hear them over the sound of Dominic pounding up the stairs.

'I've got the keys. I threatened to call the police, tell them everything. Eve handed them over.'

He throws them to me and then stands back as I fumble with the lock, my hands shaking so much I can hardly guide the key in. And then the door is open, stale, warm air escaping, my children cowering and blinking, crying, eyes red and faces snotty, but safe, unharmed, with me again. I pull them out and throw my arms around them both, sobbing. 'Oh, Archie, Rose, my babies, you're okay, you're safe, Mummy's here.'

I look behind me, to make sure Eve hasn't followed me in, but we're on our own. Dominic must have gone back downstairs. I'm here with my two beautiful, perfect children and I can't believe they're safe and I'm holding them and they never even left our house.

'Didn't you hear me calling?' I ask them. 'Didn't you hear me shouting your names?'

'We called for you, too, but you couldn't hear us,' Archie says through his tears. Rose has curled into a ball and burrowed into my arms. 'We didn't know what was going on. Eve told us to hide in here, and then she locked the door. She didn't come back. We were scared, there was this man . . .'

'What man? What are you talking about?' I stand up and lift Rose over my shoulder. I need to get them some water, something to eat. Need to get Eve out of my house. Surely Dominic can help with that.

'This big man. Rose was scared, she recognises him. She says—' That's when I hear her scream, the most blood-curdling noise I've ever heard coming from a child. The kind of cry that stops your heart and makes your knees feel weak. But I'm holding her. I can't fall to the ground.

299

'Rose, darling! What's wrong? What is it?' She slumps in my arms. She's fainted. And when I turn around, Dominic is standing in the doorway.

'That's him!' Archie shouts, his eyes wide, terrified. 'That's the man Rose saw!'

Chapter Thirty

The children are in bed now, sleeping, their trauma confined to their dreams. I linger on the landing at the top of the stairs. I don't want to leave them up here, alone, but I also don't want to take any chance that they might overhear our discussion. And they're exhausted. It's evening now and the events of the day, the terror, the confusion, had left them both shaking, nonsensical.

Rose had got it into her head that Dominic was the man she'd seen in the street after our London break-in. When she came around, she was hysterical – crying, thrashing against me, hardly able to get her words out. It was all I could do to comfort her and get some warm milk down her, feed her a few biscuits and tuck her under her duvet, sitting with her, stroking her hair while she fell asleep, almost instantly, the shock taking all the fight from her eyes.

After she'd dropped off, I'd gone in to see Archie, reassuring him in a low voice that Rose had just had a terrible fright. She'd come around in the morning. She'd realise it wasn't the same man. She'd been confused, panicked. There was so much going on. I never should have left them with Eve, but they'd be safe from now on. Eve and Dominic would be leaving soon, and we'd never see them again. I'd keep him and Rose with me. I'd never leave their sides.

'But she was so sure, Mum. It was all she could talk about when we were locked in there, in the dark. I held her hand, and tried to distract her, to sing songs, but she kept saying, "It was him. I know it was him." I didn't know what to do . . .' His tears came then, as he allowed himself to be held by me, comforted in the way he'd comforted his younger sister. As he allowed himself to be the little child again. He curled up in my arms, and I shushed him and sang to him and explained that sometimes shock does funny things to your brain, and you don't know what you're seeing, or how to make sense of it all.

I tucked him in, and waited for him to fall asleep, too, but I could tell he wasn't convinced. Not entirely. I could see it in his half-closed eyes, springing open every few moments, as if to check that his mother was still by his side, was still who she said she was.

And who could blame him for not trusting the adults around him? We hadn't exactly shown ourselves to be a reliable bunch. His mother, late to collect them from school, the neighbour not turning up in time either so that they were left to the deranged lodger, who evidently had an almighty row with her brother in front of them, and then locked them away and told them to keep quiet at all costs. They had called out for me, they said, when they heard me screaming their names. But they hadn't wanted to shout too loudly, in case Eve heard them. They'd been terrified, watching her fight and lash out at this man she said was her brother. And they were terrified of him, too, this big, strange, lumbering man. They didn't know what he'd do.

It's only as I watch the muscles of Archie's face relax, my beautiful boy, his long eyelashes fluttering every few minutes, his mouth slipping open a fraction, that I stop to wonder why Dominic was here at all. Wasn't he meant to be going to Eve's husband's house? To the graveyard? To some other places he'd thought of? He must have come straight back here, otherwise he'd never have beaten me. Why didn't he tell me, if that was his plan? Why pretend to be looking elsewhere? And where had he been while I was talking to Eve in the woods? He hadn't shown himself then. Hadn't let on he was here.

I think about Eve's husband. Her son. How could she have kept all of that from us, all this time? A fifteen-year-old boy we didn't even know she had. How was it even possible that she didn't talk about him all the time, didn't live with him? That he wouldn't speak to her, wouldn't see her. And so she'd left him to be looked after by her husband while she moved into our barn. She'd called him Jack, just like her little brother. Carrying on that legacy of sadness and loss. I wonder how much her grief for one has affected the other.

When I'm sure Archie's asleep, I walk slowly down the stairs, still trying to piece it all together, unsure what I'm going to find when I reach the kitchen.

I open the door to see Eve and Dominic sitting opposite each other at the table, glasses in front of them, Pete's whiskey on the table between them, both watching me. Waiting.

'We weren't sure what to . . . We didn't think you'd mind . . .' Dominic nods towards the drinks, while Eve shrugs and looks away. They were clearly deep in discussion.

'Why did you come here?' I ask Dominic. I want them both out of my house, but not before I get some answers. 'You said you'd go to Carl's house, to the graveyard. But you came here instead.'

'Yes, sorry.' Dom looks at his hands. 'I'd already been to Carl's this morning. I'd heard all about the split, the custody battle. But when I realised Eve knew I'd met up with you, I needed some time to talk to her alone. So I came straight here. The children were playing upstairs, that's what she told me. I saw them watching us from the top of the stairs, so I knew they were fine. And then Eve went up to deal with them, as she put it. I didn't realise she was locking them away. We had a row. I stormed off, drove off to find you, but then I couldn't get through to you. So I came back here. I didn't know where the children were . . .'

'So the children did see you then. Rose thinks . . .' I stop and shake my head. 'It's crazy. It doesn't make any sense.'

I hear a car door slam. We all do. I hadn't been aware of the engine, but someone is here. I run to the front door, just as it flies open. It's Pete. I feel like I might collapse with the relief.

'Jess, there you are. Where are they? What's happened?'

'They're upstairs, asleep. They're okay.' I run to him and throw my arms around his neck, tears flooding my eyes so that I can hardly see his face, pressing my lips against his collar. Pete's home. Thank God.

'Not the children. Where are Dom and Eve? What have they done?'

'What?' I pull away from Pete, looking at his face, trying to work out what he's talking about. 'Didn't you get my messages? Isn't that why you've come home early?'

'Your messages? My phone died this morning. I was on the move; I haven't been able to charge it. I got your messages yesterday, about the necklace and all of that. But I haven't seen any from you today.'

'The children were missing!' I shriek, and then, remembering that they are sleeping, and all they've been through, I quieten

304

my voice. 'Eve took them.' I hiss. 'She hid them. I didn't know where they were! It's been awful. I thought that was why you'd come home.'

Pete's looking from my tear-stained face to the kitchen door and back again.

'Eve took the children?' He echoes. 'Where did she take them?'

'That's the thing. I didn't know. And she wouldn't tell me. But they were in the house all along. Locked in the cupboard in Rose's room. They're fine. They're both in bed. A bit traumatised, but they're unhurt. They're okay.'

'Eve did that?' Pete looks at me, his pupils huge, his jaw clenched. 'They must have been terrified. And you . . . I can't even imagine.' He puts his arms around me. 'But, where is she now?'

'In the kitchen. Dominic's here, too. Her brother. He said you'd been trying to get hold of him?'

'Dom's here? Where is he? What's he said?' Pete spins around, as though he might find this strange man lurking behind him, standing in the living-room doorway, coming down the stairs.

'What do you mean?' I take a step back, a tightness in my stomach. 'He told me about Eve. How she pushed her little brother out of a tree and then covered up his death. Did you already know that? You knew what she was capable of and you let her look after your children? Left her alone with them? Left me alone with her, without telling me!' I think of Pete's text, then: *Keep them close.* Was this what that was about?

'I don't know what you're talking about, Jess. I don't know anything about Eve's little brother. Dom didn't tell me any of that.'

'But you do know him. You called him Dom, just then.

You were trying to contact him. Why, Pete? What's going on here?' But Pete's looking over my shoulder now, and as I turn around, I see Dominic standing in the kitchen doorway. Behind him Eve is still sitting at the table. I look from one face to another. Pete, drawn and anxious. Dominic, closed, unreadable. Eve calm, composed even. No indication of what she put my family through this afternoon.

'What the hell is going on here?' I demand. 'Somebody say something, right now, or I'm going to scream, or call the police, or something.'

'Let's all sit down.' Pete takes off his coat and walks into the kitchen. 'There's no need to get hysterical. We can get to the bottom of everything if we all stay calm.'

'No need to get hysterical? This woman kidnapped our children. She threatened me with a knife. She tried to get me to sign over the deeds to our house. She's got a son, did you know that?' I look at Pete, who shakes his head, and then back to Eve, who shrugs and rolls her eyes.

'I don't see why my son has anything to do with you. And it was hardly a kidnap. They were just upstairs, playing hide-and-seek. I thought it was better to keep them out of the way while we talked business.' She says this for Pete's benefit, but he just looks at her coldly, getting a beer from the fridge and sitting at the table.

'This isn't some kind of drinks party, you know!' I shout. 'Why is everyone pretending nothing's the matter? Why are you all so calm? What's going on?'

'Sit down, Jess.' Pete says this quietly, not looking at me. 'We'll work it all out. There's nothing to worry about.'

'Nothing to worry about? You didn't see your children this evening, shaking and sobbing. Rose fainted, you know. And when she came around, she was terrified, still convinced that she recognised Dominic. That he was the man she'd seen breaking into our house in London. That's how panicked she was. How out of her mind with fear.'

I look at Pete, expecting him to belittle me again, tell me I'm making a drama out of nothing. But his face has gone white, grey even. Dominic stands up, paces to the kitchen window and looks out.

'I hate being in this house. Hate it. Don't know what you want with it anyway,' he says to Eve, who's watching us all, an amused look on her face.

'Am I to assume that the two of you know one another?' she asks, looking from Dominic to Pete.

'Yes, why *were* you contacting Dominic?' I ask Pete. 'You only met him that once, when he showed you around the house, didn't you?' I'm so tired after the trauma of the afternoon, I can barely piece together everything I'm hearing.

'Now it makes sense!' Eve slams her hand on the table, sending a jolt through us all. 'I knew no one would be stupid enough to buy the house at the price the estate agent had it on for. Not with all the decay, and the damage, and the knotweed.'

'All thanks to you!' I interject, but Eve bats me away with a flick of her hand.

'No, you did the deal directly, didn't you? Cut out the estate agent altogether. That's why they were cagey when I called them. Why it went off the market so quickly. Why you moved in practically the same day the sold sign went up. You did a dodgy deal, Dom. Naughty boy . . .' She shakes her head.

Dominic looks at Pete, panic in his eyes. He's scared of Eve. She can clearly run rings around him.

'I . . .'

'Yes, we did a deal,' Pete says in a low voice. 'And yes, I was trying to get hold of Dom. To talk to him about how things were going with the house, to discuss our options.'

307

'What options?' I demand. 'What are you talking about?'

'Come on, Jess. You must have been able to see what a money pit this place is. And now we're running out of cash. We're nowhere near finished. You hate it here. I hate it here. And I don't know how we're going to get it all done.' His voice cracks. He puts his head in his hands.

'But that's the kind of thing you can discuss with me. We can work it out. We can find a solution. And that's why you've been working late, isn't it? Why you went off on this work trip – so you can get a promotion. Then you'll be earning more and we'll be able to pay for the build. We can get it finished and put it on the market, if that's what you want.'

'We can't afford to get it finished,' Pete snaps. 'We've run out of money. Completely. Sheffield was just a story. I went to find Dom. I didn't know what else to do. I didn't realise he'd be coming here to find me.' I look at him, struggling to process what he's saying.

'I came to warn you.' Dominic turns to face both of us. 'When Pete mentioned you had a lodger, when you said her name was Eve, I put two and two together. I worked it all out and I came to warn you about my sister. To tell you to stay away.'

'You? Put two and two together? That'll be a first!' Eve laughs drily and drains the rest of her drink. 'Just how well do you two know each other, then? Sounds like you're pretty chummy from what I can make out. Chatting about lodgers and money troubles and renovations . . . Jess seems to have a point, for once: what is going on here?'

'It wasn't meant to end up like this.' Pete's staring at the table, hands on his temples. 'It was meant to be a solution, not the cause of more problems.'

'A solution to what?' I ask the question slowly. 'Pete, you better tell me what's been going on here, or I'm going to put the children in the car and drive them straight to Mum's, tonight, and I'm not coming back.'

'To our money problems. To *my* money problems.' Pete looks up at me now, his face drawn, dark rings around his eyes. 'I didn't know what else to do. It started off with the occasional night at the casino – after work with clients. The odd flutter. But then I got hooked. I got into all these money problems, taking out loans to cover the gambling losses. I couldn't keep on top of the repayments and it just spiralled.' He puts out a hand, tries to hold mine, but I shake it away. 'I knew Dom, from the casino. I needed to find a way to pay off some of the debts, and one night we got talking. He told me he was trying to shift this house of his in the countryside, but no one would take it off his hands – problems kept coming up with it. He needed the money, too. And I knew how much capital we had tied up in our London house. I thought, if I could only convince you to move out here, to sell up, I could pay off all the debts with the profit we'd make, and we could start again. We needed to get away, anyway. None of us were happy.'

'I was happy,' I say, still trying to catch up with everything Pete is telling me. All this time he's been keeping me in the dark. All those late nights and grey hairs, the weight loss, the worry – he's been racking up huge amounts of debt. He's gambled all our money away.

'So *that*'s why you needed the money then, Dom,' Eve says, turning to him. 'You're a gambler. Who'd have thought? You sold our family home to pay off all your debts.'

'It wasn't just that. I wanted to be rid of it. And there's still money left,' Dominic grunts. 'But it's my money. I can do what I like with it.'

'*Our* money,' Eve corrects him. 'Or it should have been. And I suppose Pete was the perfect solution, with all his

309

financial problems. Here I was thinking the troubles in your marriage were romantic – the old roving eye . . .' Eve looks towards me and I freeze, panicked. She's not going to tell Pete about Miles right now, is she? In front of everyone. It will come out all wrong, Pete won't understand. I need to tell him myself, on my own terms.

But Pete interprets her dig in an entirely different way. 'It was never serious with you, Eve – you know that. Just a flirtation. You were the one who tried to turn it into something more.'

'And you couldn't go through with it, could you? Couldn't betray your darling, *innocent* wife.' Eve smirks at me. 'I'm not talking about that, anyway. I'm talking about all those texts, all those messages . . .'

'I was dealing with my debts!' Pete stands up, pushes his chair back. 'I was looking for solutions. I know it looked bad that I was always on my phone. But I was trying to find a way out of the hole I'd dug us into.' He turns to me now, and the guilt rolls over me like a wave. Pete doesn't know which messages Eve's referring to. He doesn't even know about my other phone. And now he's about to find out, and it will all be over. I might be furious about the money, the house, but this is a different kind of betrayal we're talking about. Miles was one of our friends. I feel sick just thinking about it.

Eve's waiting. Daring me to reveal myself. And in the meantime, Pete's got sidetracked by his own worries, his own confession.

'I'm so sorry, Jess, but I honestly did think this house would be a good move for us. You know I wanted to get out of London, get away from all the partying. And this seemed like the perfect solution, a chance for us to start again.'

'You did say you needed to get away, Jess,' Eve says to me pointedly.

'But you wouldn't leave, you wouldn't be convinced,' Pete carries on. 'I thought the viewing was going so well, and then you heard about the knotweed and it all fell apart. I needed to find a way to change your mind. I was desperate by then; I couldn't see any other way and—'

'Pete,' Dominic interrupts, his voice sharp.

'She's going to find out anyway. It's not fair on Rose . . .' He turns to me. 'I needed to find a catalyst, a way to get you to move.' He's pleading with me now, tears forming in his eyes. Suddenly it clicks into place what he's trying to tell me. I can hardly believe it.

'The break-in?' I ask in a whisper, and then I turn to Dominic. 'It *was* you.'

Dominic looks away. He doesn't speak.

'It was my idea,' Pete says. 'I just thought it would be a little scare, nothing major, nothing stolen, no harm done . . . It never even occurred to me how much it might affect you all.'

I stand up. 'So Rose was right. She *did* see you!'

Dom's pacing by the back door. I feel like I'm going to scream, or faint. This man. This man, standing in our kitchen, who I had a drink across a table from just a few hours earlier. It was this man who broke into my home, who traumatised my daughter, who caused us to move to this godforsaken house. And it was Pete, her own father, who arranged the whole thing. My husband. Who has made me feel as though I'm going mad, imagining things, as though I'll never get over the trauma of the break-in *he* arranged.

I can hardly take it all in. Can't even look at him. Can't be in the same room. I run from the kitchen and up the stairs, two at a time, panting, breathless, afraid of what I might do. I want to smash in all the windows and scream from the top of my voice. But most of all, I want to see my children. I want to see with my own eyes that they're safe, that they're still sleeping, and nothing can harm them now.

I peek into Archie's room and see the familiar shape in his bed, his back to the door, just a slight stirring as I linger in the doorway. And then I creep to Rose's room. She's in her bed too, facing me, her dark lashes resting on porcelain cheeks. I feel the tears start to run down my face and I don't know how I'll ever stop them. These two children are my entire world. I would do anything to keep them safe, and I've failed them. I've allowed them to become entangled in this twisted family, caught up in a situation that has nothing to do with them. Anything could have happened to them. How will I ever leave their sides again?

But what really haunts me, what leaves me hunched and sobbing on the floor in her doorway, is the fact that I silenced Rose. I told her she was wrong.

I allowed her and her brother to get into a dangerous situation with someone I knew, deep down, wasn't to be trusted. A woman who locked them up, who terrified them, who exposed them to a man who had committed a crime against them. And then I told her she was imagining it all. Just as Pete has done to me for so many months.

I curl up on my side, my back slumped against her door, feeling as though I will never move from this position again, never stop guarding her room, keeping her safe.

How can she ever forgive me? And how can I forgive Pete?

Chapter Thirty-One

It's a smaller sign this time, more discreet, blue lettering on grey. *TO LET* instead of *SOLD*. It's so unremarkable I can barely make it out as we drive slowly down the narrow, terrace-lined street, looking for a parking space. We'd forgotten what it was like, for all those months, not being able to park outside your own house. Not able to simply pull up, but having to carefully reverse park, making sure not to knock a car on the opposite side as you pull in to the only space available, and then traipse up and down the street, carrying box after box after box. The children are with us, lending a hand, or trying to. No Mum for this move. Too much explaining to do this time around. We need to wait until we've got our story straight, then I'll go and visit her, give her the edited version. Reassure her that we're all fine. And we are, I think, just about. For now, anyway.

The removal team are in and out in no time, which is lucky as they've had to double park. We hadn't got around to buying any new furniture for the Maple House. We were waiting until the grand renovation project was complete. So it's just the contents of our Walthamstow home – yellow sofa, battered pine table, our beds and wardrobes – transported once again, this time to another redbrick, two-storey terrace, small front room, narrow kitchen, three bedrooms. I prowl through the rooms once they've finished, to check everything is in its place, all the labelled boxes have found their right homes. Our old furniture fits perfectly, though this house is a bit smaller, a bit more run-down, than the one we left behind in Walthamstow.

This could almost be a London street, I think as I peer out of the grubby window in the front bedroom that will be mine and Pete's. A line of terraces, small front gardens, row upon row of wheelie bins, net-curtained bay windows, pavements in need of repair. But we can never go back there. We'd never afford it, for one thing. This place is a rental, until we work out our next move. We've washed up in Ipswich for now. It means that the children can stay at their school. I want the minimum disruption to their lives, for now at least.

Rose is still recovering from the shock of seeing the man who broke into our old house. I told her the next morning, as soon as she woke, that she'd been right. It was him, and I was wrong to say otherwise. I didn't want to deny her the truth, to make her doubt her own mind, the way I'd been encouraged to doubt mine all the months we lived in that house. She knows what she saw – that's what I'd said to Pete. The least we can do is allow her to believe herself.

So we told her Dominic had come to say sorry. He'd wanted to find us and tell us he'd never do it again. It seemed to work. In her child's-eye view, it's a natural thing to do when you've wronged – you apologise. She even said she'd like to see him again, to forgive him so that he doesn't feel bad. It had brought tears to my eyes, and I'd sat on her bed, holding her close, this precious girl who only thinks of others. But I told her it can't happen. I don't ever want to see a member of that family again. I don't want anything to do with their dark, twisted past. I'd be happy to leave that behind forever. Whether we'll be allowed to is another question.

I can hear them all downstairs – Pete, Archie, Rose. The clatter of plates as they unpack the boxes and find everything we need to make a meal in this unfamiliar house, the poky kitchen, the bare, yellowing walls. The bedroom I'm in smells of old smoke, damp, overlaid with the musty-sweet scent of dust. I know I should go down and find the box of cleaning things, begin scrubbing these walls, the windows, the floors so that we can start afresh, with a clean slate, a new beginning. Once again.

But I can't muster the energy. Instead, I sit back on the bed, on the old mattress that has been through two moves now, unmade, our sheets packed away in yet another one of the boxes piled high in these small rooms.

Eve is moving back into the Maple House today. She packed up her bags and left the barn that night, after Pete, Dominic and I had thrashed through all the details. I didn't want her anywhere near my children when they woke in the morning. Anywhere near our family. She'd gone with Dominic, presumably to get a room in the hotel where he was staying. I didn't ask. I didn't care where she went, as long as it was away from us. But I knew she'd get what she wanted in the end. She had too much on Dominic, on all of us.

How easy it would be for her to report Dominic to the police for our break-in. The e-fit the police had put together with Rose was eerily accurate. I thought he looked familiar when we met in that bar, but I'd never have guessed it was from Rose's descriptions of that night, from my brief glimpse of that wide back, the thick hand. It wouldn't take much for the police to place him in the area. He didn't have an alibi. And if it came out that Pete had been in on it too, they could both be done for perverting the course of justice, or worse.

Then there was the estate agency. Dominic told them he'd sold the house privately, accepting a price that was much lower than market value to finally get it off his hands. The estate agent had put up the *SOLD* sign believing it wasn't one of their clients who'd bought the house, but someone else entirely. If they found out we'd had viewings through them, Dominic would be liable to pay their fees. It wasn't much in the scheme of things, but they could take him to court as well, since he hadn't been upfront with them at the time.

But the biggest incentive for Dominic to buy the Maple House back from us, to give it to Eve, was the promise of peace. He'd already let slip to her that he had money left over, after paying his debts. And that night, Eve had sworn that if Dominic played his part, if he gave her a share of the inheritance towards the value of the house – which wasn't much now, after all the damage she'd wrought, the rampaging weeds she herself would now have to get removed – she would leave him alone. He'd never hear from her again. And neither would we. We accepted a lower price than we paid for the house just to be free – of her, of that family, of the renovations we had only just begun and, as Pete had revealed, couldn't afford to finish. What choice did we have, really?

Anyway, we don't need much, it turns out. Just enough for somewhere small, and a place to rent in the meantime. We still have to visit the village, for now, to take the children to school, but we can do that without ever driving past the Maple House. Eve doesn't need to see us, and we don't need to see her. We'll move further away, eventually. This is just a stopgap, while we work out what we'll do. What will happen between us. What our future holds.

Pete still doesn't know about Miles. Eve didn't say anything. I'm not sure why, but I'd guess it's insurance. So that we don't even think about coming back. As if we would. Part of me wants to get it all out into the open so that she doesn't hold anything over me any more. She's still got my other phone. I don't know when she might try to use it. What she might try to do.

She says she wants nothing more to do with our family, either. We were only ever a means to an end, to getting the house back. And I believe her on that. But still, I don't trust her. How could I, after what she did to me, to our children? She claimed that night that it was just a silly game, the kind she and her siblings used to play all the time. But it's not the same. Not with my children. Not letting me believe they were lost, or hurt, scared, alone.

I grip the mattress cover in my fists. I still haven't recovered from that shock, that trauma. I still can't bear to leave the children, even while they sleep. I check on them, hourly. At night, I find myself standing in their doorways, watching them breathe, the rise and fall of their little chests. Terrified that something might happen to them again.

I stand up and pace back to the window. Perhaps I'll feel better now that we've left the Maple House. The move couldn't come soon enough. Once all the details of the sale had been arranged between Pete and Dominic, it was just a question of waiting for a rental to become available. I was tempted to find a hotel room, to leave that house the very next day, but I didn't want the children to have to go through yet more upheaval. It was only a few weeks in the end. And then, finally, this morning we pulled away from that house for the final time. I told myself not to look back, but when we reached the end of the drive, I couldn't resist. And what did I see? It was just a house. Big, rambling, redbrick with

317

small windows. A building. Nothing more. It had lost its power over me.

Now here we are, starting all over again. It's getting dark, the streetlights throwing pools of light on the cracked paving stones, the odd stranger passing by as I stand, looking down from above. An elderly woman opposite takes her rubbish out. A younger man parks and goes into the house two doors down. Yet still I watch, searching the shadows between the streetlights, waiting for a sudden movement that will betray her presence, put me on high alert.

We have neighbours now, witnesses. Surely Eve won't follow us here. She shouldn't even know where we are. I made sure Pete didn't tell Eve, or Dominic, what we had planned. But still I can't help looking for her, waiting for that feeling, the sensation that someone is watching us, that we're not alone.

If Eve's plan works, if she succeeds in reuniting her family, perhaps she will leave us alone for good. If she gets joint custody of her son, of this shadowy boy I can still hardly believe exists. Or if she really does win her husband back, if he's that easily convinced by a large run-down house and some studio space for his photography business, then perhaps she'll forget all about us. She'll be happy. She won't need to haunt us any more.

But if she loses her family. If she's still as bitter and cruel as I've known her to be, then who knows? Even if she didn't push her brother – if Dominic's lying, or he doesn't really know what he saw – she's shown herself to be ruthless and manipulative, someone who'll stop at nothing to get what she wants. Who knows when she might decide to come back into our lives? That's why a big part of me wants to get as far away as possible, straight away.

We can never afford to move back to London though, not

now. And if we're going to uproot again, find another town to settle in, make new lives, then I only want to do it once. The kids have been through enough already. So we've agreed to wait here for a few months while we work out where to go, what to do.

Can I forgive Pete for what he did? For all the lies, the secrets, the gambling, the loans he took out, the financial security stolen from me without my even knowing. Perhaps. We've talked it all through, over and over; he's explained and apologised endlessly. I can see how the situation must have evolved, in increments and then gathering pace, becoming an unstoppable juggernaut, one he felt was headed right for our family. But can I forgive him for the break-in? For making my children feel scared and insecure in their own home? Allowing his daughter to be interviewed by the police, allowing us all to relive the experience over and over, and never saying anything. Never letting on. I'm not so sure about that.

I'm not going to report them. I agreed that much. So Dominic can go back to whatever hole he crawled out from. I don't want to know. We never need to see him again. But can I get over what Pete put us all through – the sacrifices he encouraged me to make, the way he let me question myself all those months? He says he regretted the plan instantly, that he was desperate to come clean, but he didn't know what I'd do, whether he'd ever see his children again. It's a fear he's lived with daily ever since then.

And could he forgive me? That's the other question. If he found out what I did, from Eve. Or if I told him myself, about what I got up to with our friend? I know he'd be as hurt as Arifa was when she found out. She couldn't believe I'd betrayed her in that way, and Pete would be equally wounded. For all his faults, he couldn't see it through with Eve. He could never do that to me, he said. He loves me too much; our family is too important to him. Though, surely, what he did is worse?

I watch an elderly man walk slowly down the street, a bag of shopping hooked over his walking stick, his old dog even slower than he is. And then a flash of light makes me turn my head sharply, eyes flicking to the other end of the road, where some teenagers are waiting at a bus stop, playing with their phones. That's what the light would have been. I'm sure of it.

If I told Pete about Miles, perhaps I could stop watching, looking, waiting. Maybe my conscience would be still, my startle reflex eventually returning to normal. Pete and I would be even then. I'd have to forgive him, if he's prepared to forgive me. I'd never be able to complain about his lies, his secrecy. I wouldn't be the injured party any more, the one who needs nurturing, who wins every argument.

'Jess, dinner's ready!' I've been up here so long, I've missed out on all the preparation. Pete has unpacked the kitchen, made a meal and supervised the children. He's like that these days, now he's got making up to do. He finds himself jobs, keeps himself busy, anticipating what needs to be done without me even needing to ask.

'Coming!' I move away from the window, from the darkness outside, the shifting shapes and lurking shadows. I draw the heavy floral curtains that have been left in this house and move through the darkened room towards the light of the hallway, the voices coming from downstairs, Pete's low rumble and Rose's high-pitched singing, Archie's laughter, the aroma of bolognese on the air.

I make my way past the boxes in the narrow downstairs hallway and through to the kitchen, which just about fits our table and four chairs, wedged in next to the cream shaker units and tall fridge-freezer. It may be cramped, but I can see that spirits are high, Rose twirling, her hands full of knives and forks as she sings a song about spaghetti, while Archie laughs, setting a pile of plates on the table. Pete is standing at the hob, giving the sauce a final stir, and he looks up as I walk in, throwing a nervous smile in my direction. His eyes search my face. *Is everything okay?* his expression seems to ask. *Could we be happy here?* And I smile back, meaning that he can relax again, enjoy the children's company, like a man spared his execution, permitted to remain with his family – for now, at least.

I sit at the table, allowing the children to wait on me, Pete to pass me a glass of red wine, all the work to be done while I sit back, enjoy a meal, feel the wine take its effect. It's a good position to be in, this. A hard one to give up. Pete's cut back on his after-hours drinking. He's been coming home earlier. He's even requested two days a week homeworking so I can start on an art history course.

I know I should tell him the truth about Miles. Then we really could start afresh, knowing that we've both wronged, both been forgiven. Maybe I will tell him soon. Tomorrow, even. But not now. Not tonight. Let us enjoy an evening together in our new house first, our new beginning. Let's shut out the darkness outside and focus on this moment, together, our children content, the two of us relaxed.

I look at Pete across the table, catching his eye as he picks up his fork and smiles, appreciates what he has. Perhaps he knows already and he's forgiven me, doesn't even want to talk about it.

And if he doesn't, is it worth bringing up all that hurt? Who would I be doing it for, really?

I'm sure Eve won't come back. She won't reveal the truth after what she's done.

The letter box clatters, an envelope thudding to the ground. Rose and Archie push back their chairs and race to reach it first, to be the one that opens it. But it's not going to be for us. After all, no one knows our address here yet, and I'm planning to keep it that way. Keep a low profile, until we reach somewhere we can really settle.

Rose walks in holding it above her head, triumphant. She beat Archie for once – she did have a head start.

'Don't open it, love,' I say over my shoulder. 'It's not for us.'

'Yes it is, Mum.' Archie snatches the envelope from Rose and turns it to face me. Sure enough, it has *THE MASTERS FAMILY*, written in black ink, block capitals. He's already torn the edge, got his finger in and pulled it apart. It's a card. 'Welcome to your new home!' A country cottage, a woodland scene. For a moment, my stomach plummets, but it's not one of Eve's. It's a generic, shop-bought affair, and I wait while Archie opens it, expecting him to read it aloud. But he just turns it over, looks on the back and then inside again.

'There's nothing written in it,' he announces, turning it over again.

'It's probably from the letting agent,' Pete says, taking the card and inspecting it. 'One of those courtesy things they do for all their tenants.'

And I give him a weak smile, picking up the dishes and stacking them before I stand up, carrying the card to the counter lightly, as though it might be contaminated, unclean.

I prop it up and turn to the children, gathering them into an arm each and giving them a cuddle, as if to reassure myself as much as them. We're here, we're safe, we've made it through.

Then I look at the card again, over the top of their heads, and that's when I spot it. In the bushes beside the house, a small animal watching from the sidelines. A badger.

I shiver, my arms tensing around the children so that they both look up at me, alarmed. But I'm just being paranoid. It's probably nothing. Pete's right. The letting agent sent us the card. It's a coincidence. Nothing more.

Eve can't harm us now. Can she?

Acknowledgements

I wrote my second novel in early 2021, in the depths of lockdown, so the first people I have to thank are my husband and children for all their support, patience and for (at least some) moments of peace. Nigel, Sammy and Matilda, I can't think of three people I'd rather spend so many months shut away with.

I felt very lucky during those months to be able to retreat to another world, and I'd also like to say a big thank you to my colleagues at the *Guardian*, especially Liese Spencer, who worked overtime so that I could have some much-treasured writing leave.

Thanks, always, to my agent Sophie Lambert and editor Phoebe Morgan – your thoughtful and perceptive insights have been invaluable, as has been your unfailing support through a period when it hasn't always been easy to put aside time for writing. Thank you to all at C&W and HarperCollins, especially Jaime Witcomb, Alice Hill and Liz Dawson.

A huge thank you goes to my family: my mum, Ellie, who has become a trusted and eagle-eyed early reader, dad Andy and sister Laura, for their wisdom and advice, Gregg, Kit and

Cassia, Matt, Aisha, James, Sarah, Sheena,Tony, Gill and Des, for their support during my debut year. A special thanks to Maureen, for all the help, support and childcare – and for hand-selling more signed copies of *The House Guest* than anyone.

Thank you to my early readers, Gemma Loughran and Ruth Tanner, for their invaluable feedback. To all the writers who so generously read and supported my debut, in particular Erin Kelly and Fiona Cummins. And to all those friends who rallied around online and in person during what turned out to be an unusual debut year: Jo, Georgie, Lucy, Victoire, Sarah, Rufus, Gemma, Megan, Helen, Marta, Davina, Grainne, Charlotte, Rosie, Clare, Zoe and many more.

Thanks to all at Curtis Brown Creative, particularly my ever-supportive writing group, and to all the friends I've made since relocating from London. Luckily our big move turned out to be nothing like Jess and Pete's, and I found so much local support as I launched my first book, mostly on a screen. Hopefully this time around there will be parties, drinks and laughter in real life.

The perfect family.
The perfect chance.
The perfect lie.

**Kate trusts Della, and Della trusts Kate.
Their downfall is each other.**

When Kate moves to London after the disappearance of her
sister, she's in need of a friend. A chance meeting leads Kate
to Della, a life coach who runs support groups for young
women, dubbed by Kate as 'the Janes.'

Della takes a special interest in Kate, and Kate soon finds
herself entangled in Della's life – her house, her family, and
her husband. It's only when she realises that she's in too
deep that Della's veneer begins to crumble, and the
warnings from 'the Janes' begin to come true.

Why is Della so keen to keep Kate by her side? What does
Kate have that Della might want? And what really lies
beneath the surface of their friendship?